AS GOOD AS DEAD

W0081427

LOOK FOR THESE EXCITING WESTERN SERIES FROM BESTSELLING AUTHORS WILLIAM W. JOHNSTONE AND J.A. JOHNSTONE

The Mountain Man

Luke Jensen: Bounty Hunter

Brannigan's Land

The Jensen Brand

Smoke Jensen: The Early Years

Preacher and MacCallister

Fort Misery

The Fighting O'Neils

Perley Gates

MacCoole and Boone

Guns of the Vigilantes

Shotgun Johnny

The Chuckwagon Trail

The Jackals

The Slash and Pecos Westerns

The Texas Moonshiners

Stoneface Finnegan Westerns

Ben Savage: Saloon Ranger

The Buck Trammel Westerns

The Death and Texas Westerns

The Hunter Buchanon Westerns

Will Tanner: U.S. Deputy Marshal

Old Cowboys Never Die

Go West, Young Man

Published by Kensington Publishing Corp.

AS GOOD AS DEAD

SMOKE JENSEN AND THE TAMING OF THE WEST

WILLIAM W. JOHNSTONE

AND J.A. JOHNSTONE

PINNACLE BOOKS
Kensington Publishing Corp.
kensingtonbooks.com

PINNACLE BOOKS are published by

Kensington Publishing Corp.
900 Third Avenue
New York, NY 10022

All Kensington titles, imprints, and distributed lines are available at special quantity discounts for bulk purchases for sales promotion, premiums, fundraising, and educational or institutional use.

Special book excerpts or customized printings can also be created to fit specific needs. For details, write or phone the office of the Kensington Sales Manager: Kensington Publishing Corp., 900 Third Avenue, New York, NY 10022. Attn. Sales Department. Phone: 1-800-221-2647.

First Printing: October 2025
ISBN-13: 978-0-7860-5109-0

10 9 8 7 6 5 4 3 2 1

Printed in the United States of America

The authorized representative in the EU for product safety and compliance
is eucomply OU, Parnu mnt 139b-14, Apt 123
Tallinn, Berlin 11317, hello@eucompliancepartner.com.

THE JENSEN FAMILY
FIRST FAMILY OF THE AMERICAN FRONTIER

Smoke Jensen—*The Mountain Man*
The youngest of three children and orphaned as a young boy, Smoke Jensen is considered one of the fastest draws in the West. His quest to tame the lawless West has become the stuff of legend. Smoke owns the Sugarloaf Ranch in Colorado. Married to Sally Jensen, father to Denise ("Denny") and Louis.

Preacher—*The First Mountain Man*
Though not a blood relative, grizzled frontiersman Preacher became a father figure to the young Smoke Jensen, teaching him how to survive in the brutal, often deadly Rocky Mountains. Fought the battles that forged his destiny. Armed with a long gun, Preacher is as fierce as the land itself.

Matt Jensen—*The Last Mountain Man*
Orphaned but taken in by Smoke Jensen, Matt Jensen has become like a younger brother to Smoke and even took the Jensen name. And like Smoke, Matt has carved out his destiny on the American frontier. He lives by the gun and surrenders to no man.

Luke Jensen—*Bounty Hunter*
Mountain Man Smoke Jensen's long-lost brother, Luke Jensen, is scarred by war and a dead shot—the right qualities to be a bounty hunter. And he's cunning, and fierce enough, to bring down the deadliest outlaws of his day.

Ace Jensen and Chance Jensen—*Those Jensen Boys!*
The untold story of Smoke Jensen's long-lost nephews,
Ace and Chance, a pair of young-gun twins as reckless and
wild as the frontier itself . . . Their father is Luke Jensen,
thought killed in the Civil War. Their uncle Smoke Jensen
is one of the fiercest gunfighters the West has ever known.
It's no surprise that the inseparable Ace and Chance Jensen
have a knack for taking risks—even if they have to blast their
way out of them.

CONTENTS

STRIKE
OF THE
MOUNTAIN MAN

CHAPTER 1

Deekus Templeton had once ridden with Frank and Jesse James. It wasn't particularly a matter of pride for him, especially since the James brothers were well known figures . . . even idolized in some places, while few had ever heard of Deekus Templeton.

What bothered Templeton the most was that he was the one who had planned the train robbery in Muncie, Kansas, where they got $30,000. That was the biggest haul from any train robbery the James gang made, and it was Frank and Jesse who were celebrated, not the one who planned it. Shortly after that, Templeton decided to go into business for himself.

He had learned that the Red Cliff Special would be carrying a money transfer of $50,000 from a bank in Pueblo, Colorado, to the bank in Big Rock, Colorado, which was more than any job the James brothers had ever pulled. To stop the train, he had piled wood and brush onto the track.

"The train's acomin', Deekus!" one of his men shouted.

"Torch the pile," Templeton called, and a moment later a rather substantial fire flamed up from the pile of brushwood.

Smoke Jensen had gone to Denver with Pearlie and Cal to set up a plant that would ship beef, already butchered and processed, in refrigerated cars to markets in the East. Handling already processed meat was much cheaper than shipping live cattle, and the result was a greater profit to the rancher.

Smoke built the plant, not only for himself, but also for other cattlemen in Colorado as well as in Wyoming. He had left Pearlie and Cal in Denver to see to the final details, and was on the way back home, changing trains in Pueblo so he could take the Red Cliff Special on its overnight run. He would be arriving in Big Rock at six o'clock in the morning.

There were no sleeper cars on the train so Smoke was napping as best he could in the seat. The train had been under way for five hours when it came to a sudden, shuddering, screeching, and banging halt, stopping so abruptly it awakened Smoke with a start. He didn't know what was going on, but he knew it certainly wasn't a normal stop. He looked through the window to see where they were, but the lanterns that lit the inside of the car cast reflections on the windows, making it difficult to see through them, and into the dark outside.

"Why did we stop?" someone asked.

"Did we hit something? I was thrown so, that I nearly broke my neck," a man complained.

Though he couldn't see anything through the windows, Smoke could hear voices outside, rough and guttural, and he had a feeling the train was being robbed. He pulled his pistol and held it down in his lap.

"Everyone stay in their seats!" a man shouted, bursting into the car from the front. He was wearing a hood over his face, and he held a pistol pointed toward the passengers in the car.

"What is the meaning of this?" a man shouted indignantly. He started to get up, but the gunman moved quickly toward him and brought his pistol down sharply over the man's head.

The passenger groaned and fell back. A woman who had been sitting with him cried out in alarm.

"Anybody else?" the gunman challenged. "Maybe you folks didn't hear me when I said everyone stay in their seats."

Another gunman came in to join the first. "What happened?"

"Nothing I can't handle. Is everything under control out there?"

"Yeah, ever'thing is fine. Just keep ever'one in here covered." The second gunman left the car.

The remaining train robber took off his hat. "Now folks, this is what I'm goin' to do. I'm goin' to walk down this aisle and hold my hat out." He chuckled. "You know, sort of like what they do in church. But I don't just want a coin or two like you do when you're in church. I want ever'thing you have. And if I see any of you holdin' out on me, why, I'll have to shoot you."

The gunman started down the aisle making his collection, and though the first few people cooperated, when he got to a young woman holding a baby, she protested.

"Please, this is all the money I have. I'm taking it to my husband so we can buy a house."

"I said, don't nobody hold back," the gunman said menacingly. "Now you just empty that bag of your'n into my hat."

"Leave the lady alone," Smoke said.

The train robber looked over at Smoke. "Mister, this here is a train robbery. Maybe you don't understand how train robberies work. You see, I take the money, and people like you give the money. So you might as well get your money out, 'cause soon as I get the money from the little mama here, why I'll be takin' yours."

"If you want to live, put the hat down now so the people can get their money back, and leave this car," Smoke said.

"If I want to live?" The gunman's laugh was a high-pitched cackle. "Mister, I'm the one holdin' the gun here. Or ain't you noticed?"

"Leave this car now, or die," Smoke said calmly.

"I've had about enough of you, mister." Pointing his pistol at Smoke, the train robber pulled the hammer back. That was as far he got before, in a lightning move, Smoke brought his own pistol up from his lap and pulled the trigger. Dropping his gun, the robber clutched his chest, and staggered back a few steps. "What the hell?" he asked in a pained voice.

One of the other train robbers jumped onto the train. Seeing his partner down, and an armed man standing, he fired at Smoke. His shot went wide and the bullet smashed through the window beside Smoke's seat, sending out a stinging spray of glass but doing no other damage. Smoke brought his own pistol around and squeezed off a second shot. The robber staggered back, hit the front wall of the car, then slid down to the floor in a seated position, already dead.

"What's going on in there?" Deekus Templeton shouted from outside the train.

One of the other men looked into the car, then jerked his head back. "Clay and Dooley are both shot dead!" he called. "I'm gettin' out of here!"

"You can't leave, McClain! We ain't got the money yet!" Templeton shouted.

"Get it yourself! There's only the two of us left!"

McClain started to ride away but Templeton raised his pistol and shot him off the horse.

"Now there's only one of us," he said as he rode hard to get away.

When the train reached Big Rock the next morning the bodies of the three would-be train robbers were laid out on the depot platform. Each one had his arms folded across his chest. The hoods had been removed, and all three had their eyes open. A dozen or more citizens of the town were standing there looking down at the bodies.

Sheriff Carson was there as well, and he was talking to Smoke. "You say you only got two of them?"

"Yes, these two," Smoke said, pointing to the two men he shot.

"Yeah, that's Clay Brandon and Dooley Waters," Sheriff Carson said, pointing to the two men Smoke had shot. "The other one is Len McClain. If you didn't shoot him, who did?"

"There were four of them. It was the fourth one who shot this man."

"I don't suppose you heard his name called out," Sheriff Carson said. It was more of a wishful declaration than a question.

"No, I didn't."

"Well, the bank will certainly be thanking you. There was a fifty thousand dollar shipment on that train."

"That's funny," Smoke said. "If there was that much money in the shipment, why were they bothering with trying to steal the few dollars they could get from the passengers?"

One of the men in the crowd of onlookers was Deekus Templeton. He had already learned that Smoke Jensen was the man who had foiled his robbery attempt and stood behind the others, watching Jensen and the sheriff as they were engaged in conversation. He had heard of Smoke Jensen. Who in that part of the country had not heard of him? But it was the first time he had ever seen him, and he wanted to get a good look at the man. He didn't want to ever blunder into some foolish mistake as had Clay and Dooley.

Templeton smiled as he realized he had an advantage. He knew what Smoke Jensen looked like, but Jensen didn't know what he looked like.

Then he heard Jensen ask the same question that had been puzzling him. *Why were they bothering with trying to steal the few dollars they could get from the passengers?*

* * *

Phil Clinton, the publisher and editor of the *Big Rock Journal* had heard about the attempted train robbery and came down to the depot with paper and pen to interview the passengers. He also brought a camera with him, set up a tripod, then took a photograph of the three dead men. A good newspaperman, Clinton knew a picture would supplement the story, and he employed a very good woodcut artist who could make that happen.

His article appeared in the *Big Rock Journal*.

Attempted Train Robbery Foiled

THREE OUTLAWS MEET THEIR FATE

The residents of Big Rock, and indeed of Colorado and other Western states and territories, are well acquainted with the many attributes, skills, and talents of Smoke Jensen. To his long list of accomplishments may be added preventing a robbery of the Red Cliff Special on Friday last.

It is to the fatal detriment of Clay Brandon, Dooley Waters, and Len McClain that they were unaware they were about to encounter Mr. Jensen and, as their final lesson in life, learn of his artistry with a pistol. Mr. Jensen, who owns Sugarloaf Ranch, located some seven miles west of Big Rock, was a passenger on the Red Cliff Special last Friday night, when the ill-fated robbery attempt was made. It was Mr. Jensen's presence, and especially his quick response, that saved the passengers' money, and perhaps even their lives.

That an attempt was made to rob the train is not surprising when one considers that locked in the safe of the express car, and being watched over by a bonded special agent, were fifty thousand dollars in negotiable United States currency. What is surprising is that, despite the large prize available to them, the robbers chose to augment that bounty with the meager collection of money they could glean from the passengers.

It was that particular ill-advised venture that caused two of the robbers to step onto the cars and there encounter Smoke Jensen. The result of that encounter was that Mr. Jensen has added further luster to his already illustrious career. It is said that the fourth would-be robber left the scene empty-handed. The identity of the fourth robber is not known.

CHAPTER 2

Dijon, France

Pierre Mouchette was a French Army Officer and an 1869 graduate from St. Cyr, the leading military academy of France. After St. Cyr, he'd entered Saumur, France's premier cavalry school, and after leaving Saumur, he'd taken part in the Franco-Prussian War. It was there that he encountered the American general Phil Sheridan who was in France to observe the war. Sheridan had told him of the American West, and though it had no immediate bearing on Mouchette's military career, he remembered it later when, after his third duel, he was told he had gone as high as he was going to go in the French military.

In January of 1879, orders were cut appointing Capitaine Pierre Mouchette as disbursement officer. These orders called for him to transfer two and one half million francs from Paris to the army finance office in Dijon. Mouchette made very careful plans, selecting as his assistant a sergeant who was approximately his same build. They picked up the money in Paris, then went by train to Dijon.

In Dijon, they mounted horses and started toward the division headquarters. When they were but a mile out of town, Mouchette turned off the road.

"Capitaine Mouchette, where are you going?" Sergeant Dubois asked. "The headquarters is this way." He pointed down the road.

"This is a shorter way," Mouchette said.

"Shorter? How can it be shorter? This road goes straight to the headquarters."

"Would you argue with an officer, Sergeant?" Mouchette scolded.

"*Non, mon capitaine.*"

"Then this is the direction we will go."

"*Oui, mon capitaine.*"

The sergeant followed Mouchette dutifully until they were deep into a wooded area. "Capitaine Mouchette, forgive me, but we are now some distance from headquarters. I think we should turn back."

Mouchette turned toward the sergeant. "Do you?" he asked with a humorless smile on his face.

It was then Sergeant Dubois saw Mouchette holding a pistol leveled toward him. "Capitaine, what are you doing?" Dubois shouted in fear.

Mouchette pulled the trigger, and the bullet struck Dubois between the eyes.

Working quickly, Mouchette removed his uniform and put on the civilian clothes he had previously packed in his saddle-bags. Then, stripping Dubois of his uniform, he replaced it with his own. "There now, Sergeant, you have just been promoted to capitaine. I salute you, Capitaine Mouchette."

It was not by chance Mouchette had chosen that particular spot, for earlier he had hidden a can of kerosene in the bushes. He poured kerosene on Dubois' face and set a match to it, keeping the fire going until all the sergeant's features were burned away and only a blackened skull remained. After that, he put his billfold in the pocket of the uniform Sergeant Dubois was now wearing. In it, were Mouchette's identity papers, the orders appointing him as disbursement officer, his membership card to the officers' mess, and a letter he had recently received from a military clothier in Paris, quoting the price of a new dress uniform.

With his deception completed, Mouchette crossed the border into Switzerland and journeyed to Geneva. There, he presented himself to the bank as a French businessman. "I shall be going to North America shortly to invest in a business opportunity in New York and I should like to change some French currency into American dollars. What is the current exchange rate?"

"It is five francs for one dollar," the teller said. "How much do you wish to exchange?"

"Two and one half million francs."

The teller made no reaction to the large sum. He picked up a pencil and began figuring the amount.

"Your amount comes to four hundred eighty-seven thousand dollars. That sum is, of course, less the twelve thousand five hundred dollar conversion fee."

"Very good."

The teller counted out the American dollars. "Do you care to recount it, Monsieur?"

"No, I'm sure it is all there."

"Then if you would sign this certificate, please?"

Mouchette signed it as Antoine Dubois.

It was as Pierre Mouchette that he devised the plan to steal the payroll. It was as Antoine Dubois that he exchanged the francs for U.S. dollars. And it was as Colonel the Marquis Lucien Garneau that he boarded a ship in Hamburg, Germany, bound for New York. Lucien Garneau was how he would be known.

New York, New York

Garneau got off the ship in New York and immediately bought a local newspaper. He saw an article that caught his interest.

Intelligence From Overseas

KILLER OF CAPTAIN MOUCHETTE STILL AT LARGE
SERGEANT DUBOIS SUSPECTED OF HEINOUS CRIME

Captain Pierre Mouchette was appointed
military finance officer with the
responsibility of transporting a large sum of
money from Paris to Dijon, but was foully
murdered by one he trusted most. When
Captain Mouchette did not show up at the
appointed time, a search was launched,
resulting in the gruesome discovery of the
charred remains of the gallant captain and the
discovery that both the money and the
sergeant were missing.

It is believed that the cowardly Sergeant
Dubois, animated by greed and a lack of
personal morals, betrayed the trust so
necessary in the military between the officers
and the ranks, and when least expected, killed
Captain Mouchette. The foul deed done, the
disgraceful sergeant tried to cover his action
by burning the captain's body. The attempt
was unsuccessful as he was identified by his
uniform and personal papers. The despicable
Sergeant Dubois remains missing.

Garneau smiled as he realized everything had worked out
exactly as he had intended. He went directly from Castle
Garden, his point of entry, to Grand Central depot to continue
his plan, recalling a conversation he'd had with General
Sheridan, when the American general had talked about Colorado. He'd told how beautiful the mountains were, but what
had most interested Garneau about Colorado was Sheridan's
off-hand comment. "A person could go into the Rocky

Mountains of Colorado and, if he wanted to, just drop off the face of the earth."

Finding a map of Colorado, Lucien Garneau put his finger on the chart with no particular destination in mind. The closest town to the tip of his finger was Big Rock, in Eagle County, so he bought a ticket for that destination and boarded the train.

Dijon, France

Inspector Andre Laurent of the French Military Police was shown into General Moreau's office.

"Colonel Durand said you had information for me," General Moreau said.

"I do, my General," Laurent said. "The body we found was not that of Capitaine Mouchette."

"What? But the body was wearing Mouchette's uniform. His billfold was found with the body."

"Those were plants, to make us believe it was Mouchette's body."

"Who would do that?"

"I believe Mouchette himself did it," Laurent said. "The body was that of Sergeant Antoine Dubois."

"Dubois?"

"I believe Mouchette murdered Dubois, stole the money, then made it appear as if Dubois was the guilty party. He burned Dubois' face so he could not be identified."

"Then how was he identified?"

"The body was missing two toes on its left foot. It is well known by Sergeant Dubois's friends that he lost two toes in the war. Mouchette had no such wound."

"Then Mouchette is guilty of murder and theft of the money."

"Yes, my General."

General Moreau drummed his fingers on his desk. "Inspector Laurent, you have full authorization to go after

Mouchette. Find him, wherever he is, and bring him to justice for France."

Inspector Laurent saluted General Moreau. "That will be my pleasure, General."

Big Rock, Colorado

On August first, the day that three years earlier, Colorado had become a state, the entire town of Big Rock was turned out to celebrate Statehood Day. There were food booths, horse and foot races, horseshoe throwing competitions, shooting matches, and of course, music and dancing.

Smoke hadn't entered any of the shooting contests because he had been asked to judge. In the match for rifle marksmanship, Humboldt Puddle and Dwayne Booker had survived all the others and were the last two shooters remaining. Each had just put three shots into the bull's eye, after having moved the targets to the far end of the street.

"What are we going to do now, Smoke?" Sheriff Carson asked. "If we move the targets any farther, they are going to be in another county."

Those close enough to hear the sheriff laughed.

Smoke took out a silver dollar, then set it up on top of the bale of hay being used as a backstop for the target. Standing it on its edge, he pushed enough of the coin into the hay to keep it erect. The result was that just over half the coin was showing. "Let them shoot at this."

Despite the fact that many other things were going on to attract the people of the town and county, word of the intense shooting competition had spread, and hundreds were drawn up to watch the final two shooters. They flipped a coin to see who would shoot first, and Dwayne Booker was selected.

The crowd grew very quiet as Booker raised the Winchester .44-40 to his shoulder, sighted down the barrel, then pulled the trigger. A few stems of hay fluttered up right beside the coin, but the coin wasn't hit.

"It's a miss," Smoke said, looking through a pair of binoculars.

It was Humboldt's turn. He looked down range at the target, which was at least one hundred yards away. After staring at it for a long moment, he raised the rifle and fired, almost in the same fluid motion.

Smoke didn't have to look through the binoculars, nor did he have to make the announcement. The cheers of at least four hundred people made the announcement for him. The coin flew away from the top of the hay bale, the result of a direct hit.

Humboldt's feat of marksmanship was still the talk of the town as everyone gathered for the dance held in the commodious dining room of the Dunn Hotel. Sally dragged Smoke out on the floor to form the first square. Sheriff Carson stood in front of the band, calling the steps through a megaphone he held to his mouth.

> *Chew your tobacco and rub your snuff,*
> *Meet your honey and strut your stuff.*
> *Right foot up and a left foot down,*
> *Make that big foot jar the ground,*
> *Promenade your partner around.*

"It's too bad Pearlie and Cal aren't here," Sally said. "They so enjoy these things."

"No doubt Denver is also celebrating Statehood Day," Smoke said. "And I expect they are doing just fine."

CHAPTER 3

Denver

Cal had entered a pie-eating contest and it was down to three contestants. The other two contestants had a combined weight of nearly six hundred pounds, compared to Cal's weight of one hundred seventy-five pounds.

The three remaining contestants had been given a five-minute break before the contest was to resume, and Cal and Pearlie were back in one corner of the room, talking quietly.

"I don't know if I can do it," Cal said. "I'm stuffed."

"You're stuffed?" Pearlie said. "This is pie we're talkin' about, Cal. In all the time I've known you, I've never known you to pass up a piece of pie."

"This isn't a piece of pie, Pearlie, it's a whole pie. And I've already eaten three."

"Then what's one more? Here, let me rub your stomach, that'll move some of what you've already eaten aside and give you a little more room."

"All right, gentlemen, the time is up," the judge called. "Please return to the table."

Initially, there had been several tables, but the final three contestants were moved to one round table and seated across from each other. A pie was put in front of each of them.

"All right, gentlemen, you may commence," the judge said.

One of the heavy contestants stared at the pie for just a moment, then without so much as touching it, he stood up and walked away. That left only two people.

The two began eating their pie. Cal called out to the judge and pointed to the pie the big man had left behind on the table. "Hey judge, since he's not going to eat that pie, can I have it when I finish this one?"

The spectators who were gathered around the table laughed and exclaimed in amazement. "There's no bottom in that man's stomach!"

When Cal asked for the abandoned pie, the other contestant got a very sick look on his face, then pushed away from the table. "I quit," he said.

Everyone cheered, but the judge held up his hands to call for quiet. "You must take at least one more bite to be declared the winner," he said to Cal.

Smiling, Cal not only took another bite, he consumed half the pie, then held his hands up over his head in triumph.

The crowd cheered and offered their congratulations as Cal was crowned the "pie-eating champion of Colorado."

After what seemed an interminable length of travel—he'd had no idea America was so large—Garneau reached Denver. From there, he took a train to Pueblo, and from Pueblo he began the final leg of a journey that had started in Dijon almost a month earlier.

Six and one half days after he left New York, Garneau arrived in Big Rock at six o'clock in the morning. He was tired from the overnight trip, for there had been no sleeping arrangements on the train. He inquired of the station agent where he might find a hotel.

"Well sir, we've got two of 'em," Phil Wilson replied.

"We've got the Big Rock and the Dunn. One's just about as nice as the other, so I wouldn't know which one to recommend."

"Which is the closest?"

"That would be the Big Rock. You just go down Tanner Street for one block, and it's on the corner of Tanner and Center Street."

"Merci."

Although the Big Rock Hotel was but one block away, Garneau arranged for him and his luggage to be transported there. He was very tired, and wanted nothing more than to go to bed, but he knew there was something he had to do first. Before he could rest, he had to go to the bank.

He looked at his two cases on the floor of his room. One contained clothes, and a casual look into the other would suggest it also contained nothing but clothes. However, under the first layer of clothes, were forty-seven bound packets of hundred dollar bills, one hundred bills in each packet.

Garneau had been very nervous with the money in his possession for the last month.

Finally, when he was certain the bank was open, he took the suitcase containing the money and walked downstairs. As he started across the lobby, the desk clerk called out to him.

"Sir? Is something wrong with your room or our service? Are you leaving?"

"I'm not leaving," Garneau said. "Monsieur, could you direct me to the bank, *s'il vous plaît?* "

"Certainly." The desk clerk pointed. "Just go this way one block to Ranney Street, turn left one block to Front Street. You can't miss it. It's the third building on the right, next to the Dunn Hotel."

"Merci," Garneau replied.

Although it was the middle of the day, and he was in the middle of town, Garneau was nervous as he carried the suitcase to the bank. He felt a sense of relief when he reached the bank a moment later. When he stepped inside, he stood for just a moment as he had a long look around.

"Yes, sir, may I help you?" a man sitting at a desk just inside the door asked.

"*Oui*. I am just moving here and would like to open an account, *s'il vous plaît*."

"I can do that for you, sir," the man said, picking up a printed form and a pen. "How much would you like to deposit in the account?"

"Four hundred and seventy-five thousand dollars," Garneau said.

"What?" the bank clerk gasped. "How much did you say?"

"Four hundred and seventy-five thousand dollars," Garneau repeated. He sat the suitcase on the desk and opened it, then began removing the packets of money."

"No, sir, not here," the bank clerk said. "Come into the back with me to speak with the president of the bank. I don't think it is good to show so much money in public."

Joel Montgomery looked at the money that was piled up on his desk.

"We can handle your deposit, Mr. Garneau—"

"Colonel Garneau," Garneau insisted.

"Yes, sir. Well, here is the thing, Colonel Garneau. We can handle your deposit, but there is no way we are going to keep all that money here. We are going to have to lay off ninety percent of it to other banks."

"Why?"

"The risks. We are capitalized at fifty thousand dollars, and it would be much too risky to keep this much money in one bank, so over the next few days we will be making deposits in other banks. That it won't all be kept in this bank will not affect you. You will still have a demand account, and can draw against it at any time."

"*Merci*," Garneau said.

Half an hour later, he left the bank with one hundred dollars in small denominations in his pocket, along with a deposit slip for the four hundred seventy-five thousand dollars he had left at the bank. He returned to his room at the hotel and slept through the rest of the day.

Waking up that evening, Garneau decided to walk through the town to get a look at the rather quaint place that was to be his new home. He took his dinner at Delmonico's, then went next door to Longmont's, which he perceived to be a drinking establishment.

"What will you have, sir?" the bartender asked.

"I don't suppose you would have any cognac, would you?"

The man standing at the far end of the bar overheard Garneau's accent and his order. He smiled and came toward him. "*Bonsoir, monsieur. Par votre accent, je suppose que vous êtes un homme de bonne taste. Vous demandez pour le cognac, j'ai J.V.C. Aumasson.*"

"How delightful," Garneau said. "You speak French, though with an accent I can't place. As I am in America now, I wish only to speak English. And J.V.C. Aumasson is a most delightful cognac."

"Very well. We will speak English. My name is Louis Longmont, and I own this establishment. The first cognac is on the house."

"*Merci*, Monsieur Longmont. And my name, sir, is Colonel the Marquis Lucien Garneau."

"What brings you to Colorado, Colonel Garneau?"

The bartender served the cognac, and Garneau swirled it about, used his hand to waft the fragrance into his face, smiled, and took a sip. "Marvelous. I have come to this place to buy land and raise cattle."

"Well, there is land for sale. And this is good cattle country. In fact, we have one of the largest and most successful ranches in the nation right here. It is called Sugarloaf, and is owned by Smoke Jensen. I'm sure you have heard of him."

"Smoke? *Fumer?*"

Louis nodded. "'*Fumer,*' yes. 'Smoke' is not his real name. His real name is Kirby, but everyone calls him Smoke."

Garneau shook his head. "What an odd name."

"How long have you been in America?"

"I have been in this country for a fortnight only."

"Well, that explains it. Anyone who has been here for six months or longer has heard of Smoke Jensen. We don't have marquis and lords and such, but if we did, Smoke Jensen would have a title for sure."

"He sounds quite successful. I should like to meet him."

Louis looked toward the door and smiled. "Well, speak of the devil. Smoke just came in."

"Smoke!" someone called, and he was greeted by at least half a dozen others.

"Smoke, over here," Louis called.

Acknowledging the greetings, Smoke shook hands with a couple and waved at the others. Then, with a broad smile he went over to Louis. "It looks like business is good tonight."

"Business is good every night, as you would know if Sally didn't keep you on such a tight leash," Louis teased. "How is it she let you come to town tonight?"

"She is on the school board, remember? There's a meeting down at the school tonight."

"I thought it must be something like that. Smoke, this is Colonel the Marquis Lucien Garneau. Colonel Garneau, this is the man I was telling you about. Smoke Jensen."

"It's a pleasure to meet you, Mr. Garneau."

"That would be Colonel Garneau," Garneau said.

"I beg your pardon, Colonel."

"I understand you are the largest and most successful rancher in the county," Garneau said.

"I've been fortunate," Smoke said.

"Well, Monsieur Jensen, I give you fair warning. My personal motto is *secundus nulli*. That is Latin for—"

"Second to none," Louis said.

Garneau glared at Louis, showing displeasure over being one-upped. But he regained his composure quickly. "Yes. And I am not used to being second to anyone. I will soon have a ranch that is larger."

Louis laughed.

"You find that humorous, *Monsieur*?" Garneau asked rather sharply.

"Not humorous, so much, as impossible," Louis said.

"Why is it impossible?"

"Because there isn't enough available land left in Eagle and Pitkin counties combined, to build a ranch larger than Sugarloaf."

"I will find the land. Thank you for the cognac." Garneau took a coin from his pocket and slapped it onto the bar. Then, turning, he walked away and left the saloon.

"Now that is one odd duck," Smoke said.

"He is a marquis," Louis replied. "I think that to be a marquis, one must first be an odd duck."

Smoke laughed.

When Garneau awakened the next morning, he donned the uniform of a colonel in the French Cavalry. Although he never advanced above the rank of captain, he felt that passing himself off as a colonel would be more impressive. Inquiring at the hotel desk, he was directed to the land office, which was just around the corner from the hotel on Ranney Street.

When Garneau stepped into the building the clerk looked up, then registered surprise at seeing Garneau in uniform. "May I help you?"

"I am Colonel the Marquis Lucien Garneau, and I have come to buy land," Garneau said.

"Yes, sir, if you'll wait here for just a moment." The clerk stepped into another room, then a moment later reappeared. "Mr. Perkins will see you, sir."

Pete Perkins was a small man with a red face and an over-sized nose. He invited Garneau to have a seat. "I understand that you want to buy land."

"*Oui.*"

"How much land are you interested in buying?"

"How much does the land cost?"

"It is about five dollars per acre."

"How much land does Monsieur Jensen have?"

"Oh, heavens, I don't know. I would guess he has around thirty thousand acres or so."

"Then I shall want thirty thousand acres as well."

Perkins chuckled and shook his head. "There aren't that many acres of unowned land available in the whole valley."

"How large is Eagle County?"

"Just over one million acres."

"You say that there are one million acres in the county, but I can't buy thirty thousand acres?"

"Oh, there might be that many acres, perhaps even more, but it wouldn't be contiguous. There are too many ranches and farms of one to three sections of land."

"Suppose enough farmers and ranchers contiguous to land that I buy could be persuaded to sell their land. Would it be possible to put together a ranch of the size I am seeking?"

"Well, yes, if you could convince enough of the smaller owners to sell. But I'm not sure you can do that. The small ranchers and farmers are doing remarkably well. I don't see any of them selling out, let alone enough for you to do what you want."

"Please buy as much land for me as you can, and let me worry about the adjacent land owners."

Perkins did some math on a sheet of paper, then whistled. "Colonel Garneau, this is going to require quite a sizeable outlay. With just the land I know is available, we are talking about at least eighty-seven thousand dollars."

"If you wish, you may go with me to the bank and inquire as to available funds," Garneau said.

Perkins stood, then retrieved his hat from the hat rack. "The bank is just around the corner." He exited the bank and Garneau followed.

"Colonel Garneau!" the bank president said when Garneau and Perkins stepped into the bank a few moments later. "What can I do for you?"

"You can inform Monsieur Perkins that I have sufficient funds to buy land," Garneau said.

"Mr. Perkins," the bank president said, "it would not be ethical for me to disclose just how much money Colonel Garneau has on deposit with us. Suffice it to say that he is good for any amount of land you can find for him to purchase."

Perkins smiled at the Frenchman. "Colonel Garneau, I can see that you and I are going to have quite a profitable relationship."

CHAPTER 4

DIED

Early on the morning of August 25th,
GEORGE MUNGER, *owner*
of the successful ranch, Long Trek.

Death is a solemn event, but one which all must meet sooner or later. Sometimes the pain and sadness occasioned by its touching the hearts of the bereaved is of more than an ordinary character. It is so in this case. George Munger's six thousand acre ranch, Long Trek, is the envy of all in Eagle County who have taken up that profession.

Munger arrived in Colorado nine years previous, and in that time not only began a successful ranch, but fathered two children, a boy, Seth, and a daughter, Meg. His widow, Ann, was the apple of his eye. He had spoken to others of his hope to raise Seth to be of great help on the ranch and to prepare him for eventual ownership, but that is not to be.

Barely two weeks have gone by since George Munger took ill, and though he initially passed it off as something of no consequence, the illness quickly took control, and he died. His last wish was that his widow sell the ranch and move back to Ohio where she has family, believing that a woman alone and raising two children would have a better life there than she would find here.

Mrs. Munger acquiesced to her husband's last wishes by placing the ranch on the market. As it was adjacent to land recently bought by Colonel the Marquis Lucien Garneau, the Frenchman made her a generous offer and she accepted. Out of respect for its previous owner, Colonel Garneau will keep the name Long Trek, and states that whatever property he may henceforth acquire will be assimilated into and retain the name Long Trek.

Mrs. Munger can take comfort in the knowledge that while the body may be committed to the tomb, there is a bond that reaches beyond the grave and it will ever hold her in affectionate embrace.

Lucien Garneau bought Long Trek, complete with house and outbuildings. Over the ensuing four months, he bought several more acres contiguous to Long Trek, so by spring he had 15,000 acres, making Long Trek the second largest ranch in the valley. Every ranch he had bought had been one the owners were willing to sell. But his 15,000 acres were locked in by at least eight other ranchers, all who had property that abutted his, none who wanted to sell.

* * *

"I don't believe you're goin' to get anyone else to sell out to you, Colonel." Otis Nance had been foreman of Long Trek when it was owned by Munger, and he had stayed with the ranch when Garneau bought it.

"They will sell," Garneau said. "I will have the biggest and the best ranch in the entire valley."

"Well, I tell you, Colonel, you might talk enough of 'em into sellin' out to you to wind up bein' the biggest ranch in the area, though that ain't likely. And it's even less likely that you'll be the best."

"And why not, if I may ask?" Garneau replied, obviously miffed by the comment.

"First of all, 'cause you cain't grow no more 'lessen you can get some of the folks around you to sell their land to you, which I can tell you right now, there ain't no more of 'em goin' to do it. And then even if you can wind up with more land, well, sir, I've worked some over at Sugarloaf and it's about the best run place I've ever seen. And it ain't just Smoke Jensen, it's his wife, 'n the men that work there. Jensen, he don't let all his people go in the wintertime like most of the other ranchers, and so the ones that's workin' there, stays just real loyal to him."

"Then perhaps you should go back to work for him," Garneau said angrily.

"There ain't no need for you to go gettin' all riled up now. I was just tellin' you the truth 'cause I thought you might want to know," Nance said.

"Leave my ranch, now, Monsieur Nance," Garneau ordered.

"Wait a minute. Are you firin' me?"

"I am."

"Then in that case, you owe me half a month's wages,"

Nance said, realizing that he wasn't going to be able to talk Garneau into keeping him on.

Two days later, Nance was in the Four Flusher Saloon in Wheeler, Colorado, drinking beer and still complaining about being fired. "I got fired for tellin' the truth. A fella ought not to ever get fired for doin' nothin' more than tellin' the truth. The problem is the colonel has more money than he's got sense. He's tryin' to buy up the whole county, only there ain't no more people goin' to sell to him."

The bar girl Nance was talking to was paying attention to him only as long as she could entice him into buying more drinks. But a solitary drinker at the next table over was listening, and he turned to Nance. "Who is this man you are talking about?"

"He's a Frenchman, by the name of Garneau. Lucien Garneau. Calls himself a marquis, and he likes for folks to call him Colonel. I think a marquis is supposed to be like a lord or something."

"And he's a rich man? This Garneau?"

"Oh yeah, he's rich all right."

Deekus Templeton smiled. It was good information to know.

"The thing is, he's wantin' to make his ranch the biggest and the best in the valley, but I told him, he ain't never goin' to get the better of Smoke Jensen."

"Who?"

"Smoke Jensen. You've heard of him, ain't you? Hell, I thought ever'one had heard of Smoke Jensen."

"Yes, I've heard of him."

Smoke, Templeton knew, was the one who had prevented his train robbery, but he thought it best to suggest that he had only marginally heard of him.

"Well, Smoke Jensen is the one who owns Sugarloaf. I

told Garneau that there weren't no way he would ever make his ranch bigger. Hell, he can't, 'cause he can't grow no more. Puddle and all them other little farmers and ranchers has got their land right up next to his, and if they don't sell to him, then there ain't nowhere else he can go."

"Has he tried to buy them out?" Templeton asked.

"Oh, yeah. He's tried a bunch of times. And he got Turner an' Daniels to sell out to him. But there ain't nobody else goin' to sell to him."

"Darlin', do you want to sit here all day and talk to him? Or do you want to buy me another drink and talk to me for a while?" the girl asked.

"Ha! That's an easy question to answer," Nance said. "Get yourself another drink, then come back and sit with me."

Templeton left the saloon then. He had been thinking about how to get even with Smoke Jensen ever since he had interrupted the train robbery. It just might be the way he could do that. Not only would he be able to get even with Jensen, he could make some money as he was doing it. And if this Garneau man was rich, there just might be a way to make a lot of money.

Long Trek Ranch

Templeton passed through the gate that arched over the road leading up to the main house. The name of the ranch, LONG TREK, was burned into the wood, and to either side of the name was a fleur-de-lis, though Templeton had no idea what it was, or what it meant.

As he rode past the bunkhouse he saw three men out front, sitting in chairs that were tipped back against the front wall. None of the three made any effort to greet him. Tying his horse off at the hitching rail in front of the main house, he stepped up onto the porch and knocked on the door. It was opened a moment later by a short, red-faced man wearing a jacket and tie.

"Mr. Garneau?" Templeton asked.

"I am Garrison Reeves, sir. I am Colonel the Marquis Garneau's valet," the man replied in a very English accent.

"His what?" *Valet* was not a word with which Templeton was familiar.

"Do you wish to speak with Colonel Garneau?"

"Yes."

"Your name, sir?"

"Templeton. Deekus Templeton."

"You may wait in the parlor."

Templeton was shown into the parlor and as he waited, he saw, in a felt-lined case, two pistols, though they were unlike any pistol he was familiar with. He picked one of them up for a closer examination. It didn't have a cylinder, and when he pushed a button on the side, the barrel dropped down. It was a single shot, breech-loading pistol.

"That is a perfectly matched pair of dueling pistols by Gastinne Renette, and they are very valuable."

Turning, Templeton saw a tall, dark-haired man with eyes so light blue they were almost colorless.

"Who would duel with something like this?" Templeton asked. "Hell, the barrel is so long you'd have a hard time gettin' it out of your holster."

"When a gentleman duels, the pistol is already in his hand. There is no need to withdraw it from a holster."

"The hell you say." Templeton shook his head. "I've never heard of a gunfight like that."

"It isn't a gunfight, Monsieur. It is an *affaire d'honneur.* Mr. Reeves told me you wish to speak to me."

"You are Mr. Garneau?"

"I am Colonel Garneau."

"Yes, sir. Well, Colonel, I'd like to come to work for you."

"I have too many employees now. I have no need for more cowboys."

"Yes, well here's the thing, Colonel. I'm not exactly what you would call a cowboy," Templeton said.

"Then if you aren't a cowboy, why do you ask for employment? What are you, a cook?"

Templeton chuckled. "No, I'm not a cook either. I'm what you might call someone who makes things happen."

"I don't understand. What does that mean . . . you are someone who makes things happen?"

"I've heard you want your ranch to grow larger, but you are blocked in by some small ranchers who won't sell out to you."

"They are cretins," Garneau said.

"Well, Mr. Garneau, I believe I can convince those folks to sell to you. And not only that, I can get 'em to sell to you at a price that's less than what their land is worth."

"That is most interesting," Garneau said, paying a bit more attention to what Templeton had to say. "You can convince all eight to sell?"

"We won't have to convince all eight of 'em. All we have to do is convince two or three to sell, and the others will fall into place. I can do that."

"And how, exactly, are you going to do that?"

"By hunting down cattle thieves," Templeton said.

"I don't understand. How does hunting down cattle thieves have anything to do with my intention to grow my ranch?"

"Well, if cattle are disappearing from your ranch, don't you have a right to go after the people who are stealing them?"

"I suppose so," Garneau replied, still not sure where Templeton was going with this.

"It has been my experience these small ranchers can only survive by stealing cattle from the larger ranchers."

"And you think the smaller ranchers are stealing cattle from me?"

"We can make sure they are," Templeton replied with a smile.

Garneau nodded. Finally, he understood. "I see. And you can take care of that problem for me?"

"That depends on how particular you are about how I go about it."

"How particular I am? I don't understand, Monsieur Templeton."

"I mean, what if something was to happen to one of the people who have been stealing your cattle. Something bad enough to make him want to sell?"

"Am I to assume you can make that happen?"

"I can and I will, if that's what it takes to get someone to listen to reason," Templeton said.

"I see."

"How would you feel about that, Colonel Garneau?"

"I am more interested in results, Templeton, than I am in how those results are obtained."

Templeton smiled. "Then I am your man."

"What sort of compensation will you require?"

"Ten thousand dollars, plus expenses," Templeton said.

"Ten thousand dollars?" Garneau replied with a gasp. "You think most highly of yourself, Monsieur."

"Plus expenses," Templeton said again.

"And just what would these expenses be?"

"I'd say about two thousand dollars," Templeton said. "I would need that money up front. You don't have to pay the ten thousand dollars until you have acquired all the land you need."

"Very well, Monsieur Templeton. Return tomorrow, and I will have the expense money for you. How soon will you get started on your . . . project?"

"First things first, Colonel. I have to take care of someone who might be a problem."

"Who would that be?"

"Now, Colonel, you really don't want to know that," Templeton said. "The less you know about what I'm doing, the better off you will be. This way, none of it will come back on you."

"Yes," Garneau said with a nod of his head. "Yes, I believe you may be correct."

"I'll be here tomorrow for the expense money."

CHAPTER 5

A MEETING
of the
EAGLE COUNTY CATTLEMEN'S ASSOCIATION
~ Monday Next ~
County Courthouse
Red Cliff, Colorado

The signs had been posted in all the towns of Eagle County: Mount Jackson, Dillon, Frisco, Wheeler, Eagle Park, Mitchell Wells, Swan, Preston, and Big Rock, so it was well attended by the larger landholders of the county.

Smoke got a cup of coffee from the table in the back of the room, then took his seat as Wes Gregory, president of the Cattlemen's Association called the meeting to order. "Gentlemen, the purpose of this special-called meeting is twofold. First, it is to introduce you to our newest member, Colonel the Marquis Lucien Garneau. Colonel Garneau, as some of you may know, bought Long Trek from George Munger's widow and has subsequently added to it, so it is accurate to say he is now one of the larger landholders in our county. The second reason I have called this meeting is because Colonel Garneau has encountered a problem all of us have faced from time to time, and if what is happening at Long Trek is any indication, we may all be facing it again, soon."

"What problem would that be, Joel?" Adam Dickerson asked.

"Cattle rustling."

"Cattle rustling? Why, I ain't had no problem with that, other than some transient killing a steer now and then for meat."

"Perhaps I had better let Colonel Garneau talk," Gregory said.

"*Merci*, Monsieur Gregory," Garneau said, then he smiled at the audience. "And I promise you, saying thank you to Mr. Gregory will be the last French I use. I will speak only in English, because I want to make certain everyone understands the severity of the problem.

"I have been here but a short time. I bought the ranch from the widow of George Munger, along with all the livestock. I have added to the size of the original ranch by purchasing property adjacent to the ranch. I can expand no farther, because the holdings of small ranchers and farmers have me blocked.

"That would not be a problem except for this." Garneau held up a finger to emphasize his point. "I am losing cattle at an alarming rate, and I am convinced the culprits are those same small ranchers and farmers who have me locked in."

"Garneau, I think you may be mistaken there," Smoke said. "I know all the ranchers and farmers you are talking about—they have been my neighbors for some time. Speer, Woodward, Turner, Babcock, Logan, Clayton, Daniels, Keefer, Drexler, Butrum, and Puddle. Why, you couldn't ask for a finer neighbor than Humboldt Puddle. Anytime anyone runs into trouble, Mr. Puddle is the first one to offer help."

"Perhaps, Monsieur Jensen, it is because you are a longtime, established resident that they leave you alone. Perhaps it is only because I am new here, and I am a foreigner, that I have been singled out."

"Have you gone to the sheriff about it?" Dickerson asked.

"The sheriff is as Monsieur Jensen, I'm afraid. He thinks his neighbors can do no wrong," Garneau said. "But I don't need the sheriff. I am in the process of putting together my own *régulateurs*."

"Regulators? You mean, vigilantes?" Dickerson asked.

"Yes, to guard my cattle and to stop the thievery."

"Look here, Garneau, are you expecting us to join you in hiring a bunch of vigilantes?"

"No, no, that isn't at all necessary," Garneau said. "I just want to make you aware of the problem . . . and how I plan to solve it."

Big Rock

When Smoke stepped into Longmont's Saloon three days later, he saw Tim Murchison, the owner of the leather goods store, and Dan Norton, the lawyer, sitting at a table with Louis Longmont, and he walked over to join them.

"Hmm," Louis said. "What are you doing here at this hour? Another school board meeting?"

"Do you think the only time I can come in at night is when Sally is at a school board meeting?"

"Yes."

"Well, you're wrong," Smoke said. "I also come in when she's at a garden meeting, like tonight."

The others laughed.

"Smoke Jensen, there's not a gunman in the country that you won't face down, but I think Sally's got your number," Murchison said.

"Listen, have you ever seen Sally with a gun?" Louis asked. "She's as good as anyone I know."

"I believe you there, my friend. I have seen her give shooting exhibitions," Norton said.

"How did the Cattlemen's Association meeting go up in Red Cliff the other day?" Murchison asked.

"It seems our newest rancher is being plagued with cattle rustling," Smoke said.

"Cattle rustling? That's strange. I haven't heard anyone else talking about cattle rustling. Have you had any trouble with it?" Norton asked.

"No, I haven't."

"Hmm." Louis was staring at the entrance. "There are three men I haven't seen before."

Smoke looked toward the front of the saloon as three men entered. "Probably more cowboys coming to work for Garneau. He's bringing them in from everywhere," Norton said.

"Uh-uh. Those men aren't cowboys," Smoke said.

"What do you mean?"

"Look at their hands. Most working cowboys have hands that are callused or crooked fingers from being broken. Those men have smooth hands. They've never done any real work."

"And look how they are wearing their guns," Louis said.

In cut-down holsters, their guns hung rather low from the hip. They carried themselves with the swagger of someone who not only knew how to use a gun, but had used it.

"Barkeep!" one of them called out. "Three beers. And which way to the Long Trek Ranch?"

"I'll be right with you, sir."

"No, by God, you'll be with us now," the man said belligerently.

"Sir, I am with a customer."

"Well, what the hell do you think we are?"

"I'm sorry, sir, please be a little patient. I'll be with you shortly," the barkeep said.

"Is that a new bartender?" Smoke asked.

"Yes," Louis responded, paying close attention to what was going on at the bar.

The man slammed his fist on the bar. "By damn, I said you'll be with us *now*!"

"Monsieur," Louis called over to him.

The belligerent man looked over toward the table where Louis, Smoke, Murchison, and Norton were sitting. "Are you talking to me?"

"I am, sir. The Long Trek is five miles west of town. I suggest you go there now. If you want a drink, you might be happier with the service at the Brown Dirt Cowboy. That is another saloon one block east of here, on the corner of Front Street and Sikes," Louis suggested.

"Yeah? Why should we go to another saloon, when we are already in a saloon?" He turned back toward the bar. "Barkeep, are you comin' down here, or do I have to do something to get your attention?"

"Perhaps I was too subtle for you," Louis suggested.

"Too . . . what?" the man replied, his face screwing up in confusion over the word *subtle*.

"I will say it in words even someone like you can understand. Get out of my establishment."

"Your establishment? You mean you own this place?"

"I do."

"You ain't all that careful about how you treat your customers, are you?"

"The customers I value, I treat very well. The others, I ask to leave. As I am asking you."

The belligerent one turned toward Louis then, and the two men with him stepped out beside him. All three faced Louis. They were standing, and Louis was sitting, which put him at a significant disadvantage if the situation developed any further.

"Suppose we don't want to leave, what are you going to do about it?"

"I will force you to leave."

The man smiled an evil smile. "Is that so? Now just how are you going to do that? You seem to have gotten yourself into a little pickle, here. I mean, you are sitting down, and we're standing."

"I believe you wanted my attention, sir?" the bartender said at that moment.

"Not now. I may have some business with this man."

The loud sound of two hammers being pulled back was heard, and the belligerent one got a shocked expression on his face, then turned toward the bartender. He was holding a sawed off, double-barreled twelve-gauge shotgun about twelve inches from the belligerent one's head. "And I've got business with you. I believe I could get all three of you with one shot."

"No, wait!" the man shouted, holding his hand out. "Look here, now. There ain't no need in this goin' on any further. It was just a little misunderstandin' is all. If the man don't want our business, we'll take it down to that other saloon he was talkin' about."

"That would be the Brown Dirt," the bartender said. "And as Mr. Longmont explained, it is one block east, then south on Sikes Street. You can't miss it. It's rather loud and unruly, just your kind of place."

"All right, all right. We'll go."

"Thank you," Louis called out to the three men. "I would appreciate that. Oh, and if you three would like to come back in here again sometime . . . and act like gentlemen . . . I would welcome your business."

"We ain't never acomin' back here. Come on, let's go," the man mumbled to the other two, and laughter from the bar patrons chased the three men out.

"If those three men aren't cowboys, why do they want to find the Long Trek?" Norton asked.

"Over the last several days, I've noticed quite a few men like that have gone to work for Garneau," Murchison said.

"What on earth for?" Norton asked.

"Garneau is recruiting a private army to, as he explains it, control the cattle rustling," Smoke said.

"What a dumb thing for him to be doing." Louis looked toward the bar and waved the barkeep over.

"Yes, Mr. Longmont?"

"Mr. McVey, I want to introduce you to some friends of mine," Louis said. "Smoke, Dan, Tim, this is my new bartender, Johnny McVey."

"What happened to Poke?" Norton asked.

"He still works here. He won't come in until eight o'clock tonight," Louis answered. "He and Johnny are splitting the time."

"Well, Mr. McVey, you looked as if you were at home with that scattergun," Smoke said.

"Yes, sir, I've deputied some, and I've been a shotgun guard on a stagecoach," McVey said.

"It certainly came in helpful a few minutes ago," Smoke said.

McVey smiled. "Not really. The three of them standing were no match for the two of you, even if you were sitting down. I don't think they had any idea who they were dealing with. What I got was a cheap moment in the limelight."

"You wouldn't think to look at him that he is a pianist, would you?" Louis asked.

"So, you're a piano player, are you?" Murchison asked.

"No, sir. I'm a pianist," McVey said.

Murchison looked confused. "What's the difference?"

"A piano player plays *Buffalo Gals*. A pianist plays *Tchaikovsky's Piano Concerto Number One*."

"Smoke!" Norton shouted.

The three belligerent men had come back into the saloon, bursting through the batwing doors with their guns in their hands. Dan Norton, Tim Murchison, and Johnny McVey, none of whom were armed, dived for the floor. Smoke and Louis came up from their chairs, bringing their pistols to bear.

The saloon was filled with women's screams, the shouts

and curses of men, and the bang of gunfire as all five guns were brought into play.

One of the bullets from the three intruders hit the sleeve garter Louis was wearing, cutting it in two. Because it was elastic, it flew from his arm and hit Norton in the face.

"I'm hit!" Norton yelled.

Another bullet smashed Norton's mug, sending out a spray of beer and tiny shards of glass. The third bullet hit the heating stove, cold for the summer, then went screaming off to bury itself in the wall.

It wasn't hard to track the three bullets fired by Smoke and the two fired by Louis. All three of the intruders went down with fatal wounds.

For a long a moment after the explosive sounds of the gunshots were gone, there was absolute silence in the saloon. Gun smoke curled upward, then formed a cloud that hung just under the ceiling, the acrid smell burning the eyes and noses of the witnesses and participants alike.

Smoke and Louis, with smoking guns still in their hands, approached the three men, all three of whom were now prostrate on the floor. Smoke prodded one of the shooters with the toe of his boot and got no response.

"Whoa, that was something!" one of the bar patrons shouted.

"Are they dead?" another asked.

"I'll say they're dead. They're deader 'n crap. Hell, I can tell that from way over here," another said, and after that, the saloon was alive with excited chatter.

"You don't mind if I look, do you?" Doc Urban asked. He'd been sitting in a card game on the other side of the room and had come over to examine the bodies."

"I'm tellin' you, Doc, you don't have to examine 'em. They're deader 'n crap. I can tell that from way over here."

Doctor Urban squatted down beside the three men and felt the carotid arteries of each of them.

"What about it, Doc?" Louis asked.

"In my medical opinion," Doctor Urban said, "these three men are deader than crap."

Nervous laughter broke out in the saloon, and they were still laughing when Sheriff Carson came sprinting into the saloon with his pistol in his hand.

"You're a little late, Sheriff. It's done all been took care of," one of saloon patrons said.

"Are they dead?" Sheriff Carson asked.

"Indeed they are," Doc Urban said. "Oh, Dan, I'm sorry. You said you were hit?"

"Uh, it wasn't anything," Dan said.

"Maybe I should look at it anyway. Sometimes the most minor wounds can be quite troublesome. You may as well get it treated."

"Like I said, it wasn't anything. It was—uh—this." Dan held up the severed sleeve garter. "This hit me in the face."

Those close enough to see, laughed again.

"What happened here?" Sheriff Carson asked, eventually getting the story, though so many were trying to tell it at the same time it took a few minutes before he got the entire story. "Anybody know these men?"

Nobody knew them, so he went through their pockets. In every man's pocket he found the same thing. A recruiting poster.

Men Wanted

To Stem the Rising Tide of Cattle Rustling

Must be Proficient with Firearms

Apply at Long Trek Ranch

Big Rock Colorado

Will Be Well Paid

Cattle rustling?" Sheriff Carson asked. "What cattle rustling would that be?"

CHAPTER 6

Loy Babcock was having his lunch when there was a loud knock at his door. "I wonder who that could be?" He got up from the table.

"Loy, be careful," Millie said.

"Be careful of what? It's just someone knocking on the door." He opened the door and saw Deekus Templeton standing there. Behind him were four men, all of whom were mounted. With the four mounted men was a steer with a rope around its neck.

"Can I help you?" Babcock asked.

"You mean instead of, can you help yourself?" Templeton asked.

"What do you mean, help myself. I don't know what you are talking about."

"I'm talking about the fifteen head of steers that are mixed in with your cattle. You tried to change the brand, but you did a sloppy job."

"You're crazy! I don't have any Long Trek stock!"

Templeton turned and called, "Bring that steer up here, Nixon."

The man called Nixon dismounted, then led the steer up to the front of the house.

"What do you call this?" Templeton asked. "Look at this

brand." He stepped down from the porch, pointing out the very clumsy attempt to change the LT brand into a Bar-B. The LT was still clearly visible.

"That's not my steer," Babcock said.

"You damn right it's not your steer," Templeton said. "That's the whole point. So what was this steer doing on your ranch? This one and fourteen others just like it."

"I don't know how they got here. Maybe they wandered over here. Cattle do that, you know. They start following the grass or the water, and there's no tellin' where they are likely to turn up," Babcock said, growing a little more frightened.

"Uh-huh. And I suppose after they quit wanderin' around, they also branded themselves."

"I'm tellin' you, I don't know how those steers got on my land. And I don't know how they got branded, but I didn't have anything to do with it."

"You're lyin'," Templeton said. "Well, I'm tellin' you right now, your cattle rustlin' days are over."

Nixon, who had been coming closer, suddenly dropped rope over Babcock, then cinched it up tight.

"What are you doing?"

"We're going to make certain you never steal anybody else's cattle."

Nixon jerked him down from the porch, then dragged him toward the barn.

"Get 'im up in the hayloft," Templeton ordered.

"What are you doing? Let my husband go!" Millie Babcock shouted.

"You'd better stay out of this, missus!" Templeton said.

Millie stepped back into the house, then came back out onto the front porch, holding a rifle."

"You let my husband go!" she shouted, raising the rifle to her shoulder.

Templeton shot her, and she fell.

"Millie!" Babcock screamed.

"Get 'im up there. Get the job done!" Templeton ordered.

Two of the four men climbed the ladder to the hayloft in the barn. Then they grabbed the rope and literally pulled Babcock up. When they got him into the loft, they took him over the open door, tied one end of the rope around the protruding hay hoist, and looped the other end around his neck.

"You got any last words, cattle thief?" Templeton asked.

"I didn't steal your cows," Babcock said. "You killed Millie so I have nothing to live for, but I'll be damned if I let you kill me."

Babcock leaped out of the door himself, hit the end of the rope, then swung back and forth as he gagged. Templeton and the others watched until he quit swinging.

"Get the rope off him," Templeton said.

"You mean cut him down?"

"No, leave him up there. Just take off the rope we used to tie him up," Templeton said.

He walked back over to the porch, where the body of Millie Babcock lay. He picked up the rifle, fired one round from it, then tossed the rifle onto the ground halfway between the house and the barn. "Let's go."

"What about the steer we brought over?" Nixon asked.

"Take him back to Long Trek. We don't need him anymore."

From the *Big Rock Journal*:

Terrible Tragedy
───────────

Loy Babcock and Wife Found Dead

Yesterday, Charles Woodward, whose land adjoins the Babcock spread, grew concerned that it had been some time since he had seen his neighbor. Riding over to see if anything was wrong, he came upon a most grisly scene. Loy Babcock was found hanging from the hay hoist at his barn, and his wife, Millie, was dead of a gunshot wound on the back porch. Halfway between the porch and the barn, was found Babcock's rifle, with one bullet having been fired.

Tom Nunnley, the county coroner, has ruled the deaths as murder suicide.

"It appears that Mr. and Mrs. Babcock got into an argument, resulting in Mr. Babcock shooting his wife," Nunnley said. "Then, unable to live with what he had done, Mr. Babcock took his own life."

Interment will be in the Garden of Memories Cemetery in Big Rock tomorrow at two o'clock, post meridiem. There will be no church services.

"I don't give a damn what Nunnley says," Woodward told the others after Babcock and his wife were buried side by side. "I know damn well Loy didn't kill Millie. Why, you ain't never seen a couple that loved one another like them two did."

"Then what do you think happened?" Humboldt Puddle asked.

"I don't know. Could be, a group of outlaws come by to see what they could rob."

Chris Logan shook his head. "Can't be that. Sheriff Carson found sixty-two dollars in the sugar bowl. Don't you think if it was robbers, they would've took the money?"

"Maybe they didn't find it," Woodward said.

"How could they not have found it? Damn near ever'one I know keeps their money in a sugar bowl," Logan said.

"I don't know why they didn't find it. Maybe they wasn't

even robbers in the first place. I just know that Loy wouldn'ta kilt Millie."

One of Babcock's neighbors who went to the interment was Lucien Garneau. After the burial, he went to the land office to see Pete Perkins.

"You didn't waste any time getting here," Perkins said. "Babcock's body isn't even cold in the ground yet."

"I'm thinking of his next of kin," Garneau said. "Surely he has someone who will inherit his land. I want to find out who that is, and make them an offer on the place. I'm sure they will be aggrieved by his death, but perhaps some money would help ameliorate that grief."

"I will see what I can do," Perkins said. "Robert Dempster should be able to find out who the next of kin might be."

Robert Dempster was a morbidly obese man. As he sat behind his desk listening to Garneau, he was eating a sugar-coated cruller. He took the last bite, then sucked the ends of his fingers. "I'll see what I can find out."

Garneau nodded and left the office.

"There is no need to find out who the next of kin is," Dempster said after two days of investigation. "In thirty days taxes will be due on every piece of property in the entire county. Babcock won't be here to pay the taxes, so title to the land will pass to whoever pays those taxes."

"How much will that be?" Garneau asked.

"That little bit of information comes under the heading of my legal fee," Dempster said.

"All right. How much is your legal fee?"

"One hundred dollars."

"Come to the bank with me, and I'll pay you."

Half an hour later, in exchange for the one hundred dollars

he had received from Garneau, Dempster handed over a piece of paper. "Go to the county assessor and pay him the amount on this form, and he will hand over a deed of possession to you."

Garneau looked at the form. "What? This can't be right!"

Dempster chuckled. "Believe me, it is right. Do you see now, how advantageous it is for you to have a good lawyer?"

"This says sixty-two dollars."

"That's right. For sixty-two dollars you will own what was Babcock's ranch."

Two days later, Charles Woodward saw black smoke curling into the sky and he called out to his wife. "Sue, it looks like there's a fire over at the Babcock ranch."

"How in heaven's name could a fire get started over there?" Sue asked. "There's nobody there."

"I'm going to go check it out."

"Why? I mean if nobody is there, what difference does it make?"

"I'm just curious, that's all."

Woodward reached the Babcock place in about twenty minutes. He saw a wagon loaded with furniture he recognized from his many visits with the Babcocks. He also saw that not only the house was burning, but so were the barn, the implement shed, and the little building where the hired hands stayed during the season. Four men stood around, watching the buildings burn. They watched Woodward as he rode up and dismounted.

Woodward recognized Templeton. "I was going to say that you did a good job of getting the furniture out before it was burned along with the house. But it looks like you took it out before the house caught fire."

"Of course we did," Templeton said. "Just because we are burning all the buildings, doesn't mean we have to burn the furniture too."

"Are you telling me that you burned the buildings?"

"We sure did."

"Why would you do that?"

"Once Colonel Garneau bought the ranch, he was only interested in the land," Templeton said. "The buildings were just in the way."

"What do you mean Garneau bought the ranch? Bought it from who?"

"You'll have to ask the colonel that," Templeton said. "All I know is, he now owns the place. And that means you are trespassing, by the way. What are you doing here, anyway?"

"I came to see about the fire."

"Well, you've seen about it. I suggest you get off the colonel's property."

Disgruntled, Woodward returned to his home.

"What caused the fire?" Sue asked as he came in the door.

"Garneau caused the fire," Woodward said. "Sue, that man Templeton, the one who works for Garneau, says Garneau owns the ranch now."

"What? How can that be possible? Why didn't it pass to Loy's younger brother? You know what store he set by that boy."

"I don't know, but something is fishy here. I don't know how Garneau got possession of the land, but I'd be willing to bet that it was something crooked. And I'll tell you something else. I wouldn't be surprised if Garneau didn't have something to do with Loy and Millie gettin' killed."

"Oh, Charles, don't ever say that to anyone. Why, if it got back to Garneau that you were accusing him . . . I don't know what he would do."

"I'll tell you what I'm going to do," Woodward said. "I'm going over to Humboldt's, and see if he won't call a meeting of all the small farmers and ranchers. I don't know where Garneau is goin' with all this, but I sure don't like the looks of it."

CHAPTER 7

Humboldt Puddle agreed to host a meeting, and word went out to every rancher and farmer whose land was adjacent to Long Trek Ranch.

He was the oldest of the landowners, and his ranch, *Carro de Bancada*, consisted of four sections, making him the largest property owner of the group. Because of his age, property, and the fact that he was a natural leader, the others tended to look to him for direction. It was natural, then, that the meeting took place in his house.

Otto Speer was the first to arrive. He was a German who had come to the U.S. just before the Civil War. He'd fought in the war on the side of the North, and after the war, brought his family to Eagle County to homestead a half section of land.

Woodward arrived next. He was from Georgia and had fought for the South. When the war ended, there was little left for him to go back to, so he, his wife, and daughter had come to Colorado to homestead. Despite the fact that they had fought on opposite sides, Woodward and Speer were friends. Lucy, who was a very pretty eighteen-year-old, came to the meeting with her parents and offered to look after the youngsters who came.

Herman Drexler was next to arrive. He and his wife had come to Colorado from Pennsylvania. They had a twelve-year-old son named Jimmy. Even though Drexler and his wife came by spring wagon, Jimmy rode Duffy, the horse he had gotten for his birthday. He wanted to show Duffy off to the others.

Jimmy showed Duffy first to the two young boys of Chris Logan, giving them a ride, one at a time. Logan had been a first sergeant in the Seventh Cavalry, making Custer's last scout with him. He was with Reno during the battle, and thus avoided the fate that befell so many of his friends. Logan's nearest neighbor was Marvin Butrum. Butrum was also married, with two young daughters, and on occasion Logan and Butrum discussed whether or not their children would marry each other when they grew up.

Tom Keefer was the remaining neighbor. He had a spotted past, and though his neighbors may have wondered about him, he proved to be affable and helpful, so no one questioned him. Nobody knew he had once been a road agent down in Texas, and it was money he stole from a stagecoach shipment that gave him the start he'd needed in Colorado. Keefer wasn't married.

Puddle had been married when he came to Colorado, but his wife, Martha Jane, had died two years ago without ever having borne a child. Because he lived alone, the wives of his neighbors brought food so there was a potluck dinner before the meeting. Finally, when the last biscuit had been buttered and the last pork chop eaten, Puddle invited the men into his parlor to talk.

"I'm goin' to have to do somethin'," Logan said. "Ever since Burt Daniels sold out to the Frenchman, my stock has been cut off from water. Frying Pan Creek ran through Daniel's land and on to mine. Me 'n Daniels had us an arrangement where we was sharin' that water. Daniels always made certain the creek was flowin', but the water has stopped, and I believe the Frenchman has blocked it, of a pure purpose."

"What are you doin' for water now, Chris?" Otto Speer asked.

"I'm keeping the waterin' troughs filled with water from my well, but I'm afeared the well's goin' to run dry."

"Tell you what, you can run your cattle across my range. I've got plenty of water," Speer said.

"That's damn neighborly of you, Otto," Logan said.

"And that's how we're goin' to get through this," Humboldt Puddle said. "If we're good neighbors to each other, and help each other out when it's needed, the Frenchman will get the idea that he can't just buffalo us like he's tryin' to do."

"Hell, the man has more land now than anybody else," Woodward said. "What does he want to do? Own the entire county?"

"He doesn't have more land than anyone else," Keefer said. "That's the problem. Smoke Jensen has the most land, and I've heard it said the Frenchman won't stop until Long Trek is bigger 'n Sugarloaf."

"Well, that's not going to happen. He's locked in now. He can't grow any bigger."

"Not unless he gets our land," Puddle said. "And that's what he's after now. He wants to buy us out . . . or force us to leave."

"Well, he'll play hell gettin' my land," Woodward said. "'Cause I ain't sellin'."

"No, and sell my land *werde ich nicht tun*," Speer said.

"What did he just say?" Logan asked.

"He said he would not sell his land," Woodward said.

"Well I'm willin' to stay as long as all the others are," Drexler said.

"I'd like to see us all make that pledge," Puddle said. "I think if we stay together, the Frenchman will quit trying, and will leave us alone."

"I'm willin' to make that pledge," Logan said, and he stuck his hand out. One by one the others extended their hand, until an eight-armed star was formed.

Geneva, Switzerland

For five months Inspector Laurent had conducted a diligent search and inquiry of every bank in France, looking for a major depositor, but none could be found. When he was about to report to General Moreau that he had come to a dead end, he got a break. He received a letter from the director of France's international currency exchange.

> *Monsieur Inspector Laurent,*
> *I am informed that you have been making inquiries of all banks and financial institutions with regard to large and unexpected monetary deposits. In accordance with your investigation, I can tell you we have recently received a transfer of two and one half million francs from the Swiss National Bank. The paperwork accompanying the transfer indicated this amount was the result of a transaction with one Antoine Dubois.*
> *I hope this information will be of some assistance to you in your investigation.*
>
> > *Most sincerely,*
> > *Jean Arnaud*
> > *Minister of Finance*

That was it! Laurent knew Dubois was dead. If someone made a money exchange in Geneva using the name Dubois, it had to be Mouchette!

Two days after Laurent received the letter, he stepped off a train in Geneva, Switzerland, then went straight to the Swiss National Bank.

"Yes, Monsieur Inspector, a French gentlemen by the name of Antoine Dubois did present exactly two and one half million francs for monetary exchange."

"Was this the man?" Laurent asked, showing the bank officer a photograph of Pierre Mouchette.

The bank official looked at the photograph. "*Oui*, Monsieur, I believe this may be the man. But he was not in uniform. He said he was a French businessman. He exchanged the francs for American dollars."

"*Merci*, Monsieur, you have been a great help."

When he left the bank, Inspector Laurent wore a big smile. He had traced Mouchette to Switzerland. Mouchette had exchanged two and one half million francs, which was the exact amount of money taken, and had passed himself off as Sergeant Dubois. It was all the evidence Laurent needed. That the bank official identified the photograph was but corroboration of what he already knew.

Mouchette had made the exchange for American dollars. That could only mean he had gone to America. It would be harder to find him, but Laurent was convinced that he would find him. And he would take him back to France to face the guillotine.

Sugarloaf Ranch

Sally and Smoke were in the kitchen. She laughed as she read a letter from Cal.

"What is it?" Smoke asked from the table where he sat drinking a cup of coffee.

She read aloud. "Miss Sally, me and Pearlie don't mind being here in Denver all that much, what with there being a lot to do and we know that Smoke needs us over here. But what is so hard is that we ain't had nary one bite of your bear sign in so long we've near 'bout forgot what they taste like. Could you cook some up and put 'em in a box, then put 'em on a train and have 'em sent here. Wouldn't take more 'n a day to get 'em here by train, and more 'n likely they'd still be good to eat when they got here."

Smoke laughed. "I'll tell you what is hard."

"What's that?"

"For you to read that letter exactly as Cal wrote it. I mean with bad grammar and all. It had to be almost more than you could do."

Sally laughed as well. "It did hurt me to misuse grammar. But I thought if I didn't read it exactly as Cal wrote it, it would lose something."

"Are you going to make some bear signs for them?"

"Now, how can I turn down a heartfelt request like that? Yes, I'm going to make some for them."

"Uh, would you, uh . . ."

Sally laughed again, interrupting Smoke in mid-request. "Of course I'm going to make a few extra." Sally looked through the window.

"Oh, there's Mr. Puddle coming up the road. I wonder what he wants."

"Only one way to find out." Smoke stepped out onto the porch to meet Puddle. "Hello, Humboldt. Climb down and come on into the house for a cup of coffee."

"Thank you." Puddle swung down from the saddle. He was in his mid-fifties, with a full head of gray hair and a gray beard. He wasn't a very big man, but he managed to project a persona bigger than his physical stature.

Sally greeted him when he came in. "Hello, Mr. Puddle. Welcome to Sugarloaf. Why don't you and Smoke go on into the parlor," she invited. "I'll bring you some coffee."

"Thank you kindly, Sally," Humboldt replied, taking advantage of his age to address Sally so.

"What's on your mind, Humboldt?" Smoke asked when the two men were seated.

"Smoke, just how much do you know about this fella, Garneau?" Puddle asked.

"Not too much," Smoke said. "He doesn't seem to be a man you can get friendly with."

"You got that right. You know, don't you, that he has taken over Babcock's place."

"Yes, I heard that he had."

"Do you know how he got that ranch?"

"I haven't heard, but I expect he pulled some sort of deal," Smoke said.

Puddle grunted. "I'll say he did. He paid the taxes on it. That's it, Smoke. He paid the sixty-two dollars tax on the land, and got title to it. And you know the real ironic thing? They found sixty-two dollars in the sugar bowl in Loy's house. He had the money for the tax and was going to pay it.

"I read in the paper that it was a murder suicide," Smoke said.

"You'll never get me to believe that," Puddle said. "Not in a thousand years would I believe that."

"I didn't know Babcock that well."

"Well, believe me, he wouldn't do a thing like that. It just seems damn convenient to me that both he and Millie wind up dead, and Garneau winds up with title to their property. He's already bought out Daniels, and he's been tryin' to buy ever'one else out, but I've managed to hold ever'one together so far."

"I don't doubt it. You're a man people listen to," Smoke said.

"Yes, sir. But here's the thing. Am I right in tellin' ever'one else to hold on? I mean, when you get right down to it, it ain't none of my business. And even if Garneau didn't have anything to do with killin' Babcock, it is still gettin' pretty ugly."

"How?"

"Well, you take Logan's property for example. Once Garneau got his hands on Daniels' ranch, he damned up

Frying Pan Creek. Daniels was lettin' it go on through so's Logan had water, but now he has none."

"That's not good."

"No, sir, it ain't. And I'm afraid it's goin' to get worse. I guess what I'm wantin' to hear from you, Smoke, is if I'm doin' the right thing by keepin' ever'one together."

"What are the others saying? Are they wanting to sell out?"

"No, sir. We had a meetin' at my house, and ever'one came. And ever'one of 'em said they was plannin' on stayin'."

"Then you aren't forcing them into anything, Humboldt. You are leading them. And any successful group has to have a good leader. I'd say you're doing the right thing."

Puddle smiled. "Thank you, Smoke. To be truthful with you, I think I rode over here just to hear you say that."

Sally came into the room then. "My first batch of bear signs will be out shortly, Mr. Puddle. I do hope you will stay long enough to have one."

"Miz Jensen, if that's the delicious thing I been smellin' ever since I got here, I ain't likely to leave 'less I get told to leave."

Sally chuckled. "We're not about to do that."

"Then yes, ma'am, it'll be a pleasure to stay."

CHAPTER 8

Long Trek

"Colonel, I'm goin' to be gone for a few days," Templeton said. "I'll check in with you when I get back."

"Where are you going?"

"I'm goin' to take care of what could be a problem for us. Believe me, you're better off not knowin' anything about it."

"All right. I won't interfere," Garneau said.

Red Cliff, Colorado

Templeton was in town to meet with a man named Jake Willard. A tall man with a narrow face and a badly burned, disfigured cheek, he was a gunman who killed for money. Templeton had money, and he wanted someone killed.

He found him sitting in the back of the Moosehead Saloon, drinking beer and dealing poker hands to himself. "Willard." Templeton pointed to a chair. "May I sit down?"

Willard nodded, and Templeton took a seat.

"Didn't you once tell me you would like to go up against Smoke Jensen?"

"If the conditions are right."

"By conditions, do you mean money?"

"Money is one of the conditions I mean. I would also like

to have an edge. A man is a fool if he goes into a gunfight without an edge, especially if it's ag'in someone like Smoke Jensen."

"Suppose I get something set up for you where the conditions are right? Would you be interested?"

"How are you going to make the conditions right?"

"I'll pay someone to back your play."

"How much will you pay me?"

"One thousand dollars, after it's done," Templeton said.

Willard took the last swallow of his beer, then wiped his mouth with the back of his hand.

"All right. Let's do it."

Big Rock

Smoke and Sally had come into town in the spring wagon. Sally was planning on doing some shopping, stopping first at Foster and Matthews Grocery, then Goldstein's Mercantile, and finally the dress shop.

"Are we going to have any money left when you are finished?" Smoke asked.

"Kirby Jensen, you have enough money to buy every store in this town. I imagine you'll have some left when I'm finished." Sally smiled. "Not much," she teased. "But some."

Smoke stopped in front of the grocery store, then handed the reins to Sally. "I'll let you keep the spring wagon so you have a place to put everything you're buying. I'll be at Longmont's," he added as he hopped down, then started up Front Street.

"Tell Louis I said hello."

As he passed Murchison's Leather Goods store, Tim stepped out to speak to him. "Smoke, I have those boots you ordered."

"Good, I'll pick 'em up on the way back."

"No need, I saw you and Miz Sally come into town. I'll just take 'em down and put 'em in your wagon."

"Thanks, Tim."

"Where's Pearlie and Cal? I haven't seen either one of 'em in coon's age."

"I've got them both in Denver, running the abattoir for me." Murchison chuckled. "I don't suppose they are any too happy about that."

"All in all, I think they would rather be back on the ranch," Smoke said. "And I expect I'll have them both back before too much longer."

"Tell them I asked about them."

"I will."

Templeton had climbed up to the top of the McCoy Building, which was the highest building in town. From there, he had seen Smoke approaching the town, even when the wagon was still far out on Gold Park Road.

He had a good view of Front Street by looking across the top of the Dress Shoppe, and he watched Smoke talking to Murchison in front of the leather goods shop. Templeton stayed there until he saw Jensen go into Longmont's Saloon.

Climbing down from the top of the McCoy Building, Templeton hurried down the street to the Brown Dirt Cowboy Saloon. There, he found Willard sitting at a table alone, drinking beer and dealing himself poker hands. His reputation was such that nobody would play cards with him. He looked up when Templeton approached his table. "Is he in town?"

"He just went into Longmont's. I knew he would go there, so I've got a man with a rifle up on the balcony. All you have to do is call Jensen out."

"Who's goin' to kill 'im? Me or the man up on the balcony?"

"You're goin' to be the one that kills him," Templeton said. "All my man is going to do is get his attention."

"How?"

"Once you call him out, my man will cock his rifle. That'll

make Jensen look around. You said you wanted an edge? That's the edge. When he looks around, that's when you'll kill him."

Willard smiled, giving him an even more skull-like appearance. "All right." He stood and loosened the pistol in his holster. "I had me a plate of beef and beans a while ago. And this beer. You take care of my tab. And have the thousand dollars ready as soon as I do the job."

"I've got the money out in my saddlebag."

"I want to see it," Willard said.

Templeton nodded, then started back toward the door with Willard right behind him. When they reached Templeton's horse, he opened the saddlebag flap.

"You can look in. I don't plan to flash that much money in public."

Willard looked into the bag, satisfied himself that the money was there, then nodded. "Don't you be goin' anywhere. I'll be back for my money in a couple minutes."

Smoke was standing at the bar, having a drink with Sheriff Carson when Jake Willard stepped in through the front door. "Jensen! I'm callin' you out!"

There was a quick scrape of chairs and tables as everyone scrambled to get out of the way. Only Sheriff Carson didn't move away from Smoke. The sheriff looked over at the bartender, who had ducked down behind the bar.

"Poke, would you draw me another beer, please?" he asked in a calm voice.

"Sheriff, are you crazy?" Poke hissed. "Get out of the line of fire!"

Sheriff Carson chuckled, then looked back toward Jake Willard, who was standing in the doorway with his arm crooked, just above his pistol.

"Don't you know who that is?" Sheriff Carson asked,

pointing to Willard. "His name is Jake Willard, a two-bit outlaw who is hardly worth the reward that's out on him. If he's serious about this foolish notion of challenging Smoke, then he's about to die. Now, how about the beer?"

Poke rose up just enough to take the sheriff's mug, then he drew another beer and handed it to him.

"Thanks." Carson blew the foam off, then turned and looked toward the gunman. "Willard, I'm glad you showed up. I have paper on you, and this keeps me from having to go look for you. Why don't you just take your pistol out real slow and put it on the table there? I'll take you on down the street to the jail and hold you until someone comes to get you."

"Do you really think I'm crazy enough to do that?" Willard asked.

"No, I think you're crazy enough to draw on Smoke and get yourself killed. And that's fine with me. Either way, it ends for you today."

Willard went for his pistol, shouting a challenge. "Draw, Jensen!"

Smoke beat the draw and fired a split second before Willard.

The gunman fired twice. His first bullet plowed into the bar right beside Smoke, and his second punched a hole through the floor as he fell.

Smoke stood in place, his pistol still ready, should Willard have any partners wishing to continue the confrontation. The smoke of the three discharges drifted toward the ceiling, joining the smoke of pipes, cigars, and cigarettes already gathered in a cloud.

"Did you see that?" someone asked in an awestruck voice.

"Well, yeah, I seen it. I'm here, ain't I?"

The response elicited nervous laughter from some of the others.

* * *

Outside, Deekus Templeton heard the shots and waited a moment to see if Willard came out. When he didn't, Templeton knew for certain it was Willard who had been shot. Joining the several curious people rushing into the saloon, he saw Willard lying dead on the floor. Tales of what happened were already buzzing around the saloon.

Templeton looked down at Willard and shook his head. No one with a rifle was on the balcony providing back up, nor was there ever intended to be. He had told Willard that only to give him the courage to face Jensen. To be honest, Templeton didn't think Willard actually had any hope of besting Smoke Jensen, but figured it was a chance worth taking, especially since no money would change hands unless he succeeded, and also, because it wasn't his own life put at risk.

Sally was just coming out of the dress shop when she heard shooting from the saloon. She knew, with a loving wife's intuition, it involved Smoke. And though she knew Smoke could handle himself in any fair encounter, she also knew there were people who would think nothing of shooting him in the back. It was for that reason she hurried to join the others as they ran toward the saloon.

Reaching the front porch she looked in over the swinging doors and saw Smoke standing just in front of the bar, still holding a smoking pistol. She breathed a sigh of relief to see that he wasn't hurt, then rushed in to embrace him.

"Are you all finished with your shopping?" Smoke asked calmly as he put his pistol away.

"Smoke! I come in here to see that you have been in a gunfight, and all you can say is whether or not I'm finished with shopping?"

Smoke smiled. "I'm sorry. Am I not supposed to ask such a thing?"

"You're impossible," Sally said with a laugh. She looked back toward the body, around which several had gathered.

"Who was he?"

"His name was Jake Willard."

"I've never heard of him. Is he someone who had a grudge for you?"

"Evidently so," Smoke said. "Though I don't know why."

"He was over in the Brown Dirt a few minutes ago," Templeton said. "I went over to talk to him, but he didn't give me any idea he was going to do something like this."

"What were you talking to him about?" Sheriff Carson asked.

"I'll be honest with you, Sheriff. I was discussing the possibility of him working for the Long Trek."

"As a cowboy?" Sheriff Carson asked.

"No, sir. As a private detective, so to speak, to see if we can't get a handle on all the cattle rustlin' that's goin' on."

"Smoke, have you had any problem with cattle rustling?" Sheriff Carson asked.

"No, I haven't."

"Neither has anyone else in the county, as far as I know. At least, nobody else has filed any complaints about it."

"When the Colonel met with the Cattlemen's Association no one else seemed to have a problem, either," Templeton said. "And I think I've got that all figured out, as to why."

"Why?" Sheriff Carson asked.

"I think it might be because Colonel Garneau is new. And he's a Frenchman. The rustlers probably think he is an easy target. Only they've got another think comin'. I'm makin' it my business to hire men who can deal with them."

"Like Jake Willard?"

Templeton shook his head. "I didn't hire him. As it turns out, I reckon it was a good thing I didn't."

The next day an article appeared in the *Big Rock Journal*:

Shootout in Longmont's Saloon

INITIATOR OF THE DEADLY ENCOUNTER KILLED

Jake Willard, who fancied himself a man of considerable skill with a pistol, learned to his sorrow yesterday that his skill was not the match of Smoke Jensen. Accosting Mr. Jensen while he stood at the bar having a beer and engaged in peaceful conversation, Willard proved to be inadequate to the task he had set for himself. Smoke Jensen, in a move that was lightning swift, pulled his .44 and energized the ball that ended Jake Willard's life of crime. There was a one thousand dollar reward for Jake Willard, but Smoke Jensen, in a move of great generosity, has donated the money to the Holy Spirit Orphanage.

As there was no one to mourn Jake Willard, he was put unheralded, and with naught but the gravedigger in attendance, into a pauper's grave this morning.

Garneau read the article with interest, but made no connection between the incident and the conversation he had held with Templeton a few days earlier. He was not aware the attempted assassination had been concocted by the gunman.

The colonel read a few more articles, thinking he should keep up with the local news. He was about to put the paper down when he noticed something under a column with the heading INTERNATIONAL INTELLIGENCE BY CABLE.

New Mystery from France

DECEASED SOLDIER NOT WHO THEY THOUGHT

It has been some time since the charred remains of a French soldier were found near Dijon, France. Those remains were initially identified as Captain Pierre Mouchette. It was suspected that Sergeant Antoine Dubois had murdered Captain Mouchette, and absconded with as much as two and one half million francs. It is now known that the body found was not that of Captain Mouchette, but Sergeant Dubois himself. The inescapable conclusion is that Mouchette, in all violation of the honor of his office, the fiduciary responsibility to the army he served, and the betrayal of the sergeant who served him, is the murderer and thief.

The current location of the wretched Captain Mouchette is not known.

Garneau was disturbed that his ruse had been discovered, that the authorities in France knew it was Sergeant Dubois' body they had found, and that they had deduced he was the thief and murderer. But he found succor in the fact that the article clearly stated his whereabouts was unknown.

CHAPTER 9

Brooklyn, New York

Malcolm Theodore Puddle was a shipping clerk for the Brooklyn Transit Company. It wasn't a job he particularly liked, but it paid well, and he was conscientious about his work. He was handling a bank shipment of ten thousand dollars in cash that had been delivered to him by an armed messenger. Malcolm had to stay beyond his usual quitting time, because the money could not be out of his sight until it was put on board one of the car floats, a barge that ferried railroad cars across the Hudson River.

Earlier, he had stepped into Henry's Café and arranged to have his dinner brought to him that evening. But it was getting close to seven and still no dinner. He was beginning to wonder if Henry had forgotten. Since it was something Henry had done for him many times, Malcolm decided he must have just gotten very busy at the last minute.

Sixteen-year-old Teddy Cline had the pork chop, roll, and a baked potato in a covered dish and started out the back door of the café. He didn't mind delivering the supper meal to Mr. Puddle, because Puddle always tipped well. The café was very busy, and he had gotten away late, so he hurried through the alley, which was the shortest distance between the café and the terminal. He could save time that way, but it always made him just a little uncomfortable.

Suddenly two men stepped out in front of him, and his worst fears were realized.

"What do you want?" Teddy asked. "I don't have any money. I don't have anything you want."

"Oh, I wouldn't say that." One of the men pointed to the covered plate. "We'll just take the supper you are carrying."

"No!" Teddy said, pulling the dish away as one of the men reached for it. "This is for Mr. Puddle over at the terminal."

"Yes, well, see, we want to meet Mr. Puddle, and we figure taking him his dinner will do it for us."

"You don't need to take him his supper. Mr. Puddle is a very nice man. If you want to meet him, all you have to do is go see him."

"How are we going to do that? The office is closed and the door is locked. We figured if we had his meal, when we knock, he would open the door to us. Isn't that how you get in?"

"Ha!" Teddy said. "I have a key. He left it with me earlier today when he ordered his meal."

"You're lyin'."

"No, I'm not. It's right here, see?" Teddy lifted the lid on the covered dish, and there, beside the pork chop, roll, and baked potato was a key.

"We'll just take that key." The man pulled a cloth from his pocket and held it over Teddy's nose and mouth. Teddy smelled a cloying odor, then everything went black.

"How long will he be out?"

"Long enough for us to get the money and be out of here." The man put the handkerchief and chloroform back in his pocket.

"Do you have enough of that stuff left to take care of Puddle?"

"Yes."

Malcolm Puddle was playing solitaire as he waited on his supper. Glancing up at the clock, he saw that it was getting close to eight. The car barge would leave at eight-thirty. If he had known it was going to take this long, he would have waited until after he got the money shipment on board, then gone to the café to eat.

He had just put a red seven on a black eight, when he heard the front door open. "Teddy," he called. "What has taken you so long, I'm about starved." He looked up, saw two men coming into the office, and didn't recognize either one. He stood up and backed away from the desk. "Where's Teddy?"

"Oh, he's back at the café. They got real busy and my friend Toby and I were coming this way anyway, so he gave us your supper. Oh, and the key," the man added, smiling and holding the key out toward Puddle. "He told me to be sure and give the key back to you."

Something about the two men made Malcolm feel a little wary of them, but he gave no indication. "Thank you. You can put the food and the key there on the desk."

"I'd rather not. Ol' Henry now, he was real particular about tellin' us to put the key directly in your hands, and if you don't mind, that's what I plan to do. Put it right in your hands."

Both men stepped around the desk toward him, and Toby took a cloth and a small bottle from his pocket. Malcolm had no idea what it was, or what Toby had in mind, but he didn't like it. "I told you, put the food and the key on the desk. Except for deliveries, no one is allowed in here."

"Ah, deliveries. You mean like the ten thousand dollars delivered to you today?"

Malcolm realized his suspicions were well founded, and he moved away from the desk into an open area.

"Grab him, Sid," Toby said.

Malcolm stood five-feet-nine-inches tall and weighed 155 pounds. Sid and Toby were longshoremen, over six-feet tall with a good two hundred pounds of muscle. They didn't expect any problem with Malcolm.

But they got it. Malcolm was a middleweight boxer who had twenty-three fights under his belt, and not one loss.

As Sid approached, Malcolm snapped a quick, hard, left jab to the dock man's nose. He felt the nose go under the blow, and Sid let out a yell of pain. Enraged, he raised both hands over his head and rushed toward the clerk. Malcolm ducked under the upraised arms, then sent a hard right into Sid's solar plexus. With a painful expulsion of breath, Sid fell to the floor with the breath knocked out of him.

Toby watched in disbelief as the little clerk of a man handled Sid.

"Why, you little creep!" Toby swung a powerful, round-house right, which Malcolm danced away from. The dock man swung again, and missed again when Malcolm bent back at the waist to let the fist fly by him.

That missed blow left Toby open, and Malcolm sent a whistling right into Toby's ear. Out of the corner of his eye, he saw that Sid was on his hands and knees, with his head lowered almost to the floor.

"Sid! Sid! Get up and help me!" Toby shouted, trying, unsuccessfully, to connect with another roundhouse right.

Malcolm danced over to Sid and kicked him in the side of the head. Sid went down and out.

Toby roared in a rage and decided to quit trying to hit Malcolm, planning to get him in a bear hug instead.

Malcolm knew if the big oaf got his arms wrapped around

him, that would be the end of it. He would have only one shot and it had to be a good one.

As Toby rushed toward him, Malcolm skipped to his right. Then, putting everything he had in his left fist, he drove it into Toby's Adam's apple. The big man gasped for breath and threw both hands over his throat. He dropped to both knees, his breathing coming in hoarse gasps.

"Wow!"

Looking toward the voice, Malcolm saw the café delivery boy. "Teddy, are you all right?"

"Yes, sir. They held something over my nose, and it made me pass out. But I'm all right now. Wow, Mr. Puddle, you sure can fight."

Malcolm picked up the bottle and sniffed it. "Chloroform."

"I'm sorry I let them take the key away from me."

"It wasn't your fault. I'm just glad you are all right. Do me a favor will you, Teddy? Run down to the corner, and tell Officer Casey what happened. Ask him to come here."

When the policeman showed up a couple of minutes later, Malcolm was sitting calmly at his desk, eating his dinner, while the two big men were sitting on the floor, one gasping for breath, the other holding his head.

"Holy Mary," the policeman said. "And would you be for tellin' me what this is all about?"

"Let's just say I had some unwanted visitors," Malcolm replied. "I think they were intent on robbing me."

"I used the call box to contact the station. There'll be a paddy wagon here shortly. Are you all right?"

"I'm fine, thanks."

"You should have seen him, Officer Casey. He whupped both of them," Teddy said excitedly.

"I should say he did," Officer Casey replied.

"Oh, I'd better get back. Mr. Wright is going to wonder what happened to me."

"Oh, Teddy, wait," Malcolm called. "I didn't tip you for bringing my supper."

Long Trek

"I think it is time to move on to the next step," Templeton said.

"What step would that be?"

Templeton smiled. "Now, Colonel, my job is not only to convince these people to sell to you, it is also to keep your name out of anything that might happen. Believe me, you will be better off if you don't have any idea about the details of how I go about getting them to sell."

"Yes, yes," Garneau said, nodding. "I think you are right."

"Now, I'm going to ask you to do something that is for your own good. I am told that you . . . uh . . . sometimes visit the girls at the Brown Dirt Cowboy."

"Is that any business of yours?" Garneau snapped.

Templeton held both his hands out, palms forward. "It's none of my business at all. But, if you ever had any interest in spending the night with one of the girls there . . . let's say to have someone who could tell the sheriff where you were in case you had to establish an alibi . . . well, tonight would be that night."

Garneau stared at Templeton for a long moment. "I see. That is to keep my name out of whatever you have planned?"

"Yes, sir, that's it exactly."

"There is a young woman named Amy," Garneau said. "I think spending the night with her could be quite pleasurable."

Garneau went into town by carriage. It was painted green and trimmed in yellow. On each door of the carriage was the fleur-de-lis, over which, written in yellow, was the name LONG TREK. Whenever he went to town his arrival was noticed, and it was no different this time.

The carriage stopped first in front of Longmont's, and the driver, after hopping down to open the door for Garneau, retook his position on the seat while Garneau went inside.

"Monsieur barman, a drink for everyone present, *s'il vous plaît.*"

With a cheer, patrons rushed to the bar to claim their drinks. Garneau spoke to no one, nor did he buy a drink for himself, though he did step up to the bar and pay for the drinks that had been delivered. After that, he left.

Louis stepped up to the bar. "Tell me, Poke, did he pay for everything?"

"Yes, sir, he did."

"I wonder what that was all about? Why would he come in here, buy drinks for the house, then leave?"

"I don't know," Poke replied. "But now that you mention it, it is rather strange, isn't it?

Two blocks away, the carriage stopped in front of the Brown Dirt Cowboy Saloon. Again the driver hopped down to open the door for Garneau. "Shall I wait here for you, Colonel?"

"No. Go board the team in the livery and park the carriage there for the night."

"No need on you wastin' your money doin' that, Colonel. If you're goin' to spend the night in town, I can drive back out to the ranch and come back to pick you up in the mornin'. I don't mind doin' that. Just tell me what time you want me to come back."

"Monsieur Calloway, I want you to do exactly as I tell you to do," Garneau said sharply. "Board the horses in the stable and park the carriage out on the street where it can be seen. Do you understand that? I want the carriage out where it can be seen."

"Yes, sir. I understand that," Calloway said, though the

expression on his face indicated he had no idea why Garneau had made such a strange request.

"Here is money for boarding the team, for your dinner, and for your accommodations for the night. You may stay at the hotel of your choosing."

"I suppose I'll stay at the Big Rock Hotel. It's the closest to the stable."

"Very good. You may call for me tomorrow morning at eight o'clock," Garneau said.

Leaving the driver to carry out his instructions, Garneau stepped into the Brown Dirt Cowboy and, as he had over at Longmont's, bought a round of drinks for everyone in the house.

As everyone was happily drinking, Garneau called Amy over to him. "My dear, I should like to engage your services for the evening."

Amy smiled. "I'll be with you soon, Colonel. I've already told another man I will spend a little time with him. He's first."

"Who is the man?"

"He's just a customer. His name is Paul, and he works at the wagon yard."

"Point him out for me, if you would, please."

"Oh, Colonel Garneau, you aren't going to cause any trouble, are you?"

"Not a bit, my dear. Please, bring your young man over to see me."

"All right," Amy said with some hesitation.

A moment later a young man, barely in his twenties, came over to see Garneau. "You wanted to talk to me?"

"I do, indeed. I want Amy's services for the entire night. I want to ask you to engage another *putain*."

"Another what?"

"Putain, uh, *prostituée*. Another young woman."

"But I want this one," Paul said.

"Would this convince you to change your mind?" Garneau handed Paul a twenty-dollar bill.

Paul looked at it, then smiled broadly when he saw the size of it. "Yes, sir. Yes, sir, I reckon this could make me change my mind. Sorry, Amy."

"That's all right, Paul," Amy said. "There will be other times for us."

"Yeah," Paul said, the smile still on his face. "There will be other times."

CHAPTER 10

The Drexler farm

On a low hill, Templeton sat in his saddle, looking down upon the farm of Herman Drexler. The house and barn were clearly visible in the moonlight. There was no bunkhouse; Drexler's farm was too small for him to have employees. Drexler, his wife, and his young son worked the farm by themselves.

There was no movement in or around the house, which was good. Templeton reached down to make certain the can tied to the saddle horn was secure as he rode down toward the barn. He stopped on the opposite side from the house, so if someone happened to be looking out the window they wouldn't see him.

Dismounting, he reached up to take the can down. Opening the lid, he started splashing the liquid onto the wide, weathered boards. From inside the barn he heard a horse whickering in curiosity. When the can was empty he tossed it aside, then lit a match and held it against one of the soaked boards. The kerosene caught quickly and flames spread up that board, then leaped over to the other boards that had been splashed with kerosene.

He heard the whinny of a horse inside the barn as he remounted, then rode away, keeping the barn between him and the house. After he had ridden a couple hundred yards away he turned back for another look. The entire backside of the barn was ablaze, and flames had leaped up to the roof, which was also burning.

Twelve-year-old Jimmy Drexler awakened in the middle of the night to see the walls of his bedroom glowing. For a moment he was confused as to what was causing the glow, then he heard the whinny of horses. Jumping out of bed, he ran to the window and saw that the barn was on fire.

"Papa! Mama!" he shouted. "The barn is on fire! The horses!"

His shouts awakened his father, who, from his bedroom, had no visual indication of the fire. "What is Jimmy yelling about?" he asked groggily.

Jimmy came running into his parent's bedroom. "Papa! The barn is on fire!"

"What?" Drexler shouted, leaping up from the bed. Running to the window he could hear the panicked whinnying of the horses trapped inside the barn.

"I've got to save Duffy!" Jimmy shouted.

"Jimmy, don't you go into that barn!" Mary Drexler shouted.

"I've got to, Mama! Duffy is in there!"

Drexler didn't bother to put on pants over the long johns he was sleeping in, but he did pull on his boots. He rushed outside, just in time to see Jimmy running into the barn. By that time, the barn was fully involved in flames.

"Jimmy, no!" Drexler screamed. He ran to the door of the barn intending to drag his son out, but the flames were so intense he couldn't go any farther. "Jimmy get out of there!" he screamed at the top of his voice. But his scream was drowned out by the loud crash of the blazing barn falling in on itself, and Drexler had to leap away to avoid having the barn collapse on him. He stood in numbed shock, looking at the fire which he knew was a funeral pyre for his son.

As the sun came up the next morning, the air was full of the smell of smoke and the odor of burned flesh. Several of Drexler's neighbors, drawn by the smoke, were at the Drexler house. The women were in the house comforting Mary Drexler. The men were outside with Drexler, looking at the blackened and smoldering remains of the barn. The bodies of the horses and the cow were easily seen as they were large enough to stand out.

It took a while before they actually located young Jimmy's body. They found his charred remains on the ground, his arm toward one of the charred horses as if he had been holding a rope to lead him out. If there had been a rope, it had been totally consumed by the fire.

"What ever possessed him to run into the barn when it was on fire?" Woodward asked.

"He ran in to save the horses," Drexler said. "His horse."

"He was a brave young man," Keefer said. "Not much comfort there, I know. But you can be proud of his courage."

"I don't want his mother to see him like this," Drexler said as he looked at the blackened remains.

"Don't worry. We'll get him out of there, and in a nice coffin before she has a chance to see him," Humboldt Puddle said.

"Mr. Puddle? Drexler? Come here. You might want to see this," Woodward called.

The two men answered the call.

"What is it, Charles?" Puddle asked.

Woodward pointed. "That's a kerosene can. There's no doubt in my mind but that this fire was started."

"Started by who?" Drexler asked.

"Who has been trying to run the rest of us out of the valley?"

"The Frenchman," Puddle spit out.

* * *

Garneau was awakened the next morning by a buzzing fly. He waved at it a couple times trying to ward it off, until finally he was fully awake. He watched the fly until it landed, then, cupping his hand he swung it over the fly, catching it when it flew up. He pulled both wings off, then lowered the sheet covering Amy, exposing her naked breast. He put the fly on her nipple and watched with interest as it crawled over her breast.

Amy twitched and groaned, then suddenly slapped at her breast, sitting up quickly.

"What?" Garneau asked as if he had just been awakened by her activity. "What's wrong? What are you doing?"

"I don't know," Amy said. "Something was crawling on me."

"*Mon Dieu,* you gave me quite a start there, waking me like that."

"I'm sorry."

"*Ce n'est rien.* It is nothing. It's time to get up anyway. Amy, *ma chère,* because you provided me with such a delightful night, I would like you to be my guest for breakfast at Delmonico's."

"Really? You want to take me to Delmonico's? Mr. Brown serves breakfast here, you know."

"Yes, I know. Biscuits and some sort of sauce that I think is called gravy. Food that is hardly fit for a *cochon,* and certainly not fit for human consumption. At Delmonico's, we can have a baguette with jam and butter, and *café crème,* which is what a proper breakfast should be."

When they stepped into Delmonico's a short while later, everyone seemed to be engaged in quiet conversation.

Garneau ordered their breakfast.

"Yes, sir. I'll have it right out," the waiter said.

After the waiter left, Garneau spoke to someone at the

table nearest his. "Tell me, Monsieur, everyone seems quite subdued this morning. Why is that? Has something happened?"

"You mean you haven't heard about it?"

"I'm afraid not."

"It's the Drexler boy."

"The Drexler boy? I beg your pardon, who is the Drexler boy?"

"Jimmy Drexler. He is the son of Herman Drexler, a farmer just out of town. Or rather I should say he *was* the son of Herman Drexler."

"Was? Oh, I see. You are saying the boy died?"

"He didn't just die. He was burned to death."

"Oh, heavens!" Amy said. "How horrible!"

"Yes, ma'am, I reckon it was. You see, the thing is, their barn caught on fire last night, and young Jimmy . . . well, for some reason, he ran into the barn. Most likely, it was to save the horses. Anyway, the barn fell in on him, and, as I say, he was burned to death."

"What a terrible thing," Garneau said as their breakfast was delivered. He smiled broadly. "Ah, the baguette looks wonderful."

Big Rock

Although Garden of Memories Cemetery was between St. Paul's Episcopal Church and Ranney Street Baptist, it wasn't affiliated with any specific denomination. It was crowded on the morning that what was left of young Jimmy Drexler was laid to rest. Mary Drexler, wearing a black dress and a long black veil sat in a chair next to the open grave, clutching a tear soaked handkerchief in one hand, while with the other hand she squeezed Herman's hand.

Sue Woodward stood behind Mary, with her hand resting on Mary's shoulder. Over one hundred people attended the funeral—a considerable number of townspeople, nearly all of the county ranchers and farmers, including Smoke and Sally, and some of the original cowboys who had worked on Long Trek when George Munger owned it. Conspicuous by his absence was Lucien Garneau.

The pallbearers lowered the pine box, which had been closed for the entire service, into the open grave, then pulled the ropes back up. Pastor E. D. Owen from the Ranney Street Baptist Church stepped up to the grave. "For as much as it hath pleased Almighty God in his wise providence to take out of this world the soul of our deceased brother, Jimmy Drexler, we therefore commit his body to the ground; earth to earth, ashes to ashes, dust to dust; looking for the general Resurrection in last day, and the life of the world to come."

He invited Mary and Herman to drop the first handfuls of dirt onto the coffin. As she heard the dirt fall onto the pine box, Mary let out a sob and turned to bury her head in Herman's chest. They stepped away as several others dropped dirt onto the coffin.

"Someone set fire to Drexler's barn, there's no doubt about that," Doc Urban said later that afternoon after several of the town folk and some of the county people gathered in Longmont's. "In my mind, whoever burned the barn also killed the boy. Jimmy set a world of store by that horse of his. Duffy, he called him. I remember the day he got him. He rode all the way into town just to show his horse off."

"I remember that too." Mark Worley was a self-employed contractor who did carpentry work around town. He was also a part-time deputy to Sheriff Carson. He sat at a table with Smoke, Doc Urban, and Louis Longmont.

"How do you know it was arson?" Longmont asked, lifting his wineglass to his mouth.

"Because they found an empty kerosene can behind the

burned out barn." Doc Urban took a swallow of his wine before he spoke again. "That arrogant Frenchman did it. Of that, I've no doubt."

"Whoa, hold on. I am French!" Louis protested.

"You aren't French, Louis. You are a Coon Ass Cajun from Louisiana," Doc Urban said, chuckling.

"But my heritage is French," Louis said.

"Is it?" Doc Urban challenged.

"Well, Coon Ass Cajun French," Louis admitted with a smile.

The others around the table laughed.

"I would have suspected Garneau as well, but it couldn't have been him," Worley said, taking a sip of his beer.

"How do you know it couldn't have been him?" Doc Urban asked.

"Because on the night the Drexler barn was burned, he was at the Brown Dirt Cowboy. He spent the night with Amy Kirsley. They had breakfast together at Delmonico's the next morning. Everyone who was in Delmonico's that morning has said he was there, and that he seemed surprised when they told him about the fire.

"Besides which, that carriage of his, you know the green and yellow one with that fancy design on the doors? Well sir, it sat out in front of the livery all night long. I was deputy that night, and I seen it there."

Smoke set down his beer glass. "Does he spend many nights at the Brown Dirt?"

Worley shook his head. "We asked Emmett Brown, and he said that was the only night Garneau had ever spent there. Brown owns the place, so he ought to know."

"Did you say the girl with him was Amy Kirsley?" Louis asked.

"Yes. Why?"

"Amy used to work here, but she started doing a little business on the side, if you get my meaning. I don't let the girls who work here do that, so she left and went down to work for Emmett at the Brown Dirt. Wait a minute, Olivia said something about Amy just this morning."

Louis looked around the room until he saw Olivia standing at a table with a bunch of cowboys, smiling and joking with them.

"Olivia?" Louis called, summoning her over.

The girl excused herself and came over to Louis' table.

"Olivia, didn't you say you saw Amy Kirsley in Goldstein's Mercantile the other morning?"

"Yes, I did, why."

"What was it you said about her?"

"Oh. I said she was buying one of those expensive new hats the mercantile got in. And I was just wondering where she got the money."

"Thank you," Louis said. When Olivia left, he looked at the others. "Maybe Garneau paid her to say that he was with her?"

"Except Emmett Brown also says the Frenchman was there all night," Worley said.

"That's convenient for Garneau, isn't it?" Doc Urban asked.

"Yes," Smoke said. "You might say it is almost too convenient. Convenient as if he purposely stayed the night just to establish an alibi."

"Well, what is the sheriff going to do about it?" Worley asked. "Next to you, Smoke, the Frenchman is now the largest rancher in the entire county. I can't see the sheriff arresting him on suspicion."

"No," Smoke said. "But we can keep an eye on him. I'm sure he didn't burn the barn himself, but I wouldn't put it past him to have hired someone to do it."

"Smoke, how much do you know about this man he has working for him? Deekus Templeton. Had you ever heard of him before he came here?" Worley asked.

Smoke shook his head. "No, I can't say as I have."

"Well, I've been hearing things about him. You know how people talk, and as much as I get around town, putting in a cabinet here, or a new window there, I hear things an ordinary sheriff or deputy might not hear. There's no proof, mind you, and as far as I know he was never arrested, or even suspected of it, but there are stories that he once rode with the James gang."

"The James gang? You mean Jesse James, back in Missouri?" Doc Urban asked.

"That's what I've heard," Worley said. "But, like I said, there's no proof of it. Just rumors."

"That's interesting," Smoke said.

"Yes, and what makes it more interesting is that whenever one of the small ranchers is approached and made an offer, it's Templeton who has been doing it. And they all say the same thing about him."

"What's that?" Louis asked.

"They say he scares the bejesus out of them."

"Has he ever threatened them in any way?" Smoke asked.

"No, Sheriff Carson asked that very same question. They all say Templeton hasn't done anything to actually threaten them, but there's just something about him that scares them nevertheless."

CHAPTER 11

The Drexler Farm

"Mary, you can't be serious."

"I've never been more serious in my life. I want to go back to Pennsylvania. Please, Herman, let's go home."

"What do you mean, let's go home? I thought this was our home. Mary, we've worked hard to make this farm go. And we are just about there. You know this. We were talking about it just last week."

"And last week Jimmy was still alive," Mary said.

"I think Jimmy would want us to stay here."

"Why? So you can be killed the way he was?"

"Jimmy's death was an accident, Mary, you know that. He wanted to save his horse, and he ran into that barn."

"Do you think I don't know that the barn didn't catch on fire by accident? Someone set that fire. Someone who wants to force us to leave."

"Maybe."

"No maybe about it, Herman. I know that you and the other men found a kerosene can."

"All right. I won't lie to you."

"Don't you see, Herman? If they tried once, they'll try again. And it might be you they kill."

"Mary, I can't just run out on the others like that. When we had that meeting over at Puddle's place, I gave my word I would stick it out."

"Please, Herman, take me home."

"All right. But, what are we going to do with all our stuff?"

"We'll take it with us," Mary said. "We'll load it up, take it into town, and ship it back home."

Herman nodded. "All right, Mary. If that's what you want."

The Drexlers had just finished loading their wagon when Chris Logan dropped by. "What are you doing? Where are you going?"

Herman helped Mary up onto the seat, then climbed up beside her and picked up the reins. "Back to Pennsylvania, Chris. We're pulling out."

"But you can't just up and leave, Herman. I thought we were all going to stick together."

"We tried that."

"Look, I just came by to tell you that we're goin' to build a new barn for you. We've already talked about it. And we're goin' to replace your horses and your milk cow, too."

"What about my boy?" Drexler asked. "Can you bring him back?"

Logan looked down. "I'm sorry about Jimmy, Herman. We're all sorry about Jimmy."

"I appreciate the offer of building the barn back and replacing my horses and cow. But Mary and I have made up our minds. We're goin' back to Pennsylvania."

"I hate to hear that, Herman. You've been a very good neighbor and important to all of us. Look, consider this. If we all stick together, just as we discussed at the meeting, we'll get through this. If we stick together, Garneau can't win."

"Yeah." Drexler snapped the reins against the back of the team. "Yes, he can." The team strained forward to pull the load.

Neither Drexler nor his wife said a thing during the forty-five minute drive into town. Then Mary spoke. "Before we go to the land office, can we stop at the cemetery? I want to tell Jimmy good-bye."

"All right."

Drexler stopped the wagon and they walked out to Jimmy's gravesite, the mound of fresh dirt still visible.

"I hate leaving before we even have a headstone for him," Drexler said.

"We don't need a headstone. We'll keep him in our hearts," Mary said.

The two stood there for a long moment, Drexler's arm around her as he pulled her close to him.

"Well, let's go see how much we can get for our farm," Drexler said, as they started back toward the wagon.

In the pastor's study at the back of his church, Reverend Owen stood at the window watching Herman and Mary Drexler. He saw them walk up to the gravesite, stand there for a moment, then go back to the wagon. He had already heard they were leaving and said a prayer for them. "Lord, bring them peace in this time of their great sorrow."

"Three hundred dollars?" Drexler said, shocked at what he heard. "That's the offer?"

"That's the offer," Perkins said.

"But I don't understand. His first offer was for one thousand dollars."

"You should have taken the offer when it was first made," Perkins said. "Then you were in a position of control. You had land that he wanted. Now you are in a position of weakness. You need to sell your land, and you want someone to buy it."

"But three hundred dollars will barely pay our way back if we ship furniture," Drexler complained.

"Take it, Herman, please," Mary said. "I want to get out of here."

Drexler sighed. "All right, I'll take it. I don't want to, but I'll take it."

Smiling, Perkins counted out the money, then presented the deed for Drexler to sign over the property to Lucien Garneau.

From the land office, they drove to the depot, bought tickets, and made arrangements for the furniture to be shipped.

"What are you going to do with the horses?" Wilson asked.

"They aren't mine," Drexler said. "My horses were killed in the fire. I rented these from the livery."

"Well, you won't have time to turn 'em back in. If you want, you can just leave them here. I'll take care of them for you."

"Thanks. Oh, and you don't even have to unhook 'em from the wagon. I traded Zeke the wagon for the use of the team."

The sound of a whistle came from the west.

"That's your train," Wilson said. "It's right on time."

Long Trek

"Three hundred dollars, Colonel," Templeton said. "That's all it cost you. We got Drexler. The others will come around."

"How are you going to do that? You can't burn everyone's barn," Garneau said.

"We don't have to burn everyone's barn. We don't have to burn any more barns. But we may have to show a little strength. And I know just where to start."

"Where?"

"With Humboldt Puddle. From everything I've been able to learn, he's their leader. If we can convince him to leave, right on the heels of Drexler leaving, the rest of them will fold like a house of cards. Daniels, Babcock, and now Drexler. I'm tellin' you, getting Puddle's land will do it for us."

"All right," Garneau said. "Do whatever you have to do to get Puddle to sell out to us."

Carro de Bancada Ranch

Humboldt Puddle had his wagon up on a stand, and the wheel removed. He was packing the wheel hub with grease when he saw a rider coming toward him. Wiping his hands as clean as he could, he reached into the bed of the wagon and turned the rifle so the barrel was pointing toward the approaching rider.

It wasn't that he was an unfriendly man. Under normal conditions, he would welcome a stranger, offer them water, maybe even invite them to take a meal with him. Since his wife had died of the fever, he actually enjoyed company every now and then. But these weren't normal conditions. Garneau was increasing the pressure on everyone to sell their land. Drexlers had sold and left right after they buried their son.

"That's far enough, mister," Puddle said when the man came within thirty feet of him. That wasn't a distance he had chosen arbitrarily. He knew from that distance he couldn't miss, even if he had to fire from the hip.

"Well now, that's not very friendly, is it, Mr. Puddle?"

"I'm not exactly in the mood to be friendly. What do you want?"

"My name is Templeton, Mr. Puddle. Deekus Templeton. I would like to talk to you. You are an important man in these parts, one all the other ranchers here in the valley look up to."

"I wouldn't say that."

Templeton smiled. "No, you wouldn't say that because you are a modest man."

"What do you want to talk about?"

"I work for Colonel Garneau, Mr. Puddle."

"The Frenchman," Puddle said, making it almost a swear word.

"He is from France, that's true. But now he is an American."

"He'll never be an American."

"I'm sorry you feel that way, Mr. Puddle." Templeton started to dismount.

"I don't believe I asked you to get down, Mr. Templeton," Puddle said.

"Well, that's not very neighborly of you."

"Neither is burning a man's barn. Especially when his boy gets killed trying to save the horses."

"Are you accusing me of that, Mr. Puddle? Because that was just a real tragedy, his boy getting killed like that. And I don't appreciate being blamed for it."

"Who said I was blamin' anyone?" Puddle replied. "All I did was say that wasn't a very neighborly thing to do. What do you want, Templeton?"

"As you may know, Colonel Garneau is trying to expand his land holdings, and he has made offers to buy many of the smaller ranches in the area. At a generous price, I might add. I'm sure you have heard by now that he bought the Drexler place."

"Yeah, I heard. I also heard what he paid for the place. And if you call that a generous price, then you and I have totally different ideas as to what is generous."

"Well, of course, if Drexler had sold his place to Colonel Garneau when the offer was first made, I think ever'one would have called it generous. But he waited too long. He waited until he had no choice but to sell the place. As it was, he was real happy to sell, even though he didn't make as much as he would have, if he had listened to reason when the offer was first made. I mean what with losin' his boy like he done, well, he was just real glad to get enough money to leave here and start over again."

"How could he possibly be happy with getting about one fourth what it was actually worth?" Puddle asked.

"Yes, well, that was a case of Drexler wanting to get on with his life, you understand." Templeton smiled a mirthless smile. "It created what you might call a buyers' market."

"What are you doin' here, Templeton?"

"Colonel Garneau wants to buy your place."

"It ain't for sale."

"He is prepared to give you forty thousand dollars for it."

"Forty thousand? That's considerably more than the place is worth. Why would he be willing to pay so much?"

"Because Colonel Garneau is a very generous man."

"I can't see him being that generous."

"Well, let's put it this way. The colonel feels that if you sell out, you being sort of a leader and all, well, the other smaller landowners will also sell out."

"So, I'm to be the Judas goat. Is that it?"

Templeton laughed. "Yes, you might put it that way. How old are you, Mr. Puddle?"

"What does my age have to do with anything?"

"You look to be a man at least in your fifties. Is that right?"

"I'm fifty-eight years old."

"A man your age . . . workin' on a ranch can't be that easy for you. But if you was to take the forty thousand dollars Colonel Garneau is willin' to give you, why, you could go to some place like Denver and live just real comfortable for the rest of your life. What do you say?"

"I say I'm not interested, and I'll thank you to get off my place."

The smile left Templeton's face, and he stared hard at the rancher. "Puddle, you are going to leave this land, and how you do it is up to you. You can do it easy, with money in your pocket, or you can wind up leaving it like Drexler did, with barely enough money to get to someplace else."

Puddle had never left his position behind the wagon and

had not exposed the fact that he was armed. He lifted the rifle, holding it cradled across his folded left arm. "Get off my land."

"You're not plannin' on shootin' me, are you?" Templeton asked. "Because let me tell you, that's an awesome thing, shootin' a man. Most men don't have the stomach for it."

"Is that a fact?" Puddle replied calmly.

"Yes, sir, that is a fact. Chances are if I was to make a move toward my gun now, you'd hesitate just a second before you pulled the trigger. I mean, thinkin' about killin' 'n all." Templeton smiled. "And that second is all I'd need."

Puddle pulled the hammer back on his rifle, then matched Templeton's smile. "Try me," he invited calmly. "I was with Berdan's Sharpshooters at Gettysburg. I killed fourteen men in one afternoon, Mr. Templeton."

Templeton said nothing, but the smile on his face faded.

"Now, like I said, Templeton. Get off my place."

Templeton stared at him for a moment longer, then turned and galloped away.

Puddle watched until he was sure the man wouldn't be coming back, then he put the rifle down and returned to the task of packing the wheel hub with grease.

CHAPTER 12

Long Trek

"He turned down an offer of forty thousand dollars?" Garneau said in response to Templeton's report. "Why, that's"—he did the math in his head—"two hundred thousand francs." He still could not comprehend the value of American money without first converting it into francs.

"He's a stubborn man," Templeton said.

"I thought you said you could convince him to sell."

"Yes, well, I thought if we could get Puddle to sell, most likely the others would come around. But maybe we are going about this backwards. Maybe if all his neighbors sell, and he is left absolutely alone, he'll have a change of heart."

"Didn't you say that as long as Puddle hangs on, the others will?"

"Babcock is gone, Daniels and Drexler both sold out. I'm certain we'll find someone else we can convince to sell to us. I'll do a little more probing."

In the bunkhouse, the Long Trek cowboys were playing a game of draw poker for matchsticks.

"I bet one," Hoyt Miller said, sliding a matchstick toward the center of the table. "You know, Templeton's in there talking to the colonel again. I swear, I don't know what that feller's job is, but he sure don't spend much time here. And what time he is here, he is mostly talkin' to Garneau."

Several men working at Long Trek were legitimate cowboys, men who had been punching cows at the ranch back when Munger owned the place. In addition to them, a few others had come over when the ranch where they worked was assimilated into Long Trek.

In addition to the cowboys who worked, there were ten men who had no apparent job. They had made it known they weren't cowhands, and would take no part in any of the work required to keep the ranch going. The fact that they were doing no work didn't mean they weren't getting paid. They were not only getting paid, they were getting paid more than the cowboys. And, because they weren't working, they managed to spend a lot of time in town.

"What I would like to know," Miller continued, "is just what the hell are all them other men good for? Why does the colonel keep hiring men like that? Has anyone figured that out?"

"I hear tell they are to protect the herd from cattle rustlers," Gately said.

"Cattle rustlers? What cattle rustlers?" Anderson asked. "I ain't seen no cattle rustlin'. You'd think if there was rustlin' goin' on those of us who actually work out on the range would know about it, wouldn't you?"

"Yes, well, I've tried to tell the boss that I don't think there's any real rustling goin' on," Calloway said. "But he just says I don't know what's goin' on."

"Well, I'm with Andy. I've yet to see the first cattle rustler, so I don't have an idea in hell what he's got all those extra folks for."

"Well, you know that feller, John Noble?" Elmer Gately replied.

"Yeah, I know 'im," Miller said. "Fact is, he's one of the men I'm talkin' about. I ain't never seen him do a lick of work."

"No, and you ain't goin' to, neither. I asked him once what he was doin' here, and he said he had been hired as a bodyguard. Him and Curtis and Nixon."

"Bodyguards?" Anderson said. "Who the hell are they guardin'?"

"They're guardin' Colonel Garneau," Gately replied. "I mean, him bein' one of them lords or dukes or somethin' fancy like that. I expect back in France where he come from, people that's royalty like he is always has to have guards around 'em."

"Well, I don't like it," Miller said. "I've heard folks talk. Did you know there's some folks that think Colonel Garneau is the one that burned Drexler's barn?"

"Only he didn't do it," Calloway said. "I know he didn't do it, because the night that barn got burned down and the Drexler boy got hisself killed, I drove Colonel Garneau into town, 'n he stayed there all night long. He didn't have nothin' to do with it, and I know it, 'cause I picked him up the next mornin' and brung him back home."

"That don't mean that Templeton, or Nixon, or one of them boys that the colonel has hired, didn't have nothin' to do with it," Miller said. "Have you seen the way them boys all wear their guns? They wear 'em like they know how to use 'em. And I ain't one for wantin' to find out whether or not it's all for show."

"I can tell you true," Gately said, "they ain't wearin' them guns for show."

The cowboys watched Templeton come out of the main house and call Noble, Nixon, and Curtis over to him. The four men then saddled their horses and rode off.

"Where do you think they're goin' now?" Anderson asked.

"More 'n likely they're goin' into town to get drunk and visit the whores," Miller said.

Gately laughed. "Well, what else do they have to do?"

"Burn barns, I reckon," Anderson said.

"They ain't headin' toward town," Miller said.

"Where are they headin'?"

"Toward the Butrum place."

Marvin Butrum wasn't a rancher. Like Drexler had been, Butrum was a farmer trying to make a living for himself, his wife, and two children on half a section of land, 320 acres. Most of his land was sowed in wheat, but he was also raising corn. The crops were coming along so well that he and his wife Emma were already making plans to add another room to their house. In addition to their cash crops of wheat and corn, they also had a rather sizeable garden. With produce from their garden, meat from pigs and chickens, and milk and butter from their cow, they were totally self-sufficient.

At the moment, Butrum was in the machine shed, thinking about how much better off he was in Colorado than he had been back in Arkansas where he had sharecropped a cotton farm. He was sharpening a plough shear when a shadow fell across him. "What are you doing out here, Clara? I thought your mama had you working inside," he said without looking up.

"Mr. Butrum, I wonder if we might have a little talk?"

Looking up in surprise, Butrum saw a man standing in the door of the machine shed. He recognized him immediately as the man Garneau had hired to run the farmers and small ranchers out of the area.

"What are you doing here, Templeton?"

"Now, Mr. Butrum, that isn't very nice of you. I call you *Mister* Butrum, and you don't have the courtesy to call me *Mister* Templeton? Oh, I've brought a few of my associates with me." Templeton stepped away from the door, and Butrum saw three mounted men. All three had their pistol holsters prominently displayed.

"I want you to meet Oliver Nixon, Pete Curtis, and John Noble. I've never worked with three finer men."

"What do you want?" Butrum asked. The presence of four armed men made him uneasy.

"We want to do a little business with you, Mr. Butrum."

"I know what kind of business you want to do. And I've told you before, I'm not interested in selling my farm."

"Colonel Garneau is willing to pay you fifteen hundred dollars. That's a fair price."

"I can earn that in two years. Why would I be interested in selling my place? Especially this year."

"Oh, I don't know. Crop failures, maybe? No drinking water, famine, fire, flood. There are all sorts of reasons a person might want to leave a farm."

"Yeah, well none of that is my concern." Butrum pointed to his well. "I've got a well full of water, and this year I expect I'll have the best crop since I moved out here from Arkansas."

"You may have a well full of water, but it's no good if the water is bad. And your water is bad."

"My water is bad? What are you talking about? Why, I've got the sweetest water in the entire county, if not the state."

"You may have *had* the sweetest water, but that was before a pig stumbled into your well and died."

"Why, no such thing. How would a pig stumble into my well?"

Templeton smiled, than reached down to pat the neck of his horse. "That's a good question. And now that I think about it, the pig didn't stumble. He was thrown in."

"What? Good Lord man, help me get him out."

"All right, we'll help you, though it might be too late. It's already too late to save your wheat crop."

"Too late to save my wheat crop? What are you talking about?" Butrum stepped out of the machine shed, then looked toward his wheat field where he saw smoke billowing into the sky.

"My God! The wheat is burning!"

"Yes, it does appear to be, doesn't it?" Templeton said.

"Emma! Get out here, fast!" Butrum called. He ran back into the machine shed where he grabbed several grain sacks.

"What is it?" Emma asked, stepping onto the back porch, but one look toward the field, and seeing all the smoke roiling into the sky answered the question for her.

Then she saw Templeton and the other three men. "Who are these men?"

"Don't worry about them. We've got to dunk these toe sacks into the well to get 'em wet so we can use 'em to fight the fire."

"Don't just sit there on your horses," Emma said. "Come help us!"

"We've come to make your man an offer on the farm," Templeton said. "We will give you fifteen hundred dollars."

"I told you, it's not for sale!" Butrum said as he lowered the bound sacks down into the well. Emma went over to help him, and when the bags came up, they were not only wet, they were red.

"What is this? This is blood!" Emma said in shock.

"Yes, they threw a pig in the water," Butrum said.

"They did what?"

"We'll talk about it later. Come on, Emma. Help me. If we don't get the fire put out, we'll lose our whole crop!"

Carrying the wet bags out to the field, Butrum started to fight the fire, but he had no more than started, when he knew it was a lost cause. It wasn't a small accidental fire that could be fought. It was a full-fledged conflagration that spread all the way across the field.

"Oh, Marvin!" Emma said, the expression in her voice saying it all.

Butrum put his arm around her, and they stood there, helpless, as the fire consumed an entire year's work and income.

Back at the main house, nine-year-old Clara was standing on the back porch, looking at the smoke roiling into the sky. She wasn't sure what it was, but from the reaction of her mama and daddy, she was sure it wasn't good. Looking toward the garden, she saw several men pulling up plants and tossing them aside.

She ran out to the garden. "What are you doing? Mama and Daddy won't like you pulling up plants like that. You aren't supposed to be in the garden."

"Why, we're just having a good time," one of the men said. "You want to come help? It's lots of fun."

"No!" Clara said. "I'm going to tell Mama and Daddy on you, and you will be in trouble!"

The man laughed. "Yes, you go tell your mama and daddy."

Clara ran out to the burning wheat field where her mother and father were standing together, watching the fire. "Mama, Daddy, those men are pulling up our garden!" Clara shouted, pointing back toward the house.

"Those sons of bitches," Butrum said angrily, starting back toward the house.

"Marvin, no!" Emma shouted as she ran after him. "There are four of them. And they are armed!"

By the time Butrum made it back to the house, the garden was completely destroyed. He saw a couple men playing with five-year-old Mickey. One of them had a ball, and he was pretending to throw it, then jerking it back, and Mickey was laughing.

"Mickey, go back inside the house," Butrum ordered.

Mickey started to turn, then he held his hand out. "Give me my ball."

"Sure thing, kid. Here is your ball," Nixon said.

Taking the ball, Mickey smiled, then ran into the house.

"You leave my children alone," Butrum said angrily.

"Yeah, well, we were just playing with him. He's a good kid," Templeton said. "It's a shame about your wheat, Butrum. I take it you didn't get there in time to save it?"

Butrum glared at Templeton, but knew he was absolutely powerless to do anything.

"All right," Butrum said. "You win. I'll take the fifteen hundred dollars."

"You'll take fifteen hundred dollars? What fifteen hundred dollars would that be?" Templeton asked.

"What fifteen hundred dollars? You know damn well what fifteen hundred dollars! I'm talking about the fifteen hundred dollars you just offered for my farm."

"Oh, but that was when you had water and a crop," Templeton said easily. "Surely you don't think it's worth that now?"

"What is it worth now?" Butrum asked.

"Five hundred dollars."

"Five hundred dollars? Are you crazy?"

"It's only worth five hundred dollars now, while you still have a house."

"You are out of your mind if you think . . ."

Emma saw one of the other men moving toward the house. "Marvin, take it," she pleaded. "For God's sake, take it!"

"All right," Butrum said. "All right, I'll take it."

"That's very smart of you, Mr. Butrum," Templeton said. "I will come back tomorrow. If you have your wagon loaded, I'll give you the five hundred dollars."

CHAPTER 13

Long Trek

Lucien Garneau poured brandy into a snifter, whirled it around, and lifted it to enjoy its "nose." He didn't offer any to Templeton.

"Tell me, Monsieur Templeton, how many *paysans* have you convinced to move?"

"Four, so far. And in every case you were able to buy the land for much less than the property was worth."

"What about those men who were killed in town the other day? I'm told they had papers on them, recruiting them to come work for me."

"Yes," Templeton said. "They were coming to join us when they got themselves killed."

"They were killed by the keeper of a *création potable*. A drinking establishment," he translated. "Monsieur Templeton, if the quality of your recruitment is such that they can't even deal with the manager of a saloon, how can I have confidence in those we have gathered?"

"Louis Longmont isn't your average saloon keeper," Templeton said. "And he wasn't alone. Smoke Jensen was with him."

"Smoke Jensen, ah yes. Am I right in assuming it is he who is my greatest adversary?"

"Yeah, he is," Templeton said. "But I don't think he will be for much longer. I've hired a couple men to solve that little problem for us. Permanently."

Two attempts had been made on Smoke Jensen, one unauthorized attempt by three men coming to Long Trek, but who had not yet been hired, and the other by Jake Willard, who Templeton had promised a thousand dollars if he killed Jensen.

Neither attempt had been successful, so Templeton decided to try again. He was discussing the problem with two men, Crenshaw and Harding.

"I don't know as I'd want to go up ag'in Jensen, even if there is the two of us," Crenshaw said.

"That's the beauty of my plan," Templeton said. "You won't actually be facing him at all. If you use the plan I've got worked out for you, you'll shoot him from an ambuscade, and he'll never even see you."

"Ha! What you're sayin' is, we'll dry gulch him, right?" Crenshaw asked.

"Yes."

"That don't hardly seem fair, do it?" Harding asked.

"Do you have a problem with that, Harding?" Templeton asked.

Harding giggled. "Hell, no! That's 'bout the best idea I ever heard."

"Then we are in agreement," Templeton said.

"Damn right, we're in agreement," Crenshaw replied.

* * *

Two days later, Crenshaw and Harding tied their horses off to one side of a line shack at the extreme edge of Smoke's Sugarloaf Ranch.

"Shouldn't we take the horses around back?" Crenshaw asked. "If we leave them tied out here, Jensen will see them, won't he?"

"We want him to see them," Harding explained. "When he sees a couple strange horses tied up at his own line shack, he'll come to investigate. We'll be waiting inside, and when he gets close enough, we'll shoot him right out of the saddle."

"Yeah," Crenshaw said. "How much did Templeton say he would give us?"

"Five hundred dollars," Harding said. "That's two hundred and fifty dollars apiece, which is damn near a year's wages if you're punchin' cows."

The two men went into the line shack and had a look around.

"Damn, I ain't never seen a line shack this clean before. This looks more like a house downtown than it does a line shack," Crenshaw said.

"There's somethin' tacked on to cabinet there. A note." Harding went over to read it.

"What's it say?"

"It says, 'Stranger, you are welcome to use this shack as shelter for a few days. You'll find the makin's of coffee in the cabinet, also a few cans of beans and peaches. Use what you need, but leave some for others if you can. And when you leave, please leave the shack as clean as you found it. Jensen.'"

Crenshaw chuckled. "Well now, that's just real nice of him, ain't it? You almost hate to kill a real nice man like that."

"Let's open us a can of peaches. I like peaches," Harding said.

"Yeah, good idea." Crenshaw took down two cans of peaches and, using his knife, opened both of them.

For the next few minutes, they ate the peaches out of the can, then Crenshaw tossed the can into the corner, spilling juice onto the floor. "Ha! How's that for leaving it clean?" he joked.

"Quiet! There he is," Harding said, holding his hand out.

Crenshaw walked over to the window and saw a single rider approaching. Both gunmen jacked a round into the chambers of their rifles and waited.

Smoke liked to ride around his ranch. He justified it by saying it was good to have a look for several reasons—to make certain no calves were in trouble anywhere, to make certain no cows were stuck in a mud wallow, and to check that there was an adequate flow of water. But the truth was, it was something he enjoyed doing. He had not inherited the ranch. He had built it himself, and was proud of it.

While making a routine ride around his ranch, he saw two horses tied alongside the line shack. Knowing none of his cowboys were there, he wondered who it might be. It was more a thing of curiosity than concern. He didn't mind the occasional itinerant using the shack for shelter, as long as it wasn't abused.

He rode over to the shack for a visit, to let them know they were welcome, and to see if they needed help of any kind. A hundred yards from the cabin, he saw a couple flashes of light in the window, and heard the report of rifle shots.

His horse went down and Smoke went with it, hitting the ground hard. The horse fell on his leg and he was pinned beneath it. He needed to be in position to defend himself, and stretched to recover his pistol that had fallen out of the holster when he hit the ground, but it had slid just beyond his grasp.

As he stretched, he saw two men leave the cabin, mount the horses he had seen tied alongside, then come riding toward him, slowly, confidently, and arrogantly.

"Well now, Crenshaw, what do you think about this? Here is the great Smoke Jensen caught like a rat in a trap."

"You know what I think, Harding?" Crenshaw said. "I don't think he looks like a rat at all. I think he looks more like a little, helpless mouse. Squeak for us, won't you, mouse?"

Both gunmen laughed.

Crenshaw was the larger of the two. He had a flat nose, no doubt the result of it having been badly broken at one time. Harding had one eyelid that drooped so it looked as if that eye was half closed all the time.

"Nah, now that I look at him, he ain't a mouse or a rat," Crenshaw said. "You know what we got here? We got us a goat, that's what we got. A goat, all staked out like bear bait. And you know what happens to bear bait, don't you? Most often, bear bait gets itself kilt."

Neither of the two men had dismounted, and both looked down at Smoke, their drawn pistols pointed at him.

"You got 'ny last words, before we kill you, Mister Smoke Jensen?" Crenshaw asked.

"I might be interested in knowing why you are going to kill me."

"He wants a reason why we are goin' to kill him. What do you think, Harding? Do you think we ought to give him a reason?"

"Ha!" Harding exclaimed. "We can give him five hundred reasons."

"Yeah," Crenshaw agreed as a broad smile spread across his face. "Yeah. We got five hundred reasons to kill you, and each one of 'em is worth a dollar."

"So, you are getting five hundred dollars to kill me?" Smoke asked.

"Yeah, we are. Does that bother you?"

"Well, yes, it bothers me. I thought I would be worth a lot more than five hundred dollars."

Crenshaw laughed. "He thought he was worth more than five hundred dollars. You're a funny man, Jensen. Did you know that? Yes, sir, you're a real funny man."

"Why are you men doing it so cheaply?"

"Why? 'Cause it's easy money, that's why. Killin' you is goin' to be about the easiest thing either one of us ever done."

"What if I pay you a thousand dollars to let me go?" Smoke asked.

"I don't trust you. How do I know you'll give us a thousand dollars if we don't kill you?"

"How do you know the person who has hired you to kill me will pay off?" Smoke countered.

"Ha! If he don't pay what he owes, we'll kill him," Crenshaw said.

"Well, if I don't pay off, you can kill me," Smoke said. "That way you'll still get the five hundred from whoever it is that's paying you."

"He may have a point, Crenshaw," Harding said.

"No, he don't have a point," Crenshaw insisted. "Ain't you ever heard about him? Once he gets a gun in his hand there can't no ordinary man, or any two men, handle him. Let's just kill 'im now and get it over with."

Smoke was not bargaining for his life, he was playing for time. As he was keeping the conversation going, he was also working his rifle out of its saddle sheath and, much more difficult, out from under the horse.

"Enough talk," Crenshaw said. "Say good-bye, Jensen."

The gunmen raised their pistols to complete the job.

At that exact moment, Smoke gave a yell and managed to yank his rifle free. He had no time to aim. All he could do was jack a round into the chamber and fire. His bullet hit Crenshaw in the chest. In a reflexive action, Crenshaw pulled the trigger, shooting his own horse. His horse spun around, causing Harding to jerk his horse out of the way.

Smoke jacked another round into his rifle and fired a second time, sending a bullet right into the middle of Harding's forehead. Both of his would-be assailants were down. He kept a wary eye on them as, finally, he was able to free himself from beneath his horse.

Still cautious, Smoke got to his feet and, picking up his pistol, walked over to have a closer look at the two men who had shot at him. It didn't take much of an examination to confirm they were dead.

"Oh, yes. I think you wanted me to say good-bye." Smoke stared down at them for a moment longer. "Good-bye."

Sally was beginning to wonder what was holding Smoke up. She wasn't worried. He was on his own ranch, just a lot later coming back to the house than normal. On the other hand, she knew if he found something that needed to be taken care of, he would do it. She was about to put it out of her mind, when she saw him in the distance. Right away, she noticed he wasn't riding the same horse he had left with. He was also leading a second horse.

Dismounting, he opened and closed the gate, then came riding up the road toward the house.

Sally hurried out on the porch to meet him. "Smoke! What happened?"

"Let's go inside. You make me some lemonade and I'll tell you all about it."

A few minutes later, Sally refilled Smoke's glass. He had told her the entire story, from the opening shots that killed his horse, to the end, when he had killed Crenshaw and Harding.

"You say they were talking about being paid five hundred dollars for killing you?" Sally asked.

"That's what they said."

"Do you believe them?"

"I don't think they would have attacked me for no reason at all."

"Who do you think was going to pay the money? Do you think it was Garneau?"

"I don't know." Smoke said. "They never said who was paying them."

"It had to be him. You know it was."

Smoke shook his head. "Not necessarily, Sally. I've made a lot of enemies in my day. It could have been any one of them."

"It could have been someone else," Sally agreed. "But you are going to have to convince me it wasn't Garneau. Please, Smoke, be careful."

"I'd better get a wagon hitched up, and get those two men downtown to the undertaker."

"I'm coming with you," Sally said.

"Why on earth would you want to ride into town with two bodies?"

"I won't be riding with two bodies. I'll be riding with my husband."

Smoke dropped Sally off in front of the mercantile, then he drove on to the sheriff's office, stopped, and went inside.

"Hello, Smoke," Sheriff Carson said. "What brings you to town?"

"Hello, Monte. I've got a delivery to make over to Tom Nunnley's shop. I thought you might want to take a look at them first."

Sheriff Carson put his hat on, then walked out front with Smoke. Smoke's load had already drawn a handful of people to look on in morbid curiosity.

"You do it?"

"Yes. They ambushed me on my own ranch. Killed my horse."

"You don't have to justify it to me, Smoke. If you are the

one who killed them, they damn sure needed killin'. Who are they? Do you know?"

Smoke shook his head. "I'd never seen them before in my life, but I did hear them call each other by name. This one is Crenshaw, this one is Harding," Smoke said, pointing out each one. "I have no idea what their first names are."

"I don't recognize the names," Sheriff Carson said. "More 'n likely they were just a couple low characters wanting to make a name for themselves by killing Smoke Jensen."

"I'd better get them over to the undertaker," Smoke said.

CHAPTER 14

From the *Big Rock Journal:*

Quick Finding in Inquiry

JUSTIFIABLE HOMICIDE

Crenshaw and Harding, first names unknown, lay in wait in order to, by stealth, kill Mr. Kirby Jensen, well known rancher and resident of Eagle County. This scurrilous attack took place on Sugarloaf Ranch, Jensen's own property.

While successful in killing Mr. Jensen's horse, they were unsuccessful in killing him. When the two villains approached Jensen to complete their nefarious scheme, Mr. Jensen was able to energize two shots, the balls taking immediate effect, sending the iniquitous pair to the One whose final judgment we must, one day, all face.

"Is this how you were going to take care of Jensen?" Garneau asked Templeton after reading the article in the paper.

"I will take care of Jensen. Don't worry. Right now I'm

more interested in moving out those people who are keeping you from expanding."

"You have succeeded with four," Garneau said. "That means seven remain."

"Yes, but we don't have to move seven. Right now it all boils down to Humboldt Puddle," Templeton said. "He's the leader of all the small land owners in the valley, and if we can convince him to leave, the others will leave as well."

"I believe you tried talking to him once before, but without success."

"Yes. That time I used the carrot," Templeton said. "This time I will use the stick."

"I do not understand."

"I just mean this time I will be more—let us say, persuasive."

"I understand he is an *obstiné* man. Obstinate," Garneau translated.

Templeton chuckled. "Yeah, he's hardheaded all right. But, like I said, if we can get rid of him, the rest of them will leave."

"Then by all means, get rid of him."

"It isn't going to be easy."

"I don't pay you because it is easy."

"What I'm saying is, we may have to get rid of him permanent, if you know what I mean."

Garneau lifted the goblet to his mouth and took a swallow of brandy. He didn't speak and Templeton took that as his approval.

"All right, I'll get right on it," Templeton said.

"Hey, Gately," Miller said. "There goes Templeton with Nixon, Curtis, and Noble again."

"Yeah, I see 'em. Ken Conn is with them, this time."

"Where do you think they're goin'?"

"I don't know, and I don't want to know. I'm beginnin' to think the less we know about what Garneau is doin' around here, the better off we're goin' to be."

Miller nodded. "Yeah, you may be right."

Templeton led the four men to within half a mile of Carro de Bancada, Humboldt Puddle's ranch.

"Are we going to do the same thing we did with Butrum?" Nixon asked. "Poison his well, tear up his garden?"

"I doubt Puddle even has a garden, and his well isn't an open well. Besides which, we aren't goin' to waste time trying to talk him into selling out," Templeton said.

"Well, what are we goin' to do?"

"You're goin' to kill 'im," Templeton said in a matter of fact manner.

"Kill 'im?" Noble asked.

"Do you have a problem with that?"

"I don't have a problem. But for killin', I get a little more money."

"Don't worry, I'll get all of you a bonus," Templeton said.

"What kind of bonus?"

"A hundred dollars apiece."

Curtis smiled. "Then what are we waiting around here for? Come on, boys, what do you say we do some killin'."

Templeton watched the four men ride off, then he returned to Long Trek.

Humboldt Puddle was at the pump, pumping water, when a bullet whizzed by his head so close he could hear it pop. He knew immediately what it was.

Dropping the water bucket, Puddle ran quickly to the wagon, where he grabbed his rifle and levered in a round. Then, looking toward his apple orchard, he saw a man on horseback pointing at him with a pistol. Puddle raised his rifle, fired, and saw the man tumble from his horse.

Puddle made a big mistake. Unaware there were more than one person, he started toward the fallen man and felt a blow to his stomach. Looking down in surprise, he saw that he had been shot. Moving as quickly as he could to a fencerow, he lay down and looked back toward the apple orchard to see if he could locate any others.

Smoke was at the southern end of his ranch when he heard the shooting. It wasn't the shooting of a hunter, or someone taking target practice. To Smoke, who had been in more gunfights than he wanted to remember, there was a distinct sound to gunfire, a tone and tint that told him those were the gunshots of men in desperate battle.

Smoke urged his horse into a gallop, the gunshots growing louder as he approached. He could see gun smoke floating over the scene, and as he rode closer he saw his neighbor Humboldt Puddle lying behind a fence, besieged by an unknown number of gunmen.

Smoke didn't know the reason for the gunfight, but he did know his neighbor and could see he was outgunned. That was all Smoke needed to see. Out of range at the moment, he fired at the assailants, just to let them know Puddle was no longer alone. The gunmen, seeing Smoke approach, turned their attention toward him.

That was their mistake. Three mounted gunman rode toward him, firing at him. Smoke fired twice, and two of the saddles were emptied.

The other rider turned and galloped away.

Smoke didn't give chase, instead hurried to check on his neighbor. Puddle sat on the ground, leaning back against the fence of his corral. The rifle he had been using was on the ground beside him, and he was holding his hands over his belly. Smoke could see blood spilling through his fingers.

"Mr. Puddle!"

"Hello, neighbor," Puddle said, managing a weak smile. "I got one of them. Thanks for givin' a hand."

"Who were they? Did you recognize them?"

"No, I never got a close enough look to see. But I don't need to. I know who they are. They work for the Frenchman, just as sure as a gun is iron."

Smoke looked at Puddle's wound and shook his head. "I'd better get your wagon hooked up so we can take you in to see Doc Urban."

"Don't waste your time, Smoke. You and I both know there ain't nothin' a doctor can do for this." Puddle pulled his hand away from his wound, and the cupped blood flowed more profusely.

He looked down at his wound. "That sure is a dandy of a wound, ain't it?" He chuckled. "You know what we used say about wounds like this during the war?"

"What's that?" Smoke asked, knowing Puddle wanted to talk.

"We used to say a deep belly wound was God's way of tellin' you to slow down." Puddle laughed at his own joke, but the laughter deteriorated into a spell of spasmodic coughing.

He reached up and grabbed Smoke by the arm, leaving a bloody handprint on his shirtsleeve. "Smoke, I need you to promise me something."

"Whatever it is, I'll do it if I can," Smoke said.

"Go into my kitchen. In the cupboard under the butter dome, you'll find an envelope. It's got my will in it, and the address of my nephew, Malcolm Puddle. He lives in New York. He's my brother's son and the only relative I got. I aim to leave this place to him. Will you promise me you'll get that to him?"

"I promise."

"I'll be gone, so there won't be much I got to say about it one way or the other. But I'm hopin' Malcolm will consider hangin' on to the place. And I'm hopin' that if he does, maybe you'll give him a hand."

"You can count on it."

"Do you reckon that once I get to the other side, I'll run into them fellas I kilt durin' the war?" Puddle asked. "Far as I know, they was good men, all of 'em. They just happened to be wearin' a different color uniform than I was, is all. I'd like to run into 'em 'n tell 'em there wasn't nothin' personal in it. I hope they ain't holdin' no grudge against me."

"I'm sure they aren't," Smoke said.

But Puddle didn't hear his response, because he was dead.

Big Rock

Smoke drove Puddle's wagon into town, with his own horse tied on behind. There were four bodies in the wagon. Humboldt Puddle was behind the driver's seat, completely covered with a blanket. The other three were sprawled out in the back, uncovered. The arrival in town of a wagon loaded with bodies created quite a stir so that by the time Smoke turned onto Center Street, at least two dozen people were following. Nobody spoke to him until he pulled up in front of the hardware store and undertaker shop. There, he set the brake on the wagon, then tied off the team.

"Smoke, that's Humboldt's wagon, ain't it?" one of the citizens asked.

"Yes."

"Is Humboldt the one under the blanket?"

"Yes." Smoke answered no more questions as he walked around the hardware store, to the back door that opened to the mortuary.

Tom Nunnley looked up as Smoke stepped inside. "I saw you coming, so I'm getting my tools ready. Who do you have for me?"

"Humboldt Puddle and three others," Smoke said.

"Four? You have four bodies?"

Smoke nodded.

"All right. Let's go have a look."

Smoke led Nunnley out to the street where several more had gathered.

"Who are these men? Do you know?" Nunnley asked.

"I don't have the slightest idea. But I'm sure they worked for Garneau, so he'll probably know."

"Yes, but the question is, will the Frenchman pay for their burying?"

"If he won't, the city will pay," Sheriff Carson said, coming over to join them. "Did you kill 'em, Smoke?"

"I killed two of them. Humboldt killed one of them before they killed him."

"Do me a favor, will you, Tom? Hold off on buryin' these three until I can find out who they are."

"All right," Nunnley said. "I tell you what I'll do. I'll get 'em in a pine box, then I'll stand 'em up out front here. Someone in town may know who they are."

CHAPTER 15

Long Trek

"Puddle is dead," Ken Conn said.

"How do you know?" Templeton asked.

"I seen 'im when Jensen brung him into town. He had Nixon, Curtis, and Noble too."

"All right. Thanks." Templeton walked over to his horse and pulled a bottle of whiskey from his saddlebag. "Here. You've earned it."

"Yeah," Conn said. "I was the only one to get away alive. Who would've thought Jensen was goin' to show up?"

Templeton went into the big house to report to Garneau. "Puddle's dead."

"Good. You're sure it can't be traced back to me?"

"I don't know."

"You don't know? What do you mean you don't know?"

"Three of our men were killed—Nixon, Curtis, and Noble. Sheriff might be able to trace them back to you."

"How? What is there to connect them to me?"

"Well, nothing, I guess. Unless you claim the bodies."

"Why would I do that?"

"No reason, I guess."

"Monsieur Templeton, I have led men in time of war, I

have lost men in time of war. As a leader, you cannot dwell upon the individuals under your command. You command an army. You do not command individuals. Losses are to be expected in battle, and when they occur, you simply move on. Those three men . . ."

"Nixon, Cur—"

Garneau raised his hand to stop Templeton. "I don't care to hear their names again. They accomplished their purpose. That is all I need to know."

Templeton chuckled. "Yes, sir, if you look at it like that, I guess you have a point."

"I shall go into town and meet with Monsieur Perkins. It would appear that Carro de Bancada has come on the market, and I intend to buy it."

"Do you want me to ride into town with you, Colonel?"

"You may if you wish."

Big Rock

"Oh," Don Pratt said when Smoke handed him Puddle's will. "I'm afraid there is an assessment due on this ranch, and this will can't be probated until the taxes are paid." The probate clerk was slightly flushed.

"How much is the assessment?"

"Two hundred dollars," the clerk said.

"All right. I'll pay it."

"If you pay it, ownership of the property will pass to you."

"I don't want ownership to pass to me. I want it to pass to Mr. Puddle's nephew, Malcolm Puddle."

"Then Malcolm Puddle will have to pay the assessment."

"Can I pay it in his name?"

"If you have his power of attorney."

"All right. I'll get his power of attorney."

"I don't think you'll have time to do that," the probate clerk said. "The money has to be paid by the end of next week. There isn't time for him to mail you his power of attorney."

"Let me see what I can do," Smoke said. "If I can't get his power of attorney here on time, I'll pay the assessment and take possession of the land, then figure out how to transfer it to him."

"Very well, but remember, you have only eight days. No, six, actually. The last day of the month is on Sunday, which means the taxes will have to be paid by Friday."

One block away from the courthouse where Smoke was attempting to probate the will, Lucien Garneau and Templeton dismounted in front of the land office, then went inside.

"Yes, sir, Colonel, how is my most valued client this afternoon?" Perkins asked by way of greeting.

"Monsieur Perkins, I understand Monsieur Puddle met with a tragic accident today," Garneau said. "Carro de Bancada may be available for purchase and if it is, I wish to buy it."

"Oh, heavens," Perkins said. "I haven't heard anything about an accident. What happened?"

"From what I understand, a group of outlaws may have come by his place in an attempt to rob him. Monsieur Puddle fought them bravely, but was killed in defense of his land."

"He killed three of 'em before they got him," Templeton added.

"That's a shame. Puddle was a good man," Perkins said.

"And he was my neighbor," Garneau said. "After I buy his land, I shall put a plaque on the property in his honor."

"Well, I'm sure he would appreciate that," Perkins said as he got out his land chart book. Opening the book he went through the pages until he came to Humboldt Puddle's land. He examined it for a moment, then shook his head.

"Well, it's not going to be easy, Colonel. I'm afraid he owned the land outright," Perkins said. "There's no chance of acquiring it just by paying off the mortgage, though you might be able to buy it from whoever inherits the land."

"And who would that be? Do you know?"

Perkins shook his head. "No, I don't. For all I know he may have died intestate, in which case the land will revert to the county. If it does, it will be auctioned off, so you will have a chance to buy it then."

"I don't want to have to deal with an auction. I want to buy it now."

"Well, as I said, that's not . . . wait a minute. Here's something," Perkins said as he examined the land charts.

"What?"

"You may remember how we were able to acquire the Babcock land by paying the taxes?"

"Yes. Will we be able to do the same thing with Puddle's ranch?"

"Perhaps. I see here that he hasn't yet paid the assessment for water improvement. That means there is an unsatisfied lien against the land. And, just as you did with Babcock, if you pay the assessment you can take possession of the land."

"Where do I pay that?"

"Well, you would pay it at the assessor's office, but if I were you, I would just go across the street to the law office and see Robert Dempster. He could make certain everything is properly done so the land is transferred to you."

"*Merci*, Monsieur Perkins," Garneau said. "I will do so." He turned and left the land office.

"Ha!" Templeton said when he caught up with Garneau out front. "Once you get Puddle's property, it'll be easy to get everyone else to come around. Puddle was their leader."

"We will not count our chickens until the eggs have *éclos*."

"Until the eggs what?"

"Hatched."

"No problem," Attorney Dan Norton said to Smoke. "If Malcolm Puddle has a certified witness on hand, he can send you the power of attorney by telegraph. That will suffice for thirty days, which will give him time to send a certified power of attorney by mail."

"Thanks, Dan."

"It's a shame about Mr. Puddle getting killed. I didn't know him that well, but from what I did know of him, he was a decent man who tended to mind his own business."

"That was Mr. Puddle, all right," Smoke said. "Well, I'd better get the telegram sent off."

Brooklyn, New York

Malcolm was in the transit office checking the items to be shipped against the invoice. It was a very detailed procedure, and he had to be very accurate. If he made a mistake, he was liable for any differences between the invoice and the actual shipment. He was good at it, but he disliked the tedium. It was to escape the tedium he'd decided to become a professional prizefighter. But the people who fought in the middleweight division made very little money, so Malcolm had to keep his job, boring though it was.

He was just finishing with one shipment and about to start another when a Western Union messenger came into the office. "Is there a Mr. Malcolm Puddle here?"

"I'm Malcolm Puddle."

"Telegram, Mr. Puddle." The messenger handed over the envelope, then waited for his tip. "Thank you, sir," he said, when Malcolm gave him a quarter.

Malcolm opened the envelope and removed the telegram.

REGRET UNCLE HUMBOLDT PUDDLE KILLED STOP
YOU INHERIT RANCH BIG ROCK COLORADO STOP TELEGRAPH
TEMPORARY POWER OF ATTORNEY TO ME STOP
I WILL PAY $200 TAX STOP MAIL CERTIFIED POA BY ONE
MONTH STOP PLEASE ADVISE BY RETURN TELEGRAM STOP
KIRBY JENSEN

"I don't know who this Kirby Jensen person is," Malcolm said to David Blanton, his lawyer. "I haven't heard from my uncle in a long time, and I don't know if he really is dead or alive. What should I do?"

"First, let's find out if your uncle really is dead, and if such a will exists," Blanton said. "We can do that by telegraphing the court in Eagle County. We can also check on this man, Kirby Jensen, who sent you the telegram."

"How soon do you think we'll hear back?" Malcolm asked.

"Oh, I expect we'll have a response within the hour," Blanton said. "Why don't we go over to the telegraph office and send off a telegram? We can wait for the reply in Ned's Bar."

They stopped at Western Union, and Blanton sent the telegram.

"We'll be in Ned's Bar when the answer comes back," Blanton told the telegrapher.

"Very good, sir."

They left the telegraph office, bought beer in the bar, then found an empty table.

"I hear it took Toby Gleason two months before he could talk again," Blanton said with a chuckle. "He swears you hit him with a club."

"I would have, if I could have found one," Malcolm said.

Blanton chuckled. "I don't blame you. He's a big, powerful man. So is Costaconti. People are still talking about how you handled them."

"Being big and strong means nothing, if you don't know how to fight," Malcolm said. "And clearly, neither of them know how to fight. They've always depended on their strength to get their way."

"About your inheritance," Blanton started.

"If there *is* an inheritance," Malcolm said.

"Yes, if there is. Will you be going to Colorado?"

Malcolm smiled. "Yeah, I think I will."

A few minutes later, a Western Union messenger came into the bar and began looking around. Seeing him, Malcolm called out. "Are you looking for me?"

The messenger smiled. "Yes, sir, Mr. Puddle." He brought the telegram over and Malcolm tipped him, then opened the envelope.

HUMBOLDT PUDDLE DEAD STOP ESTATE LEFT TO MALCOLM
PUDDLE STOP TAX DUE STOP KIRBY JENSEN UPSTANDING
CITIZEN STOP MONTE CARSON SHERIFF EAGLE COUNTY

Malcolm showed the telegram to Blanton. "What do you think?"

"I think the whole thing is legitimate," Blanton replied.

Malcolm smiled and stuck his hand across the table. "How would you like to shake hands with a genuine rancher?"

"What do you know about ranching?" Blanton asked.

"That's where you raise cows, isn't it?"

Blanton chuckled. "I assume so."

"You think they raise cows to milk? Or for meat?"

Blanton laughed out loud. "If I were you, I wouldn't ask that question once you get out there."

CHAPTER 16

Big Rock

Smoke was in Longmont's Saloon, having a beer with Louis, when Sheriff Carson came in.

"What have you got, Monte?" Smoke asked.

Sheriff Carson joined them at the table. "We've identified the three men who were killed out at Puddle's place." Carson pulled out three wanted flyers and showed them to Smoke, one at a time.

$1,000 REWARD

to be paid for

OLIVER NIXON

WANTED *for* MURDER

The other two wanted posters were exactly like the first, except the names were Pete Curtis and John Noble.

"But there was nothing noble about either of them, I can tell you that," Sheriff Carson said. "Back in Nebraska John Noble killed an entire family, the mother and father and their two little ones. Anyway, it looks like you have just earned yourself three thousand dollars."

"I only got two of them. Mr. Puddle got the other one."

"Yeah, well, Puddle is dead, so you may as well take the money."

"I tell you what. Puddle left everything to his nephew. Suppose we give the money to him. That is, if we can find him and he comes out here."

"All right. Sounds fine to me." Sheriff Carson looked at the woodcuts of the three outlaws and shook his head. "What in the world were they doing at Carro de Bancada in the first place?"

"According to Mr. Puddle, they were working for Lucien Garneau."

"I wouldn't doubt it," Carson said. "But even if we can prove they worked for him, it doesn't necessarily connect the murder to him. They could have been acting on their own. Every one of them has a record, and like I said, Noble once killed an entire ranch family."

"A real nice guy," Smoke said sarcastically.

"I know Puddle didn't get along with Garneau. It could be he just assumed the men who attacked him were working for the Frenchman. Seems more likely they were just planning to rob him."

"Rob him of what?" Longmont said. "I knew Puddle. He never had more than one beer when he came in here. He was always watching his money."

"I don't know. Maybe they wanted his horses. He did have a pretty good string of horses," Sheriff Carson said. "Where are the horses now, by the way? Are they still at Puddle's ranch?"

"Yes, I sent one of my men over to keep an eye on them."

"Pearlie or Cal?"

Smoke shook his head. "Neither one. They're both in Denver running my processing plant."

"Ha! Knowing those two boys, I don't expect either one of them is very happy about that."

"There's no doubt they'd rather be back at Sugarloaf," Smoke said. "But they are good men and do what needs to be done without much protest."

"You're right about that. They are both good men. Tell me, Smoke, what do you think is going to happen to Puddle's ranch now?"

"I don't know," Smoke answered. "I guess that will be up to Humboldt's nephew."

"I wonder what kind of man he is?"

"If he's anything like his uncle, he'll be a good man," Smoke said.

Sheriff Carson nodded. "You've got a point there, my friend."

At that moment, the Western Union messenger came into the saloon, and seeing him, Smoke called out, "I'm over here, Eddie."

Smiling, Eddie brought the telegram to him. Smoke tipped him, then read the message.

BY THIS MESSAGE MALCOLM PUDDLE TRANSFERS
POA TO KIRBY JENSEN LIMITED TO PAYING TAXES
ON CARRO DE BANCADA RANCH IN NAME OF
MALCOLM PUDDLE STOP NOTARIZED POA TO FOLLOW STOP
MALCOLM PUDDLE

"Good," Smoke said. "I'm going to the clerk's office now to pay the taxes so the will can be probated."

He left the saloon and stepped into the clerk's office a few minutes later, recognizing the very large man standing at the counter. Dempster wasn't a lawyer for whom Smoke had a lot of respect.

Smoke addressed the probate clerk. "Mr. Pratt, I'm here to

probate Humboldt Puddle's will. I have Malcolm Puddle's power of attorney to pay the taxes."

"You are too late, Mr. Jensen," Dempster said. "I am here to pay the assessment on that property. Once I do, I will assume ownership."

"Once you do? You mean you haven't paid the taxes yet?"

"I'm filling out the forms now."

"Then it isn't too late."

"Oh, but I'm afraid it is. I got here before you."

"How are you going to fill out those forms?" Smoke asked.

"What do you mean, how am I going to fill out the forms? I'm just going to do it."

"No, I mean, how are you going to write with a broken hand?" Smoke asked calmly.

"What? Are you threatening me?"

"I wouldn't call it a threat." Smoke smiled at Dempster, but there was absolutely no humor in his smile. "I would say it is more along the line of a promise."

"I will have you arrested and put in jail for this!" Dempster said. "And Pratt will be my witness."

"Witness to what?" Pratt asked. "I haven't seen anything."

"You heard him threaten me."

"Like I said, Mr. Dempster, I haven't seen anything."

"What's it going to be, Dempster? Are you going to walk out of here with no bones broken? Or do we give Pratt here something to see so he won't testify for you?"

"You! You!" Dempster sputtered. "I won't stand for this. Do you hear me? I simply won't stand for it!"

Smoke looked over at Pratt. "Has he given you the two hundred dollars yet?"

"No, he hasn't."

Smoke took two hundred dollars from his pocket and gave it to the clerk. "Here's the money. I'd say that puts me in front of him, wouldn't you?"

Pratt smiled and nodded. "Yes, sir. I would say that it does."

Smoke turned toward Dempster. "Are you still here?" Dempster glared at him, but said nothing before he turned and left the clerk's office.

Seven days after Malcolm Puddle boarded the train in New York, it rolled into Big Rock, Colorado. He sat at the window on the left side of the car, taking in the town that was to be his new home. He took in every building and sign as the train rolled by—Earl's Blacksmith Shop, GOOD WORK DONE FAST; Dunnigan's Meat Market, OUR MEAT IS FRESH AND CLEAN; the *Big Rock Journal*, EAGLE COUNTY'S LEADING NEWSPAPER; Longmont's Saloon, BEER, WINE, WHISKEY; Murchison's Saddle and Leather Goods store, CUSTOM LEATHER WORK; Delmonico's Restaurant, FINE DINING; Nancy's Bakery, PIES OUR SPECIALTY; and White's Apothecary, FINEST POTIONS AND SYRUPS.

The train stopped, and Malcolm saw the Western Union office and the Denver and Pacific depot building. The depot was constructed of red brick, and had a small white sign hanging from the end.

BIG ROCK, COLORADO

ELEVATION: 8,675 FEET

Reaching into the overhead rack, Malcolm retrieved his bowler hat and a leather case in which he had his important papers, including the notarized limited power of attorney. He was wearing a tan suit, a dark brown vest, and a yellow, four-in-hand tie. He stepped down onto the platform, listening to the sounds the train made behind him; from the popping sounds of cooling bearings and journals to the rhythmic venting of steam from the actuating cylinder. He decided the first order of business would be to retrieve his luggage, then locate a hotel, and finally look up Dan Norton, the Big Rock lawyer with whom his lawyer had been in contact.

The arrival and departure of trains was always an event of great interest in Big Rock, and it generally drew people who had no other reason to meet the train than to give vent to that interest. Two such characters were Curly Roper and Slim Taylor, cowboys who worked at the Long Trek Ranch. They'd ridden into town just after lunch, and had spent most of the afternoon drinking—first in Longmont's Saloon. When they got a bit rowdy, Louis nicely asked them to leave. Nobody who knew him ever made the error of mistaking his gentlemanly request for weakness, for to do so could be a fatal miscalculation. They spent the rest of the afternoon in the Brown Dirt Cowboy, where rowdiness was more or less expected.

Fairly well liquored up, they were at the depot watching the arriving and departing passengers.

"Hey, Slim, take a look at that little feller that just got off the train," Curly said. "He's all slicked up like some kind of Eastern dude, ain't he? Look at that hat he's wearin'. What kind of hat would you call that?"

"I don't know what you call it, but it sure ain't no sombrero," Slim said.

"I think I'm going to go over there and wear me that hat." Curly started toward the man.

Seeing the man coming toward him, Malcolm smiled. "Excuse me, sir, but would you happen to know where I might find a Mr. Dan Norton? I believe he is an attorney."

"He's a what?"

"A lawyer. I have secured his services."

Curly chuckled. "Have you now?" He pointed to the hat. "Tell me, what do you call that thing you've got on your head?"

"Why, it is a hat, sir. Specifically, it is a bowler." Malcolm took off his hat and held it out. "Would you like to examine it?"

"Yeah," Curly said with a little laugh. "Yeah, that's what I want to do. I want to examine it." He took the hat, looked at it for a moment, then took his hat off and put the bowler hat on.

Malcolm cringed a bit. He was very fastidious in his personal hygiene, and the man looked as if he hadn't washed his hair in months. Malcolm could almost feel the head lice. "I don't mind you looking at it, but I would rather you not put it on."

"Well, that's too bad, dude, because I'm already wearing it, and there's nothing you can do about it."

"Actually, there is," Malcolm said calmly. "But I would rather not have an altercation on my first day in town. Especially as I intend to settle here."

"Do you now?" Curly asked. "And just what will you be doing here? Working in some fancy restaurant? We've only got one of those, that's Delmonico's, and they ain't hirin'."

"Please, sir. My hat?"

"Why don't you take it off of me, dude?" Curly challenged.

"I'd really rather not. As I said, I have no wish to get involved in an altercation on my first day in town."

"Alterca. . . . alter. . . . alter what? What is that?"

"Altercation. You might call it a fight. I really don't want to get into a fight, my first day here."

Curly laughed. "Yeah, I'll just bet you don't. But, dude, if you want this hat back, the only way you are goin' to get it is if you take it off my head." He sported a challenging grin. "Go ahead, take it off me."

"All right," Malcolm said. "But remember, you invited this."

Malcolm reached for the hat with his left hand. and just as he knew he would, Curly brought both hands up to block him. That left his stomach open, and Malcolm drove his right fist into it, glad this finger had been only jammed, and not broken, in an earlier fight.

Curly doubled over with a loud and involuntary expulsion of breath, bringing his head down in a deep bow. It was a perfect set up, and Malcolm wanted to hit him a second time, but he eschewed the opportunity and chose, instead, to pluck the hat from Curly's head. He examined it closely for any signs of vermin before he put it back on his own head.

A few feet away, Slim had been watching, amused by the way Curly was playing the Eastern dude. When he saw a punch double Curly over, he was shocked and angered. He started for his gun.

"I wouldn't, if I were you," a calm but authoritative voice said. The warning was punctuated with the deadly sound of a .45 pistol being cocked.

Slim looked around to see Sheriff Carson holding a pistol leveled toward him.

"I wasn't actual goin' to shoot the little man, Sheriff," Slim said. "I was just goin' to keep him from hittin' Curly any more. Me 'n Curly was just going to roust him around a bit, is all."

"It looks to me like you and Curly are the ones who got rousted. What are you doing down here at the depot, anyway? Are you going somewhere? Are you seeing anybody off or meeting anyone?" Sheriff Carson asked.

"No, it ain't nothin' like that. We just like to watch the trains come 'n go, is all. Lots of people come down here to do that."

"Everyone else who comes down to watch the trains does just that. They watch the trains. They don't harass the passengers. Now, if you and Curly don't want to spend the night in my jail, I suggest you get on back to the Long Trek."

"We got the day off so we could spend time in town," Slim complained.

"You've spent all the time in town you're going to. Now get going, the both of you."

"What about this fella, Sheriff?" Slim said, pointing to Malcolm. "Maybe you didn't see what he done, but he hit Curly for no reason at all."

"That's not quite the truth. I was watching everything, and I wouldn't say it was for no reason at all, Sheriff. This fella here"—the town citizen pointed to Curly—"took the little fella's hat and wasn't goin' to give it back. That's when the little fella hit him."

"Little fella?" Sheriff Carson asked.

The citizen chuckled. "Well, yeah, I guess he looks little. But he sure don't hit like no little man, does he? He pure doubled that bigger fella over."

"See? Like he said, he doubled me over," Curly said. "Are you goin' to arrest him?"

"Arrest him? Why should I arrest him? I may give him a medal," Sheriff Carson replied. "Now you and Slim get on out of town like I told you. Otherwise, I meant it when I said you would spend the night in jail."

Grumbling, the two cowboys left the depot, with Curly still holding his hand over his stomach.

Sheriff Carson chuckled, then walked over to Malcolm. "I saw Curly start to bother you and I figured I would come over here and put a stop to it, but you seem able to take care of yourself."

"I appreciate your assistance, nonetheless, Sheriff. Especially as it looked as if the other gentleman was about to withdraw his pistol. As you can see, I am not armed, so I would have been greatly disadvantaged."

"Yes, sir, I reckon you would be. If you want some advice, you probably should start wearing a pistol."

"Why? I don't know anything about guns. I've never even fired one. I'll just try not to get into any situation that is beyond being able to take care of it with my fists."

"That's just it," Sheriff Carson said. "These cowboys don't have a lot of sense, but they do have a lot of pride. Getting whipped by someone who looks . . . and dresses . . . the way you do isn't going to go down very well with them.

I'm afraid you will always have someone like Curly or Slim to deal with."

"Do you think it would help matters if I change the way I dress?"

Sheriff Carson smiled. "Some Western duds would help, that's for certain."

"Then I shall do that as soon as I see Mr. Norton."

"Norton. Dan Norton?"

"Yes, sir. I believe he is an attorney here."

"He is, and a good one. Do you have an appointment with him?"

"In a manner of speaking, I do. At least, I have been in communication with him by telegraph. Could you tell me where I might find him?"

"I certainly can." Sheriff Carson pointed south, across the track. "This is Front Street and the street that runs south away from it is Tanner Street. Go down Tanner Street one block until you get to Center Street. Turn left on Center, go by the BR Hotel and the stagecoach office, cross Ranney Street, and you'll see the Dempster law office."

"Dempster? I think I'm supposed to see a Mr. Norton."

"I know. I just told you about Dempster's office so you wouldn't get confused. Mr. Norton's law office is in the building after Dempster's. It's the McCoy Building. You can't miss it. It's the biggest office in town. He's on the top floor.

"Thank you."

"Oh, and a word of caution?"

"Yes, sir?"

"It looks to me like you are pretty handy with your fists. I'd be a bit more careful in using them if I were you. You might wind up hitting someone with your fists, and, like Slim was about to, he might respond with a gun."

"Thank you, Sheriff, for the warning. And for coming to my assistance."

CHAPTER 17

Malcolm followed Sheriff Carson's directions, and a few minutes later was standing in front of a two-story redbrick building. An outside stairway climbed up the left side of the building and hanging from an arm that protruded from the side of the building was a sign. Painted on the sign were a clinched hand with one finger pointing up the stairs and the words *Dan S. Norton, Atty. at law.*

Malcolm climbed the stairs, then knocked on the door at the top. It was opened by a man who wasn't any taller than he was. Like Malcolm, he was wearing a suit, and he had freckles and thinning hair.

"Mr. Norton?"

"Yes?"

"Mr. Norton, my name is Malcolm Puddle. I believe you and I have communicated."

A big smile spread across Norton's face and he stepped back from the door, then made a sweeping, inviting motion with his arm. "Indeed we have, Mr. Puddle, indeed we have. Come in, sir, please come in."

Inside the office, Malcolm was offered a seat. Then Norton went over to a bar where he picked up a decanter of whiskey. "May I offer you a drink?"

"I don't drink whiskey, but when we have completed our business, I would be glad to buy you a beer."

"It's a deal," Norton said, sitting down across the desk from Malcolm. "Now, Mr. Puddle, what can I do for you?"

"First, I would like to make certain my uncle's will has been probated, and that I am, indeed, the heir to his ranch. The Carro de Bancada I believe it is called."

"I assure you, Mr. Puddle, that you are the heir to your uncle's ranch, and the deed to the Carro de Bancada has already been transferred to your name. For it to be validated, however, you will have to show the tax clerk that Smoke did have your power of attorney to pay the taxes in your name."

"I beg your pardon. Smoke? I gave no authority to anyone named Smoke."

"I'm sorry. In all our communications with you, we referred to him as Kirby. Kirby Jensen, and indeed, that is his real name. But everyone who knows him calls him Smoke. Even his wife."

"I appreciate him doing that for me, and I should like to see him so I can repay the money. I've got the money right here. Two hundred dollars, I believe it was?"

Norton smiled broadly. "Yes, but you don't need to worry about reimbursing Smoke. That's already been taken care of."

"I beg your pardon? How was it taken care of?"

Norton opened the middle drawer of his desk and pulled out an envelope. "It has not only been taken care of, but you have eight hundred dollars left over."

"What? Mr. Norton, I assure you, sir, I have no idea what you are talking about. I have sent no money here, either by wire or post."

Norton chuckled, then held up his hand. "Perhaps you had better let me explain. It seems that your uncle killed one of the men who went to the ranch to kill him. That man was a known outlaw, and there was a one thousand dollar reward posted for him, dead or alive. Since your uncle was unable to collect, I convinced the sheriff to allow me to hold the money in escrow for you."

Norton counted out eight one-hundred dollar bills.

Malcolm smiled. "Oh, wow, I certainly didn't expect this. And you say Mr. Jensen has already been paid back?"

"Yes. I'll tell you what kind of man Smoke is. Three of the attackers were killed at Carro de Bancada. Smoke killed two and could have claimed all three, since nobody was there to dispute him. But he said your uncle had killed one, and, by rights, the money should go to you."

"I can't wait to meet Mr. Jensen."

"You will. He will be your neighbor, and I'm sure that, as a neighborly thing, he and Sally will invite you over for a meal. You haven't lived until you've tasted her cooking. Come, we'll go see the clerk now, show him the power of attorney, and everything will be all squared away."

"Thank you. You have been most helpful. I do hope to pay for your services."

"We'll work something out," Norton said. "I'm not going to try and get all my money up front. I hope to make you a client, so I can bleed you for a long time."

"What?"

Norton laughed. "I'm teasing, my boy. I'm merely teasing."

Malcolm laughed. "Oh, by the way, what does the name mean?"

"Smoke?"

"Well, that too, but I imagine Mr. Jensen will tell me that in due time. No, I'm talking about my uncle's . . . I mean, *my* ranch. If I'm going to be a ranch owner, I should at least know what Carro de Bancada means."

"It means saddle," Norton said.

They came to a big building on the corner of Center and Sikes Streets.

"Here's the courthouse," Norton said. "The clerk is inside."

Don Pratt looked up when the two men went inside. "Hello, Mr. Norton."

"Hello, Don. This is Malcolm Puddle."

Pratt smiled. "I had a feeling you would show up in person."

"I have a notarized copy of the power of attorney to validate the one I sent by wire."

"All right. Let me see it, and I'll sign off on this, then turn the deed over to you."

"What are you going to do with the ranch, Mr. Puddle?" Norton asked.

"I haven't decided yet. Why do you ask?"

"You will, no doubt, be visited by Lucien Garneau or his agent, offering to buy you out."

"What is the land worth?"

"It's twenty-five hundred and sixty acres, and the last land transaction I dealt with was five dollars an acre. Though in your case it might be worth a little more because your uncle did a lot of work on the land. For example he dug a canal from Frying Pan Creek to provide water. In addition to the land, your uncle has three hundred and twenty-five head of prime Herefords. They are worth at least thirty-five dollars a head." Norton did some figuring. "With land, cattle, and improvements to include house, barn, machine shed, and smokehouse, I would say the Carro de Bancada is worth somewhere in the neighborhood of twenty-five thousand dollars.

"Wow," Malcolm said. "That's a lot of money."

"Garneau is a shrewd businessman so, no doubt, if he makes an offer, he probably won't offer that much."

"If he seriously wants it, he will," Malcolm said.

He finished his business about the ranch and stopped next at Goldstein's Mercantile.

"Yes, sir, may I help you?" Gary Goldstein asked, greeting him as he stepped through the door and into the store.

"I need some"—Malcolm recalled Sheriff Carson's description of the apparel—"western dudes."

"I beg your pardon?" Goldstein asked with a puzzled expression on his face.

"Oh, I think that is duds," Malcolm corrected. "I need some western duds."

"Very good, sir. Do you have anything specific in mind?"

"Look at me," Malcolm said, taking in his clothing with a wave of his hand. "Would you agree these make me stand out?"

Goldstein laughed. "Yes, sir, I have to say that your clothes, elegant looking though they are, do make you stand out."

"Well, what I have in mind, specifically, is clothes that don't make me stand out."

"Leave that to me, I'll take care of it for you."

Half an hour later, Malcolm left the mercantile wearing boots, blue denims, a white cotton shirt, and a white Stetson hat. He was carrying a bag in which he had three more outfits just like the clothes he was wearing, plus the clothes he had been wearing when he went into the store.

When he returned to the Dunn Hotel, he was met by the sheriff and another man as soon as he stepped into the lobby.

"Mr. Puddle?" Sheriff Carson called him out with a smile. "I almost didn't recognize you."

"Do these clothes make me fit in?" Malcolm asked with a smile.

"Well, I don't know that you entirely fit in, but the clothes do help," Sheriff Carson said. "You said you wanted to meet Smoke Jensen. Here he is."

"Mr. Jensen," Malcolm said with a big smile and an extended hand. "How nice to meet you, and to thank you in person for what you have done."

"The name is Smoke. Your uncle was a good friend."

"I can certainly see that he made friends," Malcolm said. "And for that I am most grateful."

"I see that you have taken a room here at the hotel," Smoke said. "But if you would like to ride out to your ranch, I'll be glad to take you there."

"Ride out? What would I ride? I don't have a horse."

"Yes, you do. I brought your uncle's riding horse into town. It's put up over at the livery."

"Thank you. That was very thoughtful of you. Uh, does my uncle have any employees? The reason I ask is because I was told there are three hundred and twenty-five cattle there and I'm concerned they haven't been looked after."

"No, there aren't any full-time employees there," Smoke said. "The cattle pretty much look after themselves until roundup time, or until you take them to market. Then Mr. Puddle would put on a couple hands."

"I see. Yes, I would like to ride out to the ranch."

"All right. I'll take you out to see it, then I want you to come over to my house for dinner tonight. You can even spend the night with us, and get an early start tomorrow to have a close look at Carro de Bancada."

"Carro de Bancada," Malcolm said. "Ha! I'm a landowner. And not just a landowner. I actually own a ranch. I can't wait to tell all my friends back in Brooklyn."

"Are those my cattle?" Malcolm asked, looking out over a field they were riding by. Several cattle were grazing.

"No, those cows belong to the Frenchman."

"The Frenchman?"

"That's what everyone calls him. He likes to call himself Colonel. Colonel Lucien Garneau."

"He is the one who wants to buy the ranch, isn't he? Mr. Norton told me about him."

"I expect he will make an offer," Smoke said. "He's bought out several ranchers already."

"I take it Uncle Humboldt wasn't interested in selling to him?"

"No, he wasn't. Well, there it is," Smoke said. "That's the gate into your place."

It had taken Smoke and Malcolm a little over half an hour of leisurely riding to reach the ranch. The gate Smoke pointed to made an arch over the road. A sign hung from the top of the arch, reading CARRO DE BANCADA. Positioned on top of the arch was a saddle, complete with hanging stirrups.

From the arch the road ran about a quarter mile up to the house, which was a rather modest, single story dwelling. Smoke identified the three other buildings as a barn, a machine shed, and a smokehouse.

"I know you have at least three or four cured hams in there, and a couple sides of bacon. And you've got a milk cow and a garden that's coming along fine."

"That's good to know," Malcolm said. "I guess I'll have to learn to cook."

"Nothing to it," Smoke said. "You just light a fire, then heat things up."

They dismounted in front of the house.

"Where was my uncle killed?"

"He was over there, behind the corral fence," Smoke said. "He put up quite a fight. There were four who came for him, and he held them off for quite a while."

"Who were they?"

"Your uncle was certain they were working for the Frenchman, but of course, Garneau has denied any connection to it. Since there's no way of connecting the men to him, the official word is they were outlaws come to rob your uncle."

"Do you believe that?"

"I don't know," Smoke admitted. "One of them, a man

named Noble, had a record of doing just that—hitting remote ranches, killing everyone there, and then robbing them. It's possible, I guess."

"But you think it was the Frenchman, don't you?"

"Your uncle thought that," Smoke said without being anymore specific in his reply. "What do you say we go on over to Sugarloaf now? I'm getting hungry, and my wife sure can cook."

CHAPTER 18

"Welcome to Sugarloaf," Sally said after Smoke took Malcolm to the ranch and made the introduction. "Tell me, Mr. Puddle, what do you think of Colorado, so far?"

"Please, call me Malcolm. I love Colorado so far. The mountains are quite impressive and beautiful."

"They are a bit overwhelming, aren't they? I remember my impression of them the first time I came here."

"You mean you aren't from Colorado?"

Sally laughed. "Heavens no. I'm not sure anyone is actually from Colorado. But once I got here I became so attached this is truly my home now, and Boston seems just like a place I have visited. Of course, I've visited New York as well, so I know what a tremendous difference it is for you."

"Monte told me about Malcolm's welcoming committee at the depot," Smoke said.

"Welcoming committee?" Sally asked.

"A couple of the Frenchman's cowboys decided to roust him. One of them took his hat and dared him to take it back."

"Oh, that's awful."

Smoke laughed. "Not so awful. Malcolm took it back." Smoke looked back at Malcolm. "Monte said you pack quite a punch."

"I was a professional fighter for a while," Malcolm said.

"Ha! I thought it might be something like that. It's good to be able to take care of yourself, but be careful where and how you use that skill. No matter how good you are with your fists, they're no match for a gun. And I'm sure you have noticed just about everyone out here carries a gun."

"Yes, I have noticed. But I'm not good with a gun." Malcolm chuckled. "The truth is, I've never even fired one."

"We'll take care of that soon enough." Smoke turned to Sally. "Have we got anything to feed our guest?"

"Smoke, have I ever turned anyone away?" Sally replied.

Smoke smiled. "No, you haven't. And, shamelessly, I have taken advantage of that."

"Shamelessly," Sally said, returning Smoke's smile.

"What's for supper?"

"How about fried ham? And I'll fry some potatoes and scramble some eggs in with them."

"And biscuits?" Smoke asked.

"Of course."

"Sounds good."

Long Trek

Templeton knocked on the door of the big house and heard Garneau call from inside.

"*Entrez.*"

Templeton went inside. He saw that Garneau had a large piece of paper spread out on the dining room table.

"Come, I want you to see this," Garneau invited. A very detailed map had been drawn on newsprint he had gotten from the *Big Rock Journal*.

"I wondered what you wanted with that big piece of paper," Templeton said.

"Here," Garneau said, pointing at the map, "is Sugarloaf. And here is Long Trek. Here is Carro de Bancada."

"Yeah, Puddle's nephew has come to take it. But I'll bet

you can buy him out cheap. He's some Eastern dude who doesn't know a thing about ranching."

"That may be true," Garneau said. "But one thing I learned at St. Cyr is a good officer is always prepared for any contingency. Suppose he doesn't want to sell to me?"

"I don't think it would take much to convince him to sell."

"I am told he has befriended Smoke Jensen."

"Yeah, that's what I've heard as well," Templeton said.

"Smoke Jensen is a formidable adversary. After all, he killed Willard, the three men who came to join us, the two men you set to ambush him, and Nixon, Curtis, and Noble."

"He is just one man."

"Just one man who has already dispatched nine men. Also, he is quite obviously a leader. What if he gathers the other *paysans* into an organized resistance?"

"What would he have if he did do that? They are nothing but a bunch of pig farmers and small ranchers who couldn't fight their way out of a paper bag."

"I studied your Civil War while I was at St. Cyr. Most of both armies were made up of farmers, ranchers, merchants, and mechanics. As Euripides once said, 'Ten men wisely led will beat a hundred without a head.' I wouldn't dismiss them so readily."

"All right. So what should we do?"

"We are going to form an army," Garneau said. "Turn out every man. I will speak with them."

Dressed in the uniform of a French colonel of cavalry, Garneau stood before every man who worked for him, cowboys and the gunmen Templeton had recruited. "Starting today, I am doubling the salary of everyone who works for me."

The men cheered and patted each on the shoulders.

Garneau let them express their joy for a moment, then he held his hands up to call for quiet. "You will earn that money."

The cheering stopped, and the men looked at him in curiosity.

"You may be wondering about the clothes I am wearing. This"—he took himself in with a small sweep of his hand—"is the uniform of a colonel of cavalry. I fought, honorably, in the Franco-Prussian War, and I am quite comfortable with command. You may look at me as your commanding officer because, starting today, we are going to become an army."

"We're goin' to become what?" Curly Roper asked.

"An army," Garneau said. "And an army demands discipline. Let us begin by lining up in formation. Capitaine Templeton, you will be my second in command."

"Yes, sir," Templeton said with a big smile.

"Briggs, Mathis, Carr, you three will be my sergeants. The rest of you men will take your orders from them, as they will take their orders from me."

"Why are you doin' this, Colonel?" Hoyt Miller asked.

"Because, Mr. Miller, I am trying to build something here, something grand and unique. I am building a cattle empire, and like any empire, we have made enemies and, no doubt, we will make more enemies in the future. In addition, this is not the kind of empire that can survive merely by staying in place. We must grow, and the only way we can grow is if we convince the small ranchers in the valley to sell out to me. Quite frankly, gentlemen, we must convince them to sell at a price that is right for me. That is going to take some persuasion, the kind of persuasion that must be backed by use of arms, if necessary."

"Colonel, it sounds to me like you are talking about a war, here," Miller said. "I didn't sign on to go to war. If I wanted to do that, I'd join the army and go fight the Injuns."

"Miller, do you know how much a private makes in the army?" Templeton asked.

"I ain't got no idea," Miller replied.

"Sir," Garneau said.

"What?" Miller asked.

"When you speak to Capitaine Templeton, or to me, you will say sir."

"Thank you, Colonel," Templeton said. "Miller, for your information, a private in the army makes thirteen dollars a month. Most cowboys work for twenty dollars a month and found. Because of the colonel's generous raise today, you will be getting sixty dollars a month. You don't have to pay for where you sleep at night, and you don't have to pay for your food. That means you have sixty dollars you can use any way you want."

"I'm going to be spending my money on the girls at the Brown Dirt," someone said, and the others laughed.

"You'll be making four and a half times more money working for the Long Trek than you would make in the army. Do you really want to go join the army?"

"No, I guess not."

Over the next several days, the ranch was alive with the sound of repeated gunfire, the echoes rolling back from the nearby mountains to double the intensity. Someone not aware of what it was, might have thought a battle was taking place, when in fact, it was nothing of the sort. Templeton stood beside Garneau as they watched their "army" train. The Frenchman had organized his men into three squads of nine, plus the "sergeants" he had put in command of each squad. Briggs, Mathis, and Carr were skilled gunmen, and they were conducting shooting exercises for the other men.

"How do you think they are doing?" Garneau asked.

"Some are doing better than others," Templeton replied.

"Yes, that is always the case when any army is trained."

"Colonel, I have a suggestion. That is, if you care to hear it."

"I would be a poor commander indeed if I refused to listen to a suggestion from my second in command."

"Jensen has two men who work for him, and one of them is almost as good with a gun as Jensen is. Fact is, he used to be a gunman himself. The other one isn't quite as good, but he is good enough that, if they joined Jensen, it could cause us some trouble. I think we should take care of them before we start anything."

"Who are these men?"

"Pearlie, and Cal Wood."

"Why haven't I heard of them? I've been here for over six months and I've never heard of either one of them. Shouldn't I have heard of them by now?"

"They've spent near on to a year now in Denver. It seems Jensen has started a slaughterhouse there, and Pearlie and Cal Wood are running it."

"If they are in Denver, then they are of no concern to us," Garneau said.

Templeton shook his head. "No, sir, that's not quite true. If they ever get the idea Jensen is in trouble, they'll be back here faster than a duck can jump on a June bug."

"How do you propose to take care of them?"

"I think we should send someone to Denver," Templeton said.

"Who do you suggest? If they are as good as you say they are I don't think any of our men would be a match for them, except possibly Mathis, Briggs, or Carr. And I don't want to send them right now. They are too valuable in training the others."

"If we put out a reward on Jensen's men, we won't have to send any of our men. Someone out there will do it for us."

"How much of a reward do you think I should post?"

"A thousand dollars ought to do it."

"And how am I to do this? I can't very well go to the newspaper office and have them print up reward posters for me."

"You won't need to," Templeton said. "All we have to do is put out the word. It'll spread all over, believe me."

"Very well. Put out the word that I will pay one thousand dollars to anyone who kills Cal Wood and Pearlie . . . Pearlie what? What is his last name?"

"I don't know."

"I can't put out a reward on someone if I don't know who we are looking for, can I?"

"Let me ask you this, Colonel. How many men do you think are named Pearlie?"

Garneau laughed.

"If you've got no objection to it, I'll start puttin' out the word."

"By all means, put out the word."

CHAPTER 19

Sugarloaf

Long Trek wasn't the only place where training was taking place.

It was going on at Sugarloaf as well, though there were only three people participating in the exercise, compared to the thirty-two men undergoing military instruction at Long Trek. Smoke and Sally were the trainers. Malcolm Puddle was the one being trained.

Smoke handed Malcolm a loaded pistol, then pointed to one of several tin cans sitting on a fence. "See if you can hit that can."

Malcolm raised the pistol then closed one eye and squinted down the barrel.

"No, don't raise your pistol to eye level and try to aim it," Smoke said. "In a fight, you won't have time to do that."

"How am I supposed to aim, if I don't sight down the barrel?" Malcolm asked.

"Do it kinesthetically," Sally suggested.

"I beg your pardon. Do it how?"

"You are a boxer, right?"

"Yes."

"When you throw a punch, do you raise your fist to your eyes and aim it?"

Malcolm laughed. "No."

"What do you do?"

"Well, I just sort of feel where the . . . oh! I think I see what you are talking about. You're saying I should just sense where I'm shooting."

"Yes."

"But that's not the same thing as hitting someone with your fists."

Smoke laughed. "Sure it is. It turns out that I've been shooting kinesthetically all along, but I didn't know it until Sally told me that's what I was doing."

"But can you really hit something that way?"

"Watch." Sally nodded at Smoke, and he turned his back. She picked up two bottles and gave one to Malcolm, while keeping the other. Then, silently, she indicated to Malcolm he should toss the bottle into the air. They launched both bottles at the same time.

"Now, Smoke," Sally said calmly.

Faster than Malcolm would have believed possible, Smoke whirled around, drawing his pistol as he did so. He shot twice, the bang of the two shots so close together the young man would have thought he fired only once, had not both bottles been broken.

"Wow, kinesthetically," Malcolm said.

"Does that answer your question as to whether you can actually hit anything that way?" Sally asked.

"Lord," Malcolm said. "If everyone out here can shoot like that, I would be an idiot to actually get into a gunfight with anyone."

"Trust me, not everyone can shoot like my Smoke," Sally said proudly.

"Try it," Smoke said.

Malcolm fired, but the tin cans stayed in place.

"It's not hard." Sally fired from her waist, knocking one of the tin cans off the fence.

"I thought you said everyone couldn't shoot like that."

"Sally's just showing off," Smoke said. "But she's a better shot than ninety-nine percent of the people you will meet out here."

"I thought you said you were from Boston."

"I am."

"Well, I know you didn't learn to shoot like that in Boston."

"I didn't. I came out here to teach school. I didn't learn to shoot like that until Smoke taught me."

"You taught her?"

"I did."

Malcolm smiled. "You must be a good teacher. Maybe there is hope for me." He fired again, and missed again.

"Maybe," Smoke teased. "But don't count on it."

"Smoke!" Sally scolded. "Don't talk like that. You know I couldn't hit anything when you first started teaching me. And I'm not the only one. Look at Matt. He's as good as you."

"Maybe better," Smoke said.

"Who is Matt?"

"Matt Jensen is a young man Smoke raised," Sally said without any further explanation.

Malcolm fired again, continuing to fire until the pistol was out of bullets.

"Here," Smoke said. "Reload and fire again."

"Are you sure I'm not just wasting your ammunition?"

"It's not exactly a waste. Even though you aren't hitting anything yet, you are getting a feel for the gun. And that is important."

Malcolm emptied the pistol two more times, then after reloading, he hit one of the cans with his first shot. "I hit it!" he yelled excitedly.

"Can you do it again?"

"I don't know. That may have just been luck."

"No," Smoke said. "It wasn't luck. Look at the can, then feel the pistol lining up with it."

"Kinesthetically," Malcolm said.

"Kinesthetically," Smoke agreed.

Malcolm stared at the can, then "felt" the pistol lining up with it, and pulled the trigger. The can flew off the post.

"Wow!" Malcolm said. "I can't believe it!"

He shot four more times, hitting two more cans. The next time he reloaded, he hit five out of six cans.

"I'm beginning to get the feel for this now," he said.

"Don't lose the feel. We'll do some more shooting tomorrow," Smoke said. "But now, I promised Sally we would go into town. Johnny McVey is giving a piano concert at the Reasoner Theater."

"Who is Johnny McVey?"

"He's one of the bartenders at Longmont's," Smoke said, as if that statement needed no further explanation.

Smoke, Sally, and Malcolm rode into town, then stopped in front of Lambert's, a restaurant, which proudly boasted it was the home of tossed rolls.

"What is a tossed roll?" Malcolm asked.

"You'll see," Sally said with a grin as they dismounted.

"Who wants a hot roll?" someone shouted as soon as they stepped in through the door.

"Here!"

Malcolm saw someone throw a roll, and it sailed across the room, caught by someone at one of the tables. No sooner had the three of them taken their table, than three rolls came flying toward them. Throughout the meal the rolls were tossed around, and there was a great deal of shouting and laughing.

"What do you think of the place?" Smoke asked.

"It's . . . interesting," Malcolm said.

"We have three restaurants in town, and since we have a population of less than five hundred there's no way all three could survive unless each of them carved out their own niche," Sally said. "This one is sort of a participatory restaurant, with tossed rolls and all the interplay between the waiters and the customers. The City Pig specializes in barbeque beef, pork, and chicken. But my personal favorite is Delmonico's."

"Delmonico's? There is a restaurant by that name in New York."

Smoke chuckled. "And in half the towns of the West, all of them trying to emulate their New York namesake."

"And while our Delmonico's isn't as large or as grand as the one on fifty-six Beaver Street, it does feature the finest cuisine in town . . . if not in the entire valley," Sally said.

After dinner they rode together to the Reasoner Theater to attend the concert.

"Smoke, did you say the pianist tonight is a bartender?"

"Yes. He tends bar for Louis Longmont."

"Is he a good pianist?"

"I've never heard him play, but Louis has. He is the one who set up the concert. Louis wouldn't do that unless he thought McVey was good enough."

"Good evening, Monsieur and Madame Jensen."

"Mr. Garneau," Smoke replied.

"The gentleman with you?"

"This is your neighbor, Malcolm Puddle," Smoke said.

"Monsieur Puddle, please allow me to express my sympathy to you for the loss of your uncle. It was a tragic thing."

"Yes, it was," Malcolm said.

"I would like to call on you sometime soon, neighbor to neighbor," Garneau said.

Malcolm nodded.

"Come, before all the good seats are taken," Sally said.

"Good evening to you, sir," Malcolm said with a nod of his head as he joined Smoke and Sally.

Inside, the theater was illuminated only enough to allow the audience to find their seats. The stage was bare except for the piano, and it was held in a spotlight from a carbon arc lamp.

Two hundred people filled the Reasoner Theater to hear the bartender give his first concert. The audience applauded as Johnny McVey walked out onto the stage. He looked nothing like the man who dispensed drinks in Louis Longmont's establishment. He was wearing a white shirt and black bow tie, a formal black jacket with tails, striped pants, and a black cummerbund. He approached the piano bench, flipped the tails back from his swallow-coat, and took his seat at the piano.

The auditorium grew quiet as McVey sat before the keyboard for a long moment as if composing himself. Then he began to play Beethoven's Piano Sonata no. 26 in E-flat major ("Les Adieux"), and the music spilled out into the theater, caressing the collective soul of the audience.

Sally reached over to put her hand in Smoke's, and as he looked toward her he saw tears in her eyes as she was reacting to the beauty of the music.

Smoke thought of the incongruity of the moment. There on stage was a man whose skilled hands upon the keyboard were filling the theater with beautiful music. And yet, but a short time ago, those same hands were holding a double-barrel shotgun and threatening to kill, if necessary, three men.

But, it was easy enough to put that image out of his head so, like Sally, he could enjoy the music.

* * *

The next day, the *Big Rock Journal* carried a story of the concert performed by Johnny McVey on the night before.

Wonderful Concert

JOHNNY MCVEY DISPLAYS
HIS VIRTUOSITY ON THE PIANO

To the patrons of Longmont's Saloon, Johnny McVey may appear to be nothing more than a bartender. And though he is a bartender par excellence, last night he proved to the citizens of Big Rock that he is much more.

Johnny McVey is a pianist of the first order. Performing on stage in the Reasoner Theater last night, he held the audience spellbound. It was a magical display, and with his skill he managed to resurrect the genius of the composer so that, to the listening audience, Johnny McVey and Ludwig Beethoven were one and the same.

Citizens of Big Rock know the Reasoner Theater is the scene for good entertainment, from the classical music prowess of Mr. McVey, to the elocutions of learned men and women, to the presentation of the latest plays, performed by traveling troupes of actors. Every citizen owes a degree of debt to Mr. James Reasoner for having the foresight to build his theater in Big Rock.

CHAPTER 20

Denver

Jack Emerson was at Nippy Jones' Saloon, having a drink with Bud Lane, when Lane told him something he had just learned. "I know someone who will pay a thousand dollars to anyone who can do a certain job for him."

Emerson frowned. "A thousand dollars? That's a lot of money."

"I reckon it is, but I ain't about to try and collect it. In the first place, it's blood money."

"What do you mean, blood money?"

"Just what I'm asayin'. They's two men here in Denver this feller wants dead."

"Who is it? And who is wantin' 'em dead?"

"The two men the feller is wantin' kilt is named Pearlie and Cal. They're workin' over at the abattoir, runnin' it for Smoke Jensen. And as far as who it is that's awantin' 'em kilt, it's Deekus Templeton."

"Deekus Templeton?"

"Yes."

"Do you know him?"

"Yeah, I know him." Lane looked around the saloon to make certain he couldn't be overheard before he made the next comment. "Me 'n him pulled a job together once. We held up a stagecoach up in Wyoming. Got twenty-five hundred dollars."

"Can this Templeton be trusted to pay off?"

"Well yeah, I reckon he can, but Jack, don't tell me you're actually thinkin' about doin' it."

"A thousand dollars is a lot of money. If I could be sure this Templeton person would actually pay off . . ."

"Well, I'll tell you this. I know where to find him. I expect you could persuade him to pay off . . . if you know what I mean."

"Yeah," Emerson said with a smile. "Yeah, I know what you mean."

Armed with the information about the reward money being paid to anyone who killed a couple men named Pearlie and Cal Wood, Emerson contacted Nelson Battle.

"Who wants 'em dead, and why?" Battle asked.

"I'm told it's a man named Deekus Templeton who wants 'em dead. I don't know why, and I don't care. All I know is, he's payin' a thousand dollars for it."

"A thousand dollars? That's good money," Battle said.

"You're damn right it's good money."

"Do you know this man, Templeton? Can he be trusted?"

"I don't know him, but I know Bud Lane, and I trust him. He knows Templeton, and says he will pay off."

"These two men we're supposed to kill. Do you know how to find 'em?" Battle asked.

"Not hard to find 'em. They're right in Denver, runnin' the Jensen abattoir."

"How are we going to do it? You got 'ny ideas?" Battle asked.

"Oh, yeah. I've got it all planned out," Emerson said.

"We're going to go see 'em and let on like we are cattlemen. We want to run some of our cows through there. We'll invite them out to supper, then, when they don't suspect anything, we'll kill 'em."

"Yeah," Battle said. "That sounds like a good idea. It'll be the easiest five hunnert dollars I ever made."

The abattoir was easy to find. It was adjacent to a big railroad marshalling yard and at least five thousand cattle were penned up outside the buildings that made up the complex. One building was where the cows were led in, one at a time, then maneuvered down a narrow chute until they reached a place where they could go no farther. A powerfully built shirtless man stood on a platform just above the animal. Once the animal was in place, he used a sledgehammer to strike it a mighty blow between the eyes. Almost instantly a tackle and pulley arrangement lifted the dead steer up, and it traveled down an overhead steam-operated conveyor track as men removed the hide, head, and feet. By the time the steer reached the end of the conveyor track the denuded carcass had already been split into two halves. Those halves were then sent into the next building where they were packed in ice, awaiting shipment by refrigerated cars to markets back east.

In front of the building, Emerson approached a man in a long white coat spotted with blood. "I'm looking for two men, Pearlie and Cal. Could you tell me where I might find them?"

"Pearlie and Cal? You'll find them both back there," the man said, pointing to two who were standing at the back of the building, watching the operation.

Emerson and Battle walked toward them.

"I thought this Pearlie feller was supposed to be a gunman," Battle said. "There ain't neither one of 'em even wearin' a gun."

Emerson smiled. "We'll try and keep 'em that way."

"We've been here for over six months now. How long do we have to stay here and watch over this business?" Cal asked.

"Smoke said we wouldn't be here forever. Just until the operation is goin' smooth. Then he'll hire someone to manage it," Pearlie replied. "He wants us here until everything is going well, and I figure we owe him that much. Don't you?"

"Yeah, I guess so. But I don't mind tellin' you, this place is beginnin' to give me the willies," Cal said.

"What do you mean, give you the willies?"

"Well, think about it, Pearlie. What have we done our whole lives but take care of cows? We feed 'em, we make sure they have water, we keep the wolves and big cats away from 'em. We protect them.

"And now what are we doing? We're leadin' 'em down a long chute to slaughter. And because we've took care of 'em for their entire lives, they trust us. They go along, thinkin' ever'thing is goin' to be just fine, then, *bam!*" Cal hit himself in the forehead with the heel of his palm. "We kill 'em! It just don't seem right to me, is all. It's like we're double-crossing them or something. I can see it in their eyes."

"Cal, you eat steak, don't you? Roast beef?"

"Well, yeah, I eat it."

"Where do you think it comes from?"

"I know it comes from cows . . ."

"Cows that we have taken care of for all their lives," Pearlie said.

"Yeah," Cal said. "Well, if you put it like that, I guess you're right. But it still gives me the willies, killin' 'em like that. I mean, when they are so trustin' an' all."

"I wonder what these men want." Pearlie said, looking toward the two men who were approaching. "Yes, sir, can we help you gentlemen?"

"We were told you two men are in charge here."

"That's right."

"We're cattlemen from up in Wyoming. Always before, we've shipped our cattle back to the eastern markets while they're still on the hoof. But I've been told the best way to do it now, is to get them processed here first."

"Yes, sir, that is the absolute truth of it. Doin' it this way brings you about a ten percent higher profit," Pearlie said.

"My name is Emerson, this is Battle. I wonder if we could buy you two gentlemen supper tonight and talk about bringing our cattle here?"

"You don't have to buy our supper just to do business with us," Pearlie said.

"But you are welcome to," Cal added quickly.

"Great!" Emerson said. "Suppose we meet you at Little Man's Restaurant at nine o'clock tonight."

"Nine o'clock?" Cal said. "Ain't that awful late to be eatin' supper?"

"Unfortunately that's the earliest we can do it," Emerson said. "I'm afraid we have some other business to take care of, first."

"Are you sure you want to meet at Little Man's?" Pearlie asked. "That's way on the other side of the marshalling yard. I know a lot of the yard workers take their breakfast and lunch there, but I've never known anyone to eat supper there. I'm not sure it's even open for supper."

"Oh yes, it's open. We've eaten there several times since we came down here. They set a fine supper table," Emerson said.

"All right," Pearlie said. "Little Man's at nine o'clock. We'll see you then."

* * *

Because they were staying in Denver for an extended period of time, Pearlie and Cal had rented a small house. That evening both men took a bath then got dressed in what Cal called their "business" suits.

"This is another thing I don't like about bein' here," Cal said as he pulled his shirt collar away from his neck. "We have to get all dressed up like some sort of dandy. Why couldn't we just wear regular clothes?"

"These are regular clothes for businessmen," Pearlie said.

"Yeah, well, I ain't a business man. I'm a cowboy. And what I want to know is, why this business of eating supper so late? Who eats supper when it's so dark you can't see ten feet in front of you?"

Pearlie chuckled. "I think the high toned people eat their supper real late, only they don't call it supper, they call it dinner."

"Ha. Dinner is what you have in the middle of the day," Cal said.

"You ready to go?" Pearlie asked.

"Ready. I've starving to death here, and you ask me if I'm ready to go eat."

The two men reached the front door, then Pearlie stopped and stretched out his hand to stop Cal. "Hold it."

"What?"

"I don't know. I've got a funny feeling about this."

"I've got a funny feeling too, only it's a big hollow space in the pit of my stomach. It's called being hungry."

"Wait a minute." Pearlie started back toward his bedroom.

"Where are you going?"

"To get my gun. I think you should get yours too."

"Why?"

"Just do it, Cal. I told you, I've got a funny feeling. I can't explain it, but I don't like it. I don't like it one bit."

"All right. You're the old man here. If you got a feeling, who am I to argue with you?"

The two men returned to their respective rooms, then met a moment later at the front door, both of them armed.

Little Man's was about a half mile from their cabin, on the other side of a large, crisscrossing network of tracks. It wasn't convenient to ride horses over this ground. The elevated tracks, the rails, and even the gravel and ballast could injure a horse in the middle of the night. They started across the marshalling yard, their feet making crunching sounds as they walked across the ballast and coal clinkers strewn about. In addition to the sound of their footfalls, they could hear the switch engines in the yard, making up freight trains for dispatch.

"Damn, it's dark out here," Cal said.

"Yeah, it is."

"Pearlie? You know that funny feeling you had?"

"Yes."

"Well, I've got it too. What do you say we just turn around and go back toward town?"

"I thought you were hungry."

"I am hungry. But we can stop at the first café we see."

The sound of one of the switch engines grew louder as it approached. Passing them, the headlamp threw a beam ahead, and in the beam they could see, for just a moment, the little building that housed Little Man's Restaurant. Then the train came between them and the building, so until all the cars passed, they could see nothing.

"Did you see the restaurant building?" Cal asked.

"Yeah, I saw it."

"Did it look like it had any lights on?"

"No, it didn't."

"There is something funny about this, Pearlie, like you said. And I don't like it. I don't like it at all."

The train cleared then, and no sooner had the train cleared, than a couple muzzle flashes lit up the night. One bullet hit a rail, sending up sparks, then ricocheted off into the night, screaming as it did so. A second bullet popped by Pearlie's ear, coming so close he felt the air pressure of its passing.

"Get down!" Pearlie shouted, and he and Cal leaped over to the opposite side of the railroad track, getting down behind the berm.

"Who is shooting at us?" Cal asked.

"I have a pretty good idea who," Pearlie said. "What I don't know is why."

From a distant part of the yard, they could hear another switch engine, working the cars.

"Emerson, is that you?" Pearlie asked.

"Oh, you figured that out, did you?"

"What do you want? Are you planning on robbing us? Just how much money do you think people like us would be carrying, anyway?"

"Oh, it isn't what you are carrying," Emerson replied. "It's what you are worth to us dead—a thousand dollars."

"What are you talking about? Neither of us is worth a cent. There's no paper out on us. You aren't going to collect a cent from the law."

"It ain't the law that's payin'," Emerson said.

"What? Who is paying?"

"What does that matter to you? You'll be dead."

"What makes you think we'll be dead?"

"Because Battle and I are going to kill you." Emerson laughed. "I'll just bet you didn't bring your pistols with you, did you? I mean, going to a nice business supper and all. Why would you?"

Pearlie was quiet for a long moment, then, almost hesitantly, he said. "Uh, yeah, we did. We brought our guns."

Emerson laughed again. "I'm sure you did. I'll tell you what. Just to show you what kind of men we are, we'll kill both of you real quick. You won't feel a thing."

A second train came by then, and once again Pearlie and

Cal were separated from Emerson and Battle by the passing of a long line of freight cars.

"Cal," Pearlie said, standing up. "Let's jump on this train."

Cal stood as well, and running alongside the moving cars until they matched its speed, Pearlie jumped in through the open side door of one of the boxcars. Then reaching down to grab Cal's hand, he pulled him in.

"Thanks," Cal said, breathing hard from the exertion.

"Battle, come on!" Emerson said. "I just seen 'em jump onto this train!"

Moving quickly, Emerson and Battle jumped onto the train and climbed to the top. That way, they would be able to see when Pearlie and Cal jumped off the train. They squatted down and waited as the train proceeded some distance, then stopped, preparatory to backing the assembled cars onto a sidetrack.

"Let's get out here," Pearlie said, and he and Cal jumped down from the train.

"Where do you reckon they are?" Cal asked.

"Half a mile away by now," Pearlie answered.

No sooner had Pearlie spoken, than Cal let out a sharp exclamation of pain. Concurrent with Cal's shout was the sound of a gunshot.

"Where are you hit?" Pearlie yelled.

"In the arm."

There was a second gunshot and Pearlie saw the muzzle flash coming from the top of one of the boxcars. When the flash receded, he saw two men standing there.

"There they are!" Cal shouted, having spotted them at the same time.

"Yeah, I see 'em." Pearlie fired twice, and had the satisfaction of seeing both men tumble from the top of the car. Gun at the ready, he ran to them. It was his hope they would still be alive so he could learn who had put a reward on Cal and him, and even more important, why?

He didn't get the opportunity to ask those questions, though. When he reached them, both were dead.

Pearlie ran back to Cal. "You were hit. How bad is it?"

"I think it was more of a crease than anything. I've felt around and I don't feel a hole in my arm. Are they dead?"

"Yeah, both of 'em."

"Who do you think wanted us dead? And why?" Cal asked.

"Cal, my friend, I don't have the slightest idea."

CHAPTER 21

Sugarloaf

Smoke was currying his horse when Eddie, the young Western Union messenger, rode up. He didn't see the rancher and headed directly for the house.

Smoke called out to him. "Eddie, are you looking for me?"

"Yes, sir, Mr. Jensen, I am. I have a telegram for you."

Smoke washed his hands in a basin, dried them, then walked out to retrieve the telegram.

"It's from Pearlie," Eddie said.

"I hope there's no problem at the plant." Smoke gave Eddie a quarter, then read the message.

ME AND CAL ATTACKED BY TWO HIRED KILLERS LAST
NIGHT STOP CAL WOUNDED SLIGHTLY STOP
KILLERS DEAD STOP NOT KNOWN WHO HIRED THEM STOP
PEARLIE

"Johnny wants to know if you want to send a message back," Eddie said.

"Yes, I do. Come on in. I'll get it ready."

"Yes, sir," Eddie replied. He followed Smoke into the house.

Sally had just baked a batch of cookies and they were cooling on the table. "What is it about men? Do you have some sort of secret sense that tells you when there are cookies available?"

"Oh, no ma'am. Nothin' like that," Eddie said.

Sally chuckled. "Help yourself."

"Thank you," Eddie replied, grabbing one of the cookies. It was still so hot he had to toss it from hand to hand for a second until it was cooled.

Smoke sat down at the table to compose the return telegram.

"Smoke, what is it?" Sally asked, concerned by the expression on his face.

"Someone tried to kill Pearlie and Cal last night. Cal is hurt."

"Oh, Smoke! No! How badly?"

"It's hard to tell. Pearlie says it isn't bad, but he would probably say that anyway, just to keep us from worrying about it."

"What if the men try again?"

"They won't."

Sally frowned. "How do you know they won't?"

"Because, according to Pearlie, they are dead."

"Oh, well, thank goodness for that. At least Cal and Pearlie are out of danger."

"Maybe not," Smoke replied. "According to the telegram, someone was paying the men to kill them. Whoever that was is likely to try again."

"But why, for heaven's sake? Who would want to kill Pearlie and Cal?"

"That's what I'd like to know. I'm going to bring them both back home."

"Who will run the abattoir operation for you?"

"Mr. Evans is about ready to take over. I'll just have to trust that he's ready."

Smoke wrote the message. *Turn operation over to Lloyd Evans. Return home now. Smoke.*

"Here you go, Eddie." He gave him the message, money to send it, plus a tip.

"Thanks, Mr. Jensen. I'll see that it gets sent right away."

Palmilla, New Mexico Territory

In a sane world, a world where size and strength meant something, Jeremiah Priest would be someone you would pass on the street with hardly a second glance. He was a small man, barely five feet four inches, very thin, with a prominent Adam's apple, a nose that seemed too large for his face, thinning blond hair, and pale blue eyes.

But the world Priest occupied wasn't sane. He was a shootist, a gunman whose draw was greased lightning and whose marksmanship was deadly accurate. Once people heard his name and associated the unimpressive looking man to the reputation he had acquired, even the biggest and strongest man quaked in his boots.

Priest stepped out of the sunshine and into the Pair of Aces Saloon. It was quite busy, but he found a quiet place by the end of the bar. He ordered a beer, then nursed it as he studied the dark haired, dark eyed man at the other end of the bar. A full mustache curved around his mouth like the horns on a Texas steer. He was leaning against the bar with his fingers wrapped around a shot glass.

The man was Coleman Wesley, a bounty hunter who made a good living by chasing down wanted criminals. He turned them over to the law belly down across the saddle as often as they were upright. Wesley was deadly fast with a gun, and in all the outlaw camps and hideouts, his name was brought up as someone whose path you never wanted to cross.

So far, Wesley hadn't noticed the gunman, and probably wouldn't have recognized him if he had. But he would know the name. Jeremiah Priest was a man who hired his gun out for money . . . a great deal of money.

"Mr. Wesley," Priest called.

Wesley didn't look around.

"Wesley! I'm talking to you!" Priest called again. His voice was loud and authoritative, and everyone in the saloon recognized the challenge in its timbre. For a moment, all conversations ceased. Then the drinkers, seeing that Coleman Wesley had been challenged by a little pipsqueak of a man, laughed.

Wesley looked up from his whiskey. "What do you want, little man?"

"I want to kill you," Priest said easily.

There was a universal gasp of surprise. Nobody recognized Priest, but nearly all knew Wesley, and they wondered who would be foolish enough to brace him.

"And why would you want to kill me?" Wesley asked without the slightest hint of apprehension.

"Because I'm being paid to," Priest replied as if that explained everything.

"Who is paying you?"

"Why do you want to know?"

Wesley tossed his drink down. "Because after I kill you, I'm going to kill whoever hired you."

"Don't worry about it. You aren't going to kill me."

For the first time, Wesley began to show a little emotion. Who was this little man who had challenged him with so little regard as to the bounty hunter's reputation?

Everyone moved away from the bar. Even the bartender left his position behind the bar and joined the others gathered against the back wall, as far away as they could get within the confines of the saloon.

The long moment of absolute silence was broken only by the loud tick-tock of the Regulator clock that hung from the wall, just above the piano. Several glanced toward it to fix in their minds the exact time they watched Wesley kill the insolent stranger.

Two men came in through the batwing doors.

"So I told Johnson, you've done bought back the same horse you sold last month," one of them said, and both laughed.

They started toward the bar but stopped when they saw that the bar was completely empty except for the two men who were staring at each other. Everyone else in the saloon was standing as far back from the bar as they could. Nobody was sitting at a table, and nobody was talking.

The new customers looked at each other. "What the hell is going on?" one asked.

"I don't know," the other hissed. "But I'm not goin' to get in the way."

They joined the other saloon patrons standing against the back wall.

"Mister, if you walk out of this saloon right now, I'll let you live." Wesley smiled, though it wasn't a smile of humor. "You can tell everyone you know that you once braced Coleman Wesley and lived."

"Now, why would I want to do that?" Priest wiped the foam from his lips with the back of his hand.

"I didn't figure you'd take my offer, but I thought I'd give you one last chance."

Priest set his beer mug down, then stepped away from the bar. He flipped his duster back so his gun was exposed. He was wearing it low, and kicked out, the way a man wears a gun when he knows how to use it. "Are you through talkin', Wesley? Because if you are, I reckon it's about time you and me got this thing settled."

"All right. It's your call." Wesley stepped away from the bar as well, and like Priest, wore his gun low and kicked out.

"What might your name be, mister?" Wesley asked. "We'll need it for the undertaker to carve into your headstone."

The gunman smiled at him. "The name is Priest. Jeremiah Priest."

Again, there was a gasp from those in the saloon. While few knew what the notorious gunman looked like, many had heard of him. A recent newspaper article had called him "the deadliest gunman in the West."

Wesley's face, which had been coldly impassive, suddenly grew animated. His skin whitened and a line of perspiration beads broke out on his upper lip.

The bounty hunter had been in shoot-outs before and he was fast. Maybe fast enough, especially if he had the edge of drawing first. Without another word he made his move, pulling his pistol in the blink of an eye.

But Priest, whether reacting to Wesley's draw or anticipating it, had his own pistol out just a split-second faster, pulling the hammer back and firing in one fluid motion. In the close confines of the barroom, the gunshot sounded like a clap of thunder.

Wesley didn't even get a shot off. The bullet from Priest's pistol hit him in the middle of the chest, slamming him back against the bar before he fell. His unfired pistol clattered to the floor.

The hearing lasted less than an hour. There was no shortage of witnesses willing to testify, enjoying their proximity to such an event. All testified that it was a fair fight. Some even said they believed Wesley started his draw first. No charges were filed, as it was a case of justifiable homicide, justifiable by reason of self-defense.

CHAPTER 22

Carro de Bancada

Malcolm was pumping water when two men came riding up toward him. He recognized one of them as Garneau, but he had never seen the other one. Although their presence made him a bit nervous, especially as he wasn't wearing his pistol, he smiled at them in order to maintain his composure. "Hello, gentlemen," he said by way of greeting. "Colonel Garneau." He looked at the other rider. "And I'm sorry, sir, but I've never had the pleasure of meeting you."

"The name is Templeton. Deekus Templeton," the other rider said in a gruff voice."

"Well, climb down from your horses. I'm about to make some lemonade. Why don't you come in out of the sun?"

Garneau and Templeton followed Malcolm into the house. It still reflected Humboldt Puddle's personality . . . the unit flag of the First Sharpshooter Regiment, to which Puddle belonged, framed photographs of his parents, who were Malcolm's grandparents, and antlers and game heads he had taken in hunts all hung on the walls. A dining table and chairs Humboldt had built with his own hands still sat in the kitchen.

Malcolm had squeezed the lemon and mixed it with sugar earlier. He added cool water, stirred it, and the lemonade was done. He poured three glasses, then gave a glass to each of his visitors.

"Merci," Garneau said, taking the glass.

"*Vous êtes les bienvenus*," Malcolm replied.

"*Parlez-vous français?*"

"Yes, I speak French. I found that in my old job as shipping clerk, and in dealing with shipments to foreign countries, learning other languages was beneficial to my work."

"I'm impressed," Garneau said. "Did you enjoy the work you were doing? Working as a shipping clerk?"

"Not particularly." Malcolm took another swallow of his lemonade and studied the two men over the rim of his glass. He knew it wasn't just a neighborly visit, and he was pretty sure he knew what they wanted, but he decided to wait and let them bring up the subject.

He didn't have long to wait.

"Monsieur Puddle, how would you like to return to New York with enough money that you could live quite comfortably for several years? You wouldn't have to return to a job that, by your own admission, you don't particularly like."

"And how would I do that?"

"By selling your ranch to me," Garneau said.

Malcolm figured that was what the Frenchman's trip was all about, so he wasn't surprised. He was interested, though, in finding out how much money Garneau was willing to offer him. He remembered Mr. Norton telling him his land and stock were worth about twenty-five thousand dollars. "How much would you offer?"

"Thirty-five thousand dollars," Garneau said without hesitation.

Malcolm spit out the drink of lemonade he'd just taken. "Thirty-five thousand dollars?" he repeated.

"It is a very generous offer," Garneau said.

"It is more than generous," Malcolm replied.

Garneau smiled. "Then, may I conclude that you accept the offer?"

Malcolm thought about it for a moment, remembering Smoke had told him the other ranchers were holding out because his Uncle Humboldt had held out. But, he also knew some of the ranchers who had sold or had been forced off their land wound up getting much less than their properties were worth.

Malcolm looked at Garneau and realized buying Carro de Bancada would give him entrée to the remaining ranchers. "Did you offer my uncle this much money?"

"The offer I made to your uncle was quite generous," Garneau replied.

"And he refused?"

"Yes. He believed he had some obligation to his neighbors. You, of course, having but recently arrived in the valley, have no such obligation. And, because the amount I am offering you is generous, very generous, I'm sure you are intelligent enough to accept."

"Give me twenty-four hours to consider it," Malcolm replied.

"Twenty-four hours? Why would you need twenty-four hours? Do you not understand that what I have just offered you is much more than this miserable piece of land is worth?"

Malcolm shook his head. "Anything of value is worth exactly what someone is willing to pay for it. The fact that you are offering me thirty-five thousand dollars means this land is worth thirty-five thousand. If it is worth that to you, it is worth that to me."

"Don't be foolish," Garneau said. "If you think by holding out on me I will raise the offer, you are sadly mistaken. Others have made the same mistake, only to ultimately sell to me for much less than my original offer."

"As I said, give me twenty-four hours to consider it," Malcolm repeated.

"Very well. I will give you until exactly this time tomorrow. If you have not made a decision by then, the offer will be withdrawn. Do you understand the consequences of that, Mr. Puddle? It means that you will be losing thirty-five thousand dollars."

Malcolm smiled. "No, I would be losing only ten thousand. I can easily get twenty-five thousand from anyone. And that is twenty-five thousand dollars more than I had last month."

Garneau had taken only a couple swallows from his lemonade, and he slammed the glass down angrily. "Twenty-four hours, Mr. Puddle. Not one minute longer."

"I understand."

"I'm not sure that you do." Garneau stood up and Templeton followed suit.

Malcolm walked to the front door with them, then watched as they returned to their horses. Templeton had not spoken a word since he first introduced himself. As he mounted his horse, he kept his eyes on the young ranch owner, staring at him with a malevolent intensity.

Malcolm found it disconcerting. He waited until the men left his ranch before he saddled his horse and rode over to report the visit to Smoke.

Long Trek

"I can't believe Puddle would turn that offer down," Garneau said angrily. "Why would he?"

"Maybe he wants to be the hero," Templeton suggested. "His uncle wouldn't sell out, so Malcolm Puddle decides he won't sell out either."

"I have to confess I hadn't counted on that. I was sure he would sell out if I offered him enough."

"We've made a mistake in thinking Malcolm Puddle was the key here," Templeton said.

"What do you mean?"

"There is no way Puddle would turn that money down if he didn't have someone behind him. And that someone is Smoke Jensen. He's your real enemy, not Malcolm Puddle. I think it's time we quit fooling around and get to the center of it. Take care of Smoke Jensen, and you won't have any problems."

"And by take care of, you mean?"

"Kill him," Templeton said.

"We have tried that, remember?"

"We haven't tried it with the right people. To kill someone like Smoke Jensen, we are going to have to hire someone who is even better than he is."

"And just who would that be, I ask you?"

"Jeremiah Priest." Templeton showed Garneau a copy of the *Big Rock Journal*. "You may read about him here."

By Dispatch to the Journal

DEADLY ENCOUNTER IN PALMILLA, NEW MEXICO TERRITORY

On the 5th instant, two men known for their skill with the pistol faced each other in a deadly confrontation in the Pair of Aces Saloon. It is not known what precipitated the engagement, but those who witnessed the fight say never have two pistols been so rapidly drawn, for only one to be so effectively engaged.

As in all encounters there must be one who prevails, and one who fails. He who prevailed was Jeremiah Priest, and indeed, Mr. Priest walks among us today. The other participant in this deadly pas de deux was Coleman Wesley, a well-known bounty hunter. Mr. Wesley paid for his unfortunate encounter with Priest by forfeiture of his life, he being but a split second slower than his adversary.

It is being said by those who witnessed the event, that nobody in the country could match Priest for the quickness of his draw, and the accuracy of his marksmanship.

Garneau read the article, then looked back up at Templeton. "And you think this man"—he glanced at the article again to be sure of his name—"Jeremiah Priest, can take the measure of Jensen?"

"Yes."

"Then, by all means, make arrangements for him to come."

"He won't come cheap," Templeton said.

"How much?"

"For someone like Priest? Ten thousand dollars."

"Ten thousand dollars?" Garneau said, the words exploding from his mouth.

"You were going to pay more than that to Puddle for his ranch. Without Jensen behind him, you can probably get it for a couple hundred dollars.

"But still, ten thousand dollars for one man is a lot of money."

"Colonel, you are relatively new here, so you don't know all there is to know about Smoke Jensen. You are going to have to find someone who is good—very good—to take care of the man. Someone like Jeremiah Priest. And that is going to cost you." Templeton smiled. "But the beauty of it is this; you won't have to pay him one red cent unless he actually completes the job."

"Yes, that's true, isn't it?"

"It is."

"Very well, Monsieur. Find this man, Priest, and secure his services."

Sugarloaf

Smoke was in the tack shed looking over the saddles and harness to determine if he needed to buy any new equipment, when he saw Malcolm come riding up. He stepped to the open door and called out to him. "Malcolm, I'm out here."

Malcolm turned his horse and rode over to the tack shed. Smoke chuckled. "You did that like a real Westerner."

"Did what?" Malcolm asked as he dismounted.

"The way you rode over here instead of walked." Smoke laughed again. "I once had an old cowboy tell me if God had wanted man to walk, He would have given us four legs."

Malcolm laughed as well.

"What's up?" Smoke asked. "Not that I'm not happy to have you visit, but I expect this is more than a social call."

"It's not exactly a social call. I had a couple visitors today."

"Let me guess. Garneau and Templeton?"

"Yes. They offered to buy me out."

"What was the offer?"

"Thirty-five thousand dollars."

"Thirty-five thousand?" Smoke whistled. "That's a lot of money."

"Yes, sir, it is. Especially considering my whole place, stock included, is worth somewhere around twenty-five thousand."

"What did you tell him?"

"I told him to give me twenty-four hours before I had to give him an answer."

"I see."

"Smoke, like you said, thirty-five thousand dollars is a lot of money."

"Yes, it is. And I don't think anyone would hold it against you, if you sold out to him."

"I would," Malcolm said. "I would hold it against me."

Smoke didn't answer.

"I mean, I should hold out, shouldn't I? Aren't the other farmers and ranchers sort of depending on me to hold out?"

"Malcolm, I can't make up your mind for you," Smoke said. "You have to make up your own mind."

"I . . . I just want to know that I am doing the right thing."

"Whatever you do will be the right thing," Smoke said.

Malcolm chuckled and shook his head. "That's no help."

"Malcolm, let me put it this way. If you decide to sell out and go back to New York, I won't hold any hard feelings toward you. This isn't your world. You were drawn into it through no fault of your own."

"That's true. And with thirty-five thousand dollars in cash, I could buy a small business in New York. Maybe meet a nice girl, get married, and have a family."

"That's right," Smoke agreed.

"What if I decided to stay here?"

"It could get rough."

"I know."

Smoke smiled. "But you wouldn't have to face it alone. The other ranchers and farmers will be with you"—he paused for a moment—"and so will I."

"All right!" Malcolm said, letting out a loud breath of relief. "That's what I wanted to hear. Tomorrow, when Garneau comes to see me, I'll tell him, *Je vous remercie, mais la réponse est non. Je ne vendrai pas.*"

"What?" Smoke asked, laughing.

"Thank you, but the answer is no. I will not sell," Malcolm translated.

"I'll be there when you tell him. I want to see his face."

CHAPTER 23

Carro de Bancada

Malcolm had invited his neighbors over for a "get acquainted" potluck dinner. As they arrived, he asked that they park their buggies, buckboards, spring wagons, and horses in the barn so they were out of sight. Smoke put his horse and wagon with the rest. He had come to stand with the young rancher against Garneau.

"I know you may wonder why I asked you to keep your horses and conveyances out of sight," Malcolm said when everyone was gathered in the keeping room. "Yesterday, Lucien Garneau made me an offer for my land. It was a very generous offer. And today he's coming to hear my response to his offer."

The expression on the faces of Malcolm's neighbors indicated their disappointment.

"I am going to tell him no," Malcolm said quickly, before anyone could say anything.

"You're a good man, Malcolm Puddle," Woodward said.

"When he arrives, I want him to be surprised to see you all here. I want him to know the resolve we all have, to keep our land."

"You're damn right!" Keefer said and he and the others applauded.

The meal was served then and, after the meal, the women began cleaning up while the men gathered once more in the keeping room. Cigars were lit and brandy was passed around as they discussed the situation.

"I've heard talk of Garneau putting together an army over at his place," Speer said.

"Why would he do that?" Logan asked.

"For intimidation," Woodward said. "But if we don't allow ourselves to be intimidated, it will fail."

"Here he comes." Smoke chuckled. "And he's not alone."

"Oh, he probably has Mr. Templeton with him," Malcolm said.

"Yes," Smoke replied. "Templeton and four others."

"Four others? You mean there are six of them?"

"Yes. Apparently, he wasn't prepared to take no for an answer."

"That's not the only thing he isn't prepared for," Malcolm said. "I don't expect he is prepared to see all of us here."

"Chris," Woodward said. "Tell the ladies and the children to stay in the back of the house."

"All right," Logan said.

The men waited until they heard footsteps on the front porch, followed by a knock on the door.

"Come in, Colonel Garneau," Malcolm called. "The door is unlocked."

The door opened and Garneau, Templeton, and the four other men went into the house.

"Monsieur Puddle, your twenty-four hours are up," Garneau said. "What is your . . . ?" His voice trailed off in shock to see so many men gathered in the room, one of whom was Smoke Jensen.

"What is this?" Garneau asked.

"Oh, it is too bad you weren't here earlier, Colonel Garneau.

You could have eaten with us. All my neighbors came over to welcome me. They brought food, and we had a fine meal."

"I . . . uh . . . came to hear your response to my offer."

"Yes, well, as I said yesterday, Colonel, your offer was most generous. But, now that I have met all my neighbors, I feel I would be doing them a disservice if I ran out on them. Again, I thank you for the generous offer, but I must decline."

"You are making a big mistake, Monsieur Puddle. When next we do business, and we will do business again, you will find my offer to be much less generous."

"Oh, I don't see much possibility of our ever doing business, Mr. Garneau," Malcolm said, purposely not using the military title. "By the way, please don't visit again, uninvited and unannounced. It does make for an awkward situation."

Nobody said a word until Garneau and those with him rode away. Then they broke out in laughter and self-congratulations.

"Did you see the expression on his face when he saw all of us here?" someone asked, and Keefer imitated it, opening his eyes and mouth wide as he looked around the room. His antics brought more laughter.

As the others made preparations to leave, Lucy Woodward came over to speak to Malcolm. He had noticed the pretty young woman when she first arrived, and was pleased she had come over to speak to him.

"I'm glad you are going to stay out here and not go back to New York," Lucy said.

"I'm glad too," Malcolm said. "There's nothing in New York for me." He made the pointed statement to let her know there were no women in his life.

"I don't know if anyone has told you, but every month there is a dance at the Dunn Hotel."

"Really? Well, that's very good to know." Malcolm smiled.

Lucy smiled back, nodded, and quickly followed her parents to their wagon.

Smoke and Sally had come in a spring wagon so they could meet Pearlie and Cal when their train came in. Leaving Puddle and the others, they drove straight to the depot.

"Hello, Smoke, Miz Sally," Phil Wilson greeted when they arrived. "Are you going somewhere or meeting someone?"

"We're meeting Pearlie and Cal," Smoke said. "They're coming home today."

"I'll bet those two boys will be happy to get back to Sugarloaf," Wilson said. "You goin' to sit in the wagon or come into the depot?"

"I reckon we can come in." Smoke hopped down, tied off the team, then went around to help Sally down.

"I just made some coffee," Wilson said. "Come on in and share a cup with me."

They followed him inside the depot. A woman and a small girl, about four years old were waiting for the next train.

"We're goin' to see Nana," the little girl announced happily.

"Ellen Genoa, you don't need to tell everyone that," the little girl's mother said.

"Oh, but I'm glad you did tell me, Ellen Genoa," Sally said, smiling at the little girl. "Because I think that is very exciting."

"Mama, she's glad."

"That's because she is a very nice lady," Ellen's mother said.

Smoke and Sally went back into the office, where Phil Wilson filled three cups with coffee, then handed a cup to each of them. "Say, Smoke, what's going on out in the valley? I hear the Frenchman has already run Butrum and Drexler off their property. Is that right?"

"I'm afraid it is right."

"What is he going to do, just keep on until he runs ever'one out of the valley?"

"I don't think so. I think he's probably gone about as far as he's going to go. The other settlers are standing up to him."

"Look here, you don't think this is going to break out into a range war, do you? I've been hearing reports the Frenchman has hired him a bunch of guns, and they are all out at his place now. He says it's to combat cattle rustling, but I haven't heard anyone complain about cattle thieves."

"The only thievery going on around here is Garneau's stealing of land."

"So, what's going to come of all this?"

"I'm not all that sure where it's going," Smoke replied. "I suppose we're just going to have to wait and find out."

At that moment, they heard the whistle of the inbound train and, shortly afterward, the chugging sound of the approaching engine. Sally and Smoke moved out onto the depot platform to greet their two arriving hands, though of course, they were much more than mere cattle hands. They were practically members of the family.

Cal was the first one down, jumping from the train even before it had come to a complete stop. Pearlie was right behind him. Seeing Smoke and Sally, they walked over to them quickly.

"Welcome home, boys," Sally said, greeting each of them with a hug. Smoke shook hands with each of them.

"How is the abattoir going?" Smoke asked.

"Smoke! You asked about that stupid processing plant before you ask about Cal's arm?" Sally scolded.

"My arm's fine, Miss Sally," Cal said, moving it around. "The bullet didn't do nothin' more 'n just sorta put a crease in it. Heck, I've been hurt worse gettin' hung up on barbed wire."

"The plant's going great," Pearlie said. "And you made a smart decision, turning it over to Beans. He's a good man."

"Turning it over to who?" Smoke asked, puzzled by Pearlie's comment.

"Lloyd Evans. Ever'one calls him Beans," Pearlie said. "And he knows that business from top to bottom. He used to work with de Mores, when he had his plant up in Dakota Territory."

"Say," Cal said. "As long as we're in town, why don't we go over to Lambert's and have somethin' to eat. One of his rolls would be real good about now."

"Tell me, Cal, is there ever a time when one of Mr. Lambert's rolls wouldn't be good? Or Miss Sally's? Or anybody's rolls for that matter?"

"No," Cal replied seriously. "I can't think of such a time."

With their luggage thrown into the back of the spring wagon, they walked across the street to Lambert's. Several of the patrons greeted them when they went inside. Those who knew Pearlie and Cal had been gone for a while welcomed them home.

"Here you go, Cal! Welcome home!" Lambert shouted from across the room, throwing a roll even as he greeted him.

Cal caught the roll easily, and had it half eaten by the time they took their seats at a table.

"Hey, Smoke, who is that fella over there in the corner?" Pearlie asked. "He's starin' at us, and it don't look none too friendly."

In the corner of the restaurant, a well-dressed man was sitting alone.

"That, Pearlie, is Mr. Lucien Garneau, though he likes to call himself Colonel Garneau.

"Is he a colonel?"

"Certainly not in the U.S. Army," Smoke said. "Whether or not he was ever a colonel in the French Army, we have only his word for it. And so far he has not proven himself to be a man whose word I'm inclined to take."

"Does he live here, now?"

"Yes, he bought Long Trek. And since he bought Long Trek he has bought four more spreads."

"What's he tryin' to do, own the whole valley?"

Smoke nodded. "Apparently, that is exactly what he has in mind."

Garneau didn't know who the two men with Jensen were. He thought perhaps they were men the rancher had hired as personal bodyguards. How good would bodyguards be if a concerted effort was made to kill somebody? Garneau didn't know, but he was fully committed to that effort.

Templeton had said Smoke Jensen would have to be killed for the Frenchman to accomplish his objective. But that was just one reason to kill him. Garneau wanted him dead simply because he didn't like the man.

He wondered how Templeton was doing in his task of recruiting Jeremiah Priest.

CHAPTER 24

When Deekus Templeton stepped off the train in Palmilla, New Mexico Territory, he headed for the nearest saloon. It had been his experience a person could find out more by visiting a saloon than he could by reading a month's worth of local newspapers.

"A beer," he ordered. When it was delivered, he paid for it with a dollar bill.

"Beer only costs a nickel," the bartender said. "Ain't you got no change?"

"If I get the right information, I don't need any change," Templeton said.

The bartender squinted his eyes. "What kind of information?"

"I'm looking for a man named Jeremiah Priest."

The bartender opened the cash drawer, pulled out ninety-five cents, and slid it across the bar. "I've never heard of him."

"Sure you have. He killed a man in this town. It was in the paper."

"I never read the paper," the bartender said. "And if you want to stay alive, you won't be readin' it, either. Jeremiah Priest ain't the kind of man you want to be askin' questions about."

"I thought you said you didn't know him."

"Mister, finish your beer and go somewhere else to ask your questions."

"You've got the wrong idea," Templeton said. "Priest is a friend of mine. I'm just trying to find him, that's all."

"Well, try somewhere else."

Templeton finished his beer, then took the bartender's advice. He visited another saloon, and was in the third saloon when he finally found someone who would talk to him. Templeton offered him two dollars if the man would tell him where he could find Priest.

"What do you want with him?" asked the man who identified himself as Dagan.

"What I want with him is my business," Templeton replied. "Like I said, if you can tell me where he is, I'll give you two dollars."

"The reason I asked," Dagan said, "is 'cause if you're plannin' on goin' up against him, you're goin' to get yourself kilt and I won't get my money. You give me the two dollars now, and I'll tell you where to find him."

"All right," Templeton said. "Here's the two dollars."

Dagan took the two bills, examined them for a moment, then slipped them in his pocket. "You see that fella back in the corner. The one with two women?"

"Yes, what about him? Does he know where to find Priest?"

"Ha. Mister, you don't know it, but you are lookin' at Priest."

"Wait a minute. Are you telling me that little runt of a man is Jeremiah Priest? There must be some mistake. The Priest I'm looking for is a . . ." he hesitated before saying the word *killer*.

"If you're lookin' for the man who kilt Coleman Wesley, that there is him," Dagan said. "And if you think there ain't nothin' to that little fella, well that's what Wesley thought. Don't let the way he looks fool you."

"Thanks." Templeton started toward the table, then stepped over to the bar. "What are Priest and the two women drinking?"

"Mr. Priest don't drink nothin' but beer. The women drink their special whiskey."

Templeton knew he meant the women were drinking tea. They had to. They drank with men all day long. If they were actually drinking whiskey, they would be passed out drunk by midday. "Let me have a beer and two of their drinks."

"If you're wantin' Mr. Priest's autograph, he don't give it," the bartender said.

"I'm not after his autograph."

The bartender poured the drinks and Templeton took them to the corner of the room where Priest sat. He put the women's drinks down on a separate table, then laid a five-dollar bill alongside each glass. "If you ladies would have drinks here, and give me a moment with Mr. Priest, I would appreciate it. I'll only be a moment and you can come right back."

The two women smiled broadly at the unexpected largesse.

One of the bar girls patted Priest's hand. "Honey, we'll be back as soon as this gentleman is finished."

"Yeah? Well, he may be finished a hell of a lot sooner than he thinks." Priest turned to Templeton. "What do you mean, running my ladies off?"

"I didn't run them off. They'll be right back. I just need a moment of your time." Templeton put one hundred dollars on the table in front of Priest.

"You're not plannin' on buyin' me with a hunnert dollars, are you?" Priest asked.

"Not at all," Templeton said. "For that money, all I want is a few moments of your time."

Priest picked up the money and put it in his pocket. "All right, you got a couple minutes. For what?"

"I want to make you a business proposition."

"What kind of business proposition?"

"Your kind of business."

Big Rock

Pearlie and Cal had gotten back just in time for the monthly dance at the Dunn Hotel. Neither man had a particular woman friend. Cal explained as they finished up the day's work, "This way we get to dance with all the ladies, and nobody gets their feelings hurt because we aren't dancin' with them."

By evening, the entire town was aware of the impending dance. A platform, built just for the occasion, had been brought out of storage and placed in the front of the ballroom for the musicians and they could be heard all along Front Street. The floor was cleared of all tables and chairs, and the room gaily decorated with bunting and flowers. Children began to gather around the glowing, yellow windows on the ground floor of the hotel and peered inside.

Buggies, spring wagons, buckboards, and horses began arriving from out in the county, and soon every hitching rail on Front Street, and even down Sikes Street all the way to Center Street, were full. Men and women who lived in the town walked along the boardwalks toward the hotel, the women in colorful ginghams, the men in clean, blue denims and brightly decorated vests.

As always, there were more men than women at the dance, but most of the ladies, even those who were married, made themselves available so everyone could have a good time.

"Pearlie, Cal! Where have you boys been?" Hoyt Miller asked as the two cowhands entered the hotel.

Pearlie told him about the abattoir in Denver. "What about you, Elmer, and Andy? What have you been doing since Mr. Munger died?"

"You mean you haven't heard? A man named Colonel

Garneau bought the Long Trek, and we're still workin' there."

"What about Homer Nance? He still the foreman there?" Cal asked.

Miller looked down. "No, he got fired."

"Fired? What for? Nance was one of the best foremen in all of Eagle county," Cal said.

"Yeah, that's what I thought, too. Don't nobody know for sure why he got fired. There's some strange things goin' on at Long Trek."

Somebody called to Miller and, excusing himself, he left.

Another young man approached them. "Are you Cal and Pearlie?"

"Yes," Pearlie answered.

The young man extended his hand. "Smoke told me about you two. He thinks very highly of you. I'm Malcolm Puddle."

"Oh, yes," Pearlie replied with a smile. "You're Mr. Puddle's nephew. You own Carro de Bancada now, don't you?"

"Yes."

"Well, it's good to meet you, Mr. Puddle."

Malcolm shook his head. "Mr. Puddle was my uncle. I'm Malcolm."

"Then it's good to meet you, Malcolm," Pearlie said.

As the ballroom continued to fill, the excitement grew. A very pretty young woman came up to Malcolm. "I see you came to the dance."

"I wouldn't have missed it for the world," Malcolm replied. "Oh, uh, Lucy Woodward, this is Pearlie and Cal." Malcolm looked a little embarrassed. "I didn't find out which one of you is Pearlie and which is Cal."

"This is Pearlie and this is Cal," Lucy said, identifying them.

"Oh." Malcolm laughed. "Here I was going to introduce you, and you wound up introducing me."

"Dancers, form your squares!" the caller shouted through his megaphone.

"Who's that callin'?" Pearlie asked. "How come Sheriff Carson ain't callin'?"

"The band brought their own caller," Lucy answered, as she held her arm out toward Malcolm, who took it.

Pearlie and Cal joined the cowboys advancing toward the unattached girls, and when a couple girls accepted their invitation to dance, they made up the final two sets for Malcolm and Lucy's square.

The music started and the caller began to shout, dancing around on the platform as he called, bowing and whirling as if he had a girl and was in one of the squares himself. The dancers moved and swirled to his commands.

Lucy danced with Pearlie and Cal during the evening, but most of the time she danced with Malcolm. It was apparent to all who paid any attention that there was a growing attraction between them.

"Folks, me 'n the band is goin' to take us about a fifteen minute break," the caller shouted through the megaphone. "So why don't you just visit with one another or enjoy some of that fine punch the ladies put together for us tonight?"

"And that the cowboys have improved!" someone shouted from the floor and everyone laughed. All were aware of the "doctoring" the cowboys had done by adding whiskey to the fruit drink.

It was then two new men came in. Unlike everyone else at the dance, they were wearing guns.

"Who are those two?" Pearlie asked as he stood with a group of cowboys. "And what are they doing wearing guns at a dance?"

"You don't want to mess with them two boys, Pearlie," Miller said. "That's Manning and Gilchrist. They are part of Colonel Garneau's army."

"Colonel Garneau's army? What do you mean, *army*?"

"I mean army," Miller said. "Colonel Garneau has done recruited him a bunch of gunmen, and he's trainin' 'em all like an army."

"Why?"

"I don't know. He says it's because of cattle rustlin', but I'll be honest with you, Pearlie, I ain't aware of any rustlin' goin' on at all."

Across the room, Lucy and Malcolm were enjoying some of the nondoctored punch.

"Malcolm, my mother asked me to invite you to dinner tomorrow. Do you like chicken and dumplings?"

"I don't know that I've ever had chicken and dumplings."

"You haven't? Why, how can you have never had chicken and dumplings?"

Malcolm laughed. "I'm from New York. It's just not something I've ever eaten."

"I think you will love it. I don't know anyone who doesn't. Will you come?"

"Lucy, I would come if your mother was serving nothing but cauliflower. And I really don't like cauliflower."

Lucy laughed.

"Hey, you pretty thing," someone said. "My name's Earl Manning and this here fella is Billy Gilchrist. What is your name?"

"As you can see, I'm talking to this gentleman," Lucy replied. "It is very rude of you to interrupt."

"Gentleman? Are you talking about this little pipsqueak?"

"Malcolm, it's a little close in here," Lucy said. "Do you suppose we could go outside for a little air?"

"Yes, of course." Malcolm offered his arm to Lucy and they started toward the door.

Manning stepped in front of them. "I tell you what, honey. Why don't I just take care of this little feller for you, then it'll just be me 'n you?"

From where he stood, Pearlie watched. "Uh-oh. It looks like our new friend is in trouble."

Pearlie and Cal started toward the couple just as Manning grabbed Malcolm by the shoulder and spun him around. The armed man made a sweeping swing with his fist, but Malcolm ducked under it easily and landed a right uppercut on the point of Manning's chin, knocking him down.

"Damn you!" Gilchrist said, stepping in from Malcolm's side and sending a straight jab toward his head.

The young rancher leaned back and watched the punch slip by him without effect. Dancing back, he answered with a hard left to Gilchrist's stomach, doubling him over. Malcolm followed that with a right cross to the jaw, and Gilchrist went down to join Manning.

"We'd better get their guns," Pearlie said, reaching to pull Manning's gun from its holster. "I don't expect they're goin' to be any too happy when they come to."

Following Pearlie's example, Cal took Gilchrist's gun.

The excitement had gathered a crowd. Malcolm, embarrassed by the scene, apologized. "I'm sorry folks. It wasn't my intention to create a disturbance."

"It wasn't your fault, mister. Most of us seen what happened," one in the crowd said.

Manning was the first one to come to, and he leaped to his feet with an angry shout. "I'm goin' to blow your head off!" He reached for his pistol, only to find his holster empty. "What the hell?"

"Are you looking for this?" Pearlie asked, showing Manning his pistol.

"What are you doin' with my gun?"

"Right now, I'm holding it on you. And I'm going to keep it on you until Sheriff Carson gets here."

"I'm here, Pearlie," Sheriff Carson said. "Mr. Miller came for me."

The sheriff pulled Gilchrist up from the floor and turned

to Manning. "Come on, boys. I think you two need to spend the night in the jail."

Hamburg, Germany

While in Geneva, Inspector Laurent had learned that Mouchette had exchanged nearly all the stolen francs for U.S. dollars and he was certain the man was going to America. But some of the stolen money had been exchanged for German marks. Putting two and two together, Laurent had come to the conclusion Mouchette had probably left from Hamburg.

He walked into the port authority office on the Elbe River and introduced himself to the director, then told him who he was looking for.

"*Nein*, no passenger named Mouchette has departed from this port, *Herr* Inspector."

"What about a man named Antoine Dubois?"

"No, nobody named Antoine Dubois."

"Have any Frenchmen departed from this port in the last six months?"

"I must examine all the records. I am afraid that will take a few days," the director replied.

"Please do so, Monsieur Director," Laurent said. "It is very important we find this man. He may also have passed himself off as Belgian or Swiss."

"I will do what I can, Herr Inspector."

"*Merci*."

Two days later Laurent was called back to the director's office where he received a stack of papers listing the names of all French, Swiss, and Belgian passengers. He thanked the port director profusely for the information.

Laurent took the papers back to France so he could investigate all five hundred names.

Long Trek

"I will do it for ten thousand dollars," Priest said. "But I want five thousand dollars up front."

"Why should I do that?" Garneau asked. "What if I pay you five thousand dollars, and Jensen kills you? I'll be out five thousand dollars, and Jensen will still be a problem."

"That's a chance we are both taking," Priest said. "All you stand to lose is money. I would be losing my life. But you won't lose any money, and I won't lose my life. I will kill Jensen."

"Are you really that good?"

"I'm really that good."

"I would like to see some sort of demonstration."

"What do you want me to do? Shoot at a target?"

"No. Target shooting is for children. I would like to see a demonstration as to how you act in a kill or be killed situation."

"How are you going to see that?"

"I will arrange it, if you are willing to participate."

"How are you going to arrange it?"

"Oh, it's quite simple, really. Over the last few months, I have collected some of the most skilled gunmen in the West. I will offer a thousand dollars to any of them who can kill you in a fair fight."

"Wait a minute. Are you saying you are going to pay someone to kill me?"

"Yes. That is, I'm going to pay someone to *try* to kill you. Does that prospect frighten you?"

"No."

"Very good. Monsieur Templeton, would you visit with some of our . . . soldiers . . . make the offer, and see if anyone is willing to accept the challenge?"

"All right." Templeton left the house to carry out Garneau's instructions.

"Are you serious, Garneau? You want me to kill one of your own men, just so you can test me?"

"I'm quite serious," Garneau replied. "Unless, of course, you find it . . . distasteful."

"Distasteful? No, I don't find it distasteful. A little weird, maybe. But not distasteful. But I do have a condition."

"And what would that condition be?"

"If I kill the man who decides to take the challenge, I want the thousand dollars you are promising him."

"But of course. You will get ten thousand dollars if you kill Jensen."

Priest shook his head. "No, you don't understand. I want the thousand dollars you are promising the other man, in addition to the ten thousand dollars. And I want it paid the moment I kill him."

"All right," Garneau agreed. "If that is what it will take for you to give me a demonstration, I'll do that."

At that moment, Templeton came back into the house. "Colonel, I've got a man who says he'll do it."

"Very good," Garneau said. "Who is it?"

"It's Strode."

"Strode, yes, an excellent choice," Garneau said.

"Strode? Vince Strode?" Priest said.

"Yes," Garneau replied. "Do you know Vince Strode?"

"I know him," Priest answered. "He's a friend of mine. Me 'n him wintered together a year or so back."

"You're friends, and he has agreed to try to kill you?"

Priest laughed. "We used to wonder which one of us would kill the other if it ever came down to it. I reckon we're about to find out."

"If neither of you are bothered by the fact that you are friends."

"There's a thousand dollars riding on it. For a thousand dollars, I'd shoot my own brother."

* * *

Since gathering his army, Garneau had decided to house the gunmen in an additional barracks away from his working cowboys in the bunkhouse. At the moment, Strode was in the barracks oiling the barrel and frame of his pistol. He had already checked the loads in the cylinder.

"Strode, are you sure you want to do this?" Ken Conn asked.

"Yeah, why not? A thousand dollars is a thousand dollars." Strode spun the cylinder, then put the pistol in his holster. He drew it a couple times, and smiled. "Besides, I always did think I was faster than that little pissant."

"Strode, I don't know," Conn said. "They say Priest has killed twenty men."

Strode chuckled. "I ain't exactly a virgin, you know. I didn't get into this game yesterday. Tell you what. After I kill the feller, what do you say you an' me go into town, have us a good meal, get a few drinks at the Brown Dirt, and then a couple women?"

"Strode, you know I ain't got enough money to do all them things."

"Don't worry. I'll pay for all of it. I'll have the thousand dollars by then. And I need somebody that'll be pullin' for me, when I go up ag'in Priest."

"Hell, Strode, you're my friend," Conn said. "You don't need to pay me to pull for you."

Templeton came back into the barracks then. "Strode, did you mean what you said about facing Priest?"

"You're damn right, I meant it."

"Well, then you might want to get on outside. Priest is out there waiting on you."

Once again, Strode loosened the pistol in his holster, then looked over at Conn and smiled. "Only thing is, I get first pick of the woman tonight. "You got that? I get first pick."

"You got it, Strode," Conn said as he followed the gunman outside.

In addition to Jeremiah Priest, every other person on the ranch was standing around, waiting to see the show. Garneau and Templeton were sitting in chairs up on the front porch of the big house. Garneau held a drink in one hand and a fan in the other.

"Is that him?" Conn asked, pointing toward the small man standing about fifteen feet in front of the steps.

"That's him," Strode said.

"I've heard about him, but I ain't never seen him before. Hell, he ain't no bigger 'n a dog turd. There ain't a man on the place but couldn't slap him around."

"Yeah, well, his guns make him bigger."

"Hello, Strode. I ain't seen you in a while," Priest said. "When was it? Two years ago? Three maybe?"

"I think it might have been three years. How you been getting' along, Priest? Ever get rid of that disease you caught from that squaw?"

"Yeah, it took a while. How come you didn't catch nothin' from her?"

"Hell, Priest, I knowed she had been Frenchified. I thought it was a big joke on you."

"Takin' the mercury cure ain't much of joke," Priest said.

Strode laughed. "I thought it was funny. Bein' as it was between friends 'n all."

Garneau stood up and walked out to the edge of the porch. "Gentlemen, I want it clearly understood the two of you are entering into this . . . contest . . . of your own free will. I also want it clearly understood that I have not used coercion on either of you."

"I don't know what that word means, Colonel," Strode said. "But I was told if I kill Priest, you'll give me a thousand dollars. Is that right?"

"*Oui*. If you are willing to risk your life in this *affaire d'honneur*, I will give you one thousand dollars."

"All right then. That's why I'm here."

"And you will make the statement here, in front of all these witnesses, that you are entering into this competition, deadly though it may be, of your own free will?" Garneau said.

"Hell, yeah, I'll say that. What about you, Priest?" Strode asked. "Are you doin' this of your own free will? I mean, bein' as we're friends 'n all?"

"Yes," Priest replied.

"There you go, Colonel," Strode said. "You heard 'im. This ain't no more than a game between two friends."

"Very well. You may proceed," Garneau said.

Strode moved toward Priest, then stopped when he was about twenty feet away. Priest smiled at him. For a long moment the two men just stared at each other, and those who were watching the macabre dance of death, held their collective breath.

Out in the stable, a horse whickered.

Overhead, a circling crow called.

A freshening breeze ruffled leaves in the trees.

"Now!" Strode said as his hand flashed toward his pistol.

Priest's draw was so fast the men watching it were unable to see when the pistol actually appeared in his hand. They saw only a jump of his shoulder, concurrent with the sound of the gunshot.

Strode had not even cleared his holster, and when the bullet hit him in the chest, he let go of his pistol, and it dropped back into the holster. He staggered back two steps, then clamped his hand over the wound. Conn and the others who had gathered for the grisly show saw the blood streaming through Strode's fingers.

"I'll be damned," Strode said as he fell. "I had no idea the little pissant was that fast."

Conn ran over to him. "Strode!"

The gunman smiled up at him. "I reckon you'll be gettin' first choice of the women tonight, after all."

Conn watched Strode die. He was the closest thing to a friend Conn had. Suddenly, and unexpectedly, he grabbed Strode's gun from its holster and swung it toward Priest. "Damn you!" he shouted in anger.

Conn beat Strode, in that he was able to bring the gun up, but that was as far as he got. Priest, who had already holstered his pistol, drew and fired again. Conn was hit in the middle of the forehead, dead before he fell back on the ground.

"Damn!" someone said. "I ain't never seen nothin' like that in all my borned days!"

"I believe, Colonel, you had a question as to whether I would be up to the task you have chosen for me. Have I answered that question for you?" Priest asked.

"You have indeed."

"And it is my impression the one thousand dollars you were going to give to Strode is now mine."

"That is correct," Garneau replied.

"Very good." Priest turned to the others, all of whom were looking at him with eyes wide in wonder.

"Men, I am going into town to find a saloon. I will be buying drinks for anyone who comes with me."

The men who made up Garneau's army cheered loudly, though the cowboys were somewhat more reserved. It was Gately who quietly made the comment that brought the rest of them around. "Hell, boys. It wasn't one of us that got killed. I say we go into town and drink on the man's money."

"Yeah," Anderson said, and all started toward the corral to saddle their horses for the night on the town.

CHAPTER 25

Having been released from jail and paid their fine, Gilchrist and Manning had watched the shoot-out.

"Ten thousand dollars?" Gilchrist said. "Are you serious? Garneau is going to give Priest ten thousand dollars to kill Smoke Jensen?"

"That's what I've heard," Manning answered.

"Well, hell, what if somebody else kills him? Would he get the ten thousand?"

"I don't know why not," Manning said. "Garneau wants him dead. I don't think it really matters much who kills him."

"That's good to know."

"So are you coming with the rest of us to spend some of Priest's money?"

"I guess so. I mean, I liked Strode, and Priest killed him. So I may as well drink up some of his money."

"They're all goin' to the Brown Dirt. Come on, we can prob'ly catch up with 'em."

"All right," Gilchrist agreed.

Big Rock

"Mr. McVey, why are you tending bar when you can play the piano as well as you do?" Smoke was standing at the bar in Longmont's Saloon.

McVey was wiping glasses and putting them back under the bar. He smiled. "Because it is my time to tend bar. Besides, I have this habit I can't seem to break. I like to eat."

Smoke laughed. "You aren't telling me you can't make enough money as a pianist to make a living, are you?"

"I suppose I could, if I worked at it hard enough. My basic problem is that I'm too lazy."

Smoke laughed at his answer. "I don't believe that for a minute. Would you play something for us now?"

McVey looked toward Louis.

"Go ahead, Johnny. I'll run the bar for a while," Louis said.

"I won't be playing any cowboy ballads," McVey said.

"I don't want you to. You choose what you want to play."

"All right."

Gilchrist and Manning had reached town. As they rode past Longmont's Saloon, Gilchrist pulled up. Manning rode on for a short distance before he realized his partner had stopped. The gunman stopped as well, and looked back toward him. "What are you doing? They're all at the Brown Dirt."

"I think I'm going to step in here for a minute or two. You want to come with me?"

"No. Longmont's is too highfalutin a place for me. Besides, the free drinkin' is over at the Brown Dirt, not here."

"I'll be there in a few minutes," Gilchrist said.

"All right. But you better get there before all the money is drunk up."

"You go along. Like I said, I'll be there in a few minutes."

When Gilchrist stepped into the saloon he saw Smoke standing by the piano, his back to the entrance. The gunman smiled. He was about to earn ten thousand dollars.

He pulled his pistol, pointed at Smoke, and shouted, "Turn around, Jensen!"

Turning slowly, Smoke saw that Gilchrist had his pistol drawn, pointing it at him.

"You're worth ten thousand dollars to me, Jensen," Gilchrist said.

"You're mistaken," Smoke said easily. "There is no paper out on me."

"I ain't talking 'bout the law. I'm talkin' about a fella wants you dead, and he's willin' to pay ten thousand dollars for it."

"Do you really think you'll be able to collect that money?" Smoke asked. "Think about it. You've just admitted in front of all these witnesses that you are being paid to do this. If you kill me, you'll be arrested and hanged. Either that or you'll have to go on the run, and you'll never get the money."

"I'll take that chance." Gilchrist smiled. "I don't think I'll hang."

"No, you won't hang," Smoke said. "Because I'll kill you."

"Ha! Maybe you ain't noticed, but I've got my gun in my hand. Your gun is in the holster. When you get to hell, I got a couple friends that just went there—Strode and Conn. Tell 'em I said hello."

"You can tell them yourself," Smoke said, his voice as calm as if he were discussing the weather.

Gilchrist lifted his thumb up from the handle of his pistol, preparatory to pulling back the hammer, but his thumb never reached the hammer. Smoke drew and fired. His bullet slammed into the middle of Gilchrist's chest. The gunman looked down with an expression of surprise on his face. He looked back up at Smoke. "How? How the hell did you . . . ?" Gilchrist collapsed.

Mark Worley, who had joined the others in moving out of the way when the confrontation started, hurried over to him. The first thing he did was kick the pistol away, then he dropped down to one knee beside him. He put his hand on Gilchrist's neck. "He's dead."

* * *

"It's the damndest thing I ever seen," Andy Anderson told the others in the Brown Dirt. "Gilchrist was standing there with his gun in his hand, but Jensen drew his pistol and shot him before Gilchrist could even pull the trigger."

"That's impossible," Manning said.

"Yeah, well, I woulda thought so too if I hadn't seen it for myself. But I'm tellin' you the truth. Gilchrist had his gun in his hand and Jensen's gun was in his holster. But he pulled it and shot Gilchrist dead."

"I still say that's impossible," Manning said. "There ain't nobody that fast."

"I am," Priest said. "I can do that."

"I don't believe it," Manning said.

"Take your gun out of your holster and point it at me. When you see me start my draw, pull the trigger."

"Don't do it, Manning. Don't you 'member what happened out at the ranch? Conn was already pointing his gun at Priest, when Priest shot him."

"Oh. Yeah. Yeah, I do remember."

"Do you want to try it, Manning?" Priest asked.

"No. Uh, no. I take it back. I reckon you could do it."

"Glad to hear you say that." Priest smiled. "It means I don't have to kill you."

"Come on. Let's have a beer," Anderson said. "Priest is buyin'."

"Damn," Manning said as he wrapped his hands around a beer mug. "I was wonderin' why Gilchrist wanted to stop at Longmont's. I believe he had it in mind to make ten thousand dollars by killin' Jensen."

"That's exactly what he had in mind," Anderson said. "I heard 'im tell Jensen he was goin' to make ten thousand dollars by killin' 'im."

* * *

Sheriff Carson was at Longmont's having been summoned after the shooting. "And that's what you heard him say? That he was goin' to make ten thousand dollars by killin' Smoke?"

"We all heard it, Sheriff," Louis replied.

"I wonder what he meant by that. Smoke, do you think there's some old paper out on you?"

Smoke shook his head. "I used the name Bucky West when I was on the dodge. As far as I know, all that paper has been pulled back."

"Then what did he mean that killing you would be worth ten thousand dollars?"

"I'll tell you what I think it means," Hoyt Miller said.

"Miller, what are you doing in here?" one of the saloon patrons asked. "I was just over at the Brown Dirt. Seems like every hand the Frenchman has working for him is there. It's almost like a party."

"It is a party," Miller said. "Jeremiah Priest is buying everyone drinks."

"Jeremiah Priest?" Sheriff Carson said. "He's here?"

"He's one of Garneau's new hands."

"What do you mean, he's one of the Frenchman's new hands? Are you saying he's a cowboy?"

"No, I ain't sayin' that," Miller said. "Half the men Garneau has hired in the last month ain't never punched a cow in their lives. They don't do nothin' but practice target shootin'. That is, the ones that's still alive. Jensen kilt Gilchrist, and just before I come into town, Priest kilt Strode and Conn."

"What?" Sheriff Carson asked. "I haven't heard anything about that."

"It just happened," Miller said. "And truth is, there prob'ly wouldn't be nothin' you could do about it anyhow. It was a fair fight. All of us that was there seen it. Strode braced Priest, an' Priest kilt him."

"What were they fighting about?" Louis Longmont asked.

"They weren't fightin' at all."

"Wait a minute. Didn't you just say Priest and Strode faced each other, and Priest killed Strode?" Sheriff Carson asked.

"Yes."

"But they weren't fighting over anything?"

"Word I got is Garneau wanted to see how good Priest was, so he offered a thousand dollars to anyone who thought they could beat 'im in a gunfight. Strode tried and lost."

"You also mentioned a man named Conn," Smoke said.

"Yeah, well, turns out Conn and Strode were friends. When Strode got hisself kilt, Conn grabbed the gun and tried to kill Priest. Priest had already put his gun away, but he drew it and kilt Conn."

"Miller, you said you could tell us what it meant when Gilchrist said that killing Smoke was worth ten thousand dollars to him. But I got you off track," Sheriff Carson said. "You want to tell us what you meant?"

"The way I heard it, Garneau is going to give Priest ten thousand dollars if he kills Jensen."

"You actually heard Garneau say that, did you?" Sheriff Carson asked. "Because if you did hear him say that, I'll go out to Long Trek and arrest him right now."

"Arrest him for what?" Miller said. "He ain't actually done nothin' yet."

"I would arrest him for solicitation of someone to commit murder," Sheriff Carson said. "But to make the charge stick, you would have to testify that you heard him do that."

Miller shook his head. "I can't do that."

"If he actually did solicit for murder, he'll go to prison, and he can't hurt you. Understand he is just as guilty if the murder isn't committed as he is if the murder is committed. So you don't have to be afraid to testify."

"That ain't it," Miller said. "I can't say nothin' about it, 'cause I didn't actual hear him say it. I just heard some of the other boys talkin' about it. Besides which, I ain't stayin' around no more. Nance had the right idea when he left. I shoulda left then too. I don't like some of the things Garneau is doin'."

Paris, France

Inspector Laurent had papers spread out on the desk before him, matching records with the five hundred names he had been given by the port authority in Hamburg. He'd matched up eighty-seven Swiss names with Swiss records. For every name on the passenger list, he found a corresponding name in the Swiss records, and saw nothing extraordinary. He had done the same thing with the one hundred and twelve Belgian names. That left him three hundred and one French names to go through.

The first name was Gaston Abadie. He listed himself as a mechanic and was traveling with his wife and two children. Laurent was sure Abadie wasn't Pierre Mouchette.

He went on to the next name.

CHAPTER 26

Big Rock

"Hey, piano player. Play *Buckskin Joe*," Manning said to the piano player.

Gordon Beaver began to play the song.

In the Brown Dirt Cowboy Saloon, the atmosphere had changed with the onslaught of all the Long Trek riders. Although somewhat more animated than the patrons of Longmont's, the regulars were overshadowed by the men of Long Trek, who were exceptionally loud and boisterous. They were argumentative with the customers and with each other.

"Hey, piano player. Play *Buckskin Joe*, again," Manning shouted.

The piano player complied.

"That was very good," Manning said. "Play *Buckskin Joe* again."

Again the piano player complied.

"All right, how about *Buckskin Joe*?"

"For heaven's sake, I've played the song three times already," Gordon said.

"Play it again."

One more time, Gordon played the song.

"All right. Now, I want you to play 'Buckskin Joe,'" Manning said.

"I have played it four times. I definitely will not play it again."

Manning pulled his knife, then walked over to the piano player and laid the sharp side of the instrument at the top of the piano player's ear, right where it was connected to his head. "Mister, you'll damn well play what I tell you to or I'll carve off this ear," he said menacingly. "Now, play 'Buckskin Joe' like I told you to."

Shaking, with his face reflecting his fear, the piano player played "Buckskin Joe" again.

"Now, ain't that the prettiest thing you ever heard?" Manning said when the piano player was finished. "Play it again."

"Piano player, don't you dare play that song again," one of the other patrons said. "It's driving me crazy."

"Well now, ain't that just too bad?" Turning around, Manning saw the man who had called out had a pistol in his hand.

"Peterson, what are you doing? Put that gun away," Emmett Brown said.

"What am I doin'? I'm goin' to shoot that crazy piano player if he plays that song again. That's what I'm doin." The tone of Peterson's voice clearly showed his agitation. He cocked his pistol and aimed it at the piano player.

"And I'm going to cut your ear off, if you don't play it," Manning said, giggling. "That kind of leaves you in a pickle, don't it?" He demonstrated his willingness to do so by cutting into the ear just enough to make it bleed.

"Mr. Brown, what am I going to do?" Gordon called out to the saloon owner in fear.

"I don't know, Gordy. God help me, I don't know what to tell you to do," Brown said.

There was a gunshot, and Gordon jerked, causing more of his ear to be cut. He called out in pain, though also with some relief as he realized he hadn't been shot.

Peterson got a shocked expression on his face, then dropped his gun. Looking around he saw a small man, holding a smoking gun. "What . . . what did you do that for?"

"Me 'n my friends was enjoyin' the music," Priest said. "It looked like you was about to stop it."

Peterson staggered back against the bar, then slid down and died. The bar kept him in a sitting position.

Once more, Gordon began pounding away on the keys. Amy, one of the bar girls, came over to hold a towel against his ear to stop the bleeding.

"Hey, girlie. Sing the song he's playin'," Priest ordered.

"I'm not a singer."

"Sing it or I'll shoot the piano player," Priest said.

"Please! I don't know the words!"

"The words are here," Gordon said. "Sing it, Amy. Please, sing it."

"Gordy, you know I can't sing."

"It doesn't matter. Please, Amy," Gordon begged. "They will shoot me if you don't sing."

Amy cleared her throat, then began singing.

"He ties up one foot, the saddle puts on,
With a swing and a jump he is mounted and gone.
The first time I met him, 'twas early one spring,
Riding a bronco, a high-headed thing.
He tipped me a wink as he gaily did go,
For he wished me to look at his bucking bronco.
The next time I saw him, 'twas late in the fall,
Swinging the girls at Tomlinson's ball:
He laughed and he talked as we danced to and fro,
—Promised never to ride on another bronco."

Just as the song finished, Sheriff Carson came into the saloon. "Brown, I heard a shot."

"I reckon you did, Sheriff. Peterson just got hisself kilt."

"Got himself killed? You mean he committed suicide?"

"No."

"Then you tell me how a man 'gets himself killed.'"

"By pointing a gun at me," Priest said.

Sheriff Carson looked over at the man who spoke. He was a small, thin man with a prominent Adam's apple and a big nose.

"Are you saying you killed him?"

"Yeah, I killed him. But it was in self-defense. Everyone in here will tell you he had a gun in his hand. Hell, look at 'im. He's still holdin' the gun."

Sheriff Carson looked over at Peterson's body, and, as Priest said, his fingers were still clinched around the handle of his gun.

"This has been a busy day for me and for Tom Nunnley." Sheriff Carson looked at Priest. "And for you. I understand you killed two men out at Long Trek."

Priest smiled. "News gets around fast, doesn't it?"

"Fast enough."

"I suppose you also heard that was self-defense. Both Strode and Conn drew on me."

"Like Mr. Peterson?"

Priest shook his head. "No sir, this one was different. You see, Mr. Peterson already had his gun out. He was threatening to shoot not only me, but the piano player."

Sheriff Carson frowned, then looked toward the piano. "Is that true, Beaver? Peterson was going to shoot you?"

"Tell him, piano player. Did he threaten to shoot you or not?"

Gordon was standing by the piano, holding a towel to his ear. Many red spots of blood were on the towel.

"That's true, Sheriff. He threatened to shoot me if I played *Buckskin Joe* one more time."

"One more time? What do you mean one more time? How many times had you played it?"

"I don't know," Gordy said. "Six or seven times, I suppose. I lost count."

"Good Lord, man. Why were you playing the same song so many times?"

"I-I play requests, Sheriff. You know that. What money I make is in tips. If the customers don't like what I'm playing, they won't give me tips."

"I see. What happened to your ear?"

Gordy looked over toward Manning, then toward Priest. "I cut it shaving."

"Are you sure there isn't more to it than that?"

Gordy shook his head. "No, that's all there is to it. I cut it shaving."

"Sheriff, are you through lookin' at the body?" Brown asked. "Because if you are, I'll get a couple men to carry it next door to the undertaker."

Sheriff Carson stared for another long moment at the piano player, then he studied Priest and the other Long Trek riders in the bar. If he pushed the issue too far, Priest and the others might turn on him. He wished Smoke had come with him. He wouldn't be nearly as anxious, if Smoke were there.

"Sheriff, the body? Can I have a couple men carry it out?" Brown repeated after the long, drawn out silence.

"Yeah," Sheriff Carson answered, and he turned and hurried out of the Brown Dirt.

"You two men, I'll give you five dollars apiece if you'll carry Peterson's body next door to the undertaker."

The two men nodded, then with one man at Peterson's head and the other at his feet, they picked him up and carried him to the building next door.

Tom Nunnley already had three bodies laid out in the embalming room, when the two men came in with a fourth.

"Lord Almighty, is there a war going on? This is the fourth gunshot victim I've seen today."

"Yeah, and a man named Priest kilt three of 'em," one of the two body bearers said.

The other man laughed. "You ought to give him a percentage of what you're makin'."

"Oh, my Lord, this is Clem Peterson," Nunnley said. "I just buried his wife last month. He's been actin' strange ever since. I guess I'm not all that surprised to see him."

It was nearly midnight when Chris Logan dismounted and walked over to look down at the dam on Frying Pan Creek. He was carrying three sticks of dynamite, tied and fused together, and he laid the dynamite on top of the wooden dam, rolled out a long piece of fuse, trimmed it, then lit it and backed away quickly.

He watched the fuse spark and sputter until it reached the sticks. There was a big explosion and the dam was destroyed. Once more, water began flowing through the natural channel of Frying Pan Creek.

Satisfied with his work, Logan mounted his horse to ride home. It had been his intention to pick up any bit of evidence that would suggest anything other than the natural failure of the dam, but as he rode off, a small, overlooked coil of fuse lay on the ground behind him.

Returning home he saw, with great satisfaction, that once again, water was flowing through his land.

When he went back into his house, he saw his wife sitting at the kitchen table, drinking coffee by the light of a single candle. Logan smiled at her. "We've got water again."

"Chris, please tell me you didn't do something to the dam," she said, the tone in her voice reflecting her concern.

"I can't tell you that, because that is exactly what I did do.

That damn Frenchman had no right to dam up the creek, and you know it."

"What did you do?"

"I blew that damn dam to hell, that's what I did." Logan laughed. "Damn dam, that's funny."

"No, Chris, it's not funny. That was a dumb thing for you to do."

"Nobody saw me, Ethel."

"It doesn't make any difference whether they saw you or not. We are the only ones the dam had any effect on. How hard is it going to be for the Frenchman to figure out who did it? I'm afraid."

Logan put his hand on Ethel's shoulder. "Darlin', I was with Reno at Little Big Horn. I don't think I can ever be afraid again."

"Look there," Gately said the next morning, pointing to the spot where the dam had been. "The dam is gone."

Anderson, who was riding with him, dismounted and walked over to have a closer look. He saw several pieces of splintered wood lying about.

"It's not just gone. Someone took it down." He picked up a piece of wood and examined it more closely. "Like as not, it was dynamited."

Gately dismounted. "Let's toss these pieces into the stream," he said, picking one of them up and throwing it into the water."

"Why?"

"If Garneau finds out the dam was dynamited, it could get dangerous for someone. If he thinks the dam just failed due to water pressure, it would be much better."

"Yeah," Anderson said. "Yeah, I see what you mean." He joined Gately in tossing the shattered remnants of the dam into the water.

"What are you men doing?"

Startled, Gately looked around to see that Manning had ridden up on them.

"Nothing," Anderson said. "Just cleaning up a bit, is all."

"What happened to the dam?" Manning asked.

"I think the water pressure must have caused it to give way," Anderson said.

Manning dismounted and picked up one of the pieces for a closer examination. Shrugging, he started to toss it into the water, then he saw the small coil of fuse. Reaching down, he picked it up for a closer examination. "Water didn't do this. This dam was dynamited."

"Oh, I don't think so," Gately said.

"Really? What do you call this?" Manning held out the piece of fuse he had found.

"Damn, I didn't see that," Gately said.

CHAPTER 27

Paris, France

Inspector Laurent was in General Moreau's office. "General, I believe I have found the man I have been looking for."

"You've found Mouchette?"

"Well, I haven't actually found him yet, but at least I am certain I have discovered the name he is now using."

Laurent placed some papers on General Moreau's desk. "He is Colonel the Marquis Lucien Garneau."

"Colonel the Marquis Lucien Garneau?" General Moreau replied with a puzzled expression on his face. He shook his head. "Inspector, I am aware of no such colonel."

Laurent smiled broadly. "Precisely so, *mon général*. But someone using that name booked passage from Hamburg, Germany, to New York in America. And since there is no such person, I am certain it must be Mouchette."

General Moreau returned Laurent's smile and nodded. "Yes. Yes, I am sure this must be so." The smile left his face. "But if the *coquin* has escaped to America, I fear he has eluded us. America is a very large country."

"I would like to go to America to look for him."

General Moreau stroked his chin as he considered the request.

"General, this man not only stole two and a half million

francs, he also murdered Sergeant Dubois," Laurent said, pushing his request. "And now, using a false name and rank, he is, no doubt, bringing discredit upon the French Republic. He must not get away with it."

"What makes you think you can find him in America?"

"Because, *mon général*, I have right on my side."

General Moreau nodded. "Very well, Inspector. Go to America with my blessings, and with the hope of all France that you find this criminal."

Laurent saluted. "I will find him, *mon général*."

Sugarloaf

"Pearlie?"

The cowhand was in the barn when he heard someone call out to him, and he went to the door. "Gately, what are you doing here?"

"I'm afraid there's goin' to be some trouble over at Logan's place."

"What kind of trouble?"

"Bad trouble. Garneau put up a dam on Frying Pan Creek to keep the water from flowing onto Logan's ranch. I think Logan must have blown the dam last night. One of Garneau's gunnies found out about it. I think Garneau plans to send some people over to teach Logan a lesson."

"Why are you tellin' me this, Gately? I thought you worked for Garneau."

"I did, but I don't work for him no more. Me 'n Andy has quit. I don't like the way the Frenchman does business."

"Thanks for tellin' me," Pearlie said. "I'll tell Smoke and see what he wants to do about it."

"I'm goin' with you," Malcolm said when Smoke, Pearlie, and Cal stopped by Carro de Bancada on their way to Logan's ranch.

"You don't need to go. We just stopped by to tell you what's happening," Smoke said.

"If I am the one who has talked all the others into staying, should I not subject myself to the same dangers I'm asking of them?"

"There's likely to be some shooting. You said yourself, you have no experience with guns."

"My father told me the story of Uncle Humboldt," Malcolm said. "He was a boy raised in Brooklyn, just as my father was. He had never even fired a gun until he went into the army during the war. At Gettysburg, my Uncle Humboldt was mentioned in the dispatches for what he did with a rifle."

Smoke chuckled. "Yes, I saw some examples of your uncle's marksmanship. He was very good with it. Very well, you can come along if you wish."

"Thank you. I'll just get my guns."

"Make sure you bring a rifle."

Concerned they might get to Logan's place too late, they were glad to see Logan, his wife, and his two sons working in the garden when they rode up. Logan looked up as the riders approached, at first with some apprehension, then with a smile when he recognized them.

"Well, Smoke, Malcolm, Pearlie, Cal. Welcome. What are you all doing here?"

"Chris, did you dynamite the dam on Frying Pan Creek last night?" Smoke asked.

The smile left Logan's face. "What if I did? I don't see where the Frenchman has the right to dam off a creek."

"Whoa. We're on your side, Chris," Malcolm said. "But the thing is, Garneau might be sending some men over here."

"Let 'im do it. If Crazy Horse and Sitting Bull didn't scare me, that peckerwood isn't going to. I'll stand up to him."

"You won't have to stand up to him alone," Smoke said.

"We are going to be here with you. But it might be a good idea for Mrs. Logan and your two boys to leave. They can go to my place and stay with Sally for a while."

"Yeah," Logan said. "Now that you mention it, that might be a pretty good idea. Ethel, I'm going to get the buckboard hitched up. Take the boys over to the Jensen place."

"Chris, I . . ."

Logan took his wife's hands in his. "Ethel, you were a soldier's wife. You know how things are."

"But I'm not a soldier's wife anymore."

"Yes, you are. Once a soldier, always a soldier. And you're still my wife. Now, do like I tell you."

"All right."

"Mrs. Logan, go around by Cottonwood Pass Road," Smoke suggested. "That way there's little chance you'll run across any of Garneau's men."

Ethel nodded, then stood there with her sons until Logan brought the buckboard around a few minutes later. He kissed her, then helped her and the two boys into the buckboard.

"Stay with Sally until we come back," Smoke said.

Ethel nodded, then slapped the reins against the back of the team, and the buckboard left.

"Cal, why don't you ride out toward the south and keep an eye out. Let us know if you see anything," Smoke suggested.

"Will do," Cal agreed, and remounting, he left at a trot.

Logan watched his wife drive off for a long minute, then he turned back to Smoke and the others. "I lied."

"What?"

"When I said that Crazy Horse and Sitting Bull didn't scare me, I lied. They scared the hell out of me."

Smoke laughed. "Good."

"Good?"

"Yes, good. I don't want to be standing here, facing Garneau's men with a fool beside me."

Logan and the others laughed as well.

"Well, we may as well get ready for them," Smoke said. "Chris, this is your place, and you're an old army sergeant, do you have any ideas on disposition of the troops?"

"Yes. One of you should be in the hayloft over there. You'll have a good field of fire from the open door."

"I'll go there," Pearlie said.

"Another could be on top of the machine shop. Get on the other slope of the roof, just behind the peak."

"I'll do that," Malcolm said.

"Smoke, if you'd like, you can be down here on the ground, waiting just behind the cottonwood over there. I'll be by the watering trough. I can get down behind it quickly, if I need to."

The men heard the sound of an approaching horse, and looking in that direction, saw Cal coming back at a gallop.

"They're comin'," Cal said as he swung down from the saddle.

"How far, and how many?" Smoke asked.

"I'd say they're still a mile to a mile and a half away. I counted ten of 'em."

"That means they have us exactly doubled," Malcolm said.

"Is Garneau with them?"

"To tell the truth, Smoke, I don't know if he is or not. I've only seen him one time, and they were too far back to make out any actual features."

"No matter, we'll handle it all right. You get up into the hayloft with Pearlie. Malcolm, you may as well get yourself in position as well."

"Right," Malcolm said.

"Come on, Cal, let's get to our places," Pearlie said.

The three men left to climb into their perches, so that only Smoke and Logan remained behind.

"How do you think we should handle this, Smoke? Let

'em get close enough to talk? Or start shootin' as soon as we see 'em?"

"Yell at them and stop them just out of pistol range," Smoke said. "If they try to pass that point after you have warned them, start shooting."

Armed and ready, they stood next to each other, waiting for Garneau's men.

Templeton held up his hand to stop the riders. They were on the rest of a ridgeline, and Logan's house and outbuildings were spread out before them.

"What do you think, Templeton?" Jerry Briggs asked.

"I think we should just ride in and shoot the man. And leave no witnesses."

"He's got a woman and kids," Mathis said.

"Like I said, leave no witnesses."

"Don't you think, maybe, we could have a little fun with the woman first?" Carr asked.

"Have you seen his woman, Carr?" Briggs asked. "She's so ugly she'd make a train take ten miles of dirt road."

The other men laughed.

"Hell, what does that matter?" Carr asked as he grabbed himself. "I just want to have a little fun with her. I don't plan to marry her."

Again, the men laughed.

They continued to advance toward the Logan place until they were within about two hundred yards. Templeton stopped them again.

"What it is?" Mathis asked. "What'd you stop us for?"

"Let's spread out and advance in . . . in . . . what was it Garneau called it during our practices?"

"A frontal line attack," Briggs said.

"Right. Spread out and advance at a trot. When I give the word, we'll continue at a gallop."

* * *

"Smoke," Logan said. "I've seen this before. There ain't goin' to be no talkin', no callin' out for them to not come any closer. They're comin' at us in a full blown attack."

"All right. Get down behind the water trough." Smoke used his hands as a megaphone and called, "Pearlie, Cal!"

"Yeah?" a voice called back.

"Start shooting as soon as they're in range."

"Right."

"Malcolm?"

"Yes, sir, I heard," Malcolm said.

Smoke levered a round into the chamber of his rifle, then got behind the cottonwood tree and waited.

The line of trotting horses came within a hundred yards of the barn, which was the closest building to them.

"Now!" Templeton shouted.

The ten riders broke into a gallop, firing pistols as they advanced.

Cal was the first one to fire. Standing in the open window of the hayloft, he fired at the rider closest to him, and that rider went down. Pearlie fired next, then Smoke, Malcolm, and Logan all fired at about the same time. The defenders had not picked out individual targets, so only two more attackers went down, a couple of them hit twice.

"What the hell?" Briggs shouted. "He ain't alone! We've been ambushed!"

"Let's get out of here!" Templeton shouted, and he jerked his horse around, leading the retreat as all seven remaining men galloped away.

"Hah!" Cal shouted from just inside the window in the hayloft. "Did you see them boys run?"

Cal, Pearlie, and Malcolm came down from their perches, and the five men gathered just in front of the watering trough.

Pearlie laughed. "You know what I think? I think them boys got a huge surprise."

"Yeah," Cal said.

"How did you know they were comin'?" Logan asked.

"Believe it or not, one of Garneau's men told us," Smoke said.

"Who was it? Gately or Anderson?"

"Both of them, actually."

Logan nodded. "Yeah, I thought so. They were about the only two men still workin' over there who had any good left in 'em."

CHAPTER 28

From the *Big Rock Journal:*

Gun Battle at Logan's Ranch

On Thursday previous, several mounted gunmen attacked Chris Logan and some of his neighbors at Mr. Logan's ranch. Long time residents of Eagle and Pitkin counties will recognize that Logan's ranch is near Carro de Bancada, which once belonged to the late Mr. Humboldt Puddle. They will also remember that Humboldt Puddle was killed in an occasion similar to the most recent gunfight.

Colonel the Marquis Lucien Garneau, owner of Long Trek Ranch, suggests the assailants were cattle rustlers, with the intention of stealing Chris Logan's entire herd. "This validates the concern I expressed to the Cattlemen's Association recently, when I explained my reason for hiring skilled gunmen who could provide protection, not only for my cattle, but for the cattle of my neighbors, such as Chris Logan."

Lucy Woodward to Visit Atlanta

Lucy Woodward, the winsome lass who is the daughter of local farmer Charles Woodward, will be taking the eastbound train on Monday next. The purpose of the trip is to visit her cousin and to enjoy the sights of Atlanta. Mr. Woodward brought his family from Atlanta six years previous, and this will be the first time any member of the family has returned to the old homeland.

New York City

Inspector Laurent stood in the office of Captain Warren Haggardorn of the New York Police Department. "I am Inspector André Laurent of the Gendarmerie Nationale, the French Police, and I am looking for one of my countryman, a person who identifies himself as Colonel the Marquis Lucien Garneau."

"Inspector, if there is such a person as Colonel the Marquis Lucien Garneau in New York, I know nothing of him," Haggardorn said. "How much money did you say he brought with him to America?"

"Half a million dollars in American money."

Haggardorn let out a low whistle. "That is a lot of money. I don't think anyone would keep that much money on his person. I'll do a very thorough check of all the banks in the city. If he made a deposit anywhere, we'll find him."

"Thank you, Monsieur."

"You want this man pretty bad, do you?"

"*Oui.* He not only stole the money from the French Army, he murdered a soldier who was under his command, then attempted to blame that murdered soldier for the robbery. He is a man who is completely without honor. I want to take him home to face the guillotine."

"I don't blame you," Chief Haggardorn said. "I don't know what I can do to help, but I promise you that we'll do everything we can for you."

"*Merci*, Monsieur Chief Haggardorn."

Big Rock

Charles Woodward was driving a buckboard taking his daughter to the depot in Big Rock. In the back of the buckboard was the train case Lucy would carry on board with her, as well as two suitcases that would be checked through to make the trip in the baggage car.

"Now, you are sure you are taking enough clothes?" her father teased. "I wouldn't want you to get to Atlanta and suddenly find that you didn't have a dress, a hat, a pair of shoes, or the pitcher and basin from your bedroom."

"Father, you know what Atlanta is like," Lucy said. "Why, Cousin Doreen will have all sorts of balls and cotillions for me to attend. You wouldn't want me to embarrass you by not being properly dressed, would you?"

Woodward chuckled. "Oh, heavens no. The last thing I want is to be embarrassed because my daughter, who more often than not can be found wearing men's pants, shirt, hat, and straddling a horse, wouldn't be properly dressed at some fancy ball."

"Then you needn't worry, because I won't embarrass you."

They reached the train station and Woodward parked the buckboard under a tree. He grabbed the suitcases, Lucy carried the train case, and they entered the depot. After securing a ticket and checking the suitcases, they took a seat to wait until it was time to board.

Woodward turned to his daughter. "I see you are wearing your mother's cameo brooch."

"Yes, isn't it beautiful? She said I could wear it while I was in Atlanta."

"You be careful that you don't lose it. Your mother sets quite a store by that."

"I'll make sure I don't lose it. I will wear it pinned to my dress, every day."

"I'm surprised you are going anyway. I thought you and young Malcolm Puddle were sparking one another."

"Why, Father, whatever gave you that idea?" Lucy asked, though her cheeks flamed red as she blushed over the comment.

Woodward chuckled. "Nothing, my dear. Absolutely nothing." He leaned over and kissed his daughter on the forehead. "I was just teasing you a little. I want you to have a wonderful time. Give your cousin my regards."

"I will, Father."

"And I want you to send me a telegram as soon as you arrive in Atlanta. I want to know you got there safely."

Lucy laughed. "I swear, Father, you are a bigger worrywart than Mama. Don't worry about me. I'll be just fine. I'm not a little girl anymore, you know."

"It's just that Atlanta is very large, not like the small towns we have here. You must watch yourself while you are there."

"Father, I will be all right."

"Board!" the conductor called.

"Oh, I must get aboard now." Lucy kissed her father, then hurried to the train and stepped up onto the car vestibule.

Woodward went down to the track as well, and as the cars began to move, he walked alongside, keeping pace with the train as it pulled away from the depot. "Remember, as soon as you arrive . . ."

"Send you a telegram. Yes, I promise," Lucy called back through the open window. "And I'll write to you in a few days to tell you what a wonderful time I'm having."

"Bye!" Woodward said, waving and calling to her.

"Bye!"

Woodward remained on the platform as the train pulled out of the station, watching it until, moving quite rapidly, it receded in the distance. Not until the train was a remote whistle and a distant puff of smoke in the clear, blue sky, did he return to the buckboard. Untying the reins, he snapped then against the back of the team, and started home.

"Ticket, please, miss," the conductor said.

Lucy showed him the long roll of tickets and he perused them before punching a hole in one.

"All the way to Atlanta, is it?"

"Yes, sir, to see my cousin."

"Well, you'll change trains in Pueblo, Denver, St. Louis, and Nashville. You are certainly going to be seeing a lot of the country."

"Yes, sir, I suppose I will."

"Well, Miss . . ."

"Woodward. Lucy Woodward," she replied with a smile.

"Miss Woodward, if you need anything, just let me know. My name is Murtaugh, and I am the conductor. You make friends with all the conductors from here to Atlanta. It's their job to keep an eye on young, unaccompanied ladies."

"Yes, sir, Mr. Murtaugh, I will. Thank you."

Four hours later, the eastbound train, on which Lucy Woodward was a passenger, made a late night stop for water. Lucy, who was sleeping in the front seat of the car, was only vaguely aware the stop had been made. She was too comfortable and too tired from all the packing and preparation for her visit to Atlanta to pay too much attention to it.

Turning her head away from the window she closed her eyes again and listened to the bumping sounds from outside as the fireman lowered the spout from the trackside water tower and began squirting water down into the tank.

"Whoowee. This is one thirsty train," the fireman called.

"It should be thirsty. We haven't taken on a drop of water in the last sixty miles," the engineer called down.

Lucy could hear the two men talking, and she thought of them working hard to drive the train while she was inside on a comfortable and padded seat.

The train was alive with sound: from the loud puffs of the actuating cylinder relief valves venting steam to the splash of water filling the tank to the snapping and popping of over-heated bearings and gearboxes. Lucy, the fireman and engineer, and everyone else on the train were unaware of Briggs and Carr outside the train, slipping through the shadows alongside the railroad track.

They had been in position for nearly an hour, waiting by the tower where the train would have to stop for water. Behind them, tied to a willow tree, were two horses. One of the horses was pulling a travois.

"Which car is she on?" Carr asked.

"Well, according to what we was told, she was goin' to be in the first car," Briggs answered.

Glancing up toward the tender, they saw the fireman standing with his back to them as he directed the gushing water from the spout into the tank. Satisfied that his attention was diverted, the two men stepped up onto the vestibule plat-form between the mail car and the first car. They remained there for just a moment to make certain they had not been dis-covered. Satisfied they were safe, they pushed open the door and stepped inside. The car was dimly lit by two low-burning, gimbal-mounted lanterns, one on the front wall and the other on the rear. The aisle stretched out between two rows of seats. Nearly all the passengers were asleep.

"Is that her?" Briggs whispered, indicating a woman who was sleeping in the front seat.

"Yeah, I think so," Carr answered.

Briggs reached out and touched the young woman. She

awakened with a start, and looked at the two men with her eyes wide in anxious confusion.

"Are you Lucy Woodward?" Briggs asked.

"Yes, why do you ask?"

"Your mama has had a terrible accident. Your papa sent us to get you and bring you back home."

"Oh! What has happened?"

"Come with us. We have a buckboard and a fast team outside."

Concerned about her mother, Lucy got up to follow the two men outside. They approached two saddled horses, one of them dragging a travois.

"What is this? I don't see a buckboard," Lucy said.

One of the men dropped a looped rope around her to hold her arms close to her side. She screamed, but the scream was drowned out by the sound of the locomotive whistle. Before she could scream a second time, a gag was stuffed in her mouth.

No one on the train had even noticed when she left the car, nor did anyone see them putting her on the travois.

"Let's go," Briggs said.

The two men mounted and rode off, even as the train, its tank full of water, got underway again.

It wasn't until half an hour before the train pulled into Cañon City the next morning that the porter, who had been told by the conductor to keep an eye on the young, unaccompanied woman in the front seat, realized that she was gone. He made a thorough search of the two cars he was in charge of, but didn't see her.

When he checked with Julius, the other porter, a look through his two cars was also fruitless.

"What happened to her?" Julius asked.

"Lord, I wish I knew," the first porter answered. He took his concern to the conductor.

"Well, she has to be on the train somewhere. Let's look through every car."

"Mr. Murtaugh, me and Julius done looked through ever' car on this train, and we ain't found her."

"Conductor, are you looking for the woman who was sitting there?" one of the passengers asked, pointing to the front row of seats.

"Yes. Do you have any idea where she might be?"

"No, sir. But I see a piece of paper on the floor under her seat, and I know it wasn't there before. Maybe it's a clue."

The porter picked up the folded over piece of paper and handed it to the conductor.

Woodward—
   We've got your daughter. It's going to cost you $5,000 to get her back. We will tell you where to deliver the money.

"What are we going to do, Mr. Murtaugh?"

The conductor thought a moment. "We'll turn this note over to the sheriff as soon as we reach Cañon City."

From the *Big Rock Journal:*

Mysterious Disappearance of Woman from Train

The fate of Miss Lucy Woodward, daughter of prominent Eagle County farmer, Charles Woodward, is still unknown. The porter on the Pueblo Special noticed she was missing shortly before the train reached the Cañon City station. He reported her disappearance to the conductor, Miles Murtaugh, and a search of the train was conducted, but to no avail.

Subsequently, a note was discovered which leads the sheriff's department to believe the woman was snatched from the train, though nobody remembers seeing the event actually happen.

The local train agent reports the note, which demands a five thousand dollar ransom, has been turned over to the sheriff.

"We've done all we can do," a railroad official reported. "All the stations along the line have been notified and we are asking that anyone who has any information on Miss Woodward's whereabouts to please contact any Denver and Pacific Railroad official."

CHAPTER 29

Malcolm was sitting in a chair on the front porch of Woodward's house. Charles Woodward sat across from him. Sue Woodward was in the house, taken to bed with worry over her daughter.

"Sheriff Carson said the train only stopped twice between here and Cañon City, once for water, and once at Buena Vista," Woodward said.

"Did anyone notice her at either of those stops?" Malcolm asked.

"They don't know if she was on the train at Buena Vista or not. Nobody noticed that she was missing until shortly before the train reached Cañon City."

"It seems unlikely anyone could have taken her off forcefully without being seen," Malcolm said.

"But I don't think Lucy would have left the train on her own."

"She might have, if she was convinced to."

"How could someone convince her to leave the train in the middle of the night?"

"If she thought something had happened to either you or Mrs. Woodward, perhaps," Malcolm suggested.

"Yes, I see what you mean. That is possible, I suppose.

Say, did you see in the paper that the Frenchman is offering a reward for her safe return?"

"I saw it. I don't believe it."

"I don't know. Maybe he realizes he's gotten off on the wrong foot with everyone, and he's trying to make it up. After all, nobody would want all of his neighbors hating him, would they?"

"I'm still mighty suspicious," Malcolm said. "Say, who's that coming up your drive?"

Woodward squinted as he stared at the man approaching in a buggy.

"I don't know. He's too far away to— No, wait, there's only one man I know who takes up the entire seat of a buggy. That has to be Robert Dempster."

"Who?"

"Robert Dempster. He's a lawyer in town. I wonder what he wants?"

"Maybe it has something to do with Lucy," Sue Woodward said, her comment surprising both Woodward and Malcolm, who had not seen her come out onto the porch.

Woodward reached over to take his wife's hand. "Don't get all worked up over it one way or the other. Let's find out what this is about."

They stood as they watched the buggy approach. Malcolm went down the steps, and Dempster halted the horse, then handed the reins to him. Malcolm tied the reins around a hitching post.

The buggy tilted to one side as Dempster, wheezing and puffing, climbed down. He was sweating profusely and held a handkerchief to his face as he climbed the steps to the porch.

"Can I help you, Mr. Dempster?" Woodward asked.

"Actually, Mr. Woodward, I rather hope I can help you," Dempster replied. "It's in regards to your daughter."

"What about Lucy?" Woodward asked anxiously. "Do you know where she is?"

"No, no. I'm sorry if I've given you the wrong impression," Dempster said, waving his hand. "I don't know where she is . . . but . . . I may be in a position to facilitate her safe return."

"What do you mean you can facilitate her safe return?"

"The amount of ransom being asked is five thousand dollars. Do you have five thousand dollars, Mr. Woodward?"

"Mr. Dempster, what does it matter to you whether I have five thousand dollars or not?"

"Because I told you, I may be in a position to help you. You see, Mr. Woodward, my office has been contacted by the person, or persons, who took your daughter. They have asked me to act as the agent in negotiations between you and them."

"Where is Lucy?" Malcolm asked. "You tell me where she is!"

"Easy, young man. I don't know where she is. As I told you, they contacted me and asked me to be the go between."

"How do you know they have her?" Woodward asked.

"They sent me something to give to you, something they said would prove they have her."

"What is it?" Sue Woodward asked.

"This," Dempster said, taking an ivory cameo brooch from his pocket and showing it to them.

"Oh!" Sue put her hands over her face and began sobbing.

"Give that to me," Woodward said, grabbing the brooch.

"Is that Lucy's brooch?" Malcolm asked.

"Yes. Well, it is her mother's brooch, but she was wearing it for her trip to Atlanta."

Sue reached for the brooch then clasped it in her hands again, bringing her hands to her face as she wept.

Dempster frowned. "So, Mr. Woodward, I ask you again. Do you have five thousand dollars?"

"No, God in heaven, I don't have it."

"That's too bad," Dempster said.

"Too bad? What do you mean, too bad?" Sue asked. "Are you saying that they are going to . . . that they will . . ." She was unable to finish the question.

"No, they want the money. They don't want to hurt the girl," Dempster said. "All you have to do is come up with five thousand dollars, and they'll release her unharmed."

"Where am I going to get that kind of money?"

Dempster stroked his triple chins as he fixed his gaze on Woodward. "I tell you what. I don't want to see this innocent girl hurt, any more than you do. I don't believe it is just by chance that they chose me as the agent between you and them. I can't promise you anything, but it just may be that I will be able to arrange the money for you."

"How?"

"You let me work on that. I'll be back tomorrow with a proposal that just might work."

"Oh, bless you, Mr. Dempster. Bless you," Sue said, reaching her hand out toward him.

"Don't despair, Mrs. Woodward. I'm almost certain I can work something out." Dempster walked back down the steps, climbed into the straining buggy, turned it around, and started back toward the road.

"I wonder what he means by saying he will work something out," Malcolm said.

"I don't know," Woodward said. "But I do know he is a pretty smart lawyer. You ask anyone in town and they'll tell you Dempster is a smart lawyer."

Malcolm grimaced. "Yes, that's what bothers me."

Sugarloaf

"That looks like Malcolm coming up the road," Sally said as she stood looking out the kitchen window.

"Yes, I believe it is," Smoke said, joining her at the

window. He went out onto the porch to meet his young friend. "Hello, Malcolm. Climb down and come on in."

Malcolm followed Smoke inside, then accepted a cup of coffee. "I just came from Mr. and Mrs. Woodward's place."

"How are they doing?" Sally asked.

"They're both very frightened. To tell the truth, I'm also frightened."

"Have they heard anything else from whoever took Lucy?" Smoke asked.

"Yes, that's why I've come to see you."

"What have they heard?"

"Well, nothing directly, but they have heard indirectly. By that I mean Mr. Dempster drove out to speak to them. He said the people who took Lucy have gotten in touch with him, and asked him to be an agent between them and the Woodwards."

"Were you there when he came to see them?"

"Yes, I was visiting with Mr. Woodward. Uh, the truth is, Smoke, you may not know it, but I've got me sort of a personal reason for wantin' Lucy back all safe and sound."

Smoke smiled. "Malcolm, I don't think there's a man in the whole county who doesn't know about that personal reason."

"Oh. Well, then you can see why this has me about as anxious as the Woodwards are."

"Did you believe Dempster, when he said that he had been contacted?"

"Oh, yes. He's been contacted all right. There's not the slightest doubt about that."

"Really? Why do you say that?"

"Because he gave Mr. Woodward an ivory brooch Lucy was wearing."

"That sounds like proof enough," Smoke said. "Did he have anything new to add?"

"Well, not about Lucy. I mean, not about where she was

or how she was doing. He says they want five thousand dollars, just like the ransom note said."

"And he's supposed to transfer the money?"

"I don't know. He didn't say. But here is something strange that he did say. When Mr. Woodward told him he didn't have five thousand dollars, Mr. Dempster said he would come back tomorrow with a way that Mr. Woodward could get the money."

"Did he?"

"Yes, sir."

"Now, that's interesting," Smoke said. "In fact, that is very interesting. Suppose you and I go over to Woodward's farm and be there when Mr. Dempster returns tomorrow."

Malcolm smiled. "I was hoping you would suggest that."

CHAPTER 30

New York City

Inspector Laurent was standing at the window of his hotel, looking down on Forty-second Street when there was a knock on his door. Opening the door, he saw one of the hotel staff.

"Mr. Laurent?"

"*Oui*?"

"Could you come to the lobby, sir? There is a telephone call for you."

Puzzled as to who would be calling him on the telephone, Laurent rode the elevator down to the lobby, then followed the messenger over to the check-in desk.

"This phone call is for you," the desk clerk said, inviting Laurent around behind the desk. The telephone was mounted on the wall, and the receiver was standing on a shelf just below the instrument.

Laurent picked up the receiver, held it to his ear, then leaned in to the phone. "*Oui,* this is Monsieur Laurent."

"Mr. Laurent, this is Captain McKenzie of the New York Police. Could you come down to the Fifth Avenue station, please, sir? I think we have something here that you might find interesting."

"*Oui*, right away."

In front of the hotel, Laurent summoned a hansom cab. "The police station on Fifth Avenue, *si vous s'il vous plaît.*"

The city was alive with activity. Jangling bells from the harnesses of horses played against the staccato beat of hooves and the ring of iron-rimmed wheels on cobblestone streets. The cab driver maneuvered the two-wheeled vehicle expertly through the heavy traffic—omnibuses, carriages, freight wagons, other cabs, and even chugging locomotives.

It took but a few minutes before the cab came to a stop in front of the police station. Paying him, Inspector Laurent went inside to inquire about Captain McKenzie.

"I am Captain McKenzie," a uniformed man said, coming to greet him.

"You said you had something that I might find interesting, *Capitaine?*"

"Yes," McKenzie said. "I believe you were searching for one of your countrymen, a man named Garneau?"

"That is the name he has assumed. His real name is Pierre Mouchette."

"Would someone going by the name of Colonel the Marquis Lucien Garneau be of any interest to you?"

A broad smile spread across Laurent's face. "You have him, *Capitaine?*

"No, but I know where he is."

"Please, Monsieur, I beg of you. Arrest him."

"I can't do that, Inspector. He isn't in my jurisdiction. In fact, he isn't even in New York. But I can show you where he is, and you can go make your case with the local authorities."

"Where is he?"

"Of course, this may not be your man. It could be another Colonel the Marquis Lucien Garneau."

"There is no Colonel in the French army, nor is there a marquis, by the name of Lucien Garneau. If you have located someone who is using that name, Monsieur, he is my fugitive."

"Take a look at this, Inspector," Captain McKenzie said, opening the *New York Times* and laying it before him. "This is an article the *Times* picked up from the Associated Press. It has the name of the man you are looking for."

McKenzie put his finger on a specific article.

Gun Battle at Logan's Ranch

BIG ROCK, COLORADO (AP)—(From The Big Rock Journal)—On Thursday previous, several mounted gunmen attacked Chris Logan and some of his neighbors at Mr. Logan's ranch. Long time residents of Eagle and Pitkin counties will recognize that Logan's ranch is near Carro de Bancada, which once belonged to the late Mr. Humboldt Puddle. They will also remember that Humboldt Puddle was killed in an occasion similar to the most recent gunfight.

Colonel the Marquis Lucien Garneau, owner of Long Trek Ranch, suggests the assailants were cattle rustlers with the intention of stealing Chris Logan's entire herd. "This validates the concern I expressed to the Cattlemen's Association recently, when I explained my reason for hiring skilled gunmen who could provide protection, not only for my cattle, but for the cattle of my neighbors, such as Chris Logan."

"*Oui!* Yes!" Laurent said excitedly. "This must be Mouchette. It can be no other. Where is this place, this"— Laurent looked back at the article—"Big Rock, Colorado?"

"Come over here to the map. I will show you," McKenzie said.

Laurent followed McKenzie to the wall where there was a large map of the United States.

"Here is New York where you are now," McKenzie said.

"And way over here"—he reached far across the map with his other hand—"is Colorado."

"Mon Dieu, that is a long way."

"Yes, it is. But we have trains that go there. You can be there in less than a week. You aren't going to let a little thing like a long trip get in your way, are you?"

"*Non, monsieur*. If Mouchette is in a place called Big Rock, Colorado, then that is where I shall go."

"I thought you might."

"May I take this newspaper, Capitaine?" Laurent asked.

"Certainly, be my guest."

"*Merci*."

With the newspaper under his arm, Laurent returned to the hotel where he packed his bag, checked out, then took a cab to Grand Central depot where he bought a ticket to Big Rock, Colorado. Before boarding the train, however, he sent a cablegram to General Moreau.

HAVE DETERMINED LOCATION OF MOUCHETTE STOP
AM PROCEEDING THERE NOW STOP
INSPECTOR LAURENT

Ajax Mountain Range, Pitkin County, Colorado

Lucy had been in the small cabin for two days, tied up for the entire time. Her back and legs were cramped and her wrists were raw from the rubbing of the ropes. "How long are you going to keep me here?"

"We're going to keep you here until your papa pays us five thousand dollars," Briggs said.

"My father is not a wealthy man. There is no way he can raise that much money."

"If he wants to get you back in one piece, he'll raise the money," Carr said.

"Are you hungry? Do you want something to eat?" Briggs asked.

"No, thank you," she replied.

"Here, take a piece," Briggs said, offering her a piece of jerky.

Lucy shook her head. "I don't want it. I would like a drink of water, though."

"You got to eat something. It's been two days and you ain't et nothin'. All you've done is drink water. Maybe you'd like somethin' to drink other than water. You want some whiskey?"

"No."

"Come on. It'll make you feel better." Briggs held the bottle out toward her.

"Please, no," she said.

"Leave her alone if she don't want it," Carr said harshly. "It don't make no sense tryin' to give whiskey to someone who don't want it. You'll just be wastin' good whiskey."

"Why won't you eat somethin'?" Briggs asked.

Lucy didn't answer.

"Miss, we're just tryin' to be nice to you. I don't really care whether you drink or not, and that's the truth of it."

"Nice to me? You haul me off the train by telling me a lie about my mother, then you bring me here and tie me up, but you say you are being nice to me?"

"Miss, maybe you don't know what sometimes happens to women when they get took," Briggs replied.

Lucy gasped in quick fear as she realized what he was saying to her.

"Don't be threatenin' her with that," Carr said. "The colonel was just real particular about that."

"The colonel? Who is the colonel?" Lucy asked.

"You got a big mouth, Carr," Briggs said.

"She don't know what I'm talkin' about. Hell, you heard her. She don't have no idea who he is."

"Just don't say nothin' about him no more."

CHAPTER 31

Smoke, Pearlie, and Cal were waiting on a road about a mile east of the farm of Charles Woodward. They were expecting Dempster to call on Woodward, and when he left the farm, Smoke wanted to know where he planned to go.

"Don't stop him," Smoke said. "And don't let him see you follow him. I just want to know where he goes after he leaves Woodward's farm."

"All right," Pearlie said.

"What if he leads us to the girl?" Cal asked. "Can we rescue her?"

"I don't think he'll be going to the girl, but if he does, and you see the opportunity to rescue her without getting her hurt, of course you can do it."

"I'll bet she would give me a dance at the next dance if I did that," Cal said with a broad smile.

"If she did, it would only be the one dance to thank you," Pearlie replied with a chuckle. "Ever'body knows she has her cap set for Malcolm."

"Yeah, well, all I'd want is one dance anyway."

"You two get over there, on the other side of that ridge-line," Smoke said. "When he leaves, this is the way he will go. And if I have this figured correctly, when he gets to the T in the road, he'll turn left."

"Left? Town is to the right," Cal said.

"Uh-huh."

"The Long Trek is to the left," Pearlie said. "You're thinkin' the Frenchman is behind this, aren't you?"

"That's exactly what I'm thinking," Smoke said. "And today, we're going to call his bluff."

"Smoke, you don't really think the Frenchman is that evil, do you?"

"I don't think it's a coincidence that someone has tried twice to kill me, and someone has tried to kill you two. I think the Frenchman believes that if he can get us out of the way, he'll have a clear track to owning the entire valley."

"Yeah? Well, he don't know Miss Sally, does he?" Cal said. "He might kill you, but he would still have Miss Sally to contend with."

Smoke chuckled. "Well now, Cal, that's just real comforting."

"Yeah, well, that's what I'm saying."

Pearlie laughed as well. "Cal, quit while you're ahead."

"What'd I say?"

"I see dust way up the road," Pearlie said. "I'll bet that's him."

Smoke nodded. "I'm sure it is. I'm going on up to the house. You boys get out of sight." He sat his horse until he saw that Pearlie and Cal were well out of sight, then he rode on the rest of the way to Woodward's farm.

Woodward and Malcolm were sitting in chairs on the front porch. Because they were expecting Smoke, there was a third chair on the porch, empty and waiting for him. At Woodward's invitation, Smoke took it.

"Is he coming?" Malcolm asked.

"I saw someone coming up the road. I didn't wait around long enough to see who it was, but I'm sure it's Dempster."

"I'm sure it is, too," Woodward said.

"Have you got the money with you?" Smoke asked Woodward.

"Yes, sir," Woodward answered. "And I can't thank you enough. But I have to be honest with you, Smoke, I don't know how, when, or even if I can ever pay you back."

"I'll pay him back, Mr. Woodward," Malcolm said. "I can borrow enough money against my ranch to do that."

"Neither one of you will have to pay me back," Smoke said. "I'm pretty sure I'll be able to get it back on my own."

"I think that's our man coming, now," Malcolm said.

Looking up the road they could see dust roiling up, though as yet, they couldn't see the buggy. Then a moment later, the buggy came into view, and they watched as Dempster drove all the way up to the porch. He sat there for a moment as the dust cloud rolled over him, but didn't bother to climb down from the buggy. "I've got good news for you, Mr. Woodward. Very good news."

"Mr. Dempster, the only good news you can have for me is that my daughter has been found and is safe."

"Well, unfortunately, it hasn't advanced that far yet. But I'm reasonably certain we aren't far from a successful end to this terrible ordeal. I think you will be happy to know that I've arranged to get the five thousand dollars for you."

"Have you, now?" Woodward asked.

"Yes, sir, I have. It wasn't easy, mind you. It took a lot of talking before I could convince Mr. Montgomery to go along with it. But, I have the five thousand dollars."

"Do you have the money with you?" Woodward asked.

"What? Oh, heavens no. It's still in the bank. You'll have to come to the bank with me and sign some papers before the money can be released. But not to worry," he added with a big smile. "The money is there for you, and Joel Montgomery has agreed to make the loan."

"I'm not signing any papers," Woodward said.

"What?"

"You heard me. I'm not going to the bank to sign any loan papers," Woodward repeated.

"But you must! Mr. Woodward, I don't know if you understand the seriousness of the situation here. The ransom demand is for five thousand dollars. This is your daughter's life you are dealing with. Surely you aren't going to balk at signing a few loan papers, are you?"

"I'm not going to sign any loan papers, because it isn't necessary. I have the money." Woodward reached around behind his chair, and brought forth a small cloth bag. He held the bag out toward Dempster. "It's all here. Five thousand dollars. You can count it."

"What?" Dempster asked, his voice weak with shock and disbelief. "But I thought, that is, you told me you didn't have the money."

"I lied," Woodward said. "I wasn't going to let the outlaws know I had the money until it was absolutely necessary. But, it's like you said, Mr. Dempster. This is my daughter's life I'm dealing with, so I'm not going to let five thousand dollars get in the way of her safety."

Dempster made no effort to take the money, so Malcolm took the cloth bag from Woodward, then stepped down to Dempster's buggy. He held the sack up, but the lawyer still made no effort to take it.

"What's the matter, Dempster?" Smoke asked. "Why aren't you taking the money? Aren't you the agent for this?"

"Oh . . . uh . . . yes. Yes, of course. I'll . . . uh . . . I'll take the money."

"Count it," Woodward said.

"No need to. I'm sure if you say it is all there, then it is all there," Dempster replied.

"Count it in front of these witnesses," Malcolm said. "Mr. Woodward wants it well understood that the ransom money for his daughter's release has been given to his"—Malcolm paused for a long second—"agent."

"All right." Dempster opened the sack, took out a stack of one hundred dollar bills and began counting them.

"Count them out loud," Smoke ordered.

"One hundred," Dempster started, and he enumerated each bill until he reached five thousand dollars.

"What will you do with that money now?" Smoke asked.

"I don't know. Uh, I wasn't told about this."

"What do you mean? You were told to collect five thousand dollars, weren't you?" Smoke said.

"Well, yes."

"They must have told you what to do with the money when you received it. Well, you've collected the five thousand dollars. Seems to me, your next step is to put that money into motion, so Mr. Woodward's daughter is returned to him."

"Y-yes," Dempster stammered. "Yes, that's what I will do." He put the money on the floor beside him, clicked at his horse, turned the buggy, and drove away.

"Where do you think he's going now?" Woodward asked.

Smoke grinned. "I believe he is going to see Garneau to see what he's supposed to do next."

"Pearlie, looks like he's comin' back from the Woodward place," Cal said.

"Get back down behind the crest so's there no chance of him seein' you," Pearlie said.

Cal turned his horse and guided him back down. The two men waited until they heard the buggy pass on the road below the ridge, then they rode back to the top and watched. They waited until the buggy was at least a quarter of a mile down the road before they followed.

"You think we're far enough back?" Cal said. "What if he looks behind him?"

"That buggy's kickin' up so much dust, there's no way he can see us."

The two men continued to follow, then saw him turn left when he reached the T in the road.

"Smoke was right," Cal said. "He's goin' straight to the Frenchman's place.

Pearlie nodded his agreement. "You ride back and tell Smoke. I'll keep on Dempster's tail."

Long Trek

"How did it go?" Garneau asked. "Did Woodward take out the loan?"

Dempster was sweating profusely, and he wiped his face with a handkerchief. "I wonder if I might have a drink of water."

"Yes, of course. Mr. Reeves, get Mr. Dempster a glass of water," Garneau ordered. Then he glanced back at Dempster. "Would you care for a little brandy?"

"Just water is fine, thank you."

Reeves poured a glass of water from a pitcher that sat on a side table, then brought it over to Dempster. Dempster gulped it down, then handed the empty glass back. "Thank you."

"Now, how did it go?"

"He gave me the money," Dempster said.

"Good, good," Garneau said, smiling as he rubbed his hands together. "Then he took out the loan. Did you explain to Montgomery that it was to be a forty-eight-hour loan? I want to be able to redeem it and—"

"There was no loan," Dempster said.

"What?"

"There was no loan," Dempster said, "Woodward had the five thousand dollars in cash. I have the money with me."

"I don't understand. Where did he get the money?"

"I don't know for sure," Dempster said. "But Smoke Jensen was there with him. As was Malcolm Puddle. It is my belief that one of them gave him the money."

Garneau swore, hitting his fist into his hand.

"What should I do with the money?" Dempster asked.

"I don't care what you do with the money," Garneau replied. He shook his head, then went over and poured himself a glass of brandy, swallowing it down before he spoke again.

"This isn't working out the way I planned."

CHAPTER 32

"You was right, Smoke," Cal said. "Dempster went straight to the Frenchman's place."

"Is he still there?"

"Far as I know he is. I left so I could come back and tell you about it. Pearlie is still there, watchin' out."

"Well, that confirms it," Smoke said. "Garneau is the one who took your daughter. That whole loan business was just to set up a situation where you would have to pledge your ranch in order to get the money."

"Who's this comin' up the road now?" Cal asked.

"Well, I'll be," Malcolm said.

"What is it, Malcolm?"

"That is Curly Roper. I had a brief . . . uh . . . meeting with him the day I arrived in Big Rock."

"Yes," Woodward said. "I heard about that meeting."

"I know Roper. He works for Garneau," Cal said.

"I wonder what he wants," Smoke said.

"Probably bringing some offer from Garneau—my farm for my daughter," Woodward said.

"No, I don't think so. Roper isn't someone he would send for that," Smoke said.

Roper rode all the way up to the porch, then stopped.

His horse began cropping some grass and he patted him on the neck.

"What do you want, Roper?" Woodward asked.

"I think I know where your daughter is."

"What? Where? Is she all right?"

"Look, I'm not sure of any of this, but I have a pretty good idea."

"What did Garneau tell you to say?" Malcolm asked.

Roper looked over at Malcolm. "Mr. Puddle, I know me 'n you didn't get off on the right foot, and that's all my fault. I'm sorry 'bout that. As for Garneau, that damnable excuse for a man didn't tell me nothin' to say. I can't work for him no more, not after all he's done.

"Like I said, I don't know for sure, but I got me an idea that your daughter might be in a cabin up on Ajax Mountain. The reason I say this is 'cause I know there's a cabin up there. Some of us have used it now and then. Well, the other day a couple of us was talkin' 'bout maybe goin' up there to do some huntin', but we was told we couldn't use it no more. Then Briggs and Carr left with some provisions like they was goin' to be gone for a long time. It turns out they left right after there was that article in the paper 'bout your daughter goin' to Atlanta.

"That didn't mean all that much to me until today, when that lawyer come to see Garneau. Reeves—he's the English feller that works as a valet—he overheard Garneau and the lawyer talkin'. Turns out Garneau was all upset that you had come up with the money, Mr. Woodward. Seems he had set up a loan for you, that if you didn't pay it back in forty-eight hours, he would be able to pay it off and take over your farm.

"When Reeves told me that—Reeves, he says he can't work for Garneau no more neither—well, sir, it got me to thinkin'. I wouldn't be none at all surprised if Garneau didn't send them two, Briggs and Carr, out to snatch that girl, just so's you'd have to borrow that money. I can't be sure, but if

I was layin' a bet on it, I would bet that Briggs and Carr are holdin' her, more 'n likely in that cabin up on Ajax."

"Mr. Roper, I appreciate you telling us this," Woodward said.

"Yes, sir, well, I just hope I'm right and that you can find the girl and get her back safe 'n all." With a nod, Roper turned, then rode away.

"Can we believe him?" Cal asked.

"I think so," Malcolm said. "It took a lot of guts for him to come over here to tell us that. The question isn't whether or not he is telling us the truth. The question is whether or not he is right."

"It's easy enough to find out," Smoke said. "I'm going to the cabin."

"I'm going with you," Malcolm said.

"You'd better let me go alone, Malcolm," Smoke said. "This is more my kind of game than yours."

"I'm going, Smoke, whether I go with you or by myself," Malcolm said. "I've got a personal interest in this."

Smoke looked at the intense young man for a moment, then he nodded. "All right. I see how it might be something pretty important to you. You're welcome to come along with me."

"What about Pearlie and me?" Cal asked.

"I think maybe the two of you should stay here with Mr. and Mrs. Woodward. If Garneau went so far as to take Lucy off the train, there's no telling what he might do next."

"All right," Cal agreed.

Ajax Mountain

"Who's that comin' this way?" Briggs asked, looking through the cabin window to the right of the door.

Carr went to the window on the other side to have a look. "It's Templeton."

"Huh. I wonder what he wants."

The two men stepped out in front of the cabin to watch as Templeton rode up, then dismounted.

"Did you bring us any whiskey?" Briggs asked. "We're near 'bout out."

"You don't need any more. You won't be staying here much longer," Templeton said.

"Why not?"

"Because it didn't work out the way Garneau wanted. Woodward got the money for the ransom somewhere else."

"You mean the ransom's been paid?" Carr asked.

"Yes."

"So what are we goin' to do now? We can't just let her go. Hell, she's seen us. She even knows our names," Carr said.

"Who said anything about letting her go?"

"So, what are you saying? We're supposed to kill her?"

"You got a problem with killing women?" Templeton asked.

"The only problem I got is, ever'body in the state of Colorado will be lookin' for us," Briggs said.

Templeton opened his saddlebag and pulled out two packets of money. "Here's twenty-five hundred dollars for each of you. That ought to be enough money for you to leave the state."

"Yeah!" Carr said, taking the money. "That'll do it."

"I got a question," Briggs said. "Since we're goin' to kill her anyway, is there any objection to us . . . uh . . . havin' a little fun with her?"

Templeton smirked. "Not as long as I'm first."

It had been a three-hour ride from Woodward's farm to Ajax Mountain. Smoke saw the cabin at the base of the mountain. "There it is."

"What do we do now? Just ride up to it?" Malcolm asked.

"No. We'll tie our horses off here in the trees, then go up

through that arroyo until we get to the other side of the cabin." Smoke pointed to a steep-sided dry gulch that led up the mountain.

The two men worked their way up until they were even with the cabin, then Smoke climbed up a little farther to take a look. The cabin was small, no more than ten feet by ten feet, with a single window in the back. There were no windows on the side.

"Somebody's coming to the cabin," Smoke said.

"Maybe we've made a mistake. Maybe Lucy isn't there."

"Wait a minute. No, she's there, all right. That's Templeton."

Smoke watched as two men came out of the cabin and began talking to Templeton. They talked to him for a moment, then all three went inside.

"What do we do now? Wait until nightfall?" Malcolm asked.

"No. I don't know what Templeton is doing here, but I don't like the looks of it. If we wait until nightfall it might be too late. We're going to have to go in now."

"Have you got any ideas?"

"I can approach the cabin from the side, but before I go in, I'm going to need something that will divert their attention from the front door."

"What if I break the back window?" Malcolm suggested.

"No," Smoke said. "I can approach the cabin from the side because there's no window. But if you come from the back, there's no cover, and they might see you."

"I can get as far as that big rock without being seen," Malcolm said, pointing to a boulder about twenty yards behind the cabin.

"That won't do you any good. You can't break it from there."

"Sure I can," Malcolm said with a smile. "I not only boxed when I lived in New York, I also played baseball. If I can find the right sized rock, I can throw it through the window from there."

"All right," Smoke said. "You get in position behind the cabin, I'll approach the side. When I give you the signal, you count to five, then throw it. That'll give me the opportunity to get around front at the same time you break the window."

"Wait. Let me find the right rock," Malcolm said, looking at the scattering of pebbles on the floor of the arroyo. "Ah, this one will do." He picked up one about half the size of a baseball.

The two men left to go to their chosen positions. Smoke got to the side of the cabin before Malcolm reached the boulder, so he waited as the young rancher worked his way up the gulley toward the big rock. As Smoke waited, he tried to hear what was going on inside the cabin, but the logs were so thick they blocked out any sound from inside.

Lucy looked up as the three men came back into the cabin. Seeing a third man gave her some hope.

"Has the ransom been paid? Have you come to get me?" she asked anxiously.

"Ha! Yeah, it's been paid, all right," Carr said. "Five thousand dollars. I got twenty five hundred and Briggs, he got the other twenty five hundred."

"Then you're going to let me go?"

"Yeah," Briggs said. "After," he added, grabbing his crotch.

When Malcolm nodded that he was in position, Smoke gave him the signal to begin counting, then moved quickly to the front of the cabin, counting softly. A moment after he reached the number five, he heard the sound of crashing glass, then someone called out, "What the hell!?"

Pulling his pistol, Smoke kicked open the door then fell to the floor inside, rolling away from the door with his gun at the ready. Because they had been startled by the breaking window, all three men had their pistols in their hands.

"It's Jensen!" Briggs shouted as he fired.

The bullet sped by Smoke's ear and plunged into the plank floor beside him. Even as Briggs shot at Smoke, Templeton rushed by him, fleeing the cabin. For the moment, Smoke had to let Templeton go. He was busy with the two men trying to kill him.

Four more shots were fired inside the little cabin, and Smoke fired two of them. Briggs went down with a hole in his forehead and Carr went down with a bullet in his heart.

Malcolm was running around to the front of the building just as Templeton came running out.

"Hold it!" Malcolm shouted.

Templeton turned and shot at him, but Malcolm dived to the ground and rolled, avoiding the bullet. Not until then did Malcolm pull the pistol he was carrying. "Shoot kinesthetically," he told himself.

He pointed the gun and fired, then saw Templeton get a surprised expression on his face, slap his hand over a bleeding hole in his chest, and go down

Getting up, Malcolm ran over to him and kicked the pistol away from the fallen man, but that wasn't necessary. Templeton was already dead.

Malcolm looked toward the cabin, and with gun in hand, started toward it.

Inside the cabin, Smoke regained his feet and approached each of the downed men to make certain neither of them offered any more danger.

None did.

He looked up as Malcolm entered the cabin with a smoking gun in his hand. "Templeton?" Smoke asked.

"Dead."

They looked around for Lucy. She was sitting on the edge of the bed, a pair of wide-open, frightened blue eyes staring back at them. She was bound, head and foot, by ropes.

"Malcolm! Mr. Jensen!" Lucy said. "I have never been happier to see anyone in my life!"

Malcolm rushed over to her and began untying her. As soon as her hands were untied, she threw her arms around Malcolm and began smothering him with kisses.

Smoke chuckled. "If you folks don't mind the interference, I'll untie her feet."

"Did they do anything to you?" Malcolm asked. "What I mean is . . . uh . . . did they?"

"No," Lucy said. "But they were about to, just before you got here."

Malcolm smiled in relief that she had not been harmed, and also at the idea of playing a role in saving her.

"Well, there's no sense in being a hero, unless you can be a hero who arrives just in the nick of time," Malcolm said.

"Oh, the money!" Lucy said.

"What money?"

Lucy pointed to the bodies of Briggs and Carr. "The ransom money. They have it. But even though the ransom was paid, they weren't going to let me go."

"You don't even have to think about that," Malcolm said. "You're safe now, and I'm not going to let anything else happen to you."

CHAPTER 33

Big Rock

Curly Roper was standing at the bar in the Brown Dirt Cowboy, staring into a mug of beer as he tried to decide what he should do next. He no longer had a job, and was pretty sure none of the local ranchers would hire him, not after having worked for Garneau. If he was honest with himself, it wasn't just that he had worked with Garneau.

Roper had been pretty much a troublemaker all along, often getting into fights, sometimes getting drunk and destroying private property. There was nothing left for him around Big Rock.

"Roper!" a loud high-pitched voice called.

He knew at once who it was.

"Roper, I'm talking to you."

Roper turned toward Jeremiah Priest.

"The colonel's not very pleased with you, Roper."

"I don't care whether he's pleased or not," Roper said. "I don't work for the colonel no more."

"It ain't you quittin' that's got him upset. It's how you done it. Word is, you went to see Smoke Jensen, and you told him about a huntin' cabin. A cabin that the colonel wanted to keep private, just for his own men."

"What if I did?"

"Well, then that means that me 'n you are goin' to have to come to some sort of a settlement."

"I got nothing to say to you, or do with you."

"Yeah, you do. I'm callin' you out, Roper."

"You can call me out all you want. I ain't drawin' on you." Roper doubled up his fists. "But if you'd like to settle this with your fists, why, I'd be glad to oblige you."

"I said, draw," Priest repeated in a cold, flat, voice.

The others in the saloon knew there was about to be gunplay and quietly, but deliberately, moved to get out of the way of any flying lead.

Roper held his hand out in front of him. "Look here. I'm takin' off my gun belt, and I'm layin' it on the bar." He held both hands up in the air. "Now, as you can see, I ain't wearin' no gun. So whatever you got in mind, you can just forget about it."

"Go ahead and pull your gun from the holster," Priest offered. "I won't draw till you got it in your hand."

"I told you, I ain't goin' to get into no gunfight with you."

Roper picked up his drink, hoping by that action to show his defiance. What he showed instead was his fear, for his hand was shaking so badly he had to put the mug back down before all the beer splashed out.

"Pull that gun, Roper."

Roper reached out toward his gun and holster. Instead of pulling the gun, he pushed the belt across the bar, and it fell with a loud thump to the floor on the other side of the bar.

"What gun?" Roper asked with a nervous smile.

"Somebody give him one," Priest said coldly. He pulled his lips into a sinister smile. "Mr. Roper seems to have dropped his."

"I don't want a gun," Roper said.

When no one offered Roper a gun, Priest pointed to the cowboy standing at the far end of the bar. "Give him your gun," Priest ordered. "You aren't going to be using it, are you?"

"He don't want a gun," the man said.

"Oh, I think he does."

"Listen, Priest, we can all see that Roper don't want to fight. Why don't you just leave it be?"

"I said, give him your gun."

"I ain't goin' to do that. If I give him a gun, you'll kill him."

"That's right."

"Well, I don't want no part of it."

"You got no choice, friend. You'll either give him your gun so I can kill him, or you can keep the gun, and I'll kill you. Now, which one is it goin' to be?"

"Now, just wait a minute here! I don't know what kinda beef you got with Roper there, but I got none with you, and you got none with me!" the cowboy said, holding out his hands to stop Priest from doing anything.

"Give him the gun, or use it yourself," Priest said again.

The cowboy paused for just a moment longer, then he looked over at Roper.

"This ain't my doin', Roper. I want you an' ever'one in here to know this ain't none of my doin'." The cowboy took his gun out of the holster, put it on the bar, then gave the gun a shove. It slid down the bar, smashing through a few of the glasses that had been abandoned by drinkers who, when the trouble started, had stepped away from the bar.

The pistol stopped just in front of Roper.

"Pick it up," Priest said to Roper.

Roper looked at the pistol. He chewed his bottom lip, while sweat broke out on his forehead. "I . . . I ain't goin' to do it. You ain't goin' to have no excuse to shoot me."

"Do it," Priest said again.

"No, I ain't goin' to, and there ain't nothin' you can do that will make me fight you."

Priest jerked his pistol from his holster and pulled the

trigger. There was a flash of light, then a roar of exploding gunpowder, followed by a billowing cloud of acrid blue smoke.

Shouts of disapproval came from everyone in the saloon who thought Priest had shot Roper. But when the smoke drifted away, they were able to see what had actually happened. Roper was holding his hand to the left side of his head with blood spilling through his fingers. Priest's bullet had clipped off a piece of his earlobe.

"Are you goin' to fight or not?"

"I told you, I ain't goin' to fight you!" Roper yelled angrily.

A second shot sounded and flesh flew from his right earlobe.

"Pick up the gun!"

"No!" Roper shouted back, covering both ears. Blood streamed through the fingers of both hands. "You people! Do something! Stop him! Can't you see he's goin' to kill me?"

"What's goin' on in here?" a new voice said and, looking toward the swinging doors, everyone saw Deputy Worley standing just inside the door with a gun in his hand.

"This ain't none o' your business, Deputy," Priest said.

"Deputy, this man is trying to force me into a gunfight," Roper said.

"Is that right?" Worley asked.

"Hell, Deputy, I'm just tryin' to give him a little backbone is all," Priest said.

"All right, Priest, take your gun out. Do it real slow. Then drop it on the floor."

"Deputy, if I take my gun out, it ain't goin' to be slow. Now, why don't you just back on out of here and leave the two of us to settle our difference of opinion?"

"No, Deputy, don't go!" Roper said.

"Do what I told you, Priest. Take your gun out and drop it on the floor!"

"I warned you, Deputy. There can't nobody say I started this here fight between me 'n you."

"There ain't goin' to be no fight. You are going to pull your pistol out and drop it like I told you, then me 'n you are goin' to jail till whatever is goin' on here is all settled," Worley said.

Priest drew, fired, and replaced his gun in his holster so quickly that some in the room, who were looking at Worley, trying to gauge his reaction to what was going on, didn't even see what happened.

There was the sound of a gunshot, a look of shock and pain on Worley's face, then his pistol clattered to the floor. With his hand over his wound, he took a couple steps forward, then collapsed.

There were gasps and shouts of surprise from the others in the saloon.

Priest turned his attention back to Roper. "All right. Now it's just me 'n you again. Pick up that gun."

Roper made no move toward the gun, so Priest fired again, sending a bullet crashing into Roper's kneecap. Roper shouted out in pain, then bent over to grab it. "You're crazy!"

"Pick up the gun," Priest said calmly.

Roper stared at Priest through fear-crazed, hate-filled eyes. Suddenly, the fear left his eyes. They became flat and void, as if he had already accepted the fact that he was a dead man. He had one emotion left, and one emotion only, and that was absolute, blind fury. He let out a bellow of rage that could be heard all up and down Center Street, from the undertaker's establishment all the way down to the stagecoach depot.

"You pig-faced, scum-sucking—" Roper made a mad, desperate, and clumsy grab for the gun.

Priest watched, smiling broadly. He waited, not only until Roper had the gun in his hand but actually brought it to bear.

For just an instant, but an instant only, Roper thought he might have a chance, and he raised his thumb to cock the pistol. His thumb didn't even reach the hammer before Priest fired.

Unlike the other bullets that had been used to tantalize, enrage, and torture Roper, the bullet was energized to kill, hitting him in the neck. Surprised by the suddenness of it, he dropped his gun, unfired, and clutched his throat. He fell back against the bar, then slid down, dead before he reached the floor.

Priest looked around the saloon, a broad smile on his face. "Is there anyone in here who feels that I didn't give these two men a fair chance?"

When nobody responded, Priest walked over to the bar and picked up Roper's beer. "I may as well drink this." He laughed. "Roper sure as hell ain't goin' to be finishin' it."

CHAPTER 34

Carro de Bancada

The aroma of cooking meat wafted over the ground as Cal and Pearlie turned a quarter of a steer on a spit over a fire. The meat had been salted, peppered, and basted with a spicy sauce, and the forty men, women, and children gathered in Malcolm's front yard visited, laughed, and made comments as to how good everything smelled. A piano had been brought over from Sugarloaf, and Johnny McVey had been invited to the party to provide the music.

There was a dual reason for the gathering. All the neighbors had come to celebrate Lucy's safe return, as well as the announcement that Malcolm and Lucy were soon to be married.

"I reckon we don't have to worry none about you goin' back to New York now, do we, Malcolm?" Tom Keefer asked.

Malcolm put his arm around Lucy and drew her to him. "Now, if I've come two thousand miles to find someone like this, why in the world would I want to go back to New York?"

The others laughed.

"No reason at all, Malcolm," Logan said.

"Hey!" Pearlie called. "This meat's done if you folks are ready to eat."

"Ready to eat?" Keefer said. "I been smellin' that meat cookin' so long I'm near 'bout ready to come over there and start gnawin' on it while it's still on the spit."

"Come on, Johnny. You're the only one who's been working," Malcolm said. "So you get to go first."

"Hey, what if I start playing my Jew's harp?" Logan asked. "Could I go next?"

"I've heard you with that thing," Otto Speer said. "I think if you promise *not* to play it, you should go first."

Again there was laughter, but the laughter was interrupted when Keefer called out, "There's riders comin'! A lot of 'em!"

"At least four of them," Logan said. "Maybe we'd better get our guns, and get the women and kids out of here."

"No, wait," Smoke said. "I know those men. That's Taylor, Gately, Anderson, and Calloway. They're working for Garneau, but I don't think they mean trouble."

"They sure ain't ridin' in a way that would make you think they're lookin' for trouble," Keefer said.

The four riders came up to the yard, then stopped.

"Hello, Gately," Smoke said. "What brings you boys over here?"

"We've all left the Frenchman." Gately looked over at Woodward. "Mr. Woodward, it was the Frenchman what took your daughter. There didn't any of us know about it for a while. Then, Curly Roper, he found out, an' he quit. Then, this mornin', the Frenchman sent Priest into town."

"And Priest killed Roper and the sheriff," Anderson said.

"What? Monte has been killed?" Smoke asked in shock.

"It wasn't the sheriff," Taylor said. "It was one of his deputies. Worley."

"Smoke!" Sally said, grabbing Smoke's arm.

"Was Worley a friend of yours, Mr. Jensen?" Taylor asked.

"Yes, he was."

"I'm sorry to be the one to tell you about the deputy,"

Taylor said. "But, I reckon you already know that Curly Roper was a friend of mine."

"Mr. Jensen," Calloway said. "We didn't just happen to come this way. Colonel Garneau wanted me to give you a message. After the others and I found out what happened to Curly, we decided to quit Garneau. At first, I wasn't even goin' to bring you the message, but we talked it over and figured you probably should be told."

"What is that?"

"Priest is in town waitin' for you. It is Colonel Garneau's intention to have Priest kill you. With you out of the way, he intends to take over the whole valley. Sugarloaf, too."

"He's not going to be able to do that if I kill Priest, is he?" Smoke asked.

"Have you ever seen Priest in action?" Taylor asked.

"No."

"Well, I have. I've seen some awful fast gunmen in my day. I know you're fast, 'cause I've seen you. But I feel I ought to tell you, Mr. Jensen, that I think Priest is a mite faster."

"There's always that possibility," Smoke agreed.

"You also should know that Priest is settin' himself up an edge," Gately added.

"What kind of edge?" Malcolm asked.

"Merlin Mathis. He's goin' to be somewhere that'll give him a chance to take a shot at you."

"Plus, Garneau is in town his ownself," Anderson added. "So, really, you got three of 'em to worry about."

"What about the others?" Woodward asked. "What about the army he's put together? Will they be in town as well?"

"There ain't that much left of the army." Taylor said. "If Garneau gets his way, and Smoke Jensen is kilt, what's left of the army—them that ain't already been kilt—will more 'n likely stay with him. But if it winds up that Priest and Mathis was to happen to get kilt, I doubt the others will stay with Garneau. Since we left this mornin', I can tell you that Garneau ain't got no cowboys left at all."

"And you say Priest is in town now?"

"Yes, sir, he is."

"Smoke," Sally said anxiously.

Smoke reached over to put his hand on hers. "Listen, where are our manners?" He smiled broadly. "You men go tie your horses off somewhere and sit down to eat with us. As you can see, we have plenty of food."

"And it's good, too," Cal said. "I've done been sampling it."

Taylor looked quickly toward the others as if determining whether or not the invitation was from all of them.

"Yes," Woodward said, nodding his head and smiling at the Long Trek riders. "Smoke is right. You boys get down off your horses and come join us."

"We'll eat first, then I'll go into town," Smoke said. "I don't like to work on an empty stomach."

The men dismounted, secured their horses, and joined those who were celebrating Lucy's safe return and the engagement announcement of Lucy and Malcolm.

Big Rock

By midafternoon, nearly everyone in town was aware of the possibility of an upcoming gunfight between Smoke and Priest. To a person, they wanted to see Smoke triumph, and not just figuratively. They actually wanted to see the gunfight go down. To that end, nearly three hundred people were out on the streets when Smoke, Sally, Cal, Pearlie, and Malcolm rode into town.

"You folks wait here at Longmont's," Smoke suggested to the others.

"Where is Priest?" Cal asked.

"I expect he'll be here soon enough," Smoke said. "As soon as he gets word I'm in town."

Priest was waiting in the Brown Dirt with Garneau when one of the citizens of the town came into the saloon.

"You was waitin' on Smoke Jensen?"

"Yes."

"Well, he just come into town. He's over on Front Street, standin' out in front of Longmont's.

Priest smiled, then glanced over at Garneau. "Here's where I earn my money."

"Let me go first," Garneau said. "I want to be in position to watch this."

"All right." Priest smiled. "I don't mind performing before an audience."

"Well, you've got a good one today," the man who brought the message of Smoke's arrival said. "Looks to me like damn near the whole town is linin' both sides of Front Street."

Priest waited until Garneau left, then looked over at Mathis. "Get in position."

Mathis nodded, then stepped out front and pulled a rifle from his saddle sheath. He hurried down Center, cut in between the post office and the McCoy building, then stepped in between Kathy's Dress Shop, and Earl's Barbershop. He pressed up against the wall of the barbershop and looked across the street. He saw Smoke in the road in front of Longmont's. Garneau was standing on the boardwalk in front of the newspaper office. Looking to his right and down the street, he saw Priest approaching Jensen.

Most of the crowd got out of the street then, going into the buildings that fronted the street in order to see what was going on. A few of the braver ones stayed outside, though they did step back. One of those who remained outside was Lucien Garneau.

Priest stopped a few yards away from Longmont's and smiled. "Well, now, you're here. I have to tell you, Jensen, I wasn't sure you had the guts to face me. I admire you for that." The smile left his face. "But this is where it all ends for you."

"It may. But whatever happens between you and me, it will definitely end for your boss."

"Ha! Are you saying you are going to kill Garneau?"

"That is exactly what I'm saying."

"Go ahead."

"Priest!" Garneau shouted. "What are you saying? What are you doing? He means it. Can't you see that?"

"Oh, yes, I see that. But Jensen knows that I mean it too. Go ahead, Jensen. Kill Garneau."

"If he's dead, who pays you?" Smoke asked.

"Oh hell, I'm not worried about that," Priest replied. "I've already got half the money I was going to get. But this here thing between me 'n you ain't about money anymore. I can't leave town without killing you. You understand that, don't you?"

"That's probably true," Smoke said. "But that's your problem."

"Not just my problem," Priest said. "We're going to have to deal with it, both of us, right here, right now. You can see for yourself, Jensen, ever'one wants to see us shoot it out. Well, what they really want to see is you kill me." He chuckled, then took in the crowd with a wave of his hand. "I almost feel bad about disappointin' them."

"Well, I'll try not to disappoint them. I'll kill you, right after I kill Garneau."

"Look, either kill him or quit talkin' about it. I really don't care which. Then, let's you and me settle this thing, once and for all."

"Malcolm?" Smoke called.

"Yes, Smoke?"

"Keep an eye on Garneau while I take care of Priest."

"I'll be happy to do that," Malcolm said, pulling his pistol and pointing it at Garneau.

Smoke turned toward Priest. The crowd backed away even farther to give the two men more room."

"Ever since I first heard of you, I've been wonderin' which one of us was the fastest," Priest said. "I reckon we're about to find out."

"Smoke, across the street!" Malcolm shouted.

Smoke looked around to see that Mathis was raising a rifle to his shoulder. Smoke drew and fired, and Mathis dropped the rifle, then tumbled forward.

Smoke knew, without having to look, that Priest was taking advantage of the distraction to draw. Smoke fell to his stomach an instant before Priest fired, feeling the concussion of the bullet as it passed less than an inch over the top of his head.

Smoke returned fire from his position on the ground, and Priest caught the ball high in his chest. The gunman fired a second time, but it was more a convulsive than an aimed shot, and the bullet went into the dirt.

Priest took a couple of staggering steps toward Smoke and tried to raise his pistol, but it fell from his hands. He smiled, then coughed, and flecks of blood came from his mouth. He breathed hard a couple times. "I was sure I was faster than you."

"Looks like you were wrong," Smoke said easily as Priest fell to the ground.

Someone leaned down and put his hand to Priest's neck. He looked up at the others. "He's dead."

Sherriff Carson, who had watched the whole thing, walked over to Garneau. "You are under arrest."

"For what?"

"For conspiracy to murder."

CHAPTER 35

One month later

Robert Dempster was tried and found guilty of fraud and grand larceny. He was currently in jail, awaiting transportation to the state prison in Cañon City.

Lucien Garneau was tried and found guilty of conspiracy to murder. He was sentenced to hang. A gallows had been constructed at the east end of Front Street, right in front of the blacksmith shop. It was visible from the window of Garneau's jail cell.

On the day he was to be hanged, Inspector Laurent presented himself before Sheriff Carson. "Sheriff, I am Inspector André Laurent of the French Military Police. I have tried, without success, to extradite your prisoner back to France."

"Oh. Well, I have to tell you, Mr. Laurent, if you were to take the Frenchman away from us now, there would be a lot of very upset folks. You see, he has been responsible for quite a few people getting killed since he came to Colorado."

"I do not doubt that, Sheriff. Before he left France, he committed murder, and he stole two and one half million francs from the French Army."

Carson let out a low whistle. "Damn! How much money is that in American?"

"One half million dollars."

"That's how he was able to buy so much land," Carson said. "Yes, I can see why your government would want him. But, if it's any consolation to you, he has been sentenced to hang, and he will hang this very afternoon. You can watch him, if you like. We can furnish an affidavit signed by the judge that the sentence was carried out. That should satisfy your government."

"Yes, I'm sure it will. May I see him?"

"Sure, I don't see why not. He is in back. I'll take you to him."

Laurent followed the sheriff into the back of the jail. When they reached the back corner, the prisoner was staring out the window toward the gallows.

"Garneau, you have a visitor," Sheriff Carson said.

"When you address me, Sheriff, you will address me as Colonel the Marquis Garneau," the prisoner said. "You may hang me, Monsieur, but you will not rob me of my honor."

"*Vous ne pouvez pas être dépouillé de l'honneur, Mouchette, parce que vous êtes dépourvu de tout honneur!*" Laurent said. To Sheriff Carson he added, "I will translate for you, Sheriff. I told him he cannot be robbed of honor, because he is devoid of honor. He is neither colonel nor marquis. And his name isn't Garneau. It is Mouchette, Pierre Mouchette."

"*Qui êtes-vous?* Who are you?" Garneau asked.

"I am Inspector André Laurent of the Gendarmerie Nationale. I have come to see justice done for the murder of Sergeant Dubois and for the theft of two and a half million francs. Did you really think you would get away with it, Mouchette?"

"Ha! I did get away with it. There will be no guillotine for me."

"The guillotine is quick and painless. Hanging is a much slower, and more agonizing, way to die."

Involuntarily, Garneau-Mouchette lifted his hand to his neck.

Laurent turned to Sheriff Carson. "Will there be some sort of reading of the pronouncement from the gallows?"

"Yes, the judge's order and authorization must be read."

"Please, Monsieur Sheriff, when you read the orders, do not dishonor France by calling this imposter a colonel and a marquis. And could you add that he is also being executed for murdering an innocent soldier who was under his command?"

Sheriff Carson nodded. "I don't know how the judge is going to like that, but I'll do it for you."

He was no longer thinking of himself as Garneau. It was as Mouchette he was born, and it would be as Mouchette that he would die. As he stood on the gallows floor, his arms tied to his sides, his legs tied together, he looked out at the faces of the people drawn to the event. Some of them reflected a sense of fear and horror, others morbid fascination, and still others, an obvious show of satisfaction that he was paying for his crimes.

Near the back of the crowd he saw Amy, the whore from the Brown Dirt Cowboy, and recalled the night he spent with her. He smiled and nodded. Amy looked away.

He had seen his coffin when he climbed the steps, but it was beneath the gallows floor and he couldn't see it any longer.

A camera had been set up on a tripod. The photographer was taking pictures. He had just taken one, because he was removing the plate and replacing it with another.

"Hey, Garneau, when you hit the bottom of the rope, are you going to dance for us?" someone shouted.

Mouchette didn't answer. He had already vowed to himself that he would not perform for them. He would exhibit no emotion whatsoever.

A priest approached him. "Mr. Garneau, I am—"

"My name is Mouchette. Pierre Mouchette."

The priest looked toward Sheriff Carson, who was also standing on the gallows floor. "I don't understand. I thought the man I was to minister to was named Garneau."

"Garneau was his assumed name, Father. His real name is Mouchette."

The priest nodded, then turned back to the prisoner. "I am Father Sharkey, an Episcopal priest. May I minister to you?"

"I am Catholic, *Père* Sharkey. Or I was when I was a boy and actually went to church."

"It's the same God."

"Yes, well, it's a little late for all that, isn't it?"

"With God time is both instantaneous and eternal."

"Go ahead."

Father Sharkey began reading from the Book of Common Prayer. "O Father of mercies, and God of all comfort; we fly unto thee for succor in behalf of this thy servant who is now under sentence of condemnation. The day of his calamity is at hand, and he is accounted as one of those who go down into the pit."

Sharkey made the sign of the cross. "Unto God's gracious mercy and protection we commit thee. The Lord bless thee, and keep thee. The Lord make his face to shine upon thee, and be gracious unto thee. The Lord lift up his countenance upon thee, and give thee peace, both now and evermore. Amen."

Sharkey looked over at Sheriff Carson and nodded. Carson walked with him to the thirteen steps that led down to the ground. The priest continued down the steps.

The sheriff looked at the crowd. "I am instructed to read the death warrant issued by the court of Eagle County, Colorado."

He began reading the judge's warrant of execution. "For the crime of accessory to the murder of Humboldt Puddle and others, and for the murder of Sergeant Antoine Dubois, Pierre Mouchette, also known as Lucien Garneau, is to be hanged by the neck until pronounced dead by the attending physician in pursuance to the instructions contained in this warrant. Let no one present question this warrant."

A moment later, the sheriff went over to Mouchette, holding a black hood in his hand. "Are you ready?"

Mouchette chuckled. "Suppose I told you that I needed about forty more years before I was ready. Would you wait?"

"I'm afraid not."

"Wait, before you put it on, let me find Laurent in the crowd. I know he is here. Where is he?"

"He is standing just to the right of the foot of the steps," Sheriff Carson said.

"Laurent, tell those with whom I served that I died like a soldier," Mouchette shouted.

"I shall," Laurent answered.

Mouchette watched as the hood came down over his face, realizing that, as of that very second, he had seen the world for the very last time. He could see some light coming through the hood, but nothing else.

With the outside world gone, he saw—as real and present as it had been in his youth—a small boat upon the Seine. A man was rowing the boat, and a pretty woman, holding a red parasol against the sun, was sitting in the bow.

"Look, Mama, the woman in the small boat is holding a red parasol," he had said then, and, quietly, he mouthed those same words again. "*Rechercher, Maman, la femme dans le petit bâteau est la tenue d'une ombrelle rouge.*"

He held on to that peaceful and innocent scene as he felt

the rough texture of the rope when the noose was fitted over his head, and the knot pushed up against the back of his neck.

"May God have mercy on your soul," Sheriff Carson said, speaking so quietly only Mouchette could hear him.

Mouchette heard Sheriff Carson's footsteps as he walked back across the gallows floor.

He heard the pealing of church bells.

He heard the whistle of an approaching train.

He heard the sound of the trapdoor opening, then felt his stomach leap up into his . . .

EPILOGUE

Smoke and Sally were in a spring wagon, driving back to Sugarloaf after having attended the wedding and reception of Mr. and Mrs. Malcolm Puddle.

"It was nice of Laurent to sign a quit claim on behalf of the French government for Garneau's land," Sally said. "Now it belongs to the state of Colorado, but I'm wondering what is going to happen to it?"

"The ranchers and farmers who have land adjacent to his are going to buy as much of it as they can afford to enlarge their own holdings. I expect I'll buy the rest. That way, we aren't likely to ever run into any more Mouchettes. Or Garneaus, for that matter."

"What about Frying Pan Creek? What will become of it?"

"It will remain property of the state. That way nobody can ever dam it up again or use it as a weapon against other landholders."

"Good idea." Sally moved closer to Smoke, took his upper right arm in both her hands, then leaned her head against his shoulder. "Wasn't the wedding beautiful?"

Smoke chuckled. "You say that about every wedding you've ever attended."

"Well, every wedding I've ever attended has been beautiful. Ours was the most beautiful of all."

"Yeah," Smoke said. "It's almost a shame it wasn't a real preacher, and we aren't really married."

"What?" Sally shouted.

Smoke began to laugh, and Sally started hitting him on the arm. "You are impossible. Why would you say such a thing?"

"I don't know. Maybe to put a little excitement in your life?"

Sally laughed as well, then kissed him on the cheek. "Kirby Jensen, being married to you is all the excitement I will ever need . . . or ever want."

JOHNSTONE ON JOHNSTONE

William W. Johnstone was born in southern Missouri, the youngest of four children. He was raised with strong moral and family values by his minister father, and tutored by his schoolteacher mother. Despite this, he quit school at age fifteen.

"I have the highest respect for education," he says, "but such is the folly of youth, and wanting to see the world beyond the four walls and the blackboard."

True to this vow, Bill attempted to enlist in the French Foreign Legion ("I saw Gary Cooper in *Beau Geste* when I was a kid and I thought the French Foreign Legion would be fun") but was rejected, thankfully, for being underage. Instead, he joined a traveling carnival and did all kinds of odd jobs. It was listening to the veteran carny folk, some of whom had been on the circuit since the late 1800s, telling amazing tales about their experiences that planted the storytelling seed in Bill's imagination.

"They were mostly honest people, despite the bad reputation traveling carny shows had back then," Bill remembers. "There was one guy named Picky, who got that name because he was a master pickpocket. He could steal a man's socks right off his feet without him knowing. Believe me, Picky got us chased out of more than a few towns."

After a few months of this grueling existence, Bill returned home and finished high school. Next came stints as a deputy sheriff in the Tallulah, Louisiana, sheriff's department, followed by a hitch in the U.S. Army. Then he began a career in radio broadcasting at KTLD in Tallulah that would last sixteen years. It was here that he honed his storytelling skills, creating oddball characters and unusual situations to put them into, for his radio program. Bill played all the parts as well as writing them. "My favorite was a flimflam man named Skip Towne, a con artist who operated one step ahead of the law and was always trying to sell you stuff like left-handed screwdrivers and Norwegian smoke snifters. And then there was Newton Chickenheart, the most cowardly man in the West.

Bill turned to writing in 1970 but it wouldn't be until 1979 that his first novel, *The Devil's Kiss*, was published. Thus began the full-time writing career of William W. Johnstone. He wrote horror (*The Uninvited*), thrillers (*The Last of the Dog Team*), even a romance novel or two. Then, in February 1983, *Out of the Ashes* was published. Searching for his missing family in the aftermath of a post-apocalyptic America, rebel mercenary and patriot Ben Raines is united with the civilians of the Resistance forces and moves to the forefront of a revolution for the nation's future.

Out of the Ashes was a smash. The series would continue for the next twenty years, winning Bill three generations of fans all over the world. The series was often imitated but never duplicated. "We all tried to copy *The Ashes* series," said one publishing executive, "but Bill's uncanny ability, both then and now, is to predict in which direction the political winds were blowing." (The Ashes series also, Bill notes with a touch of pride, got him on the FBI's Watch List for its less than flattering portrayal of big government.)

In late 1985, Bill's first western, *The Last Mountain Man*, was published and it was here that Bill has found his greatest success. In fact, western fans couldn't get enough of Smoke Jensen, so Bill created *Preacher*. Next came *Blood Bond,* the western adventures of blood brothers Matt Bodine and Sam Two Wolves.

Today, Bill's western series, co-authored by J.A. Johnstone, include The Mountain Man, Matt Jensen: The Last Mountain Man, Preacher, The Family Jensen, Luke Jensen: Bounty Hunter, Eagles, MacCallister (an Eagles spin-off), Sidewinders, The Brothers O'Brien, Sixkiller, The Last Gunfighter, and the upcoming new series Flintlock and The Trail West, most of which have propelled him onto both the *USA Today* and *New York Times* bestseller lists.

"The western," Bill says, "is one of the few true art forms that is one hundred percent American. I liken the western as America's version of England's Arthurian legends like Robin Hood or the Knights of the Round Table. Starting with the 1902 publication of *The Virginian* by Owen Wister and followed by authors like Zane Grey, Max Brand, Ernest Haycox, and of course Louis L'Amour, the western has helped define the cultural landscape of American entertainment.

"I'm no goggle-eyed college academic, so when my fans ask me why the western is as popular now as it was a century ago, I don't offer a 200-page thesis. Instead, I can only offer this: the western is honest—we can't change the way real events turned out. Sure, we can embellish, exaggerate, and yes, I admit it, occasionally play a little fast and loose with the facts, but only to enhance the enjoyment of readers.

"Put another way, there's a line in one of my favorite Westerns of all time, *The Man Who Shot Liberty Valance,* where the newspaper editor tells the young reporter, 'When the truth becomes legend, print the legend.'

"These are the words I live by."

BUTCHERY
OF THE
MOUNTAIN MAN

PREFACE

In 1923, which is two years before this writing, I undertook the task of putting together a scholarly tome on the Vanguards of Western Expansion. Heroes, Trappers, Indian Fighters, Explorers, Scouts, and Adventurers were to be my subjects, but I faced the immediate problem of deciding who should be the focus of my study. I had many to choose from: Kit Carson, John C. Frémont, James Bridger, Jedediah Smith, Arthur "Preacher" Gregory (though the last name is uncertain), Kirby "Smoke" Jensen, Matt Jensen, Ian Mac-Callister, his son Falcon MacCallister, a cousin, Duff Mac-Callister, and John "Liver-Eating" Jackson. Most will agree that all warrant their own book, and in many cases those books have, indeed, already been written.

But the decision was made for me when I realized that as of October 1923, the time I began the project, one of the most storied of all the aforementioned heroes, Smoke Jensen, was still alive. Furthermore, my initial investigation led me to the inescapable fact that Smoke Jensen and John Jackson were not only friends, but shared the incredible adventure of Liver-Eating Jackson's personal war with the Apsáalooke, or, as they are more popularly known, Crow Indians. The decision was made. I would write about Smoke Jensen and John Jackson. I contacted Smoke Jensen and brought him to the University of Colorado, where, by making use of the magic *of voice recording, I was able to extract the story herein presented to the reader.*

Mr. Jensen proved to be an excellent storyteller, and I apologize to those readers who must absorb this account from the printed page while I was able to actually hear the story from his own mouth. And, because of the transformative power of Mr. Jensen's spoken words, I was miraculously transported back in time to actually witness the events described here.

Discerning readers will soon realize that Jensen possesses the knack for noting and relating details, which is the prime ingredient of the storyteller's art. He has preserved a detailed picture of how things were in the century previous. The varied roles he played during his active career involved him in so many different activities that his own life story constitutes a fair approach to an encyclopedia of life on the American frontier.

Quite apart from its informational value, Smoke Jensen's story provides grand entertainment for the general reader. The scholar, however, intent upon reconstructing accurately the life of the past, will naturally ask how faithfully Smoke Jensen has recorded it.

Smoke Jensen's memory is quite detailed and astonishing. He can recall all the interesting experiences of his own eventful life, and the day and date of almost everything that has happened in the mountain region within the last sixty years. I have included in this book Jensen's verbatim accounts, recalled from his personal participation, as well as his recollection of stories relayed to him by his friend John Jackson.

I have also included, at various places through the book, editorial inserts if I believe that I have ex cathedra information that will enhance the readers' appreciation of the story herein told.

Jacob W. Armbruster, Ph.D.
Professor of History, University of Colorado
Boulder, Colorado
April 9, 1925

CHAPTER 1

"I have taken your proposal to the Board of Regents," Dr. Norlin said. "And, I might add, I did so with my own, heartiest recommendation that it be approved."

"And?" Professor Armbruster said.

Dr. Norlin smiled, then slid the papers he was holding across the desk. "The approval was unanimous. You will be given the time, the resources, and an intern to help you with your project. What are you going to call it?"

"I'm going to call it *Vanguards of Western Expansion*."

"And it is our understanding that you plan to publish it?" Dr. Norlin asked.

"Yes, Runestone Press has agreed to publish it. In my proposal, I offered thirty percent of the royalties to the university. They were okay with that?"

"Well, they do have a counterproposal," Dr. Norlin replied. "They thought that because you would be researching and writing this book on university time, as well as using university assets, that a fifty-fifty split would be more appropriate."

Professor Armbruster stuck his hand across the desk. "Agreed," he said.

Dr. Norlin chuckled. "You had actually planned that all along, hadn't you?"

"Yes. I figured if I offered thirty percent . . . but agreed to giving up half, that the Board of Regents would feel a sense of accomplishment."

"I'll never say a word," Dr. Norlin replied with a smile. "What is your first step?"

"My first step is to invite Kirby Jensen to come to the university for interviews, and hope that he agrees."

"Do you think that he will?"

"I don't know. I certainly hope so. If he doesn't, this project is dead before it even gets off the ground."

"Well, I wish you the best of luck in getting him to come," Dr. Norlin said. "I really do believe in your project. I think it would not only be good for the university, I think it would also be a good resource for historians who are studying the western expansion for many years to come."

Sugarloaf Ranch

Smoke was sitting in a swing on his front porch, peeling an apple, and throwing the peels to his dog. In front of the house was a Model T Ford, which Smoke had modified. Behind the front seat and extending to beyond the rear axle was a truck bed, about the size of the bed of a buckboard. He called it his motorized buckboard, but some of the younger cowboys on his ranch called it a pickup truck.

Painted on the door of the truck, in arched letters, were the words SUGARLOAF RANCH. Beneath the arch was a picture of a horse's head, the markings on its face resembling the number seven. Under the horse's head was the name KIRBY "SMOKE" JENSEN.

Smoke was seventy-three years old, and still fast enough on the draw, and accurate enough with his shooting that he was often called upon to give demonstrations of his skills.

The speed with which he could still extract his pistol and fire continued to amaze people.

He saw a cloud of dust billowing up from the road, and because this road ended right here, on Sugarloaf, he knew that whoever it was, was coming to the house. And, from the speed at which the vehicle was traveling, he also knew who it was, even before he could actually see the car.

"You know what I think, Dog?" he asked.

Dog cocked his head at an angle to study Smoke's face.

"It's not what I think, it's what I know. That's Sally, coming up the road like a scalded-ass cat. I think she only knows two speeds: stop and fast."

He watched until the car, a light blue Duesenberg phaeton, emerged from the cloud of dust. Thankfully she slowed down before she got too close, so that the dust dissipated before it rolled up onto the porch. Smoke stood, and rested his hand on one of the support posts for the porch roof as he watched her get out of the car.

"Indians after you, are they?" he teased.

"Indians?"

"The way you were barreling up the road there, I thought a pack of wild Indians might be chasing you."

"Oh, pooh. Automobiles are made to drive fast."

"Of course, why didn't I think of that?" Smoke replied with a chuckle. "You got 'nything you need carried in?" Smoke asked.

"Two bags of groceries in the backseat," Sally said, opening the door to get one bag. Smoke came out to carry the second.

"I picked up the mail down at the mailbox," Sally said. "You got a letter from the University of Colorado."

"Maybe they want me to come play on their football team," Smoke teased.

Not until the groceries were put away did Smoke read the letter.

Mr. Kirby Jensen
Sugarloaf Ranch
Big Rock, Colorado

Dear Mr. Jensen:

I am a professor of history at the University of Colorado, and I am currently doing research on some of the pioneers of the early days of our state. I wonder if I could persuade you to come to Boulder to be interviewed. I am particularly interested in direct information regarding two of our more colorful characters: a man named "Preacher" and another named John Jackson. I believe you knew both of them.

The University would be happy to offset any expenses you might incur in responding to this request.

> *Yours Truly,*
> *Jacob Armbruster, Ph.D.*

Smoke showed the letter to Sally.

"What do you think?" he asked. "Should I go?"

"Yes, of course you should go. How often have I heard you comment about something you've read about our past, that you know is wrong? This would give you the opportunity to make certain that the facts are correct."

"Yes, I guess you're right. Okay, I'll take the truck in to . . ."

"You most certainly will not take the truck," Sally said resolutely. "Didn't the *Rocky Mountain News* recently declare you to be one of Colorado's leading citizens? How would it look if you drove onto campus in that ugly old truck. We will take the car."

"*We* will take the car?"

"Yes, I'm going with you," Sally said with a smile. "I would dearly love to do some shopping in Boulder."

"I'd better tell Pearlie we're going to be gone for a few days, so he can keep an eye on things."

"I'll get us packed."

Boulder, Colorado—October 1923

Smoke and Sally checked into a hotel the night before he was to meet with Professor Armbruster. There were several college students in the lobby, the boys were wearing raccoon coats, and the girls had on cloche hats and dresses with short skirts. Some of the young girls were smoking, their cigarettes held in long cigarette holders.

Someone said something, and there was a loud burst of laughter. The hotel clerk apologized.

"These young people today," the clerk said. "They seem to have no respect or regard for ladies and gentlemen of riper age, like yourself. But you and Mrs. Jensen will be on the top floor, so you won't be able to hear them."

"Ehh? What did you say, sonny?" Smoke asked, cupping his right ear and leaning forward.

"Smoke, stop that!" Sally scolded. But she couldn't help but laugh at his antics.

"Smoke?" the hotel clerk said. "You are Smoke Jensen?"

"Yes."

"Oh, sir, what an honor it is to have you at our hotel. If there is anything you need, please, just let me know. The telephone in your room will connect you directly with the front desk."

The clerk banged on the little bell with the palm of his hand. "Front!" he called, and a moment later a young man wearing the uniform of a bellhop arrived.

"Take Mr. and Mrs. Smoke Jensen to Room 406, please," he said. "Oh, and, sir, there is a radio in your room so that you may enjoy the broadcasts."

The bellhop escorted them to their room, carrying their

luggage, and received a generous tip. Sally waited until he left before she turned to Smoke.

"That was awful, what you did to that poor clerk, pretending you couldn't hear." Her chastisement was ameliorated, however, by a broad smile.

"Don't you think he expected something like that? I mean, after all, we are of *riper* years," Smoke said.

"Oh, hush," Sally said, laughing. She turned on the radio, then began singing along with the song.

Smoke walked over to the window and looked out over the bright lights of the city. On the street below cars were moving steadily, forming a long streak of white lights in one direction and red lights in the other. Behind him, a little box was playing music, broadcast from some remote place. They had come here from Big Rock by automobile, traveling fast enough to cover in one hour a distance that took a full day when he first arrived in Colorado.

Tomorrow he was going to discuss Preacher and John Jackson. What in the world would they think if they could be here, right now, standing beside him looking through this same window?

"How on God's earth can anyone stand all this noise and congestion? Who could live here more than a day?"

"What?" Sally asked.

Smoke chuckled. "I didn't realize I had said that aloud. I was just thinking about what Preacher would say if he were here to see and hear all this."

"Well, darling, you did say it aloud. And if you didn't know it, maybe you are of riper years," Sally teased.

"Hah. You're not that far behind me, woman," Smoke said. "Get your jacket. Let's go find us a nice restaurant somewhere."

"Oh, that sounds lovely."

"Think they might have raccoon on the menu?"

CHAPTER 2

Campus of the University of Colorado

The next morning, Smoke parked the Duesenberg in front of the Old Main building on the campus. There was a young man waiting in front of the building, and when he saw the light blue phaeton glide to a stop, he smiled and hurried over to the car.

"Are you Mr. Jensen, sir?"

"I am," Smoke said.

The young man smiled. "I am Wes Pollard. Professor Armbruster asked me to watch for you so I could walk you to his office."

Smoke returned the smile. "Well, you did a good job," he said.

"I've read a lot of books about you," the young man said.

"About ninety percent of them are fanciful," Smoke said.

"But if only ten percent of them are true, you have still led a phenomenal life."

Smoke followed the young man up the concrete steps to the redbrick building. Inside the building, the hardwood floors smelled of oil and wax, and he walked by a glass case housing athletic trophies. At the end of the hall, the last door on the right had frosted glass. The sign on the frosted glass read: DEPARTMENT OF HISTORY.

The young man opened door, stepped aside to let Smoke enter first, then came in behind him.

"Mrs. Peabody, this is Smoke Jensen," the young man said, proudly.

"Did you say 'Smoke'?"

"Kirby Jensen," Smoke said.

"Oh, yes, Mr. Jensen," Mrs. Peabody said. "Professor Armbruster is expecting you. Just a moment."

Mrs. Peabody knocked lightly on the door, then went in, shutting the door behind her. A moment later the door opened again and a tall, bald-headed man came out. Smiling broadly, he extended his hand.

"Mr. Jensen," he said. "What an honor it is, sir, to meet you. Please, come in."

Smoke followed him into the room, where the professor led him not to his desk but to a seating area that had a leather sofa, and two leather chairs facing a low table. On the table Smoke saw a basket of bear signs, and a pot of coffee sitting on an electric hot plate.

"I have read of your penchant for bear signs," Professor Armbruster said. "I know these won't be as good as the ones your wife makes . . . after all, her bear signs are famous throughout the West. And the coffee, percolated on an electric hot plate, isn't quite like making it over an open flame. But maybe it will suffice, under the circumstances."

Smoke smiled. "I'm sure it will."

Smoke picked up one of the pastries and took a bite.

"As I stated in the letter I sent you, I am currently doing a study on some of the old mountain men of the Rockies. A man called Preacher, for example. I think you knew him."

"Yes, I knew him very well," Smoke said. "I was already sixteen when I saw him first, but I figure you could say that he partly raised me."

"Despite all the research I've done, I have never been able to ascertain his real name," Professor Armbruster said. "Some sources say it was Pierre, some say it was Clyde, but most reports say it was Art. It is the last name that I've had the most trouble with. Bode? Barnes? Garneau?"

"Preacher was pretty guarded about his name, that's for sure," Smoke said. "I think that's because he ran away from a slave owner, and until the day he died, he was worried about that."

"He ran away from a slave owner? See here, was Preacher black? None of my research has indicated that."

"No. But in those days, if a slave owner claimed you had a touch of the brush, and in that same claim said that he owned you, it was hard to prove otherwise if you were no more than a fourteen-year-old boy and had no kin anywhere about to vouch for you. That's what happened to Preacher."

"I never knew that."

"Bet you never knew that Preacher was in love once, either, did you? Her name was Jenny, and she was a slave. She was mostly Creole, but her grandma was black, and that was all that was needed then. He said she was the most beautiful woman he had ever seen."

"Why didn't he marry her?"

"She got killed. Preacher killed the ones who killed her."

"I imagine he would."

"Gregory," Smoke said.

"I beg your pardon?"

"Gregory. That was Preacher's last name. Or at least that was the name he used. But to be honest about it, he once confided to me that he had just taken that name. I never did learn his birth name, and I figure I knew him better than any other human being ever knew him. He seldom even shared his taken name with anyone. Art Gregory. I don't see any reason why the name has to be kept secret any longer. With Preacher dead, there's nothing anyone can do to him now."

Professor Armbruster chuckled. "No, I suppose not."

"Mind if I have another one?" Smoke asked, reaching toward the plate of glazed pastries.

"No, of course not," Professor Armbruster replied. "Speaking of names, let's consider John Jackson. He is often referred to, and I'm sure you know this, as Liver-Eating Jackson. Though the concept of him eating the livers of the Indians he killed has never been verified."

"Would you like me to verify it?" Smoke asked, as he bit into his second bear sign.

"You mean, you *can* verify it?" Professor Armbruster asked in surprise.

"Don't tell my wife, but these bear claws are very nearly as good as hers."

"You have actually seen John Jackson eat a liver. That's what you are telling me."

"The Crow had a belief that they couldn't get into the Happy Hunting Grounds if they didn't have the liver with them." Smoke licked some of the frosting off the end of his finger.

Professor Armbruster chuckled and shook his head. "You will forgive me, Mr. Jensen, but how can you sit there calmly eating a bear claw while talking about having watched John Jackson eat a liver."

"You are the one who brought it up, Professor. And there have been many times in my life when I've been in a position to where I had to eat things that would gag a maggot on the gut wagon."

Professor Armbruster looked a little pale. "Yes, I . . . can imagine so," he said.

"Now, Professor, what is it that you want with me?" Smoke asked, wiping his hands and fingers with a damp cloth that was on the table.

"I want you to come to the recording room with me. I

intend to make a voice recording of our discussion. That is, if you don't mind."

Smoke smiled. "Well, I've been speaking into telephones for a lot of years now, but I've never spoken into a recording machine. How long after I speak into it will it be before it is developed and I can hear my voice played back?"

"Oh, it isn't like photograph film," the professor said with a laugh. "We can have an instantaneous playback if you wish."

"I guess I would sort of like to hear my voice played back to me."

"Then come with me, if you would, please."

Smoke followed Professor Armbruster out of his office, down the hall, and into another room in the building. The walls of this room were lined with thick padding.

"This room is soundproofed, so that no outside sound will interfere. That way, the machine will only record our voices, and nothing else."

There was a table in the room and on the table were two microphones. Smoke looked up at a big glass window and saw the same young man who had met him when he arrived. He was standing by some sort of shelf putting a black disc into position. Behind him there was a panel with dials.

Professor Armbruster indicated that Smoke should sit behind one of the microphones, then the professor sat behind the other one.

"Should I?" Smoke started, but the professor held his finger vertically across his lips, then looked through the glass at the young man on the other side.

The professor moved a toggle switch, and spoke into a little box. "Wes, are we about ready?" the professor asked.

"One moment, Professor," Wes's voice came back through the box. A moment later Wes held one finger up for a second as it appeared he was doing something with his other hand, then he brought the finger down and pointed directly at Professor Armbruster. The professor began talking into the microphone that was before him.

"I am sitting here with Mr. Kirby 'Smoke' Jensen, a genuine pioneer of the West, and particularly our state . . . that is, the state of Colorado. During my research on another fascinating figure from the West, John 'Liver-Eating' Jackson, I learned that the paths of these two men had crossed, many years ago. John Jackson is no longer with us, having died on the twenty-first of December, 1900, in a hospital in Pennsylvania. But Smoke Jensen is still with us, and today I consider interviewing him about John Jackson to be as close to the actual source as it is possible to get.

"Mr. Jensen, would you state in your own voice, your name, please?"

"My name is Kirby Jensen, although I have been called Smoke for most of my life."

"I suppose we could start with how you came to get the name Smoke."

"Preacher gave me that name, on the first day we ever met. I had just been firing a Henry .44, and there was a little wisp of smoke curling up from the end of the rifle barrel. I don't know why Preacher made the connection, but he called me Smoke, and that's how I've been known ever since."

"You say you had just been firing your rifle. What were you shooting at?"

"Indians," Smoke said calmly.

"Were you actually engaged in battle?"

"I suppose you could call it that," Smoke said. "The Indians were trying to kill us, we were killing them. Yes, you could say that was battle."

"When and how did you meet John Jackson?"

"Preacher and I happened to come across him one day.

It was in the middle of summer in 1869, and I was eighteen years old. But that's getting a little ahead of the story."

"Ahead of the story? What do you mean?"

"First, you need to know a little about John Jackson's background. I mean, before he came West."

"All right, please, go on," Professor Armbruster said. "I would love to hear about Mr. Jackson's background."

Smoke continued with the story, talking in a deep, resonant voice that painted word pictures of the mountains, the streams, the cold of the winters, and the heat of the summers, the smell of smoke, drifting through the woods, the sound of woodpeckers and coyote and babbling brooks.

Armbruster asked no more questions; he didn't have to. He had been transported back in time to visit with the man John Jackson before he had become known to history as, John "Liver-Eating" Jackson.

[*This was the first time the actual discussion of "liver eating" was introduced in our discussion of John Jackson. Tales around the campfire say he'd cut out and eat the liver of every Crow he killed. He became known as "Liver-Eating" Jackson and "Dapiek Absaroka," meaning "Crow Killer." Throughout the Northern Rockies and the plains of Wyoming and Montana, Crow warriors who had come for him were found with their liver cut out, presumably eaten by Jackson.*

I was most anxious to find out if this was true, but rather than press the issue at this point, I decided to let Smoke Jensen continue with the story at his own pace. And indeed, had I rushed him at this point, the story might have lost some cohesion, and that would not be fair to the eventual readers of this tale.—ED.]

CHAPTER 3

Gettysburg, Pennsylvania—July 3, 1863

There had been fierce fighting for the two previous days and if Captain John Jackson, of the 151st Pennsylvania, had to give an honest account of who was winning the battle he would be unable to do so. So far John had seen nearly one-half of his company killed, or so badly wounded as to be taken from the field.

"Captain, would you like to take your lunch with me?" Lieutenant Sanderson asked. "We've got a quiet moment; I don't know when we'll get a better opportunity."

"What are you offering for lunch, Bobby?" John asked his second in command. "Baked ham? Roast beef? Fried chicken, perhaps?"

"Ahh, you can have that anytime," Sanderson said. "How about some nice hardtack, fried in bacon grease?"

"Absolutely," John teased. "Who would want roast beef when we can have that?"

"I can also throw in a fresh peach that I took from a peach orchard," Sanderson added.

"I thought the orchard had been picked clean."

"It has," Sanderson said. He smiled. "It just so happens that I'm one of the ones who picked it clean."

"Cap'n, I believe them rebs is gettin' ready to come at us," one of his men said.

"I believe you are right, Sergeant Dunn," John replied.

"It's goin' to get pretty hot," Dunn suggested.

"Yes, but consider this. Would you rather be here, behind a stone fence, waiting for them? Or would you rather be one of those poor souls who are going to have to cross that field toward us?"

"Yes, sir, I see what you mean," Dunn said. "I'd rather be here."

"Here" was Cemetery Ridge.

At one o'clock two Confederate artillery pieces fired. John was sure that was a signal, because almost immediately afterward, a mile-long line of Confederate cannons began firing, keeping up a steady bombardment. John hunkered down against the stone fence as the missiles whistled and whizzed by overhead. Amazingly, the Confederates were, for the most part, overshooting their target, with the cannonballs bursting on the ridgeline behind the Union positions. The Federal artillery returned fire. The cannonading continued for one solid hour, with enough of the shells falling onto the waiting Union soldiers to do some physical damage, but causing considerably more fear and unease.

Then first the Confederate, then the Union artillery ceased fire and the loud thunder that had been washing across the field for nearly an hour grew silent.

As John listened, he could actually hear the sound of mockingbirds, and he marveled that nature could so turn off the folly of human warfare. Then he heard the faint notes of a bugle call as it rolled across the thousand yards that separated the two armies. That was followed by the long roll of drums.

"Here they come!" someone shouted.

"The rebs is attackin'!"

"They're a-fixin' to come at us!"

None of the proclamations were necessary, as every Union soldier in position could see the long gray line stretching out all the way across the field.

John stood up behind what was left of his company in order to be able to exercise command and control over his men. This also had the effect of inspiring his men, because while they could hunker down behind the stone wall, their commander was exposing himself to enemy fire.

For the moment all was quiet, save for chirping of the mockingbirds and the steady, rhythmic tat of the drums, urging the soldiers on. They were still too far away to separate the individual soldiers from the mass of gray. But he could see the flags . . . bits of red fluttering in the breeze, and the flag bearers who were taking the lead position of each of the committed units.

Slowly, steadily, inexorably, the Confederate soldiers, fifteen thousand in all, and under the command of General Pickett, moved across the field.

"Steady, men, hold your fire, hold your position," John ordered.

The drumbeat cadence grew louder, and as the advancing army moved closer, John could hear the clank and rattle of their equipment, and the fall of their footsteps on the open ground.

"Stay in line, men, stay in line!" a Confederate officer called to his men, his words drifting across the distance between them. He was in front, holding a saber upon which he had placed his hat, and John couldn't help but think of the courage it took to be exposed like this young Confederate officer was.

John did not believe he had ever seen a more magnificent sight, nor a more foolish one. What officer in his right mind would commit his men in such a way?

Suddenly one of the Confederate soldiers gave out a yell that John had heard before. It was what the others referred to as a rebel yell. The other Confederate soldiers joined in, and with that yell, the advancing soldiers stopped their measured march, and broke into a run. Thousands of throats roared their defiance, their shouts answered by many more thousand Union soldiers.

Union artillery opened up then, and John saw the awful effect of the grape and canister as it tore into the Confederate lines.

"Fire!" John shouted, and not only his men, but Union men all up and down Cemetery Ridge began shooting.

For a moment John forgot that he was standing in the open, then he heard the angry buzz of minié balls flying by him, and he moved quickly to the stone fence. That was when he saw the dashing young saber-brandishing young Confederate officer go down.

The deadly musket fire, to say nothing of the sustained grape and canister artillery fire, so devastated the Confederate advance that within moments the fifteen-thousand-man massed front was broken into several smaller units. Finally the front row of the Confederate soldiers actually managed to cross the stone wall, where they engaged in hand-to-hand combat with the Federals as the two bodies of men slashed at each other with sabers, thrust with bayonets, clubbed with rifle butts, and shot from point-blank range with pistols. But quickly the Confederate ranks, which had been so decimated by cannon and rifle fire during their long approach toward Cemetery Ridge, began to be overwhelmed by the superior numbers of the Union troops. Realizing they could not sustain the attack, those who could manage it broke off the engagement and retreated back across the broad field, leaving the dead and dying behind them.

Gradually the constant bang and pop of gunfire died out, and all that could be heard were the moans and cries of the wounded, and the shouts of soldiers in blue and gray, calling for assistance from hospital corpsmen.

John, who miraculously had not been wounded, walked over to sit on the stone fence and look back across the field, covered now with a low-lying fog of gun smoke. The smoke was so thick that the retreating Confederate soldiers were quickly enveloped by the cloud. What he could see, though, were the bodies of the dead, strewn across the field, many of which had been nearly cut in two.

The sounds on the battlefield which, but moments earlier had been the thunder of artillery fire, the rattle of musketry, and the challenging screams of men locked in deadly combat, had changed. Now the only sounds were the low moans and whimpers of the wounded. Many of the wounded were from John's company, and he stopped by to see each one.

One of the wounded was Lieutenant Sanderson.

"How badly are you wounded, Bobby?" John asked.

"I don't know," Sanderson replied. He chuckled. "It hurt like hell when I was first hit, but the truth is, I don't feel anything now."

"I'll get you to the aid station," John offered.

"No, sir. Not before the men," Sanderson replied.

John smiled, and put his hand on his friend's shoulder. "That was a collective 'you,' Lieutenant. I intend to get all of you to the aid station."

John mustered the rest of his company, and organized them to move the wounded, including Lieutenant Sanderson, to the aid station.

"Cap'n, do you reckon we're goin' to counterattack?" Sergeant Dunn asked.

"Do you want to leave as many blue-clad bodies out there as there are gray now?" John replied.

"No, sir."

"I'm pretty sure General Hancock doesn't want to either."

Old Main Building, University of Colorado—
October 1923

"John's prediction was correct," Smoke said as he continued to tell the story. "The next day, July Fourth, General Lee
started back to Virginia, leading a twenty-seven-mile-long
train of hospital wagons. He halted his army at the flooded
Potomac River and had his men dig in to fight another battle,
but General Meade's army was too battered and too exhausted to counterattack. Also his troops had used up almost
all of their ammunition and would have to be resupplied
before they could fight again."

"What happened to all the dead and dying?" Professor
Armbruster asked.

"The citizens of Gettysburg, the civilians, were left to deal
with the thousands of wounded. They turned private homes,
businesses, schools, and public buildings into hospitals. For
some time afterward, infection and unsanitary conditions
caused disease to spread through the town. But they didn't
have to handle it alone; volunteers came from the North and
the South. Northerner and Southerner worked together to
care for the wounded and bury the dead, regardless the color
of the soldier's uniform. They also piled up, and burned the
carcasses of horses and mules killed in the fighting."

*[It had been a grand plan with Lee proposing to take
the offensive, invade Pennsylvania, and defeat the
Union army in its own territory. Such a victory would
have moved the fighting out of Virginia, bringing some
relief to that beleaguered state, as well as strengthen
the hand of those politicians in the North who wanted
peace at any price. It was also believed that it would
undermine Lincoln's chances for reelection. It would
reopen the possibility for European support that was
closed at Antietam. The result of this vision was the*

*largest battle ever fought on the North American
continent. This was Gettysburg, where more than
170,000 fought and over 40,000 were casualties.*

*In the grand scheme of things, Lee's plans failed, but
this battle is now referred to as the high-water mark of
the Confederacy. From this point forward, victory for
the South was unachievable. How many lives could have
been saved, had the Confederacy realized then that further continuation of the war was a terrible waste.*

*It is now believed that this battle had a profound
impact upon John Jackson, causing memories which remained with him for the rest of his life. Of course, John
Jackson wasn't the only one damaged by the terrible
consequences of the battle at Gettysburg. As of the publication date of this book, it is sixty-two years since that
terrible battle was contested, and there are still many
survivors who continue to bear the scars, as does,
indeed, our entire nation.—ED.]*

"Hold it up for a moment, will you, Professor?" Wes
asked, his voice coming through the intercom box. "I have
to set up a new disc."

"Very well, tell us when you are ready," Professor Armbruster replied. Then, taking his finger away from the toggle
switch that activated the intercom, he spoke to Smoke.

"Jackson went all through the war without sustaining any
wounds, didn't he?"

"It depends on what you call wounds," Smoke said. "He
had the kind of wounds that you can't see."

"Traumatic shock."

"I beg your pardon?"

"Jackson, undoubtedly, suffered from a syndrome known
as traumatic shock. Last year, Dr. Walter Bradford Cannon,
a noted physiologist, published a book on this very subject.

It refers to a severe anxiety disorder that can develop after exposure to any event that results in psychological trauma, such as being in a war."

"Yes. I've never heard of that term before, but it certainly had an effect on him."

"You know, one of the things that I found most interesting in my research on John Jackson is that he did have a college degree," Professor Armbruster said. "But he never used that degree. Instead, he lived for many years in the wilds of Montana and Colorado."

Smoke chuckled. "I think the fact that John was an educated man did surprise a few people. But it wasn't something that ever got in the way."

"Got in the way?" Professor Armbruster replied. "What an odd thing to say, suggesting that, somehow, an education might get in the way."

"Professor, could you see any of your contemporaries in academia doing what John Jackson did? And I'm not talking about his vendetta with the Crow, I mean the many years he lived in the mountains, surviving off the land."

"No," Armbruster agreed. "No, to be honest with you, Mr. Jensen, I don't know that I, or any of my peers, could do that."

"It's because your education would get in the way," Smoke said. "You have learned to expect certain privileges as your due, because of your academic position. It is always hard for anyone to function in a milieu that is vastly different from the environment to which they have become accustomed. John Jackson was able to do this."

"I must confess, Mr. Jensen, that, given what I have read and heard about you, that I am—and please don't think this to be patronizing, because I don't mean it that way—but your language, your deportment, is considerably different from what I expected. Have I missed something in my research? Did you attend college?"

Smoke laughed. "Yes, the University of Sally."

"I beg your pardon?"

"My wife was a schoolteacher when I met her. She never quit learning, or teaching. And she shared it all with me."

"Well, I must congratulate her. She did a wonderful job with you."

CHAPTER 4

"I'm ready when you are, Professor," Wes said.

"Thank you, Wes. Give me a sign when you put down the stylus."

Wes held his finger up, then brought it down.

"As we finished with the last recording disc you were telling us about John Jackson's war experiences. Tell us, Smoke, did his war experiences have any effect on his personality?"

"Yes," Smoke answered. "And that was especially so after the war. It was as if he were having a more difficult time being a civilian during peacetime, than he had being a soldier at war."

Again, Smoke began telling the story, and again Professor Armbruster found himself transported beyond time and place so that he was an eyewitness, almost a participant, to the events as they transpired.

Media, Pennsylvania—September 1865

With a history that goes back to William Penn, Media is one of the oldest, continuously occupied settlements in Pennsylvania. Served by the West Chester and Philadelphia Railroad, it was only twelve miles from the city of Philadelphia.

And, because of the railroad and its proximity to the city, it was a summer resort for well-to-do Philadelphians.

Father Nathaniel Jackson, rector of Christ Episcopal Church, drummed his fingers on the desk in his study as he stared at his son.

"Why would you do such a thing, John? Is it your intention to embarrass the church? Is it your intention to embarrass me?"

"No."

"Then why would you say such a thing in the men's Bible study?"

John didn't answer.

"Do you really think that the reason so many men were killed during the war was because God went fishing?"

John remained silent.

"God went fishing?" Father Jackson shouted at the top of his voice, slamming his hand down on the desk so hard that a bookend fell over and several books slid off onto the floor.

John started to pick up the books.

"Leave them!" his father said loudly.

John sat up again.

"Have you nothing to say to me, John?"

"Well, didn't Jesus tell Paul that He would make him a fisher of men?" John asked with a smile.

Father Jackson stretched out his arm and pointed his finger at his son. "Don't you blaspheme! Don't you dare blaspheme!"

"I'm sorry," John said contritely.

"What were you thinking, John? When you disrupted the men's Bible study, what were you thinking?"

"You wouldn't understand."

"I am an Episcopal priest, John. And like all men of the cloth, I listen to the deepest fears, the most private sins, and the most earnest questions of my parishioners. Do you really think I can't listen to the problems of my own son? And you do have problems, John. You have manifested those problems ever since you returned from the war. You are not the same man who left."

"Pop, over three million men participated in that war, twenty percent of them were killed, and another twenty percent were wounded. How could anybody have gone through that hell, and returned as the same man who left?"

"You aren't the only member of this church who went to war, John. No one else seems to have the same degree of restlessness that you do."

"Are you talking about Frank Gilbert, who spent the war in Philadelphia recruiting other men to die? Are you talking about Mark Davidson, who spent his war in Washington? Or maybe Milt Goodpasture, who commanded a militia company that never left Delaware County?"

"They all did their part," Father Jackson said.

"Tell me one other member of this church who killed a dozen men—sons, husbands, fathers—good men—whose only sin was to be wearing a different color uniform. Tell me one other man in this church who had to wipe from his face the blood and brain matter of his best friend who had just had half his head blown off while standing right beside him. Tell me one other man in this church who shit in his pants because he was slitting the throat of another human being, and he didn't have the opportunity to go find someplace to relieve himself."

"John, there is no need for you to be vulgar about this. If you are going to discuss it, please be Christian enough to use civil language," Father Jackson scolded.

"Civil language? *Civil language?*" John shouted. "I'm talking to you about hell! Do you understand that? You preach about hell, you offer salvation to keep your flock from hell, but have you ever seen hell? Because I have seen it. I have not only seen it, I have lived there! And you complain because I am not using civil language? Well you tell me, Father Jackson—and I'm asking you as my priest, and not as my father—just how does a person describe hell, in civil language?"

The small brick building sat alongside the railroad track, not a part of, but directly adjacent to the passenger depot. The sign on the front of the building read: PENNSYLVANIA FREIGHT BROKERAGE. And though they handled railroad freight, they also handled freight that was moved by wagon, riverboat, and ship.

It was near the end of a busy day, and John was separating the bills of lading into the type of transportation required. Many of the shipments would use multiple means of transport before reaching their final destination.

John's place of employment was behind a counter that separated the entrance from the rest of the building. From this position he dealt with the public, assessing their shipment needs, suggesting the best solution for them, then, once the requirement was established, he would make all the necessary arrangements for them. He found the job boring, but for the time being it was the only job he could find. He had studied to be a teacher; the original idea was for him to start a school that was associated with Christ Episcopal Church. And, had there not been a war, he would no doubt now be the head-master of the school, perhaps with one of his own children enrolled.

But when he returned to Media he was in no mood to teach school. By his own admission, at this point in his life, he would not be a good role model for children.

Eric Coopersmith, owner of the Pennsylvania Freight Bro-· kerage company, stepped into the area behind the counter and looked over at John, who, by now, had four stacks of shipping documents.

"Mr. Jackson, did you tell Mr. Poindexter to go to hell?"

"Not exactly," John replied. "What I told him was that I was quite adept at processing shipping requirements as to carrier and destination, and I would be happy to arrange his transportation to hell."

"Did you think that was an appropriate response to a paying customer?"

"I thought it might be a little more appropriate than knocking him on his ass," John said.

"I see."

"Is this conversation going somewhere, Mr. Coopersmith? Or is it just your purpose to chastise me?"

"Oh, yes, it is going somewhere, Mr. Jackson. I'm sorry, but I'm afraid we just can't use you anymore. You don't fit in with the others."

"Fit in? What is there to fit in?"

"Were this the first incident, I would be inclined to overlook it. But this type of behavior has become far too common. In addition, our customers have told me they don't like to deal with you. There is a sense of melancholy about you that they find disturbing. Don't bother to come back tomorrow."

The oldest and most privileged of the city's old-guard clubs was located at 1301 Walnut Street. It was the club to which the most elite members of Philadelphia society belonged, and by education and social standing, John Jackson would have been considered a shoo-in for membership.

But on this day, shortly after he lost his job with the Pennsylvania Freight Brokerage, he was sitting in the outer sanctum of the club. He had been denied any deeper penetration into the building because that was reserved for members only, and he was not yet a member. He had every intention of rectifying that, however, and had applied for membership, having acquired all the necessary sponsors and recommendations. He was now waiting for the results.

He was reading a newspaper, but all the while keeping an eye on the door that led into the inner sanctum, looking for Morgan Phillips, who was his sponsor.

The expression on Phillips's face told John all he needed to know.

"I'm sorry, John," Phillips said by way of beginning. "But I have put your name in for membership three times. I'm afraid the rules of the Philadelphia Club are quite specific. You have been blackballed three times. You are not eligible to have your name submitted again."

There was no specific reason given for John's being blackballed. But John knew that it was not necessary for any reason to be given. It was sufficient reason for him to be denied entry in the club if even one person made the arbitrary decision that he didn't want John to be a member.

"I'm so sorry, John," Phillips said, apologizing again.

John went directly from the Philadelphia Club to Ye Olde Ale House, where, despite its name, one could also buy whiskey. And that's what John did, bought several whiskeys. It didn't take him too long to get drunk, and the drunker he got, the more generous a tipper he became. As a result he had at least three of the ladies at the bar hanging on his every word.

"Fired! I was fired from a job any moron could do, but I can't do it anymore because I was fired," John said.

"Honey, any man who would fire you is a fool," one of the young women said.

"Yeah, he musht be a fool," John said, slurring the words. "The very idea not lettin' me join their club. Well I din't want to be in their damn club in the firsht place. All it is, is a bunch of old stuffed shirts sittin' around a fireplace talkin' real quiet so's the devil doesn't find out where they are 'n come get 'em."

"Join their club? Honey, I thought we were talking about you gettin' fired," one of the girls said.

"My own father."

"Your own father fired you?" the first girl asked.

"Or wouldn't let you in the club?" a second girl asked.

"No. He's an Episcopal priest," John said, filling his glass and tossing it down, neat.

John was two days sober when he stepped up onto the wide, columned porch, and pulled the cord that hung alongside the door. He could hear the bell reverberating through the house. The home belonged to Swayne Manning, and it was one of the largest and most stately mansions in Chester Hill, one of Philadelphia's most elegant neighborhoods.

The butler answered the doorbell.

"Hello, Morris," John said as he started to step inside.

"I'm sorry, sir," Morris said, moving to block John. "But I have been asked to prevent you from entering."

"What? Morris, what are you talking about? What do you mean I can't come in? Is Lucinda here?"

"Miss Lucinda is not receiving, sir."

"Why not? Morris, is something wrong? Is she ill? Has she been in an accident? If so, I must see her."

"No, sir, nothing like that, I'm glad to say. She asks that I give you this letter."

Morris handed an envelope to John, who recognized at once the very small, but exceptionally neat penmanship of Lucinda Manning. He recognized it because she had sent many letters to him during the war.

"May I come in to read it?"

"No, sir, I'm afraid not."

"Morris, you know damn well that if I really wanted to come in that there is no way you can stop me."

"Yes, sir, I am well aware of that, Mr. Jackson. But it is my hope that you will be gentleman enough not to force your way in where you are not wanted."

"I'm not wanted? Is that what the letter says?"

"I have no way of knowing what the letter says, sir. But, as I say, I have been asked to deny you entrance."

"Yeah," John said. "All right." He turned away from the door, then drove off. He was at least a mile away when he stopped, then opened the letter.

Dear John,

This is a difficult letter for me to write, but I have been thinking of it for the entire year since you returned from the war. You have asked me many times when I would consent to marry you. Here is my answer.

I will never marry you. I know it is something that we had planned on, and though we were going to get married as soon as you graduated from college, it was you who suggested that we put it off until after the war. Of course at the time, neither of us realized how long the war would be.

I waited for you throughout the long war, I was faithful to you, and I maintained a correspondence. But I think now that you were right in suggesting that we wait, because the John Jackson who returned from the war is not the John Jackson I fell in love with.

I think it would be best, John, if we not see each other again. I wish you all the best.

Fondly,
Lucinda

Old Main Building

"Yes, the way you are describing John Jackson is certainly indicative of someone with traumatic shock," Professor Armbruster said. "I imagine that losing his job, and his fiancée, could well drive him to come west to lose himself in the mountains."

"Yes, but he didn't come west right away," Smoke said. "It was another four years before he showed up in the Rockies."

"What did he do during those years? Did he stay in Pennsylvania?"

"No," Smoke answered. He chuckled. "He joined the French Foreign Legion."

CHAPTER 5

Paris, France—April 1867

It was a brisk day in mid-April and John stopped out front, and looked at the sign on the outside of the building.

OFFICE DE RECRUTEMENT MILITAIRE

DE LA

LÉGION ÉTRANGÈRE FRANÇAISE

He was met just inside the door by someone in the uniform of a noncommissioned officer.

"Bist du gekommen, um die Französisch Fremdenlegion?"

"I beg your pardon?" John replied.

"Oh, you are English. I thought you were German."

"I am American."

"American, you say? And you have come to join the Foreign Legion?"

"Yes."

"Your name?"

John debated over whether or not to give him his right name, then decided that he may as well.

"John Jackson."

"Your name is Jean Jourdain," the noncommissioned officer said.

"John Jackson," John said, speaking his name a bit louder, thinking perhaps the sergeant hadn't heard him.

"*Non.* Here, we will give you a new name. Your new name is Jean Jourdain."

The noncommissioned officer pointed to a door. "Wait in that room with the others."

When John stepped into the other room he saw at least thirty more men, and he heard conversations being carried on in several languages.

"*Deutsch, Belge, Norsk, Español,* English?" someone asked.

"American."

"Oh, very good," the man answered in English. "I am Hans Frey. I am Swiss, but I speak English. We can talk as we wait."

"Is that your real name, or the name you were given?"

"It is the name that was given me by the noncommissioned officer when I reported, so now it is my real name."

"I was given a new name as well, but if we are to be friends, I prefer to use my real name. It is John Jackson."

"Yes, I think we will be friends," Hans said.

"It will be good to have someone to talk to."

"John, I have read of the terrible war in America," Hans said. "Were you in the war?"

"Yes."

"And yet you come to join the French Foreign Legion? You know, do you not, that the crazy French are in wars all over the world? They are in Mexico, and in Africa, and in Asia. And who do they send to fight their wars? They send the Foreign Legion."

"Yes, so I have heard."

"Have you a choice?" Hans asked.

"I beg your pardon?"

"I have no choice. I killed a man," Hans said. He held up

his finger. "Mind you, I am not sorry that I killed this man, for if ever a man needed to be killed, it was Max Botta. He was a most despicable person, who by his fraud and deceit, ruined the life of a good man. My father took his own life because of Max Botta."

"Yes, I can see how you would want to avenge that."

"You can see that because you are my friend. But I fear that the law may not see things my way, so I left Switzerland, and where could I go but the Foreign Legion? Look around you," Hans invited. "What do you see, besides murderers, thieves, adulterers, men who have much reason to leave their homeland and no reason to stay?"

"I see."

For the next hour John and Hans, and an Englishman, carried on but one of many conversations, the drone of voices filling the room.

The Englishman was Desmond Winthrop. Winthrop had been indiscreet enough to impregnate the daughter of the mayor of his town, and not wanting to get married, had left the country.

All during their conversation Sergeant Major Dubois, the noncommissioned officer who had welcomed them to the building in the first place, would periodically call out a name.

"Jean Jourdain?"

There was no answer.

"Jean Jourdain?" Sergeant Major Dubois said again, and this time he stared directly at John. That was when John remembered that he was Jean Jourdain.

"I'm here," John replied, holding up his hand.

"Come, you must speak with the capitaine," he said.

Capitaine Pierre Beajou had a very large moustache, but no beard. He was wearing a dark blue uniform with brass buttons, and he was looking at a piece of paper as John came in. Automatically, John saluted.

"Have a seat, Monsieur Jourdain," Capitaine Beajou said. "I see by the papers you filled out that you are a capitaine in the American army."

"Yes."

"For the North, or the South?"

"For the North."

"That is most unusual, monsieur. We have many men who were officers for the South, leaving because their army is no more, their country is no more. We do not have so many from the army of the North. You will, no doubt, be serving with many of these men. Will you be disturbed by that?"

"No."

"That is good. You do understand, do you not, Monsieur Jourdain, that even though you were an officer in the American army, that you cannot be an officer here? Only Frenchmen who have gone to school at Saint-Cyr—that is like your West Point—can be officers."

"Yes, I know."

"You were in the war, but in your war, gentlemen were fighting gentlemen. Here, the ones you fight are not gentlemen. You are likely to get your throat cut by some Arab or Tonkin. Or, maybe you'll just be wounded. In that case, the women will make sausage out of you.

"And if that doesn't happen you'll have to deal with fever, sunstroke, bad water, and bad food. All in all, it is a bad business.

"And who will you be serving with? Deserters, thieves, murderers, scallywags who have run out on their families, or who have squandered their wealth.

"Why are you here? A petticoat, is it? Were you deceived by a faithless sweetheart?"

John thought of Lucy Manning.

"I have my reasons," he replied.

"Yes, don't you all," Capitaine Beajou said. He made a dismissive motion with his hand.

"Go away, Monsieur Jourdain. Leave while you still can. Have a good dinner tonight at the Moulin Rouge. Watch the pretty girls, enjoy some wine, and think about this.

"Tomorrow, we will swear in the new recruits. If you come tomorrow, you will be sworn in with the others. If you do not come tomorrow, you are still free to go, and that, my friend, would be the wisest thing for you to do."

When the recruiting office opened for business the next morning, John was there. Hans and Desmond were there as well, as were all the others he had seen the day before.

The oath of enlistment was issued in French, German, Spanish, Norwegian, Italian, and English. Then, when all were sworn in, all the new recruits shouted: *"Vive la France. Vive la Liberté. Vive la Légion Étrangère!"*

And after shouting it in French, each new recruit repeated it in his own language. "Long live France. Long live Liberty. Long live the Foreign Legion!"

[*Part of the defining characteristic of the legion is its rule of anonymity, which says that all legionnaires must give up their civil identity upon enlisting. With their old identities set aside, recruits join the legion under a declared identity—a new name that they use during their first year of service. At the end of the first year a legionnaire may reclaim his old name through a process known as "military regularization of the situation," in which fresh identity papers are obtained from the person's home country. Alternatively, a legionnaire can choose to spend his entire career under his declared identity, and many do.—ED.*]

French Indochina—October 1867

On the 30th of October, at 1:00 A.M., John was with the 3rd Company of the Foreign Legion, consisting of sixty-two soldiers plus three officers, en route to Bien Hoa. At 7:00 A.M., after a fifteen-mile march, they stopped for a breakfast of bread and coffee. Soon after, the Black Flag force of Liu Yongfu was sighted. He was leading a cavalry battalion of over six hundred men, which meant that the 3rd Company was outnumbered by a ratio of ten to one.

Capitaine Beajou ordered the company to take up a square formation, and, though retreating, he rebuffed several cavalry charges, inflicting heavy losses on the Annamese army by use of accurate long-range fire.

Looking for a place that would provide a better defensive position, Capitaine Beajou moved his troops to a nearby *ngôi nhà trang trại*, a farmhouse protected by a stone wall that was three feet high. His plan was to keep the Black Flag forces occupied until relieved by Capitaine Ernest Doudart de Lagrée. While his legionnaires prepared to defend the farm, Liu Yongfu demanded that Beajou and his soldiers surrender, noting the numeric superiority of the Black Flag Army.

Beajou replied: "We have munitions. We will not surrender." He then swore a fight to the death, an oath which was seconded by the men who were with him.

John could not help but think back to Pickett's Charge at Gettysburg. There too, he had the protection of a stone fence. But there, he had at least ten thousand men deployed along Cemetery Ridge. Here, there were but sixty-five of them, against six hundred.

The legionnaires put up a spirited defense, but the situation was growing critical. They had lost their pack mules during the retreat, so they were without food or water, and quickly their supply of ammunition reached the critical point as they had only such rounds as they were carrying on their person.

* * *

The two lieutenants were killed early in the fight, then at midday, Capitaine Beajou was shot in the chest and died. Now under the command of Sergeant Major Dubois, the legionnaires continued to keep up a spirited fight, despite the overwhelming odds against them.

By five o'clock that afternoon, only twelve of the legionnaires remained, with not an officer or a noncommissioned officer among them. John assumed command and the others readily followed him. They continued to fight until their ammunition was nearly exhausted.

After repulsing the last charge, only three men remained: John, Hans Frey, the Swiss, and Desmond Winthrop, the Englishman.

The Vietnamese had pulled back after the last assault and were now approximately one hundred yards away, on the other side of a rice paddy.

"You both know that when they come the next time, it will be the end, don't you?" John asked.

"Yes, I know, and I have already made my peace with God," Desmond said. "But I do hope to kill at least three more of the buggers before they get me."

"I figured I would die at the hands of some jealous husband, never thought I would die in some stinking rice paddy," Hans said. "What about you, Jean? Are you ready to die?"

"I'm already dead," John replied. "I was killed at Gettysburg, and I've been on borrowed time ever since. So, what the hell?"

"I think our little yellow friends are getting ready to come again," Desmond said.

"Yeah, it looks like it," John said. "All right let's . . . wait! Listen! Do you hear that?"

The three men could hear the sound of a bugle, coming from behind them.

"Quickly," John said. "Let's get a few of these bodies up against the wall, put their rifles out, maybe they'll think relief has already come."

The soldiers of the Black Flag attacked again, but this time John, Hans, and Desmond had pulled back to the other side of the house. Each of the three had found a place to hide, and they picked off Liu Yongfu's attackers from concealment. The positions of Hans and Desmond were found, and both were killed. John fired his last round, then fitted his bayonet to his rifle and waited for the final attack.

It was at that moment that the relief element of the legionnaires arrived on the scene, twelve hundred strong. They swept through the compound, and over the walls, shooting down the Vietnamese where they could, capturing five, and chasing the rest from the field.

When General de Lattre arrived he saw John sitting on the stone fence, surrounded by the dead officers and men of his company. John stood, and saluted the general.

"Were you with Capitaine Beajou?" General de Lattre asked.

"I was, sir," John replied.

"How many of you remain?" the general asked.

"I believe I am the only survivor," John replied.

General de Lattre put his hand on John's shoulder. "I am sorry that I did not arrive in time to save your comrades."

CHAPTER 6

Cholon—November 1867

The five captured Black Flag soldiers were tried and condemned. They walked to their death without tremor or hesitation. They were chatting together, and chuckling, as if they were going to some sort of social event, instead of their own execution. They threw curious glances at those who were gathered to watch them die, the witnesses not there by choice, but by command.

They were ordered to stand five meters apart, and they did so, spitting out the red juice of the narcotic betel leaves they were chewing. Behind them, and not seen by the condemned men, the five executioners, all wearing black hoods and carrying wide-bladed swords, approached them. A French officer stood in front of the five men for a moment, then shouted, *"Vive la France!"*

That was the signal, and at the shout all five executioners swung their blades at the same time. The severed heads of the prisoners bounced off the cobblestone square, as the headless bodies tumbled forward.

* * *

Later that same afternoon, John was standing at a window in the headquarters building in Cholon, looking down at the Saigon River. A large boat was docked at a pier, an eye painted on the bow in order to allow the boat to see, and avoid, demons. A young man wearing a conical straw hat was squatted on the bow, working with fishing net.

"Bun mae! Bun mae!" The haunting calls came from an old woman who was walking the cobblestone road alongside the river, calling out for customers to buy the hot, small baguettes of bread she was selling. A man, pushing a cart that contained a steaming cauldron of soup, was using a young boy to advertise his product, the young boy walking in front, beating sticks together in a precise rhythm that was the specific signature of this man's soup.

[*This was probably very similar to the Annam soup now known as pho, though in fact pho did not become an Annam staple until 1907. It is very likely that the soup peddler Jackson refers to here was Chinese, as Cholon had already become a center for Chinese immigrants into Annam.—ED.*]

John watched as customers bought both the bread and the soup. It was nearly time for lunch and he wished he could be down there on the riverfront, buying the soup and bread, rather than standing here, awaiting his appointment with General de Lattre.

What did de Lattre want? He had asked that question of Capitaine Ernest Doudart de Lagrée, his new commanding officer, but de Lagrée told him that he didn't know.

"I am but a capitaine. Generals do not consult with me."

"Private Jourdain," a sergeant said. "General de Lattre will see you now."

John nodded, then stepped into the general's office. De Lattre had piercing dark eyes, and a vandyke beard.

"Private Jourdain reporting as ordered," John said, saluting the general. The general made a casual return of the salute.

"Private Jourdain, I am pleased to report that I am sending you back to Paris, where you will receive the *Légion d'Honneur*, the highest award that can be given to a member of the Foreign Legion."

"Why?" John asked.

John's response was totally unexpected, and the general looked up in surprise.

"Why? You ask why? It is because of your heroic stance in the battle so recently fought."

"General, I wasn't a hero, I was a survivor," John said. "If anyone is to get the medal, it should be Capitaine Beajou, Sergeant Major Dubois, and the sixty-one others who died in the battle."

"Your hesitancy to accept the medal is commendable, Sergeant Jourdain."

"I'm a private, sir."

"You were a private. I have promoted you to sergeant. And, as I was saying, your hesitancy to accept the medal is commendable, but it is being awarded to you precisely because you are still alive. You will go back to Paris, be awarded the medal, be given two weeks of leave, then assigned as a recruiter to bring other young men into the legion."

"To come to Algeria, or Indochina to die gloriously?" John asked.

"Yes, yes! You do understand!" General de Lattre said.

What was obvious to John at that moment was that General de Lattre didn't understand that John was being sarcastic.

"You are happy to go to Paris, are you not?"

"Yes, General. I am happy to go to Paris."

Old Main Building

"And did John go to Paris?"

"Oh, yes."

"All of this happened before you and John Jackson ever met, didn't it?"

"Yes."

"I must confess that in my own research, this is new to me. I never knew that he had been a member of the French Foreign Legion. Also, I am curious. How is it that you can speak in great detail and with such authority about events that transpired before the two of you met?"

Smoke chuckled. "Professor Armbruster, this is just a guess, mind you, but I would be willing to bet that you have never wintered in the mountains with just one other person."

Armbruster laughed. "You would win that bet," he said.

"Well, when there are just two of you, in a small twelve-by-twelve cabin, and you spend an entire winter together—sometimes snowed in for days at a time—all you can do is talk. There is very little about John's life that I don't know. And, though at the time I had very little history of my own to share, there was little of my life that John didn't know."

"I wonder why John never told anyone else about his experience with the French Foreign Legion. There is, after all, a certain élan about that. You would think it would be something he would speak of with a degree of pride."

"It wasn't a part of his life that he was particularly proud of," Smoke said. "For one thing, he didn't feel all that good about being part of a military establishment that was depriving a people of their freedom. And for another thing, he wasn't proud of being a deserter."

"A deserter?"

"Yes, the enlistment period for serving in the legion was five years. John served less than one year. When he returned to Paris to accept the *Légion d'Honneur* he was given a two-week leave. During that leave, he boarded a ship at Le Havre, bound for Southampton, England, and from there, took a ship back to the United States."

"All this you are telling me about John Jackson, the difficulty he was having in adjusting from the war, and his time with the Foreign Legion, was before you met him, wasn't it?"

"Yes, it was."

"I'm curious, Smoke. You say you had very little history of your own at the time, but hadn't you already located, and, uh, dealt with, the men who killed your father and brother?"

"Yes." Smoke's answer was nonspecific.

"I've read about that. The man's name was Casey, wasn't it?"

"It was. Ted Casey."

"You found him," Professor Armbruster said. It wasn't a question, it was a statement of fact."

"Oh, yes, I found him, all right."

"Since your story is so inextricably related to John's story, I wonder if you would share with me, for the purposes of my research, just what happened when you found Casey. I think that, for future historians, having the story in your own words would be invaluable."

"All right," Smoke said. "It started with Prosperity."

"Prosperity? You mean when you became a wealthy man?" Professor Armbruster asked.

Smoke laughed. "No, I'm not talking about prosperity with regard to wealth. I'm talking about a town that was named Prosperity. On the banks of the Cuchara River, it was a ranching and farming community, with a rather grandiose sign posted just outside the town limits with the proud boast:

COME WATCH US GROW
WITH PROGRESS
AND PROSPERITY
IN Colorado

[*The town of Prosperity no longer exists. It was one of many such towns in the emerging western United States of the nineteenth century. Some grew and died within a matter of a few months, towns that boomed with gold fever, then went bust when the gold played out . . . or more often, when the promise of gold never bore fruit.*

Prosperity was not a gold town, but rather a town that had been born on the promise of a railroad. At its peak, Prosperity had a population of 1,325. It lasted for three years, then when it became obvious that there would be no railroad, it disappeared quickly. The 1890 census listed its population as 25. By 1900 it was listed only as a "populated place" and by 1910, even that mention was gone.—ED.]

Prosperity, Colorado

The city marshal, having seen Smoke approaching from some distance away, met him just outside of town.

"Welcome to Prosperity, stranger," the marshal said. "The name is Crowell, Marshal Crowell." He put his hand to his badge, even though Smoke had already seen it.

"Marshal," Smoke said, touching the brim of his hat.

"I didn't catch your name," Marshal Crowell said.

"Folks call me Smoke."

"Smoke?" The Marshal chuckled, more in dismissal than in humor. "That's it? Smoke? Smoke what?"

"I've been spending some time in the mountains," Smoke said. "One name is all anybody needs up there."

"Well, Smoke, if you're just makin' a friendly visit to my town, then you're welcome," Crowell said. "But if you're comin' here for any other reason, well, I'm goin' to have to ask you to just keep ridin'."

"I'm looking for a man named Casey," Smoke said. "Ted Casey."

"What do you want with him?"

"That's my business."

"I'm the law here'bouts," Crowell said. "I reckon that makes it my business."

"Is that a fact?"

"You know what, mister, I don't much like your attitude," Crowell said. "Why don't I just . . . ?"

That was as far as Crowell got. He was reaching for his gun, but stopped in mid-draw and mid-sentence when he saw the pistol in Smoke's hand.

"What the hell?" Crowell gasped. "I didn't even see you draw!"

"Like I said, where is Casey?" Smoke asked. He neither raised his voice, nor made it more menacing. Ironically, that made his question all the more frightening.

Crowell hesitated for a few seconds. "His ranch is southeast of here, on the flats. You'll cross a little creek before you see the house. I ought to warn you, though, he's got several men workin' for him, and they're all good with a gun. Maybe not as fast as you, but there's only one of you."

"You got an undertaker in this town?" Smoke asked.

"Of course we do. Why would you ask?"

"I'm about to give him some business," Smoke said.

Ten miles out of town, Smoke encountered two rough-looking riders.

"You're on private land," one of the men said. "Turn your horse around and git."

"You're not being very hospitable," Smoke said.

"Don't intend to be. Strangers ain't welcome here."

"I'm looking for Ted Casey."

"You deef or somethin'? I told you to git."

"I'm looking for Ted Casey," Smoke repeated.

"What do you want with Casey?"

"Just to renew an old friendship from the war," Smoke said.

"From the war?" one of the men said with a laugh. "Boy, you're still wet behind the ears. You ain't old enough to have been in the war."

"I'm sorry, I wasn't very clear. I'm actually looking him up for my pa."

"What was your pa's name?"

"Jensen," Smoke said. "Emmett Jensen."

"Jensen?"

"Yeah. You remember him, don't you?" Smoke said. His words were calm and cold.

"Kill 'im!" one of the riders shouted, and both grabbed for their guns.

They were too slow; Smoke had his pistol in his hand and he fired twice, the shots coming so close together that there was no separation between them.

The two riders were dumped from their saddles, one dead, the other dying. The dying rider pulled himself up on one elbow. Blood poured through his chest wound, pink and frothy, indicating that the ball had passed through a lung.

"Figured when we killed your pa that would be the end of it," he said. He forced a laugh, and blood spattered from his lips. "You're good, a hell of a lot better 'n your brother. Casey shot him low and in the back. It took him a long time to die too. I enjoyed watchin' him. He was a coward, squealed like a pig and cried like a little girl."

Smoke made no reply.

"So was your pa a coward."

Smoke was quiet.

"What's the matter with you?" the rider asked. "You just goin' to let me talk about your folks like that? You're yellow."

Smoke turned his horse and rode around the two men, following the road in the same direction from which the two riders had come.

"Shoot me!" the rider shouted. "You yellow-bellied coward, don't leave me here to die like this! Shoot me!"

Smoke continued to ride away. Thirty seconds later he heard a gunshot, the sound muffled by the fact that the shooter had put the barrel in his own mouth.

Smoke didn't bother to look around.

CHAPTER 7

Stopping in a copse of trees a short distance from the ranch house, Smoke studied it for a moment or two. The house was built of logs and had a sod roof. If it came to it, it would burn easily.

"Casey!" Smoke called. "Casey, come out!"

"Who's callin'?" a voice shouted from within the house.

"Jensen."

"Jensen? I thought we killed you."

"That was my pa. And my brother," Smoke said.

"What do you want?"

"I'm here to settle up."

There was a rifle shot from the house, and though it missed, the bullet came close enough for Smoke to hear it whine.

Smoke took his horse into a ravine that circled the house. Fifty yards behind the house he dismounted, snaked his rifle from the saddle sheath, then lay against the bank of the arroyo. Inside, he saw an arm on the windowsill. He shattered the arm with one shot from his new Henry. A moment later he saw someone's outline through one of the other windows and he shot him, hearing a scream of pain.

"You boys in there," Smoke called. "You want to die for

Casey, do you? I've already killed two of you back on the road."

"Your Daddy ride with Mosby?" someone called from inside.

"That's right."

"You had a brother named Luke?"

"I did."

"Yeah, well, he was shot in the back and the gold he was guardin' was stole. Casey done it, not me! You got no call to come after me."

Smoke fired several more rounds into the house.

"Jensen! The name is Barry! I come from Nevada. Din't have nothin' to do with no war, never been east. They's another fella in here just like me. We herd cattle for wages; we ain't got no stake in this fight."

"Come on out and ride away then," Smoke called. "I won't shoot you."

The cabin door opened and two men came out with their hands up.

"We're just goin' to get our horses," one of them shouted.

"Go ahead."

The two men were moving toward the barn when a couple of shots rang out. Both were shot in the back by someone from within the house.

"What'd you do that for, Casey?" Smoke shouted. "They weren't part of this."

"When I pay men to work for me, I expect loyalty," Casey called back.

Smoke didn't answer. He was quiet for several moments, trying to decide what he should do.

"Jensen? Jensen, you still out there?" Casey called.

Casey's voice was getting nervous.

"Jensen? Come on down. Come out in the open so I can see you and we can talk."

Smoke still didn't answer.

"Jensen, you there?"

"I think he's gone," another voice said.

"That's what he wants us to think, you fool," Casey's voice replied.

Smoke followed the arroyo on around to the bunkhouse. In a pile behind the bunkhouse he found a bunch of rags, and in the bunkhouse, a jar of coal oil. He stuck the rags down into the mouth of the coal-oil jar, lit it, then threw it at the ranch house. The jar broke and the fire erupted almost immediately. As the logs burned they began filling the house with smoke and fumes.

From inside the house Smoke heard coughing. Then one man broke from the cabin and started running. Smoke cut him down with his rifle. A second began running and Smoke pulled the trigger on the rifle, only to hear the hammer fall on an empty chamber. He pulled his pistol and shot the man once, watching him double over with a slug in his gut.

Casey waited until the last minute before he stumbled out into the yard, his eyes blinded from the smoke and fumes. He fired wildly as he stumbled around, finally pulling the trigger repeatedly on an empty gun.

Smoke walked calmly up to him, even as Casey was trying to reload, and knocked him out.

Just outside the little town of Prosperity, Smoke dumped a bound and gagged Casey onto the ground. Curious about what was going on, several townspeople came forth to watch as Smoke took a rope from the saddle of Casey's horse and began making a noose.

"What do you think you are going to do here?" Marshal Crowell asked.

"Obvious, isn't it?" Smoke replied. "I'm going to hang the son of a bitch who killed my brother and my pa."

"I am an officer of the law. What if I ordered you to stop?" Crowell asked.

"Then I'd just kill you and hang him," Smoke answered.

"But you can't do this," Crowell insisted. "He hasn't been found guilty."

"Yeah, he has. He's already admitted it to me," Smoke said. "I also watched him kill two of his own men. He shot them in the back."

"That doesn't make what you are doing right," Crowell said.

"It's right in my book," Smoke said. He put the noose around Casey's neck, then threw the other end of the rope over a tree limb. "Get up on your horse," he ordered.

"You go to hell," Casey said, spitting at him.

"Have it your way," Smoke said. He tied the end of the rope to the saddle horn, and started to slap the horse on the rump.

"No, wait!" Casey shouted. "Not that way." Casey's hands were tied in front of him, but he put them on the pommel, then swung himself into the saddle.

"You got anything to say before I send you to hell?" Smoke asked.

"Yeah. I already sent your brother and your pa there, and when I get there I'm going to kick them both in the ass. Now, do your damndest, you son of a bitch."

Smoke slapped Casey's horse on the rump. With a protesting whinny it leaped forward and Casey, dying quickly from a broken neck, swung back and forth, the only sound being the creaking of the rope and the cawing of a distant crow.

"I'll be notifying the governor about this," Crowell said.

"You do what you think you need to do," Smoke said. Without looking back, Smoke walked over to his horse, swung into the saddle, and rode away.

"Son of a bitch," someone said, almost reverently. "That's the damndest thing I done ever seen."

[This was but the first of what would become Smoke Jensen's legacy, one of "making things right." Smoke Jensen was uncommonly fast with a gun, and could shoot with unerring accuracy.

Because much of the law, in Smoke's time, was ineffective, Smoke often took the law into his own hands. For many, this power could have been abused for personal enrichment.

This wasn't the case for Smoke, though, because he considered himself a knight, bound by rules of right and chivalry.

The number of men who fell before Smoke Jensen's gun has never been made known, but what is known, and has been recognized by every local, county, state, and federal law enforcement agency is that Smoke never misused his power. He was an invaluable asset as an unpaid deputy to Sheriff Monte Carson of Big Rock. Carson's autobiographical book, Both Sides of the Badge, *states, clearly, that Smoke Jensen had some sort of internal compass that always pointed to what was right. Therefore, according to Sheriff Carson, every killing was justifiable.—ED.]*

Old Main Building

"How much longer after you avenged your father and brother, before you met John Jackson for the first time? Did he come to Colorado right away after he got back to the United States?" Professor Armbruster asked.

"Pretty soon after he got back," Smoke said. "The first thing he did when he returned was go to Philadelphia to see Lucinda Manning. He was going to tell her that he had changed, and he was ready to settle down and become a useful citizen."

"But she didn't believe him?"

"It wouldn't have made any difference whether she believed him or not," Smoke said easily. "Lucinda had gotten married to a member of the Pennsylvania state legislature. He was just the kind of man her father wanted her to marry."

"I see," Professor Armbruster said. "What did John do next?"

"He went to a high-priced Philadelphia lawyer. He wanted to know if he was in trouble for deserting the French Foreign Legion."

Philadelphia—February 1869

"I have done some research," the lawyer, Robert Dempster, said. "It seems that desertion is higher in the French Foreign Legion than it is in any other military unit in the entire world. And, because desertion is so high, and because they have few records of the actual identity of the men who serve with them, they rarely make any attempt to look for those who have deserted. Apparently, they never do so for Americans. So I would say that you are safe."

"Good, thank you."

"But tell me, Mr. Jackson, is the training and service really as difficult as they say?"

"Yes, especially the training to be hungry," John replied.

"I beg your pardon? Training to be hungry?"

"The legion embraces the philosophy that if you want soldiers to fight hungry, you train them hungry. Breakfast might be watery coffee and a baguette, lunch a few pieces of ravioli and a pear."

"I see. But somehow I get the idea that it wasn't the rigorous training that caused you to desert. It couldn't have been. They don't award medals to those who aren't up to the rigors of training," Dempster said.

"No, it wasn't the training that drove me away. It was the killing."

"The killing? But, Mr. Jackson, you recently came through the Civil War. Surely there wasn't killing on such a scale among the Foreign Legion?"

"It isn't the number of people killed," John replied. "It is the reason they are killed. In the Civil War both of the competing armies had honor on their side. The men of the North and the men of the South thought they were fighting for the survival of their nation.

"France has no such honorable motive. France is fighting wars, not of liberation, or of survival. France is fighting wars of aggression . . . killing innocents so that the country may add to its empire. I saw that when I was in Indochina, and I have neither desire, nor intention to kill those who are defending their own homes and their own culture, merely to add to the glory of France."

"I understand."

"I'm not sure you do," John said. "Had I not been there, to see for myself what was going on, I wouldn't understand."

"What are you going to do now?" the lawyer asked.

"I'm going west."

"Texas? California?"

"No. To the mountains."

"You have to have more in mind than simply going to the mountains, Mr. Jackson. You have to have some idea of how you are going to support yourself."

"I'm going to become a fur trapper."

"Surely, sir, you jest. Have you ever read about such men?"

"I have."

"And that appeals to you?"

"It does."

Dempster shook his head. "Mr. Jackson, I wish you luck. Because I am absolutely certain that you are going to need it."

[*The Rocky Mountain fur trade is the catalyst for one of the most interesting and influential periods of America's movement west. The fur trade as well as the mountaineers who conducted it have caught the American fancy. This subject has probably received more attention, scholarly and popular, than any other phenomenon of the history of the previous century, with the obvious exception of the Civil War. The literature dealing with the mountain men is voluminous and detailed. They are unique in our history: pathfinders and trailblazers, not by design, but simply because they had a need to go from one place to another. They were men who were possessed of common sense, bravery, and coolness under trying conditions. They were noted for the ability to shoot straight, ride hard, fight ferociously, to withstand numbing cold and blistering heat. They were blissfully unaware of their unique qualities, considering them simply a matter of survival.—ED.*]

CHAPTER 8

Old Main Building

"I wonder if, before you speak of your first meeting with John Jackson, you might tell us a little about Matt Jensen? I have read some reports that he is your son, other reports that he is your younger brother, and still other reports that he is of no kin at all. Yet, he does share your last name."

"His birth name was Cavanaugh," Smoke said. "He honored me by taking my last name, shortly after he left."

"This was before you met John Jackson?"

"Yes. Matt was a fourteen-year-old boy when he ran away from an orphanage. I found him half frozen to death in the mountains and took him back with me. Once he recovered he stayed with me quite a while until he left to be on his own. He was with Preacher and me when we first ran across John."

The Colorado Rockies—1869

Smoke and young Matt were with Smoke's friend and mentor, a man who had never given anyone—and very few at that—anything more than his Christian name, Art. To his contemporaries and to history, he would always be known as Preacher.

"You two fellas hold it up there for a moment," Preacher

said, lifting his hand. He pointed to the top of some trees. "See them birds up there? The way they're actin'?"

"Yes."

"What does that tell you, boy?" Preacher asked Matt.

"They're studying something that's holding their attention pretty good," Matt said.

"You think it's a critter?" Preacher asked.

"No, I don't think it is. The way they're acting, I think it might be a man. Or men."

Preacher chuckled. "Smoke, I'd say you're learnin' this boy pretty good," he said.

"I had a pretty good teacher myself," Smoke said.

"Yeah, I reckon you did," Preacher replied. It wasn't a boast; it was a statement of fact.

"I would tell you to loosen up that hog leg of yourn, but no need to. You can get it out fast enough, I reckon. Let's the three of us ride on up there, but let's do it real quiet."

Smoke reached down to stroke his horse's neck, then, with a slight pressure of the knees, urged him on.

Preacher, Smoke, and young Matt were approaching a break in the trees without making a sound. It was as if their mounts knew to be quiet, because their hoofbeats were but soft plops in the dirt, no breaking twigs, no rattle of crushing leaves.

Then, just before they reached the opening in the woods, the three heard a long string of curses from just ahead, and Smoke reached down to put his hand on his pistol, though he didn't pull it. They rode a bit farther, then Preacher held his hand up. What they saw ahead of them was a man, probably fifteen years older than Smoke, trying to hold on to a wild turkey that had been caught in a snare. The turkey, with flapping wings and pecking beak, was fighting hard to get free.

"Grab him by the neck," Preacher called to the man.

"I'm trying to grab him by the neck, but the bird apparently has his own ideas. He just won't cooperate," the man replied.

Smoke slid down from his saddle, hurried up to the man and the flapping bird, then reached up with his left hand to grab the turkey just under his head, while with the knife in his right hand, he cut the head off. The man who had been holding on to the bird dropped him, and the four of them watched the turkey flop around until, finally, it grew still.

"Well, it would be quite ungentlemanly of me not to invite you three gentlemen to help me eat this bird," the man said.

"We appreciate the invitation," Preacher said. "But who will we be eating with?"

"The name is Jackson. John Jackson. And who would you three be?"

"I'm called Preacher. This is Smoke. The boy is Matt."

"You're a man of the cloth, are you?" Jackson asked.

"Nope."

"But you're called Preacher?"

"Yep."

Preacher's monosyllabic responses were indications that he had no intention of explaining his moniker, and Jackson didn't pursue it.

Without being asked, Matt picked up the turkey and began plucking it. Once the feathers were removed, he gutted it, then cleaned it in the nearby creek.

"You seem to be quite a capable young man," John said.

"Smoke is bringing me along," Matt replied.

All the while Matt had been cleaning the turkey, Smoke had been gathering wood, and now had a good fire going. He had made a pile of rocks in the middle of the fire, and the turkey, now quartered, was laid out on those rocks to cook.

"Are you three out hunting?" John asked.

"Sort of," Preacher replied.

"What are you hunting for?"

"Whatever we find," Preacher said.

"Were you watching me?"

"Some."

"Does this one talk?" John asked, nodding toward Smoke.

"I talk," Smoke said. "When there's something to talk about."

"Smoke," Matt said. "Look over there. Isn't that sage?"

Smoke chuckled. "It is indeed, boy. You have good eyes."

"Mr. Jackson, it's your bird. Do you mind if I rub in some sage?"

"Do I mind? No, not a bit," John replied. "Show me what it looks like. That might be something good for me to know."

Matt led John over to the growth of sage, then he picked it and began rubbing it between his hands, breaking the leaves down so he could put it on the turkey.

The four were quiet for a long moment as the four quarters of the turkey cooked, and, as it cooked, the air was perfumed with its aroma.

"Damn, that smells good," John said. "I have to confess, I would never have thought of piling up rocks like that to cook it."

"How did you plan to cook it?" Smoke asked.

"I'm not sure what I planned to do. I guess I was just going to throw it in the fire."

"It would've burned half of it away, maybe all of it," Smoke said.

"Yeah, well, when it was just me, there would probably have been enough left. With four of us, I can see how this is the best way to cook it."

Finally, Smoke went over and pulled on a wing. It came off easily.

"Turkey's ready to eat," he said.

"I'll get some salt out of my pouch," John offered.

"No need for you to waste your salt. You furnished the turkey, the least we can do is furnish the salt," Preacher said.

"Well, that's mighty kind of you."

"You're new to the mountains, aren't you?" Preacher asked.

"Is it that obvious?"

"No, it's just that I've been in these mountains for some thirty years now, and I ain't never run across you before."

"Well, sir, you're right, I just got here a few days ago. I'm from Pennsylvania, and I read about the Rocky Mountains, and how there's land here that no man has ever seen before. So I bought a book that told me everything a man might need in order to live in the mountains. It also had a list of everything I needed to buy, so I went out and bought everything it suggested.

"Now I have supplies for about six months." He laughed. "But it has left me just about dead broke."

"What do you figure on doin' after your six months is up, and you don't have any money to resupply?" Smoke asked.

Jackson chuckled. "To tell you the truth, Smoke, I don't know as I've given it too much thought," he said. "I guess I just sort of figured that something would come along. It's my plan to trap beaver, but if that doesn't work out, I've got enough to get by until I can find employment somewhere and just give up the notion."

"Pilgrim, looks to me like you are a fella in the need of a lot of education."

"Well, if it is education I need, I do have a degree from the University of Pennsylvania," he said.

"It ain't book learnin' I'm talkin' about," Preacher said. "The kind of learnin' you need out here don't come from no college or no books. It don't even come from them books you was talkin' about."

"Then where does one acquire such an education?" John asked.

"It most comes from just bein' out here, and doin'," Preacher said. "After you make the same mistake over a few times, why it just sort of sets in your mind not to do them same things again.

"But it also helps to have someone with you, to help learn you."

"You mean to 'bring me on,' like Smoke is doing with the young man?" John asked.

"Yeah, something like that."

"Well, I can't argue with that. Matt seems to be a most capable young man, despite his youthful age." John laughed, a grunting, rather self-deprecating laugh. "I must confess that my degree in fine arts does little to prepare me for the adventure I'm about to undertake."

"What do you think, Smoke?" Preacher asked. "Would you be willin' to take this pilgrim under your wing for a while?"

"What about Matt?" Smoke asked.

"What about him?" Preacher asked. "You've got a cabin, the boy can hunt and fish, I've no doubt he can take of his ownself. Besides which, I'll look in on him from time to time."

"What do you think, Matt? You think you're up to livin' on your own for a while?"

"I reckon I can," Matt said with a broad smile.

"Damn, you're looking forward to it, aren't you?" Smoke said.

"Why not? It'll be good to get away from your bossin' me around," Matt said with a teasing laugh.

"All right, I'll take him under my wing," Smoke said.

"Whoa, not so fast here," John said. "I agree that my education may be somewhat remiss, but I wouldn't feel right about burdening someone with the task of undertaking my education."

"Pilgrim, I come out here as a boy, no more 'n fourteen years old, I was, when I got here," Preacher said. "I'd done freed a slave girl that was mostly white, fought river pirates on the Mississippi, took a raft down the river, and fought the Battle of New Orleans with ole Andy Jackson hisself. I thought I was ready to take care of myself, but I run into a couple of mountain men by the name of Pierre Garneau and Clyde Barnes. They took me in, and ever'thing I know I learned from them two mountain men. Then, when Smoke come along, well, I sort of took him in, like them mountain men did me, and I taught him as much as I could.

"I reckon it would only be fittin' to give you the same kind of learnin'. And there wouldn't be nobody any better at it than Smoke Jensen. So what do you say? Are you wantin' to actual learn somethin'? Or do you plan on stayin' out here makin' a fool of yourself and maybe even windin' up gettin' yourself kilt?"

John looked over at Smoke, studying him for a long time before he nodded.

"All right," he said. "I'm not too proud to admit that I need help. It's fine by me, if it's fine by you."

Smoke grinned. "I think we'll get along just fine, Mr. Jackson."

Jackson held his hand out. "No, sir. Now we have to start this off right between us. I'm not Mr. Jackson. If we're to be friends, you'll call me John."

"All right, John it will be," Smoke said.

"Say, you ain't no kin to Andy Jackson, are you? I mean, what with your name 'n all," Preacher asked.

"He and my grandfather were first cousins," Jackson said.

"Is that a fact? Well, he was a good man, General Jackson was. Seems to me like I heard he was the president of the United States once. Is that true?"

"Yes, he was the seventh president."

"I thought so. I'll be damn. To think that I once knowed

a president of these here United States is some kind of an awesome thing."

One of the first things Smoke did was tell John that if he was serious about trapping, they were going to have to move.

"The Colorado Rockies have been mostly trapped out," he said. "I think we're goin' to have to go north."

"How far north? All the way into Canada?"

"No, there is no need to go that far. But I reckon we'd better head on up to Wyoming, or more 'n likely, all the way up to Montana."

"Montana," John said. "Yes, that sounds quite interesting. I'll bet there are more places up there that no one has ever seen, than there are down here."

"I'm sure there are," Smoke said. "It's a lot bigger area, and there are a lot fewer people."

"I'll be ridin' on then," Matt said.

"Matt, you know where the money is," Smoke said. "If you start running short of the possibles—flour, coffee, sugar, beans, bacon, that sort of thing—well, just ride on down to Schemerhorn's Trading Post and pick up what you need there. You might go there once a month or so anyway, 'cause if I decide to send you a letter, I'll send it to you care of Schemerhorn."

"All right," Matt said. "Smoke, is it all right if I practice drawing and shooting my pistol while you're gone?"

"Yeah, you've come far enough, I don't reckon you'll be shootin' yourself," Smoke said. "You might need to buy some more cartridges while you're getting your possibles."

"All right," Matt said. "I reckon I'll see you early next summer."

"Take care," Smoke said to the boy as he rode off.

"You sure he'll be all right alone?" John asked. "He seems awfully young."

"Don't let the boy's age fool you," Smoke said. "He's already a better man than three-fourths of the men I know."

They watched Matt until he was out of sight, then Preacher spoke.

"You'll be needin' a pack mule, John," he said. "And to get one of them you're goin' to have to go some way from here, maybe a hunnert miles or more. That'll be a town called Big Rock. It's sort of a new town, just growin' up, but me 'n Smoke has been there three, maybe four times, already, an' they's some pretty good folks there, don't you think, Smoke?"

"So far, the few times we've been there, the folks we've run across have been friendly," Smoke said.

"They got 'em a new sheriff there," Preacher said. "Fella by the name of Monte Carson. Folks say he's honest, and I figure if a town has an honest sheriff, then it's more 'n likely an honest town."

"Any proper town has to have a saloon," John said. "It's been a month of Sundays since I had a beer, and I would be more than willing to dip into my meager resources to remedy that situation."

"They got a saloon there," Preacher said. "It's a good one too, and it's run by a man that ain't always tryin' to cheat you. Besides, it's been a while since either one of us been in town. Might be good . . . I'd like to have a beer my ownself, 'n maybe a meal I didn't have to kill, or cook."

CHAPTER 9

Old Main Building

"I know that you ultimately settled near Big Rock," Professor Armbruster said. "Sugarloaf Ranch is only a few miles away, isn't it?"

"Yes, my ranch is just under five miles from Big Rock."

"But the time of your story is, I believe you said, 1869?"

"Yes."

"Big Rock was still quite new then, wasn't it? I believe it was founded in 1860."

"Yes, Big Rock is proud of its position in Colorado history," Smoke said. He continued with his story and, as before, Professor Armbruster was able to lose himself in the narrative, so that he was actually there as an eyewitness to the events Smoke was describing.

Big Rock

The star on the man's vest was still new because he had only been the sheriff for a short time. Before he moved to Big Rock to become their sheriff, Monte Carson had ridden the outlaw trail. It was mostly down in Texas, and most of the money he stole was from the carpetbaggers and reconstructionists who were taxing the ranchers and farmers to the point that more and more were having to sell out.

He was good with a gun too, and had demonstrated that skill many times, though almost always with someone who was also on the outlaw trail. The only exceptions had been when he killed Marcus Shardeen, a bounty hunter who was looking to take a dead Carson in for the reward, and Lou Bona, who, six months later, tried to do the same thing.

Carson looked again at the telegram he had received just this morning.

DREW CULPEPPER AND MARTIN DINGLE BELIEVED TO BE
HEADED FOR BIG ROCK STOP BOTH MEN WANTED FOR
MURDER STOP

Carson knew Culpepper; he had had a run-in with him two months earlier. Then it had been for getting drunk and throwing a rock through the front window of Murchison's Leather Goods store, a dispute over a pair of saddlebags. Carson had forced Culpepper to pay for the damages, and Culpepper, before he left town, had uttered some threat about "getting even." Carson didn't know Martin Dingle, and had never even heard of him.

Laying the telegram aside, the sheriff walked over to the stove and, using a rag to protect against the heat, picked up the blue-steel pot to pour himself a cup of coffee. He drank it black, simply because it was easier that way, and holding the cup in his hand, he walked over to look through the front window, out onto Front Street. He blew into the coffee to cool it a bit before taking his first swallow.

Big Rock was a bustling town, primarily because of the gold mines in the area. When Smoke, Preacher, and Jackson rode into town they were treated to the sight of new buildings being erected, and the air was rent with the sounds of saws and hammers. There was a sawmill on the outer edge of town, and the ear-splitting screech of its steam-powered circular saw could be heard all over town. There were freight wagons moving up and down the streets, and the boardwalks on each side of the street filled with people conducting commerce.

"Coach comin' in! Coach comin' in!" someone shouted, and looking around Smoke saw a team of six horses coming into town at a gallop. The stagecoach behind the team was rocking left and right as it was pulled at a rapid pace north, up Tanner Street.

"Surely he didn't run that team like that out on the road?" John asked.

Preacher chuckled. "No, they just like to make a point of arrivin' and leavin' at a gallop," he said. "It calls attention to 'em, and makes some people think that maybe the whole trip is fast like that."

They passed the Delmonico Café. "Now, that's where we'll eat after we have us a few beers," Preacher said. "Ain't no finer café in all of Colorado. 'Course, I ain't et in ever' café in Colorado."

The three men stopped in front of Longmont's Saloon. Preacher and Smoke dismounted, but John remained in his saddle.

"I appreciate what you men are doing," John said. "And while I can buy my own beer, I'm not so sure I should be wasting money by eating in a restaurant. Especially if I'm going to have to buy a pack mule."

"Don't you be worryin' none about that," Preacher said. "When we take a feller in, he becomes our pardner. We ain't goin' to let you go thirsty, or hungry, or without a mule."

"We'll be buying all that we need," Smoke said. "And you won't be beholden to anyone. This is just the way we are out here."

"I shall be in your debt then, and I fully intend to discharge that debt at my earliest opportunity," John insisted.

"I have no doubt but that you will," Smoke replied with a friendly smile. He held his hand up in invitation. "Now come on in before the beer goes stale."

What only Preacher and Smoke knew was that Smoke's father, Emmett, lay buried in a place called Brown's Hole, up in the northwest corner of Colorado, near the Idaho line. And buried right beside him was several thousand dollars in gold. Though he didn't show it in the way he lived, because he was always moving around, and staying in the mountains mostly, and avoiding towns and civilization, Smoke was a very wealthy man.

They tied up their animals in front of the saloon. A sign on the front of the saloon featured a beer mug containing a golden brew with a white foamy head. Beneath the sign were the words: COLD BEER HERE.

That was all the invitation they needed, and they pushed their way through the batwing doors to step inside. It was so dark that they had to stand there for a moment or two until their eyes adjusted. The bar was made of burnished mahogany with a highly polished brass footrail. Crisp, clean white towels hung from hooks on the customers' side of the bar, spaced every four feet. A mirror was behind the bar, flanked on each side by a small statue of a nude woman set back in a special niche. A row of whiskey bottles sat in front of the mirror, reflected in the glass so that the row of bottles seemed to be two deep. A bartender with pomaded black hair and a waxed handlebar mustache stood behind the bar, where he was industriously polishing glasses.

"Is the beer really cold, like the sign says?" Smoke asked.

The bartender looked up at him, but he didn't stop polishing the glasses.

"Any colder and the glass would freeze to your lip," he said in a matter-of-fact voice.

"Good. Two beers," Smoke said.

"Just two? There are three of you. What does the other one want?"

"I reckon they'll be orderin' for themselves," Smoke said. "The two beers are for me."

"I'll have two," Preacher said. "How about you, John?"

"As I said earlier, it has been a month of Sundays since I had a beer, so I think two beers would go a long way toward alleviating that situation," John said.

The bartender chuckled, filled six mugs of beer, and set them in front of the three men.

"If all my customers were like you boys, I could get rich real quick, close this place down, and go on to California," a tall, well-dressed man said, from his table near the piano.

"The sign out front says Longmont's Saloon. You would be Mr. Longmont, would you?" Smoke asked.

"I am, sir, Louis Longmont, proprietor of the finest wines, beers, and whiskeys, at your service. And you gentlemen would be?"

"I'm Smoke Jensen. This is John Jackson. And the old gentleman is Preacher."

"Preacher?" Longmont smiled. "I do believe I've heard of you, Preacher. Folks say you were here as soon as Jedediah Smith, Jim Bridger, and Kit Carson."

"Jedediah Smith welcomed me to these mountains. I welcomed Bridger and Carson," Preacher said.

"What's in California?" John asked.

"Beg your pardon?"

"You said if you got rich you would close this place and go to California. What's out there?"

"I'm afraid I can't actually tell you that," Longmont said. "I started out for California, but I never quite made it. I stopped here for a while and I haven't left. But I expect I'll get there someday."

"Why would anyone ever want to leave?" Preacher asked.

"I've been to a lot of places, never found a place I like better 'n these mountains."

"*Oui,*" Longmont said. "I will confess that there's something about the mountains that gets in a man's blood."

Smoke picked up the first beer and took a long drink before he turned to look around the place. A card game was going on in the corner and he watched it for a few minutes, drinking his beer while Preacher and John were carrying on a conversation behind him.

"Pilgrim, you'll be in good hands with Smoke," Preacher said. "I never knew anyone that learned as fast as he did."

"I appreciate it," John said.

"And here's another thing. You make this boy your friend, and you'll have a loyal friend for the rest of your life. And out here, one of the first things you learn is that the most valuable thing a man can have, is a loyal friend."

The back door opened and a tall, broad-shouldered man wearing a badge, stepped through the door. Smoke recognized Sheriff Monte Carson, and he started to speak to him, but saw that the sheriff's attention was directed to a table in the corner of the room.

"Culpepper," Sheriff Carson said. "I heard you were in town. I didn't think you'd be dumb enough to come to my town. Not after killin' those two men down in Pueblo."

The man Carson was talking to, one of the cardplayers, stood up slowly, then turned to face the sheriff.

"What gives you the idea this is your town? And anyway, am I supposed to be afraid of some small-town sheriff like you?"

Because the situation had the look of an impending gunfight, the remaining cardplayers jumped up from the table and moved out of the way.

"You had to know that if you were going to come back

to Big Rock, I was going to find out about it, and put you in jail."

"You ain't puttin' me in no jail, Sheriff."

"You're either goin' to jail, or you're goin' to die, right here, and right now," Sheriff Carson said.

Culpepper smiled. "Sheriff, have you considered the possibility that you might be the one dyin'?"

Smoke was watching the drama play out before him, when he heard something, a soft squeaking sound as if weight were being put down on a loose board. Looking up toward the top of the stairs, he saw a man aiming a shotgun at Sheriff Carson. Carson didn't see him, because the man was behind the sheriff.

"Sheriff, look out!" Smoke shouted. When he shouted the warning, Sheriff Carson turned quickly, drew, and fired. The man at the top of the stairs fired the shotgun wildly, and the heavy charge of buckshot tore a large hole in one of the tables. Sheriff Carson's shot had been right on target, and the man with the shotgun dropped his weapon and slapped his hand over the wound in his chest. He stood there just for a second as blood spilled between his fingers. Then his eyes rolled up in his head and he fell, belly down, headfirst, sliding down the stairs, following his clattering shotgun to the ground floor.

The sound of the two gunshots had riveted everyone's attention to that exchange, including Sheriff Carson, and while his attention was diverted from him, Culpepper took the opportunity to go for his own gun.

"Don't do it, Culpepper!" Smoke yelled, and Culpepper turned his gun toward Smoke. The saloon was filled with the roar of another gunshot as Smoke drew and fired at Culpepper, even though Culpepper already had his gun in his hand.

Smoke's shot hit Culpepper between the eyes, and he fell

back on the table that was still covered with cards and poker chips. He lay there, belly up with his head hanging down on the far side while blood dripped from the hole in his forehead to form a puddle below him. His gun fell from his lifeless hand and clattered to the floor.

"What's goin' on in here?" a new voice asked. "What's all the shootin'?"

When Smoke turned toward the sound of the voice he saw a man standing just inside the open door. Because of the brightness of the light behind him, Smoke couldn't see him clearly enough to identify him.

"Get out of the light," Smoke ordered.

"You don't tell me what to do, I . . ."

Smoke pulled the hammer back and his pistol made a deadly metallic click as the gear engaged the cylinder.

"I said get out of the light, or I'll kill you where you stand."

The figure moved out of the light. When he did, Smoke saw that he was wearing a badge. He put his pistol away.

"It's all right, Emile," Sheriff Carson said to his deputy. "Put your gun away. This man just saved my life."

Emile Harris put the gun away, then advanced farther into the saloon. He looked first at the man lying at the foot of the stairs, then at the other man, spread out on the card table with his head dangling over the edge.

"Damn, what happened here?" he asked.

"What happened here is that these two men made the mistake of thinking they could run roughshod in our town," Sheriff Carson said.

"And you killed both of 'em?"

"No, just that one," Carson replied, pointing to the man at the bottom of the stairs. "That one, I presume, is a man named Dingle. This is Culpepper. Carson pointed toward Smoke. This man killed Culpepper."

"Would you really have shot me if I hadn't moved out of the light?"

Smoke picked up his beer and took a drink before he responded.

"Yeah," he said.

CHAPTER 10

Old Main Building

"The event in Longmont's saloon would be termed a shoot-out, I believe. At least, that's what the western novelists call it, people like Owen Wister, Zane Grey, and Max Brand," Professor Armbruster said.

"A shoot-out, yes. They use the term accurately. I have met all of them, by the way," Smoke said. "And Ned Buntline. I've met him as well."

"Surely you don't equate someone like Ned Buntline with the more legitimate figures of western literature, men like Wister, Grey, and Brand," Professor Armbruster said.

"Why not? He was a storyteller, just as the three men you have mentioned were. In fact, all three of those men told me they had read Buntline, and it was because of his stories that they developed an interest in writing about the West."

"I . . . I must apologize," Professor Armbruster said. "I didn't mean to be pedantic, nor to give offense."

"No offense taken."

"Was that the first time you met Monte Carson?" Professor Armbruster asked.

"Yes. It was the first time I met Louis Longmont, as well."

"But you and Carson, and you and Longmont, became very good friends after that, didn't you?"

"Yes, eventually. Not right away, not until I moved there, some years later."

"How old were you when this shoot-out happened, Mr. Jensen?" Professor Armbruster asked.

"Nineteen, twenty, maybe, I don't remember exactly."

"But, it was before you established Sugarloaf Ranch."

"Oh, yes, long before Sugarloaf, even before Nicole. But I thought I was here to discuss John Jackson, not Preacher and me. You are sort of getting off the track, aren't you?"

"I am indeed. Though many times during the course of research one finds that divergent paths can lead to other fascinating subjects. And quite often, those subjects don't detract from, but rather enhance your original research, as has happened here, with you. But, you are right, we should get back to our discussion of John Jackson.

"Earlier you said that the man, Preacher, suggested you should educate him. Did you undertake that responsibility?"

Smoke chuckled. "Oh, yes, I spent the next year with John. It turns out that he required a lot of education."

"Please, continue with your story," Professor Armbruster said.

"After we left Big Rock, Preacher went one way, John and I went another."

Smoke resumed telling his story, and as it had before, his low, well-modulated voice began to paint word pictures, so that, again, Armbruster wasn't merely listening to a story, he was reliving it, traveling through time and space with Smoke and John Jackson.

Colorado Rockies

"How'd you meet up with Preacher?" John asked Smoke.
Following Smoke's instructions, John was building an

oven from stones. They had shot a possum, and Smoke was cleaning it as John worked on the oven.

"My pa and me come west right after the war," Smoke said. "Then one day this old man just sort of appeared. He was the dirtiest, most stinkingest human being I had ever laid my eyes on. I tell you the truth, John, I just about threw up smelling him."

"That bad?"

"Whoowee, you don't have any idea how bad he was. He told us he'd been watching us for about an hour, and that we were crazy for keeping out in the open the way we were. He said we were prime targets for Indians."

"And what did you think?"

"All I could think about was how bad he stunk and how much I wanted him to go away, or at least get downwind from us."

"What happened?"

"I'll tell you what happened," Smoke said with a grunting chuckle. "It wasn't fifteen minutes later we were jumped by a bunch of Kiowa. We had to fight them off. And that stinking old man? He killed as many as my pa and I did combined."

"I guess you didn't mind having him around so much then, huh?"

"I didn't mind at all. Here, let's put this meat in there and let it start cooking."

They roasted the possum, along with some wild onions and sun roots that Smoke gathered. On top of the oven he set a pan of water to boil, and cooked some cattails.

"Always be on the lookout for cattails," Smoke explained. "They have more uses than you can shake a stick at. In the summer you can harvest the tender stems. The lower part of it will be white and ready to eat, just as it is. If you eat them raw, they taste a little like cucumber. If you cook them, they taste like asparagus. Later, the green flower heads can be cooked and eaten like corn on the cob. And when the yellow pollen starts up, you can gather it up, mix it with flour. That will not only make your flour last longer, it makes a real tasty bread.

"Then, in the fall you can dig up the roots, mash them in water, and let the mix set for a few hours. What you'll get when you pour off the water is a gooey mass of starch at the bottom of the container. That will provide you with a thickening base for soups, whether it be squirrel, rabbit, bird, or, if no meat is available, it's not a bad soup all by itself. Especially if you are in a position where you're near about to starve. Of course, if you pay attention to what's around you, you won't ever actually starve."

"You talk as if a true mountain man never needs to come into the store for supplies," John said.

"Well, the truth is, you just about don't. As long as you've a good supply of salt handy, you'll find that you can make a meal out of almost anything," Smoke said.

"We'll see about that," John replied.

Later, as John chewed the last bit of meat from a bone, then finished up with the boiled cattails, he nodded. "You know, you may be right," he said. "This is about as tasty as anything I've ever eaten. And these things, what did you call them?"

"Sun roots."

"Damn if they don't taste just like potatoes."

"I thought you might like that."

Over the next three days the rain was hard and cold, and Smoke showed John how to build a shelter under an overhanging rock by draping canvas across the front to keep the rain out. Such meat as they could find they cooked over a fire they made just in front of their shelter, and Smoke continued with his lessons.

"There will come a time when you will want to build yourself a cabin against the weather. One with a fireplace and chimney so you can keep warm on the coldest days. I'll help you build it."

"Do you build a new cabin every winter?"

"No, Preacher's been in his same cabin for more than twenty years now. I reckon we can build one that you'll be proud to come back to, every winter. But there's no need in building you one down here. We'll wait until we get to Montana. That way you can be where you can still trap."

"What is the value placed on a beaver skin? How much can you get for one?"

"They are called plews," Smoke said. "And they aren't worth as much as they once were. It used to be one beaver plew was worth three martens. Now martens are worth more than beaver, so it's martens you want to go after. You'll get about three dollars apiece for martens, two dollars for beaver. In a good year, you can trap maybe two hundred marten, and three hundred beaver; you could make as much as twelve hundred dollars."

"Well, now," John said with a broad smile. "That certainly makes the endeavor worthwhile."

"It does, indeed, my friend, it does indeed. I tell you what. If we survive the winter, we'll go to Rendezvous come spring," Smoke said.

"If we survive the winter?" John replied with a bit of a start in his voice.

Smoke laughed. "Most likely, we will," he said.

"What is Rendezvous?"

"They aren't quite as big now as they were back when Preacher was younger, but they are still fun to go to. They are almost like a county fair. Merchants come from the east to sell supplies, whiskey, books, candy, and such. There's music, and generally some women around for dancing. There's shooting contests and knife- and ax-throwing contests. And it's a place where you can sell all the skins you've managed to trap in the past year."

"Where is it held?"

"A different place every year. I guess we'll find out from some of the other trappers."

It was one week later when the two saw their first Indians. There were six of them, all mounted, and painted up.

"I was afraid of that," Smoke said.

"What?"

"Pawnee. They've been following us for the better part of an hour. I thought, or maybe I was just hoping, that they would go on their way. But now they've showed themselves to us, I don't think they have any intention of leaving."

"Are the Pawnee friendly?"

"Not friendly enough so's you can count on it," Smoke said.

"You think they're going to attack us?"

"Yeah, I think maybe they are. You were in the war, so I reckon you can use that long gun."

"Yes, I can use it," John said.

"Problem is, you've got a lot of range and hitting power with that Sharps, but you've got to reload it after every shot."

"Then I shall just have to make every shot count, won't I?" John replied.

The six mounted Indians let out loud war whoops, then, slapping their legs against the sides of their horses, they started galloping toward Smoke and John. Smoke and John stood their ground.

"Now would be a good time to make one of those shots count," Smoke said, and he no sooner spoke the words, than the big, large-bore Sharps boomed loudly beside him. John rolled back from the recoil of the big rifle, but one Indian was knocked down from his horse, and, even from here, Smoke could see the fountain of blood that gushed forth from the strike of the heavy, .50 caliber bullet.

Smoke had a lever-action Henry and he fired once, jacked a new shell into the chamber, and fired a second time. Within less than five seconds the attacking Indians had seen their number cut from six to three. Now, only three, they realized that they no longer had a substantial numerical advantage. The remaining Indians hauled back on the reins so hard that the horses nearly squatted down on their hindquarters. They turned and started galloping away.

Because the Sharps was a breech-loading weapon, and not a muzzle-loader, John had managed to reload more quickly than Smoke had anticipated. John raised his rifle to his shoulder to take aim.

"No, John, don't shoot!" Smoke said, reaching out to push the barrel of John's rifle down before he was able to pull the trigger.

John looked at him in surprise.

"We've got them on the run. By not shooting, we are shaming them as they are running from us; we are showing them that we don't fear them."

"What if they come back?"

"They won't come back today."

Boulderado Hotel, Boulder, Colorado

The university had put Smoke and Sally up in the finest suite in the hotel, or, as the hotel advertised it: "seven hundred square feet of pure luxury." The suite, consisting of a living room, dining room, and bedroom, was on the corner so that there was an excellent view of the city.

Sally was sitting on a leather sofa in the living room, her legs folded up to her side, reading a *Saturday Evening Post* magazine when Smoke came in.

"Finished already?" she asked.

"Just for the day," Smoke said.

"How is it going?"

"It's going well, I think. He has me talking into a microphone, and my words are being recorded on a record, just like the ones you play on the Victrola, only I'm not singing," Smoke said with a smile.

"Too bad. I've heard you crooning. You have a good voice," Sally said.

"They played it back for me today, and I heard my voice. You should hear it."

Sally laughed. "Smoke, I've been hearing your voice for a long, long time now."

"Oh, yes, I guess you have. But I have to tell you that it did sound strange to me. It didn't sound like me. The professor said it did, and he said the reason it sounded different to me is that we never really hear our own voice as others hear it. We hear by the waves caused by sounds in the air, but at the same time we also pick up the vibration of the bones in our skull.

"That's why, when I hear myself recorded and played back, it sounds completely different, because all I hear back from the recording is sound coming through the air, minus the skull vibration and bone conduction."

Sally laughed. "And you understood all that, did you?"

"Yeah," Smoke said with a crooked grin. "It might sound strange, but it makes perfect sense to me."

Sally got up from the sofa and kissed Smoke. "I'm proud of you," she said.

"What are you looking at in the magazine?"

"An ad for a new car."

"A new car? You don't like the Duesenberg?"

"No, I love the Duesenberg," Sally said. "I mean, for your truck."

"I'm not getting rid of my truck."

"Listen to this," Sally said. She cleared her throat, then began reading the ad, as if reciting on stage.

"'Somewhere west of Laramie there's a bronco-busting, steer-roping girl who knows what I'm talking about. She can tell what a sassy pony, that's a cross between greased lightning and the place where it hits, can do with eleven hundred pounds of steel and action when he's going high, wide, and handsome. It's a hint of old loves, and saddle and quirt. The truth is, the Jordan Playboy is built for her.'"

"What is that?" Smoke said with a puzzled expression on his face. "'High, wide, and handsome, hint of old loves, saddle and quirt'? That says nothing about the car."

"I think the idea is to create a feeling," Sally said. "I think the words are beautiful. And so is the car. Look at the picture."

Sally showed Smoke the ad.

"Doesn't look very practical," Smoke said. "It only has one seat, and you can't haul anything in it. I can't see trading the truck for it."

"You're right. Okay, keep the truck. Just buy the car."

"What if we wanted to go somewhere and take some folks with us? There's no room in this car."

"Well, then we would just go in the Duesenberg," Sally said.

Smoke laughed. "So what you're saying is we'll have two cars and a truck?"

"Smoke, don't tell me we can't afford it."

"I'll tell you what we can afford. We can afford to have something good to eat. How about we order up room service for supper, and use this fancy dining room table?"

"Oh, no," Sally said. "We don't get to come to a city that often. You're taking me out, Kirby Jensen. And not for supper, for dinner."

CHAPTER 11

Old Main Building

"Are you ready to resume, Mr. Jensen?" Professor Armbruster asked the next morning when Smoke returned to the Old Main building on campus.

"Yes, sir, I am," Smoke said. "Where did I leave off yesterday?"

"You and Jackson had just been attacked by six Pawnee," Professor Armbruster said, "but you drove them off."

"So we did."

"Did you have any more Indian encounters?"

"Not immediately. We kept moving north until we left Colorado, then we wound up at Fort Laramie, in Wyoming."

"Laramie?"

Smoke thought of the car ad Sally had read to him yesterday—"Somewhere west of Laramie"—and he smiled. "No, sir, we were at Fort Laramie," he said.

Fort Laramie

When Smoke and John reached Fort Laramie, they were stopped by the guard at the front gate of the post.

"What is your business here?" the guard at the gate asked.

"We have no particular business, private," John said. "We are just passing through and thought we would take shelter here for a couple of days."

"You're both civilians, I can't let you through."

"I realize that you can't authorize our entry. But your post commandant can. So I'm asking you to call the corporal of the guard so that he may escort us to the post headquarters where we will secure permission from your commanding officer."

"The corporal won't take you there."

"Oh, I think he will," John said. "Army regulations twenty-two-dash-five specifically state that civilian personnel may be billeted on a military reservation under certain conditions where safety is concerned, and permission for such visits may be granted at any time by authority of the post commandant."

The guard looked at John with a shocked expression on his face, but he was no more shocked than Smoke.

"Go ahead, Private, call him," John said. There was an air of authority in John's voice that Smoke had not heard before.

"Corporal of the guard, front gate!" the private called.

The other sentries repeated the gate guard's call until, after a few moments a corporal came strolling up to the gate.

"What is it?" the corporal asked.

"Corporal, under the provisions of army regulations twenty-two-dash-five, my friend and I wish to petition the post commandant for permission to spend a few nights inside the fort," John said.

"I ain't never heard of no regulation like that," the private said. "Have you ever heard of it, Corporal?"

"Of course I have," the corporal replied. He stared at John and Smoke for a moment, then nodded. "All right, come with me."

"John, is there such a regulation?" Smoke asked, quietly,

as they followed the sergeant across the open area toward the headquarters building.

John chuckled. "I don't have the slightest idea," he said. "But it has gotten us this far."

Smoke laughed. "Yeah, it has."

"Wait here," the corporal of the guard said when he led them into the orderly room. The first sergeant and the company clerk were both sitting at their desks.

"Top, these men want to see the commandant," the corporal of the guard said.

The first sergeant gave Smoke and John a cursory glance, then nodded and stepped into the CO's office. A moment later a major stepped out of his office. At first there was a rather irritated look on his face, but when he saw John, he broke into a wide grin.

"Captain Jackson!" he said.

"Lieutenant Sanderson," John replied. "I haven't seen you since Gettysburg. What happened to you? Other than the fact that you made major?"

"I went to the hospital in Washington, D.C., and when I recovered, I was assigned to General Grant's staff."

"Ha. I can see why you made major then. Oh, this is my friend, Smoke Jensen."

"Mr. Jensen," Sanderson said.

"Smoke, during the war Bobby Sanderson and I served together."

"Served together? Don't you mean you were my commanding officer?" Sanderson replied.

"Congratulations on making major, though I'm sure the congratulations are late," John said.

"What brings you to Fort Laramie?" Sanderson asked.

"I'm in a new business now," John said. "I'm a fur trapper, and my friend, who knows about these things, tells me that the best place to trap now is in Montana. So we're headed up that way, and I thought you might be generous enough to put us up here for a couple of nights."

"Of course I will," Sanderson said. "And you are here just in time to help us celebrate Independence Day."

"Independence Day? What day is this, anyway?"

"July third," Sanderson said.

"Yes, we would love to celebrate the Fourth with you and the troops."

"First Sergeant, get these gentlemen billeted in the officers' quarters," Sanderson said.

"Yes, sir. If you gentlemen will come with me?" the first sergeant invited.

The first thing Smoke did after being assigned a room in the bachelor officers' quarters, was to take a bath, and get into clean clothes. Although he had bathed in streams, this was his first real tub bath in over a year, and he sat in the tub for a long time, just luxuriating in the water. He heard a knock on the door.

"Smoke? Smoke, are you in there?"

"Yeah, John, if you don't mind seeing me in the bathtub, come on in," Smoke said.

When John came in, Smoke was surprised to see that he was wearing the uniform of an army captain.

"I'll bet you didn't even know I had this uniform with me, did you?"

Smoke chuckled. "Hell, John, I didn't even know you had ever been in the army. Let alone an officer. And a captain, no less. That's pretty damn impressive."

"Not all that impressive. The army was huge during the war, and it required a lot of officers. Those of us who had college educations sort of had a leg up on the rest of the troops."

"Well, it impresses me," Smoke said.

"Bobby has invited us to his quarters for supper tonight," John said. "I took the liberty of accepting the invitation for both of us. I hope you don't mind."

"No, why should I mind? I never turn down a free meal. But I'm afraid the best I can do for clothes would be a buckskin outfit that's clean, instead of the dirty one I've been wearing. Hand me that towel, would you?"

"Your buckskins will be fine," John said, handing Smoke the towel as he stepped from the tub.

"I have to tell you, I'm a little out of place here, on an army post," Smoke said. "I wanted to go to the war, but my pa and my brother went, and my sister ran off, so that left me to take care of ma."

"You would have been too young anyway, wouldn't you?" John asked.

"I could have lied about it."

"Well, for the time being, you and I will be trading places," John said. "You have the lead when we are in the mountains; I'll take the lead while we are here, on the army post."

"Sounds like the best way to handle it," Smoke said.

Major Sanderson lived in the commandant's house, which was a rather large, two-story home with Corinthian columns supporting the porch roof. Smoke and John were met at the front door by an enlisted man who was Sanderson's striker.

"Come in, sirs, the major is expecting you."

"Thank you, Private," John said.

Major Sanderson and his wife were waiting in the parlor.

"Hello, John. I would like you to meet my wife, Cindy."

John smiled. "You have done well, Bobby, both in your military career and your choice of a wife. What a lovely lady you have married. I'm most pleased to meet you, Mrs. Sanderson."

"Mrs. Sanderson," Smoke said with a slight nod of his head.

"I have heard much about you, Captain Jackson," Cindy said. "It is good to finally meet you."

For the next half hour, and even after they were called to dinner, Smoke listened, with interest, to the stories John and Major Sanderson exchanged.

"Were you in the war, Mr. Jensen?" Major Sanderson asked.

"No, I missed it. My father and my older brother were." Smoke smiled. "But I'm afraid they fought on the opposite side from you gentlemen."

"Men of good conscience fought on both sides," Sanderson said. "Who was your father with?"

"He was with Mosby's Raiders."

"Mosby? Wait a minute," Major Sanderson said. "Jensen? Your father wouldn't be Emmett Jensen, would he?"

"Yes."

"My, what a warrior he was," Sanderson said. "John, it was before I came to your company. I was on General Stoughton's staff when Mosby's Rangers showed up. Two men went into the general's quarters and awakened him, most rudely I must say, by a slap on his rear. General Stoughton was incensed and, pulling himself up in righteous indignation, said, 'Do you know who I am?'

"One of the two men replied by saying, 'Do you know who John Mosby is?'

"'Yes! Have you got the rascal?' General Stoughton asked.

"'No, but he has got you!' The two men in the room with the general that night were John Mosby"—Major Sanderson looked over at Smoke—"and your father."

John laughed out loud. "How did the men take it?" he asked.

"I have to tell you, John, that General Stoughton was

a pompous ass. The truth is, I think at least half the men applauded Mosby, and Emmett Jensen. Myself included," he added.

"Good," Smoke said. "I wouldn't want to make enemies from new friends."

John and Major Sanderson continued to discuss the war. The incident where General Stoughton was captured happened in March 1863. In May, Lieutenant Sanderson joined Captain Jackson's company and fought under him in the greatest battle of the war, the Battle of Gettysburg.

In Smoke's young life he had already faced death many times, and smelled the acrid smell of gunpowder, so he was not unfamiliar with violent death. But the scale of Gettysburg, with thousands of men on either side facing shot and shell, advancing and withdrawing across battlefields strewn with the dead and dying, was enough to hold even his attention.

John and Major Sanderson continued to share such stories.

"What made you decide to go into the fur-trapping business?" Sanderson asked. "I thought you had some girl you were anxious to marry back in, where was it? Boston? Philadelphia?"

"Philadelphia, and it didn't work out," John said.

"That happened to a number of people, I think," Sanderson said.

"Yes. But not everyone did something as foolish as I did."

Sanderson chuckled. "What did you do that was so foolish?"

"I joined the French Foreign Legion."

"What? You did? But wait . . . I've read about the Foreign Legion. The term of enlistment is five years, isn't it? If you joined the Foreign Legion, how is it that you are no longer a member?"

"Let's just say that I altered my contract with them."

"You altered your contract? What do you mean?"

"I deserted."

"Oh," Sanderson said. "Are you afraid that . . . what I mean is, do you think they'll come looking for you?"

"No. They would have to come, not only to America, but to the Rocky Mountains to find me. They won't waste their time, they'll just recruit someone to take my place."

"Bobby, can't we find a more pleasant subject to discuss?"

"Yes, forgive me, my dear," Major Sanderson said. He smiled. "Because tomorrow is Independence Day, it will be a day of no work for the men. We plan to have a day-long celebration, and a barbeque. You'll probably smell the meat cooking tonight."

Smoke did smell the meat cooking all night long, two beef halves on spits that were suspended over glowing coals. By the next morning morale on the post was high, not only because of the barbeque, but because the day was given over to celebrations and games. One of the games was baseball, the first time Smoke had ever seen the game played.

That night there was a dance. Held at the sutler's store, it was for everyone on the post, enlisted and officers alike, though it was somewhat limited, due to the lack of women. The wives of the post did their part by allowing their dance cards to be filled by the bachelor officers and men, and it wasn't all that unusual to see Major Sanderson's wife, Cindy, dancing with a young private.

There were very few single women at the post, mostly laundresses who lived on "Soapsuds Row" washing and iron-ing the post laundry. As a rule, the laundresses did not stay single very long. They were prime candidates for marriage to the noncommissioned officers of the post.

Both John and Smoke danced once with the major's wife, but generally stayed out of the dance in order to give the men of the post more opportunities. There were a few of the women, though, who made it known by looks and gestures that they would welcome a dance with the two handsome strangers.

The next morning, the two men left immediately after breakfast.

CHAPTER 12

Two weeks later Smoke and John reached the town of Theresa, Montana. Theresa was a one-street town that had grown up at this location in order to take advantage of the only water in the area. They surveyed the town as they rode in, and realized it could be any out-of-the-way town, anywhere in the West. There was almost an ethereal quality to them.

The Cattleman's Saloon wasn't hard to find. It was the biggest and grandest building in the entire town. Inside, the saloon was out of the sun, but the air was still and stuffy, and the dozen or so customers who were drinking had to use their bandanas to continually wipe the sweat from their faces. Behind the bar was a sign that read: PLEASE USE THE SPITTOONS. Despite that admonition, the floor was stained with tobacco juice.

There was no gilt-edged mirror, but there was a real bar and an ample supply of beer and decent whiskey. The saloon had an upstairs section at the back, with a stairway going up to a second-floor landing. When Smoke glanced up, he could see rooms opening off the landing. A heavily painted saloon girl was taking a cowboy up the stairs with her. Smoke had never been upstairs with a bar girl, but he had a pretty good idea of what went on there.

The upstairs area didn't extend all the way to the front of the building. The main room of the saloon was big, with exposed rafters below the high, peaked ceiling. There were three tables with drinking customers, and a fourth table that had a card game going on.

Smoke and John bellied up to the bar.

"What'll it be?" the barkeep asked as he moved down to the two men. He wiped up a spill with a wet, smelly rag.

"Beer," Smoke said.

"I'll have the same."

Smoke slid a dime across the bar and the bartender drew two mugs of beer from the barrel behind the bar.

Smoke turned his back to the bar and looked out over the room. A bar girl sidled up to him then. She was heavily painted and showed the dissipation of her profession. There was no humor or life left to her eyes, and when she saw that Smoke wasn't interested, she turned and walked back to sit by the piano player.

The piano player wore a small, round derby hat and kept his sleeves up with garter belts. He was pounding away, though whatever music he was playing was practically lost amidst the noise of the many conversations.

A girl came down the stairs and went up to the bar. Glancing over at her, Smoke saw that one eye was red and swollen nearly shut. It still had the glowing look of a very fresh injury.

"Millie, what happened?" the bartender asked.

"Nothing happened," the girl said, putting her hand up to cover the eye. "Don't worry about it."

"What do you mean, don't worry about it? It's clear to see that someone just hit you."

"Please, don't say nothin' about it," Millie said. "He wants a bottle of whiskey." Millie put some money on the table.

"The hell he does. Did Colby hit you?" The bartender tried to touch her eye, but Millie pulled away from him.

"Please, Don, just drop it," Millie said. "It's no big thing and I don't want to . . ."

"You don't want to what?"

"I don't want to make him mad at me."

"Honey, looks to me like he's already mad at you. And if he isn't already mad, looks like it makes no difference to him one way or the other."

"It's all right, please, don't make any trouble."

"No trouble. I'll just go up there and tell him his time is up." Don started from around behind the bar.

"No, don't, please!" Millie said. "I told you, nothing is going on." She reached out to grab him. "Don, I'm afraid he'll kill you. You know how good he is with that gun, and how he's always lookin' to use it. He'll use it on you."

Don hesitated. "All right," he said. "I won't go up 'n say anything to him, but you don't go back up there neither."

"We ain't . . . done nothin' yet," Millie said. "He'll just say he ain't got what he's paid for."

"Then I'll give him his money back. But you don't have to go back up there. Not if he's beating you."

As the two were talking, Colby, bare-chested, and wearing only his trousers and gun belt, appeared at the railing on the upper balcony.

"Hey, you! Bitch!" he shouted down at the girl. "What the hell's keeping you? You've been down there long enough. Get back up here!"

"Colby, she's not coming back up there," Don said. "You've had her long enough."

"What do you mean, I've had her long enough? I'll by damn have her as long as I want her. Do you understand? How long I have her ain't none of your business."

"No, now, your time is up. There's another gent wantin' her."

"Yeah? Just who would that be?" Colby looked down over

the floor of the saloon. "Who else is wantin' her?" he asked. "Who wants her bad enough to come through me to get her?"

Millie looked out over the rest of the saloon patrons, the expression in her eyes showing her fear of Colby, and her desperate bid for someone to help her.

There was absolute silence as all the other men in the saloon found something on the floor, or the back wall, or the front window to examine. Not one man would meet Millie's eyes.

"Well, now, turns out you was lyin', doesn't it?" Colby said. The smile that spread across his face was totally devoid of all humor.

"Why don't you leave her alone, Colby?" The other bar girl said. This was the same one who had made a tentative advance toward Smoke and John when they first came into the saloon.

"There ain't nobody asked for your opinion," Colby replied with a snarl. "Besides, if she don't come with me, who would she go with? You done seen that nobody else wants her. Hell, she's nothin' but a whore, same as you. Now, you, Millie, if you know what's good for you, you'll get your ass back up here, now!"

Millie clinched her hands into fists and shook her head resolutely. "No," she said, her voice so quiet that Smoke could barely hear it. "No, I'm not coming back up."

"What do you mean you ain't comin' back up? I paid for you. You hear me, girl? I paid for you! You belong to me."

"Your time is up," Millie said.

"My time is up when I say my time is up."

Millie put her hand down in a dress pocket, then pulled out two pieces of silver.

"Here is your money," she said. "I'll give it back to you."

Colby pulled his pistol and pointed it toward Millie.

"I don't want my money, bitch. I want you. Now you get back up here or I'll shoot you dead where you stand."

"Like the lady said, your time is up," Smoke said. "I believe I'm next, miss, if you don't mind." If the girl had actually gone back upstairs, then he wasn't going to try and stop her. But she was showing courage enough to refuse, and Smoke felt that her courage should be rewarded. He intended to see to it that she didn't have to go up if she didn't want to.

Millie looked at Smoke with an expression of hope, but when she saw how young he was, the expression of hope died.

"No," she said quietly. She held her hand out and shook her head. "No, honey, I appreciate it, but you don't need to get involved."

"Ha!" Colby said. "I say let him get involved. You want to take me on, do you, sonny?"

"If I have to," Smoke said.

Colby chuckled. "Oh, you don't have to, sonny. You can just tell me you're sorry, then tell the bitch there to get on back up here where she belongs."

"Well, I don't plan to apologize, and I don't plan to tell her to go back up there. It seems pretty obvious to everyone here that she doesn't want to."

"Now, do you want to tell me why the hell I should care what she wants? She's got no choice," Colby said. "Neither do you, mister. Or haven't you noticed that I happen to be holding a gun in my hand."

"Oh, yeah, I see the gun," Smoke said. "And I'm asking you, nicely, to put it away."

Colby laughed out loud. "Do you people hear this young punk? He's asking me, nicely, to put the gun away."

"Or drop it," Smoke said.

"And if I don't do either?"

"I'll kill you," Smoke said easily.

"You," Colby said to John. "You're a dumb son of a bitch

to be standin' there next to him like that. When I start shootin', I ain't goin' to be all that particular about where I'm shootin'."

John leaned back against the bar and took a swallow of his beer before he replied.

"I'm in no danger," John said.

"You're in no danger, huh? And what gives you that idea?"

"I'm in no danger because you won't be shooting," he said.

"What do you mean, I won't be shooting?"

"I mean if you don't do what my friend says, if you don't put your pistol away, or drop it, he'll kill you before you can even get a shot off."

It was the calm and very understated way John made his comment that made everyone's hair stand on end.

With a shout of rage, Colby swung his gun toward Smoke, but in one smooth and incredibly fast motion, Smoke drew and fired. Colby dropped his gun over the rail and it fell with a clatter to the bar floor, twelve feet below. He grabbed his chest, then turned his hand out and looked down in surprise and disbelief as his palm began filling with his own blood. His eyes rolled back in his head and he pitched forward, crashing through the railing, then turning over once in midair before he landed heavily on his back alongside his dropped gun.

Colby lay motionless on the floor with open, but sightless eyes staring toward the ceiling. It had all happened so fast that no one else in the saloon had made so much as one move . . . it was as if they had all been frozen in position, an eerie tableau, watching the action take place around them.

The gun smoke from the single shot formed a cloud which drifted slowly toward the door. Beams of sunlight became visible as they stabbed through the cloud. There were rapid and heavy footfalls on the wooden sidewalk outside as more people began coming in through the swinging doors. One of them was wearing a badge.

"What happened here?"

Everybody began talking at once.

"Hold, hold it!" the lawman said, holding up his hands. He walked over and looked down at Colby's body.

"The world is a better place without this son of a bitch," he said. "All I need to know is, was it a fair fight?"

"Fair fight? Marshal, Colby had his gun out and was fixin' to shoot before the young feller there even drawed his gun!" the bartender said.

"Then I see no reason to get the judge to come here and hold a hearing," the marshal said. "You the one that did it?" the marshal asked.

"Yes."

"You're a stranger here, ain't you?"

"Yes, my friend and I are going up to Montana to trap beaver and marten."

"Tell you what. I got no quarrel with you. Seein' as ever'one in here says you was in the right. And, seein' as Colby was one worthless son of a bitch. But it might be better if you moved on tonight."

"Do you mind if we stay long enough to have our supper?" Smoke asked.

"Yeah, you can. Go on over to the café and order anything you want. I'll even pay for it. For the both of you."

"That's very nice of you, Marshal."

Finishing their beer, Smoke and John followed the marshal over to Waggy's Café. They were met by a small, gray-haired man.

"Gentlemen, this is William Wagner, owner of Waggy's Café. And you'll not find a better café in town."

"Well, now, James, I'd just feel real complimented, if I wasn't the only café in town," Wagner said.

"Waggy, I want you to give these two men anything they want, and bill the city."

"All right, Marshal," Waggy replied. "Have a seat, gentlemen."

John started to sit at a table in the middle of the room, but Smoke shook his head no.

"We'll sit back there in the corner," he said. "That way we'll both have our backs against the wall."

"You really think that's necessary?"

"Yeah, I do," Smoke said. "It's hard to imagine someone like Colby with friends, but if he does have any, I wouldn't want them coming toward us without our seeing them."

"Yeah, I see what you mean," John said. John smiled. "I have to tell you, I'm really looking forward to this meal."

"Now I'm hurt," Smoke teased. "Why, that sounds like you aren't all that pleased with my cooking."

"Oh, don't get me wrong, I'm pleased, all right. But it's been a month of Sundays since I've had fried chicken, and I see that they have that here. I intend to enjoy myself."

"Yeah, me too," Smoke admitted.

The men ordered, and the waiter began bringing food to the table. Between them they ate an entire chicken, a dozen biscuits, mashed potatoes, gravy, and green beans. They finished the meal off with two slices each of black and blue pie, made with a combination of black- and blueberries. Their eating was of such a prodigious nature that it drew the attention of everyone else in the café.

"I'll tell you two boys the truth," Waggy said. "If the city wasn't payin' for your meals, I'd just about let you eat for free. Seein' you boys enjoyin' your food that much is about as good a job of advertisin' as I could hope for."

"It's not hard to appreciate good food, and we thank you," John said.

Old Main Building

"I've read about that shooting in the Cattleman's Saloon," Professor Armbruster said. "The town of Theresa doesn't even exist anymore, and when you look it up, turns out that the shooting you just described is one of the highlights of its entire history. The man you killed was Braxton Colby. He is said to have killed more than twenty men, and, after he was killed, turned out that he had murdered at least three women."

"I gave him a chance to back out of it," Smoke said.

"Yes, the way you just told the story squares with everything I've read about it. Did you have any repercussions from killing Colby?"

"Do you mean did anyone come after us for revenge?"

"Well, did they?"

"Yes, that very night," Smoke said.

"I thought that might be the case, though I must confess that in the reports I have read the stories vary so that I've never been able to ascertain which one was true or even if it actually happened."

"It happened," Smoke said.

CHAPTER 13

Theresa

Smoke opened his eyes. Something had awakened him and he lay very still. The doorknob turned and he was up, reaching for the gun that lay on a table by his bed. He moved as quietly as a cat, stepping to the side of the door and cocking his Colt .44. His senses were alert, his body alive with readiness. Smoke could hear someone breathing on the other side of the door. A thin shaft of hall light shone underneath. Outside the hotel he heard a tinkling piano and a burst of laughter.

Smoke heard a rattling of the doorknob. He had locked the door but whoever was on the other side either had a key, or was very good at picking locks, because in less than a minute, the door opened, and an increasing wedge of light spilled into the room.

Was it John?

He didn't think so. John wouldn't have let himself into the room that way. He would have knocked.

Smoke watched as a hand stuck in through the opening. The hand was clutching a pistol, and the pistol was aimed toward the bed, exactly where Smoke had been but several seconds earlier.

Smoke watched the thumb pull the hammer back, but just before the intruder pulled the trigger, Smoke stuck a pencil just in front of the hammer so that when it fell, it made only a slight clicking sound.

"What the hell?" the intruder asked in surprise.

Smoke grabbed the gun arm and pulled the intruder on into the room. The intruder called out in surprise, and Smoke jerked his arm around behind his back, then twisted the arm up behind the intruder's back.

"Who are you?" Smoke hissed.

"Emile Colby," the intruder replied.

"What are you doing here, Colby?"

"I come to avenge my brother."

"Yeah? Well, it isn't goin' to work out like that, is it?"

Smoke grabbed Emile Colby by the scruff of his neck and the seat of his pants, then rushed him out into the hallway.

"Hey! Leggo of me! Leggo of me!" Colby started shouting. His shouts and the loud disturbance caused half a dozen other doors to open onto the hall.

"Here, what's goin' on here?" someone shouted.

"Nothing much," Smoke replied. "I'm just taking out the trash."

"You've got no right to . . ."

"To what?" Smoke said.

By now everyone was laughing at Colby.

When they reached the head of the stairs, Colby had pretty much quit his shouting, and was now quiet, the silence brought on by fear.

"What are you going to do?" Colby asked. "Where are you taking me?"

"You don't understand," Smoke replied. "I'm not taking you anywhere. This is as far as you go."

Smoke bent Colby over, then gave him a kick in the rear. Colby tumbled down the stairs, screaming all the way.

[*In presenting to the public this story of Kirby Jensen and John "Liver-Eating" Jackson's life and adventures, I was cautioned against embellishing any particular incident too highly, and to leave out of the book any element of fiction.*

"I have observed," Smoke Jensen said, "in reading much of the work written about me and my contemporaries, that the tendency has been to exaggerate nearly everything. The effect of this has been to give the public a wrong idea of the character of the men who found their way into the young West in search of wealth and adventure. Please tell the story so that those who read it may draw from it correct conclusions as to the kind of lives we really lived, and avoid such coloring of the truth as might lead them to think I am boasting of my own prowess, or exaggerating my own importance."

There have been many books written about Smoke Jensen, and as he is generally considered to be a true treasure of Colorado, there will be many more. And, no doubt, many of these books, especially those that make no pretense of being anything more than a novel, will attempt to build upon a basis of truth, a degree of fact and fiction ingeniously combined.

I am attempting in this endeavor to present the stories of Smoke Jensen and John Jackson's life as truthfully as I can. But the plain fact, perhaps not understood by those of us in the twentieth century, is that men like Jensen and Jackson lived the kind of lives that are written about by such men as Owen Wister and Zane Grey, or portrayed by Tom Mix and William S. Hart. Such men are passing from the scene, but they will never pass from our history.—ED.]

Montana—late September 1869

The trapping didn't really start until the cold came because, as Smoke explained, it wasn't until then that the beaver and marten would have their full coats.

"All right, this looks like a good place," Smoke said.

"The old man, Preacher, has he been out here long?" John asked, as the two men started unloading their traps.

"He came out here soon after the War of 1812," Smoke said. "And he was taken in by a couple of old-timers who had been here since the late seventeen hundreds."

"Late seventeen hundreds? That was before Lewis and Clark."

"Which Preacher's friends described as nice young men, who were wet behind the ears."

"Ha! It would have been interesting to meet them. But then, Preacher is an interesting man too."

"More than interesting. He is one of the finest, if not the finest man I have ever met. Let's get some traps out. *La langue n'attrape pas le castor.*"

"What did you just say? I know that it is French, but I must confess that I learned very little while I was in the Foreign Legion."

Smoke laughed. "It's a saying that Preacher learned from his friend, Pierre Garneau. It means 'the tongue does not catch the beaver.'"

John laughed as well. "*La langue n'attrape pas le castor.* Very good, I shall have to remember that."

After trapping for several weeks, and skinning and cleaning the beaver pelts, several buffalo came by.

"John, have you ever eaten buffalo?" Smoke asked.

"I can't say as I have."

"Your Sharps fires a heavy enough bullet to take one down. I'll give you the honor. Come with me."

The two men approached the buffalo . . . not part of a large herd, there were no more than six in the group.

"Do you think you can hit one from here?"

"Yes."

"That one," Smoke said, pointing one of them out.

John slipped a .50 caliber bullet into the chamber, closed the block, and took aim, and fired.

A puff of dust flew up from the buffalo's coat, its front legs buckled, then straightened as the animal fought to stay on its feet, then it went down. The sound of the gunshot rolled back in repeating echoes.

"Great shot, John!" Smoke said.

"They didn't run," John said, puzzled.

"That's because you shot the leader. Since he didn't run, none of the others did either. Now, shoot that one, and we'll both have a robe for the winter."

John shot the second buffalo, and this time the remaining four did run. Smoke and John hurried out to the downed buffalo and discovered that both were dead by the time they got there.

[*Less than twenty years after the experience described above, the buffalo were very nearly extinct. Dr. William T. Hornaday of the National Museum directed public attention to the impending extinction of the buffalo. In 1889, he conducted a census which disclosed only 1,091 living buffaloes in the entire world. Another census taken in 1903 turned up only 969, in forty-one herds in the United States, and an additional 675 in Canada, for a world total of 1,644.*

It is easy to point to the cause. Some might say that they were hunted out during the westward expansion of the railroad, and to a degree that is true. But it is also true that the survival of the buffalo did not have a very high degree of importance among the western settlers, whose economy was incompatible with the continued existence of the buffalo. Today the cattle on a thousand hills provide a far greater economic resource than the buffalo, if left to thrive in their primitive paradise, could possibly supply.—ED.]

"We've got some work to do," Smoke said, pointing to the two dead animals.

After skinning the two buffalo, their hides had to be fleshed and thinned. Smoke started at the edges, and began removing the meat and the fat, using a very sharp knife, and working his way toward the center.

The buffalo had already been butchered into chunks of meat that weren't too heavy to carry, and those chunks were hanging from the limbs of a tree to keep the wolves away.

"We'll have meat all winter," Smoke said. "The cold will keep the meat fresh."

"I have got to get me a better knife than this," John said as he tried to emulate Smoke's work on the hides. "This damn thing is as worthless as tits on a boar hog."

"You need a Bowie knife," Smoke said, showing his.

"Well, since I'm not helping much with the cleaning of the skin, suppose I get a fire started and we carve off some of that buffalo for supper."

"Sounds like a good idea to me," Smoke said, without looking up.

Smoke continued to work on the buffalo skin while John began gathering wood for the fire.

"Smoke?" John said a moment later. There was quiet urgency in his voice.

"What?"

"We've got company coming."

"Trouble?" Smoke asked.

John shook his head. "I don't know. I don't think so, though, because there are women with them."

Smoke dipped his hands in the icy cold water to wash off the blood and tissue that had been collected from the inside of the buffalo skin. When his hands were clean, he stood up to watch the Indians approach. There were seven of them, three men and four women. One of the men and one of the women were very old.

Smoke held his hand up, palm out as the Indians approached.

"I am Ketano," the oldest of the men said.

"I am Smoke."

The Indian looked confused, and he made the symbol of smoke with his hand twirling around and lifting.

"Smoke?" he asked, not sure he understood the name.

"Yes, Smoke," Smoke said, repeating the hand sign, then pointing to himself.

The old Indian smiled. "It is a good name," he said, then he repeated to the others, saying the name both in English and his own language.

"What kind of Indians are these?" John asked.

"Mandan, I expect," Smoke said. "More than likely if they were Crow, they would be after our scalps."

"Trade?" Ketano asked, again backing up his English with sign language.

"Yes, we will trade," Smoke said. "What do we have that you want?"

"Buffalo meat," Ketano said, pointing to the hanging chunks.

Smoke walked over to the meat and put his hand on one of the two humps. "This you cannot have," he said. He pointed to the rest of the meat. "You may take some of the remaining meat."

Again Ketano spoke to the others. They laughed, and one of them said something.

"He says you know what part of buffalo is good," Ketano said.

"What have you got to trade?" Smoke asked.

The Indians had honey, corn, dried berries, and wild greens. They also had a beaded knife sheath that John wanted.

Before they left, Ketano gave Smoke and John a warning.

"The Crow do not like the white men trapping here," he said. "I think if they can, they will kill you."

"But we aren't on Crow land. This is public land," Smoke said.

"The Crow believe that any land they want is their land," Ketano said.

With other signs of friendship, the Indians left, carrying bundles of buffalo meat with them.

On the Missouri River—December 1869

A bright sun, reflected back by the mantle of snow, made it necessary for both John and Smoke to keep their eyes at a squint. The river whispered slowly on its never-ending journey to St. Louis where, joining the Mississippi, it would flow all the way down to the Gulf of Mexico.

"Smoke, you do know we're being trailed, don't you?" John asked.

"Good for you, John, you're picking it up fast," Smoke said. "Yes, I know. I just wanted to give you the chance to mention it first. How many do you make?"

"Four, I think. Crow?"

"More than likely," Smoke said. "You remember, Ketano told us they were trying to keep white trappers out."

"Do we confront them? Or try and elude them?" John asked.

"We may as well face them down," Smoke said. "We won't have any peace, otherwise."

"Look, just ahead," John said. "See how that rock juts out toward the edge of the water? It will give us cover and concealment. And it's big enough for both of us."

"Yeah," Smoke said. "Let's get up there quickly enough to get our horses out of the way."

Smoke and John urged their horses into a gallop, and the

pack mules came along without much urging. They rode around behind the big rock John had pointed out, secured their animals, then climbed up onto the rock.

The rock was absolutely perfect for their purposes. It was in two steps, one step that allowed them to get into a kneeling position behind the second step, which was high enough to conceal them.

The four Indians were very skillful in their approach. Not one word was spoken, and they were handling their animals so adroitly that their unshod hooves could not be heard.

"When they get to about fifty yards from us, we'll challenge them," Smoke said. "Use my Henry. You can get your shots off faster that way."

"What will you use?"

"If we wait until they are within fifty yards, I'll use my pistol," Smoke said.

The two men waited until the four Indians came around the bend. Then, suddenly, Smoke stood up. And seeing him stand, John did so as well.

"Stop there!" Smoke cautioned.

"Ayiee!" one of the Indians shouted. He was armed with a bow and arrow, and he raised the bow and loosed an arrow.

The arrow flashed by so close that Smoke could hear the wind of the arrow passing.

"You take the two on the right, now!" Smoke said, firing even as he said the word "now."

John didn't need a second invitation; he fired almost as quickly as Smoke, and jacking another round into the chamber he fired a second time as Smoke was also firing. In less than the time it took to tell about it, all four Indians had been knocked from their horses.

"Looks like at least two of them had repeating rifles," Smoke said. "I see no sense in letting them go to waste, do you?"

John chuckled. "I see no sense at all," he said.

Keeping wary, because Smoke knew that sometimes an Indian would fake death to get an advantage over his adversary, the two men approached the four Indians.

Extreme caution wasn't necessary. All four were dead.

John picked up the two Henry repeating rifles, and examined them very carefully.

"Well now," John said with a broad smile spreading across his face. "These are superb weapons. Absolutely superb. I'll be quite happy to keep these."

"Good," Smoke said. "Let's go find a place to get our traps in the water."

Although there had been periodic snowstorms beginning in late fall, they were hit by a blizzard in the middle of December. They had no wagons to use in the construction of a shelter, but Smoke showed John a time-proven trick of survival he had learned from Preacher. They each carried a buffalo robe with them, and they wrapped the robes around themselves and dug in under a protecting bank. With the rifle set up, and the breech open, the barrel acted as an air vent. That way, they could let the snow drift and pile over them. The snow helped insulate them from the cold and, under the buffalo robes, their natural body heat, trapped by the insulated shelters, managed to keep them warm. They had a third rifle running between them, the barrel pointed toward John, and the open breech under Smoke's robe. That way they could talk to each other, the rifle barrel carrying the sound between them.

"Can you hear me, John?" Smoke asked, speaking into the open breech.

"Yes, I can hear you," John's voice replied.

"Good, that means we can talk to each other while we're waiting out the storm. But if you notice, the breech is on my side. So I would advise you not to say anything to piss me off."

John laughed, then he stopped. "Uh . . . I assume you are joking."

Smoke laughed. "All I'm saying is, watch your p's and q's."

"Oh, I will. Believe me, I will."

Old Main Building

"I take it you got through the blizzard with no difficulty."

"Yes. We came through it fine."

"How did the trapping go that winter?" Professor Armbruster asked.

"It went exceptionally well. I was used to trapping down in Colorado, and as I had told John, the rivers and streams there had been just about trapped out. But when we got to Montana, it was all virgin territory. First of all, you have to understand that the population of the entire state . . ." Smoke paused, then corrected himself. "Well, it wasn't a state then. But the population of the entire territory of Montana at that time, wasn't much over five thousand people. Not counting Indians, that is."

Smoke chuckled. "Just for the fun of it, John and I figured out what the population density was then. It worked out to about one person for every thirty square miles."

"Yes, I can see how that would have given you a lot of elbow room," Professor Armbruster said. "Shall we walk over to the cafeteria for lunch?"

"Sounds like a good idea," Smoke said.

Outside the Old Main building, several students had gathered, and they were singing:

> *"Glory, Glory, Colorado*
> *Glory, Glory, Colorado*
> *Glory, Glory, Colorado*
> *Hurrah for the Silver and Gold!"*

After the song, a cheer went up.

> *"Co lo ra dah*
> *Sis boom bah*
> *Rah rah rah!*
> *Co lo ra dah"*

"We are playing a football game against Denver tomorrow," Professor Armbruster said. "It's our fourth game, and the aggregate score of the first three games has been 152 to zero. So you can perhaps understand the excitement."

"I guess I can," Smoke said.

All during lunch the students were abuzz about the undefeated football team, and they were talking about the shellacking they were going to give Denver the next day.

After lunch Smoke and Professor Armbruster returned to the recording room.

"I'd like you to talk about Rendezvous, if you would," Professor Armbruster said.

"All right."

CHAPTER 14

[Rendezvous was an annual gathering held at various locations by fur-trading companies. The purpose of the rendezvous was to allow the fur trappers and mountain men to sell their furs and hides, and to make purchases of supplies and other goods from those vendors who accompanied the representatives of the fur-trading companies. The large fur companies put together teamster-driven mule trains which packed in whiskey and supplies into a preannounced location each spring-summer and set up a trading fair—the rendezvous—and at the season's end, hauled the furs out.

The trappers, most of whom had lived in total isolation for many months previous, very much looked forward to the rendezvous. It was here that the trappers and mountain men could mingle with other human beings, renew old friendships, and make new friends. The gatherings were known to be lively, joyous places, where all were allowed: trappers, Indians, Native trapper wives and children, travelers, and later on, even tourists who would venture from as far as Europe to observe the festivities. As Smoke Jensen described, there was "mirth, songs, dancing, shouting, trading, running,

jumping, singing, racing, target shooting, yarns, frolic,
that entertained and delighted white men and Indian
alike."—ED.]

Rendezvous, Montana Territory—Spring 1870

The smoke of scores of campfires could be seen from some
distance away. Then, as John and Smoke got closer, they
were also aware of smells, and sounds of Rendezvous,
aromas of roasting meat from the many cooking fires, but also
odors that were considerably less pleasant, being the stench
of scores of mountain men who had neither bathed, nor
changed clothes for the entire winter.

In addition to the mountain men, there were also merchants, photographers, painters, writers, and more than a
hundred Indians. The air was alive with the sound of drums,
Indian flutes, Indian chants, as well as guitars, and even a
bagpiper.

And of course, there was the fur trader. Only one fur trader.

There was a time, in the early days of trapping, back
before the war and the western migration, when Rendezvous
would be the biggest city between the Pacific Ocean and St.
Louis. And though those days were over now, and Rendezvous was no longer the mountain men's only contact with
civilization, Rendezvous were still big and important events,
still attended by everyone who called himself a trapper.

This rendezvous in 1870 would be Smoke's third but it
was John Jackson's first and he was very much looking forward to it. The two men rode in to the rendezvous leading
mules that were laden with both beaver and marten skins.
They were greeted by a representative of only one fur-trading
company, which meant there was no haggling for the best
price. You took what the fur company offered, or you would
have to take your furs to someplace like St. Louis and try and
sell them there.

"*Ahch,*" one old mountain man said in disgust. "In the old days there were many dealers who came, and we could find the best price."

"Well, there you go, old-timer. This isn't the old days. Now the price we're paying this year is seventy-five cents for a beaver plew and a dollar and a half for marten fur. Beavers aren't that much in demand anymore. The beaver hats have gone out of style, and the womenfolk think the marten fur is prettier. Are you going to take my offer, or not?"

"What choice do I have?" the trapper complained. "Yes, I will take your unfair offer."

"Hell, Seth, what does it matter to you, anyway?" one of the trappers said. "You'll be spendin' it all on whores and trinkets and such while you are here, anyway. By the time you leave, you won't have two coins to jangle in your pocket."

The others laughed.

"I might want one or two extra whores, and an extra trinket or two," Seth replied, and again, there was laughter.

After John sold his plews, he had money in hand for the first time in almost a year.

"Look at this," he said, displaying his new wealth. "I've got twelve hundred and thirty-five dollars. Why, I'm practically rich."

"I didn't do bad myself," Smoke said. "I've got a little over a thousand dollars."

"You've actually got more than that. I feel like at least half of my money is rightly yours for coming along with me, and teaching me the ropes. To say nothing of the liquor and food and pack mule you bought me whenever we were able to get into town."

"Nonsense. I learned everything from Preacher. It's only right I should pass along what I know to you. The liquor and food is nothing, you were my and Preacher's guest. You can pay for the mule, but it only cost forty dollars."

"I don't know, it doesn't seem right to me." John smiled as he counted out forty dollars. "But who am I to argue? If you say this money is rightly mine, I have no compunctions about keeping it."

"What are you going to do with all your money?" Smoke asked.

"First off, I've got to buy a few of the necessaries," he said. "Some more ammunition, maybe a rubber slicker, never knew how much one would come in handy. And a knife, boy, do I need a good knife. I want you to help me pick one out."

"Nothing to it," Smoke said. "We'll find you a Bowie knife with a good handle. That's all you'll need."

"You stay right there until I come get you. Do you understand that, you ignorant bitch? You don't move, you don't say nothin' to nobody, you don't do nothin' till I come back."

The speaker was a wiry-looking man with a hawklike nose and pockmarked skin. His hair was long and stringy. The person he was talking to was a young Indian woman, probably in her early twenties. She was pretty, but there was a cowed look about her, obviously the result of being browbeaten by the man who was yelling at her. John looked at her and smiled in an attempt to cheer her up, but she looked down at the ground, as if frightened to be caught returning his smile, or even his glance.

"Who is that most unpleasant gentleman?" John asked.

"I don't know who he is, but I know who he isn't. He isn't a gentleman."

"You certainly have that right."

"Let's pick you out a knife," Smoke suggested.

"All right. I need some ammo too, some more .50 calibers, some .44s for the carbine and pistol."

"Sounds like a good idea."

"Are you going to stock up for the next season?" John asked.

Smoke shook his head. "No, this is it for me. After Rendezvous, I'll be going my own way. I've taught you about as much as can be taught. The rest of it you're going to have to learn on your own. But I expect that you have acquired enough skills that you can move around without getting yourself killed."

"I would certainly hope so," John said.

"Mister, if you ain't plannin' on a-buyin' one of them blankets, move on out of the way so the others can have a look at them," a harsh voice said, and looking around toward the speaker, John and Smoke saw that it was the same man who had been yelling at the young Indian girl a few minutes earlier.

"I'm sorry about that," John said. "I didn't know I was blocking your merchandise."

"You dumb-assed mountain men are so damn stupid that it's a wonder you can even find your way here ever' year."

John said nothing but he did move away. He was smiling as he did so. "Did you hear that, Smoke? He called me a mountain man. All right, it was a dumb-assed mountain man but a mountain man nevertheless."

Smoke chuckled. "You are a mountain man, John, and there is absolutely nothing dumb assed about it. Like I said, you have acquired all the skills you need."

John reached out to take Smoke's hand, and he covered it with his other hand.

"Skills aren't the only thing I've acquired, Smoke. I've acquired a friend, a good friend. And I'm telling you now that if there is ever anything I can do for you, all you have to do is let me know. If I have to, I'll soak my britches in kerosene and walk into hell to kick the devil in the ass for you."

Smoke laughed. "Well, I haven't been that much into churchgoing since I came out here. But I sort of have a hope that I won't ever be needing someone to go into hell on my part. I'd just as soon not be there, if it's all the same to you."

"Friend, if I had followed my father's avocation, I would grant you absolution right here on the spot." He made the sign of the cross. "Have mercy upon you; pardon and deliver you from all your sins."

"You do that well," Smoke said.

"I should, my father is a priest. I was raised listening to him grant absolution every Sunday."

"A priest?" Smoke asked, curious at the pronouncement. "How can that be? I didn't think priests could be married."

John laughed. "He is an Episcopal priest. Oh, what about this knife?" he asked, picking up a Bowie with a beautifully polished, wide blade, sharp on one side, as it was also on the arch that led away from the point on the other side. The handle was a stag's horn.

"Great-looking knife," Smoke agreed.

John bought the knife, then slipped it into the beaded knife sheath the Mandan Indian had given him.

"Yeah, that looks good on you," Smoke said.

"It feels good on me," John agreed.

After all the purchases were made, Smoke and John went into one of the tents where there was a sign that read: DEER AND BEER. It referred to a meal of deer meat, and a mug of beer.

"Well, the deer isn't all that inviting, seeing as we had plenty of it over these last eight months," Smoke said. "But the beer sure is."

The men bought their meals—the deer served with fried potatoes and freshly baked bread, the beer in large mugs— and took them over to a table.

"Here's to a good winter," John said. He lifted his beer mug, and held it out over the table.

"A good winter indeed," Smoke replied, and lifting his mug, he clicked it against John's.

They took a drink and were just setting their mugs back down when, once again, they heard a familiar voice.

"Here, you worthless bitch!" someone shouted. "Pick that up! There ain't nobody goin' to pay no five dollars for a blanket that you have dragged through the dirt."

Both Smoke and John looked toward the loud voice and saw that it was the same man they had seen earlier, again yelling at the same young Indian girl.

The man went over to the young woman and jerked the blanket away from her.

"Look at this!" he said loudly. "Do you see the dirt on this blanket? Look at it."

The woman looked away.

"Don't look away, you bitch! I told you to look at it!" The merchant shoved the blanket into the young woman's face, and when he did so, she dropped the rest of the blankets she was holding.

"Now look what you have done, you ignorant slut! One blanket isn't enough? You have to ruin them all!" the trapper shouted. He slapped her, hard.

Smoke started to say something but before he said anything John got up and walked over to pick up the things the woman had dropped.

"Here, let me help you," he said.

"Who gave you permission to talk to my woman?" the merchant asked, angrily. "This is none of your business. You just stay the hell out of it."

"A little courtesy is everyone's business," John said. "Apparently, you are too dumb to comprehend that."

"What did you say? Did you just call me dumb?"

"Yes, as a matter of fact, I did," John said. "And if you would like me to be more specific about it, I will say that you are a low-assed, piss-complexioned, terminally ignorant, inconsequential, dumb son of a bitch! Do you need me to repeat any of that?"

"Did you just call me a inconse . . . uh, a termin . . . uh, a son of a bitch?"

"I did, indeed, sir."

"Look here, you! Just who the hell do you think you are talking to?"

"I thought we had already covered who I thought I was talking to," John said. "Do you really want me to repeat it?"

Suddenly the man drew a knife, then he crouched in a fighting stance. "I told you, you got no business bein' around my woman," he said. "And you got no business talkin' to me like that, neither. So unless you get away from her and apologize to me right now, I reckon I'm just goin' to have to carve your heart out."

John smiled and pulled out his knife. "Well now, it appears that I am going to have the opportunity to try out this brand-new knife I just bought. And here, I thought the first use for it would be to skin a bear. But I believe I would just as soon skin your hide."

"Mister," one of the bystanders called out to John. "I ain't never seen you before, so I reckon you be new. But iffen I was you, I'd be apologizin' to Dan Cooper. He's done kilt hisself three men with a knife."

"And about to make it four," Cooper said. Catlike, he lunged toward John, but John, even though he was much larger, managed to pivot around the lunge as adroitly as a ballet dancer. Cooper's knife found only thin air.

As Cooper leaped back, John struck him in the face with the butt of his knife. He felt Cooper's nose go flat under the blow.

"Arrgh!" Cooper shouted in pain and anger. His beard and teeth were covered with the blood that was streaming from his nose. He made a swipe at John, and though John jumped back again, this time he wasn't quite quick enough and Cooper's knife opened up a slice on his arm. Instinctively, John covered the cut with his hand and that gave Cooper the opening he was looking for.

"I've got you now, you son of a bitch!" Cooper said, putting his hand behind John's neck as he stepped up to him to make the killing thrust.

Smoke watched, as did all the others, as the two men closed to within inches of each other, so close that for a moment no one could see the knives, or what was going on. A knife fell to the floor, but was kicked away in the scuffle before Smoke could see it.

Then Cooper gasped and stepped back. It wasn't until then that Smoke saw John's arm extended, the Bowie knife in his hand now embedded in Cooper's side, all the way up to the knife hilt. John had slipped the blade in, sideways, between the ribs, and now he twisted it so that the blade turned up. As Cooper fell, the weight of his body against the very sharp, and upturned blade opened up his stomach, causing his intestines to spill through the wound.

John pulled the bloody knife out as Cooper, with his hands over the wound and an expression of surprise on his face, collapsed to the floor. He lay there with his guts spilling out of the wound, dead within two more gasps.

John leaned down and used Cooper's pant leg to wipe off the blood from the wide blade of his knife. He put the knife back in the beaded scabbard he had traded for with the Mandan Indians, and looked up at the fifteen or so people who gathered to watch the fight.

"What do I do now?" he asked. "Is there a sheriff or someone I need to see?"

"Ain't no law within two hunnert miles of here," one of the onlookers, a trapper by the name of Emerson, said. "Hell, mister, as far as I'm concerned, there ain't no need for you to do nothin' at all."

"Yeah," another added. "Ever'body here seen what happened. Cooper's the one that started it. I figure the son of a bitch got what he deserved."

"Me too," another man said. "And truth to tell, there ain't nobody what liked that low-life bastard anyway, so there ain't goin' to be nobody pissed off about it. Good riddance, I say."

That seemed to be the general consensus, which eased John's mind. Then he looked over at the young Indian woman who had been the catalyst behind the fight.

"What about the girl?" John asked.

"What about her? She's a hell of a lot better off without Cooper, I can tell you that for sure."

"Was she his wife?"

"No, I don't think you'd call her that. I think he bought her."

"Bought her? What do you mean, he bought her? I just fought four years of war so people couldn't be bought and sold no more."

"This here's a Injun girl," one of the men said. "Far as I know, the war was fought so's black folks wouldn't be slaves no more. It didn't have nothin' to do with Injuns."

"It most indubitably did," John said. "Nobody can be bought or sold as slaves anymore."

"Don't matter now, nohow. Cooper's dead; that means the girl is free."

"Yeah, she's free, but where does she go?"

"That's her problem."

"Do you speak English?" John asked the girl.

"Je ne parle pas anglais, mais je peux parler français," the girl said.

"I'm sorry, I don't speak French well enough to understand what you said."

"She said she doesn't speak English, but she can speak

French," a man said. The man who spoke was speaking with a French accent.

"What is your name, sir?" John asked.

"Mouchette. Jean Mouchette," the man replied.

"Monsieur Mouchette, will you translate for me?"

"*Oui.* What do you want to say?"

"Tell her she is free. She can go wherever she wants to go now."

Mouchette translated John's words.

"*Quel est le nom de cet homme?*" the Indian girl asked.

"She wants to know your name."

"It's Jackson. John Jackson." John said the words very slowly and very distinctly.

"*Je veux aller avec John Jackson,*" the girl said.

Mouchette laughed. "I don't know how you're going to take this," he said.

"What did she say?"

"She says she wants to go with you."

"Go with me? Go where with me?"

Mouchette asked the question.

"*Je veux être sa femme, que j'étais la femme de Cooper.*"

Mouchette shook his head as he looked at John. "She says she wants to be your wife, as she was the wife of Cooper."

"I, no, that's impossible," John said. "Tell her no."

"Wait a minute, Mouchette," Smoke said. "Let me talk to my friend here for a moment before you say anything else."

"All right," Mouchette said. "Talk away."

"John, you might want to think about this before you just dismiss it out of hand."

"Smoke, do you expect me to marry this girl?" John asked.

"No, and I don't think she expects it either. In the first place, when she said 'wife,' I don't think she actually meant it in that way. You know damn well she wasn't Cooper's wife. I think she just wants to come with you, that's all."

"That's all? If you ask me, that's asking quite a bit."

"Look at it this way. If she was sold by her father, or her tribe, she can't go back to them. She can't go into some town and live with white people, and she can't survive on her own. It's easy to see why she wants to come with you. If she is left on her own, she'll more than likely be dead within a month. And in a way, you are responsible for her."

"How am I responsible for her?"

"You killed Cooper. And regardless of how he treated her, she is still alive because of him. And now she will live, or die, because of you."

John let out a big sigh of frustration.

"What am I going to do with her?" he asked.

Smoke smiled. "Whatever you want to do with her, I'm thinking."

John looked at the woman who had been following the conversation with great intensity.

"Damnit," John said, though he spoke the word quietly. "Damnit," he said again. Then, "Mouchette?"

"Oui, monsieur?"

"Ask the girl her name."

"Quel est votre nom?"

"Hanhepiwi. Cela signifie 'clair de lune.'"

"Her name is *Hanhepiwi*."

"I heard her say 'Claire.'"

"Hanhepiwi means *clair de lune*, or, in English, the clear moon."

John looked her and smiled. "Tell her, her name is Claire. And, yes, she can come with me."

Mouchette translated, and Claire smiled, then looked down at the floor.

CHAPTER 15

Old Main Building

"That is a most amazing story," Professor Armbruster said. "And did he take her with him?"

"Oh, yes," Smoke said.

"Professor, it's four o'clock," the young man who had been handling the recording said.

"Very well, Wes, we'll call it quits for today," Professor Armbruster said. He smiled at Smoke. "You've spoken about all the saloons you have visited; how would you like to visit one of ours?"

"One of your saloons?" Smoke replied with a puzzled look on his face. "Professor, have you forgotten prohibition?"

"Oh, my, indeed, there is that pesky little problem, isn't there?" Professor Armbruster answered with a conspiratorial smile on his face.

"But, if you will come with me, I believe I know a place where people wink at prohibition. In fact, you might say they ignore it altogether."

"Would this be one of those speakeasies I've heard about?" Smoke asked.

"Indeed, it might be," Professor Armbruster replied. "As you know, Colorado went dry January of 1916, but thanks to

Clyde Smaldone and dozens of others like him, we have never been totally dry. In fact, we got a four-year head start on the rest of the country in learning how to beat the system. I know that Louis Longmont is a long-time friend of yours. How is he dealing with it?"

"Louis is a wealthy man," Smoke said. "He closed his business down and is totally retired." Smoke smiled. "He does, however, have a private reserve of, as he likes to call it, fine liquors, which he shares with his friends from time to time."

"I tell you what. If you would like to drive me to the establishment, I'll show you where it is. I'll get a ride home."

"Are you sure? I can bring you back."

"No need."

Professor Armbruster followed Smoke out to his car.

"Duesenberg, nice car," he said.

"Thanks. What do you think of the Jordan Playboy?"

"I beg your pardon?"

"The Jordan Playboy. Apparently it is a sports car, and my wife would like one. I believe she's going through a second childhood."

Professor Armbruster laughed. "Wouldn't you rather have her young and vibrant, than an old fuddy-duddy?"

"I suppose you have a point there," Smoke said.

Smoke parked in an empty lot on High Street in what looked like an industrial section of the town. He followed Professor Armbruster across the road to a two-story brick building which had all its windows boarded over. There was nothing outside the unmarked building to indicate that it was anything other than a deserted building. There was a wooden door with a small window which, like the large ones, was boarded over.

Professor Armbruster knocked on the door, and when the little window opened, he passed a dollar bill and a card through the door. A moment later, the door opened.

"Good evening, Professor," the doorman said.

"Hello, Marty. Good crowd tonight?"

"If you ask me, the whole student body is here," Marty said. He looked, suspiciously, at Smoke.

"It's all right, Marty, this gentleman is my guest," Professor Armbruster said.

Marty stepped aside to let them in.

Inside was a large room, tall and majestic with beautifully molded ceilings. The bar itself was worn, and could have been taken directly from any of several hundred saloons Smoke had visited over his lifetime. Conflicting with the bar were booths that looked brand new, running around the outer edge of a large, open space. The open space was a dance floor, the dancers being painted by hundreds of glowing dots reflecting from a rotating mirrored ball that was hanging down from the ceiling.

Professor Armbruster led Smoke to the bar. "The whiskey is good and safe here," he said. "It's not moonshine; it's brought down from Canada."

Smoke ordered a whiskey.

"Hey, old man," someone said from the bar. "Ain't you a little old to be out with the young people? What are you, some old pervert looking to pick up some young girl?"

"I'm afraid I'm beyond that," Smoke said. He picked up the whiskey and held it out toward the man, who didn't appear to be a student. "Here's to you."

"Hey, old man, aren't you afraid that whiskey will make your false teeth fall out?" He laughed, and the three people with him, another man and two women, laughed as well.

"They aren't students, are they?" Smoke asked Professor Armbruster.

"Not on your life," Professor Armbruster replied.

"Hey, old man, look here. Don't you wish you could do this?" He had his hand stuck down inside the top of the dress of the young woman he was with. His hand was, clearly, gripping her breast. "I'll bet you don't even remember what a young woman's titty feels like."

"Hell, Vinnie, women didn't even have titties when he was young," the other man said.

"Come on over, old man," Vinnie said. "I'll let you feel Linda's titty."

"Vinnie, no you won't," Linda said, pulling his hand away from her. "You act like that, I'm not even goin' to let you feel it."

"Ah, ha, Vinnie, you've stepped in it now," the other man said, laughing at him.

"Hey, old man, this is all your fault," Vinnie said, continuing his harassment of Smoke. "Now, you come here and apologize to my girl. You hear me? You come over here and apolo—"

That was as far as Vinnie got before Smoke, in a lightning, and totally unexpected move, brought a roundhouse right, connecting with Vinnie's jaw and dropping him to the floor. It was doubly effective as the first half of the swing had been hidden from Vinnie's view because of Smoke's position at the bar.

"Hey, you old son of a bitch! That was my friend you just hit!" the other man shouted and he picked up a barstool, lifting it over his head.

"Huh, uh, not a smart move," Smoke said, and to the surprise of the man holding the barstool, as well as everyone else in the speakeasy, Smoke was holding a .44 pistol in his hand, the hammer back.

"You . . . you have a gun," the man said, surprised.

"Yes, I do, don't I?"

The man started to put the barstool back down.

"No," Smoke said. "If you move that barstool so much as one inch, I'll kill you where you stand."

"I'm not going to hit you with it, I'm just going to put it down."

"No, you aren't. You're going to hold it until I tell you, you can put it down."

"What? Are you crazy?"

Smoke shook his head. "I might be. Or maybe I'm just senile. I am an old man, as you and Vinnie have been pointing out to me."

The man continued to hold the stool over his head, and by now the dancers had stopped dancing, and the band had stopped playing. Everyone was watching the drama play out before them.

"Please, mister, this stool is getting heavy."

"Is it, now? And that's what you were going to bring crashing down on my head? A barstool? Aren't you ashamed of yourself? You were going to hit an old man in the head with a heavy barstool? Something like that could have killed me. You know, I believe I could shoot you right now, and claim that it was self-defense. I don't believe any jury in the state would convict me."

"No, mister, please, no! Don't kill me!"

"It's your own fault, Eddie," the other woman said. "Vinnie was being a fool. You had no business getting involved."

Eddie's arms started shaking.

"My God, mister, I can't hold it any longer! I'm going to drop this stool and you're going to shoot me!"

"That's right," Smoke said calmly. "If you so much as move that stool by one inch, I'm going to shoot you."

A wet stain appeared on the front of Eddie's pants.

"Miss, would you take the stool from him, please?" Smoke said. "Eddie seems to have had an accident."

"Look at that, he peed in his pants!" one of the college students said, pointing to Eddie.

The young woman took the stool down, and Eddie doubled over in pain and embarrassment.

Vinnie sat up, groaning, and rubbing his jaw. "What happened?" he asked.

"Apparently, you tripped over the footrail," Smoke said.

By this time nearly everyone else in the speakeasy had gathered around, and confident now that there wasn't going to be a shooting, they all laughed.

"What the hell is everyone laughing at?" Vinnie asked. Then seeing the front of Eddie's pants, he laughed as well. "Damn, Eddie, you pissed in your pants!"

"Let's go," Eddie said.

"I'm not ready to go anywhere," Vinnie complained.

"Stay if you want to. Remember, I drove."

Eddie started toward the door, and both of the women went with him.

"Wait a minute, what's goin' on here?" Vinnie shouted. He turned toward Smoke. "I've got a feeling you're behind . . . you're holding a gun in your hand. Are you crazy? I'm going to call the cops."

"Right, you are going to call the police and bring them to a speakeasy," Smoke said. "Where everyone in here would be subject to arrest. And by the way, I'm a deputy United States marshal. I not only have the right to have a pistol, I also have the authority to arrest you right now, for consuming alcohol."

"What are you talking about, arresting me? Everyone in here is drinking."

"Really? It looked to me like they were all dancing. You are the only one I actually saw drinking."

Very pointedly, Smoke picked up his glass and took a drink of whiskey.

"Get out of here, mister," one of the college kids said to Vinnie. "Or we'll throw you out."

With a final look of hate and anger toward Smoke, Vinnie turned and hurried toward the door, chased by the laughter of the others.

When Smoke turned back to the bar, Professor Armbruster was laughing. "Last night I told Edna I would like to have seen you in your prime. By damn, I think I just did."

When Smoke returned to the Boulderado Hotel, he saw that china and silver had been laid out on the table in the suite's dining room. Two unlit candles were in the middle of the table, and Sally was standing by the table, dressed in an evening gown.

Smoke smiled at her. "I don't know who you are, you young hussy, but you can just get out of this room now. I'm happily married to a sixty-eight-year-old woman, and I don't need some floozy here, trying to make me go astray."

Sally laughed. "How you do carry on. You are so full of blarney. Your tuxedo is laid out on the bed. Please change into it."

"My tuxedo? What are you talking about? I didn't bring a tux."

"Yes, you did. I packed it. And tonight, I want you to wear it."

Reluctantly, Smoke went into the bedroom, where he saw his tux laid out on the bed. The last time he had worn the tux was at the world premiere of the movie *Guns of the West*, in which the actor Tom Mix portrayed Smoke. In fact, that was the only time he had ever worn the tux.

When he came out of the bedroom, Sally flashed a big smile. "My, my, it's true what they say, you know."

"What is true?"

"Men, at least, some men, never age. They just get more distinguished looking, and more handsome. I'm glad we are dining in tonight. I would hate to have to fight off all the young ladies who would be throwing themselves at you."

"Now who is full of blarney?" Smoke teased. He kissed

her, and was still kissing her when there was a knock on the door.

"Room service," a voice called from the other side of the door.

Sally tried to pull away, but Smoke continued to hold her.

"Uhmm, that's our dinner," she said. "It'll get cold."

"Let it," Smoke teased. "Don't forget, you are the one who started this."

"Smoke," Sally said, laughing.

Smoke opened his arms and stepped back from her, but he continued to smile.

The white-jacketed bellhop brought their dinner in on a cart, the various dishes protected by domed silver covers. He lit the two candles, then served the meal.

"Thank you, Reginald," Sally said,

Dinner was a lobster bisque, followed by a filet mignon with asparagus and baked potato.

CHAPTER 16

Old Main Building

There were several young people out in front of the Old Main building when Smoke parked his car the next morning. Many of the young men were wearing gold sweaters, with the block letter C.

"Hello, Mr. Jensen."

"Hi, Mr. Jensen."

"Good morning, Mr. Jensen."

The greetings were friendly and numerous, and Smoke returned them all as he went into the building.

"What's going on out front?" he asked Professor Armbruster.

Armbruster chuckled. "Don't you know? It is all over campus what you did last night, putting Vinnie Sarducci and Eddie DeSchamp in their place. Those two have made themselves very unpopular around here, and I think what you did was much appreciated. You have become a campus hero."

"There must be a scarcity of heroes," Smoke said.

"Not at all. It's just that they have put you up there with them, and given your history, rightly so."

"So you say."

"Well, shall we go on? What happened with John and the Indian girl?"

"John and I separated after Rendezvous. He and Claire went back into the mountains of Montana, I went back to Colorado."

Upper Missouri River, Montana—1870

John Jackson and Claire rode west along the upper reaches of the Missouri. Because of his experience with Smoke the year before, John was well aware of the potential danger that threatened from behind every stand of trees and every butte or rock. They were just crossing a tributary when Claire called out to him.

"John Jackson," she said. She pointed up the tributary. "We go that way."

"What? You speak English?" John asked, surprised to hear the words.

"Yes."

"But you said you only speak French."

"I did not want Cooper to know I can speak English. He was not a good man."

John chuckled. "That is as true a statement as I've ever heard. Why do you think we should go up this tributary?"

"When the cold returns, the trapping there will be good. There would be a good place to build a house, because there is water and shelter from the cold winds in the winter, and shade from the hot sun in the summer. Also, the only Indians are friendly Indians."

"And you say that is where I should build the house, huh?"

"Yes."

"All right, if you say so, that's where we'll go."

The tributary took them into a wide ravine that, as Claire had pointed out, kept them shaded from the hot sun. It also tended to shield them from observation.

"We'll camp here, tonight," John said. He led his horse

and pack mule to the stream so they could drink. Claire, by agreement of everyone at Rendezvous, had inherited Cooper's saddle horse and pack mule, and she led them to the stream to drink alongside John's animals.

"I'll gather up some firewood," John said. "Can you make us a fire pit from stone?" He picked up a couple of rocks and put them on the ground, then made a circle with his hand. "We'll make the fire here."

"Yes," Claire said, nodding her head.

John wandered off into the trees, where he started gathering old, downed limbs, branches, and even a piece of rotted-out log. When he came back he saw that Claire had laid the fire pit, but he didn't see her. Concerned, he put the wood down and started looking around. When he found her, he stopped in his tracks.

Claire was standing knee-deep in the water, and she was totally nude. Her back was to him, and he couldn't help but enjoy the gentle curves, and the smooth golden skin. She was taking a bath, and though he felt that he should turn away, he couldn't make himself do so. He leaned against a tree and watched as she splashed water on herself. Then, unexpectedly, she turned and started out of the water, affording a total view as she did so.

When Claire glanced up, she saw that John was looking at her, but she showed no alarm, nor did she display any modesty. She smiled at him, then reached down and picked up a clean dress and pulled it down over her still-wet body.

"Did you start the fire?" she asked.

"Uh, no," John replied.

"We cannot cook if we have no fire."

John chuckled. "I guess you have a point there. I'll get a fire started, then carve off a piece of ham for us."

"Not ham," Claire said. "Fish."

"Fish? Might be good but we'll have to catch . . ." John stopped in mid-sentence when, with a broad smile, Claire walked over to the edge of the stream and picked up two good-sized salmon that he hadn't seen earlier.

"How did you catch those? Where is your hook and line?"

"I use my hands," Claire said, making a swooping motion with her hands to demonstrate.

John started the fire as Claire cleaned the fish, then she ran a green stick down through each of them and leaned them out over the fire to cook.

That night, John lay in his bedroll by the fire, watching the red sparks ride the rising columns of heat into the sky, there to blend with the stars. He thought back over the last few years of his life . . . the fiancée who promised to wait, but who spurned him after he returned from the war . . . the friends he had met, and who were killed during the war . . . and the difficult time he had adjusting to peacetime civilian life, then his experience with the French Foreign Legion in Annam.

He recalled his last conversation with his father, just before he left Pennsylvania to come west.

"I don't know what is wrong with you, son," his father told him when he returned from Europe. "When you came back from the war you said you just needed a little time to readjust, so you went to Europe and joined the French Foreign Legion. I told you then that you were making a mistake, but you didn't listen to me.

"So, what happened to you in Europe? You were just as disturbed when you came back from there as you were when you came back from the war. You've told me nothing of your experiences with the Foreign Legion. Was it an unpleasant experience?"

"There is nothing to talk about," John replied.

"You've said nothing about going into battle with the Foreign Legion, but you have returned with a medal that you can only get by being in battle. Was it bad?"

John didn't answer.

"John, you have been much in my prayers for these last

several years. While you were in the war, I prayed for your physical survival. But since the war, I have prayed for the survival of your soul. You just aren't the same sweet boy, or even good man, you once were. You are too quick to anger, you have too little patience, you don't enjoy the things you once did, you haven't reconnected with your old friends, and you can't sleep at night. I know the stress you went through during the war, and maybe even when you were with the Foreign Legion, is causing that. Maybe someday there will be a name for it . . . but nothing I have ever read addresses it."

"You don't understand," John had told his father. "I can't sleep at night, because when I do, I hear the gunfire . . . I hear the moans of the wounded and the dying."

"I know you were upset when you returned from Europe, and found that Lucy had married another. But you've made no effort to meet any other young women. You shouldn't let what she did keep you from seeing other women."

"To tell you the truth, Pop, I'm actually glad she found someone else. I just don't feel like being around any women now."

"I know you said you wanted to go west, into the mountains where you would be away from everyone. Maybe that's not such a bad idea. Maybe if you are alone long enough, you'll get back to normal."

And so here he was, the sum total of his entire life had brought him to this time and this place, in the mountains, alone. No, he wasn't really alone, nor had he been alone. There had been Preacher and Smoke. But he was thankful to Smoke. What he had learned from Smoke in the last year was worth a four-year college degree. It was certainly more valuable than the degree he had earned at the University of Pennsylvania.

Claire was lying in her blankets, not five feet away from him. She had certainly not been a part of his plans. There was no room in the life he wanted now for any kind of a companion, let alone a female companion, and especially not an Indian woman. He had been forced into taking her, convinced that the circumstances were such that she would not survive had he not done so. He had tried, to the degree that it was possible, to maintain a separation between them. He had thought that the difference in language would help in that regard.

Then he learned that she could speak English.

All right, it was probably a good thing that she could speak English. If they were going to be together, there would be times when it would be necessary for them to communicate. He would just put her out of his mind as much as he could.

But tonight, he saw her naked, and he saw, for the first time, what an exceptionally beautiful woman she was. And now she was lying beside him, totally dependent upon him for her survival, and for all intents and purposes, his to do with as he pleased.

If he went to her now, what would she do? Would she acquiesce to his advances? Or would she fight him off?

What about her time with Cooper? Had she been with Cooper?

Of course she had, there was no way she could have avoided it. And she did say that she had been Cooper's wife.

For a moment the thought of Claire having been with Cooper disgusted him, and he thought the less of her for it.

Why? Why did he think that? She was absolutely helpless. How could she have possibly controlled her own fate?

Now John felt guilty for having such negative thoughts about her. The truth was, in the few days they had been together, he had grown comfortable with her. Yes, she was dependent upon him for her survival, but to a degree he was dependent upon her as well.

She knew the country and had offered suggestions from time to time, such as following this tributary from the river. She was helpful around the camp, she could make a fire, she could cook, she was able to point out what plants were edible, she could find wild, sweet berries, as well as honey. And tonight she had shown him that she could fish.

Yes, having her with him was not the burden he thought it would be.

A gas bubble, trapped in one of the burning logs, popped loudly, and sent up a shower of sparks. A couple of them landed on Claire's blanket, and John, afraid that the blanket would catch on fire, moved over quickly to brush the sparks off.

Claire opened her eyes and looked up at him. Her eyes reflected bright orange points of light, and her face gleamed in the glow of the fire. She stared up at him for a long time with those big, brown, trusting eyes, and when John put his hand on her cheek, she reached for it, not to push it away, but to hold it in her own hand.

With Claire's other hand she opened the blanket in invitation and he saw that she was as nude as she had been when he saw her in the water. Quickly taking off his own clothes, John got under the blanket with her.

John was awakened the next morning by the loud, rapid hammering of a woodpecker. The first thing he realized was that Claire wasn't in bed with him. Raising up on his elbow, he saw her by the fire, cooking something in the skillet. He could smell it, and it smelled very good.

"What are you cooking?" he asked.

"Breakfast."

"Yes, but what?"

"You eat first, then I will tell you," she said.

John chuckled, then he started to get up from the blankets. That was when he realized that he was naked and, inexplicably, he felt a sense of embarrassment. He reached for his clothes and dressed, all the while keeping himself covered with the blanket.

The breakfast meal consisted of Indian fry bread, which John had eaten for the first time at Rendezvous, bacon, and something else, something that resembled scrambled eggs, though it was more orange than yellow.

Claire spooned it out of the frying pan and onto two tin plates. She gave one plate, and a fork, to John.

"Eat," she said.

John knew that he liked bacon, and he knew that he liked the fry bread. He didn't know what the orange stuff was, but he took a bite.

Claire studied his reaction, intensely.

It wasn't at all an unpleasant taste, but John had never tasted anything quite like it. It had sort of a salty taste, but not overly so. He took two or three bites, hesitantly, then with a little more confidence, and by the time he finished he discovered that he was actually enjoying it.

"What was that I just ate?" he asked.

"Come, I will show you."

Claire led John to the water's edge, then she pointed to some leaves that were growing in the water. Clinging to the leaves were hundreds of little, round, almost translucent balls.

"What is that?" he asked.

"Fish eggs," Claire replied with a broad smile.

John chuckled. "I'll be damned," he said. "I know that some rich folks back in Philadelphia serve fish eggs. They call it caviar. If I ever get back there, I'll have to tell them how good it can be when it's fried in bacon grease."

"You like?"

"Yes, I do. Claire, what do you say we build our cabin here?"

"I think here is a good place," Claire replied.

CHAPTER 17

Old Main Building

"Let's see," Professor Armbruster said. "Just to make certain that I have the time line straight, we are now up to 1870, is that correct?"

"Yes."

"And where is Matt at this time?"

"Matt had left by then. Our paths continued to cross after he left and of course we remained friends. Actually we are still friends; he spent last Christmas with us at Sugarloaf. But, for the most part by then, Matt was on his own."

"And, I believe, if I remember correctly, 1870 is when you met your wife."

"It is when I met my first wife, Nicole."

"As I intend to blend yours and John Jackson's stories together, I wonder if you might share that with us now."

Uncompahgre Plateau—Spring 1870

Shortly after Smoke returned from his almost year-long stay with John, he joined Preacher in pushing a herd of mustangs south. They had been on the drive for three days when Preacher stopped and held up his hand.

"What do you smell, boy?" he asked.

Smoke sniffed the wind. "I'm not sure," he said. "It's not new growth, I know that. It's more like . . . well, I want to say smoke, but it isn't exactly smoke. It's something else."

"It's burnt hair," Preacher said.

"Yes," Smoke said, realizing that burnt hair is exactly what he was smelling. "That's not good."

"No, it ain't," Preacher said. "It ain't good at all. It's comin' from that way."

"You want me to ride over there and check it out?" Smoke asked.

"Not by yourself, I don't. Ain't no tellin' what we'll find over there. It might take the two of us to handle it."

"What about the horses?"

"I've been here before, they's a box canyon just ahead. We can put the critters in there, then block off the entrance. They's water and grass in there too, so they ain't likely to be tryin' to get out."

"All right," Smoke agreed.

Putting the horses into the box canyon that Preacher spoke of, they blocked off the entrance, then rode over to investigate the smell. As they got closer, the smell became more cloying.

"What is that?" Smoke asked.

"It ain't only the hair what was burnt, Smoke. It's the flesh too."

They followed their noses until they found a wagon that had been burned, but not entirely consumed. They also found the source of the burnt flesh odor, a man, suspended by his ankles from a tree, was hanging head down over a fire. His head, face, and shoulders were burned black. They found another man lying on the ground, his body mutilated, and a third man tied to the wheel of the wagon, also dead. All three men had been tortured.

"They died hard," Preacher said.

Tied to the side of the wagon, and undamaged by the fire, was a shovel.

"I'll get them buried," Smoke said.

"No need in diggin' more 'n one grave," Preacher said. "They was either friends or family. They all died together, so they may as well lie together."

Smoke dug only one grave, but he dug it large enough to bury all three men. Then he and Preacher covered the grave with rocks, to prevent wolves and coyotes from digging them up.

After they buried the dead, they took a closer look at the burned-out wagon, and that was when Smoke found a dress.

"Preacher, there were women with them. Or at least a woman."

"Most likely the Injuns took 'er with 'em."

"No, I don't think so. Look." Smoke pointed to a set of small footprints, shoes, not moccasins, leading away from the wagon.

"Praise be, maybe she got away. Let's find her," Preacher said.

It didn't take long to find her; the tracks led right to some brush.

"Girl, come on out from there," Preacher called. "You're among friends now. You ain't goin' to be hurt."

The young woman came out. She was an exceptionally pretty woman and Smoke was so struck with how beautiful she was that for a moment, he just stared at her.

"What's your name?" Smoke asked.

"Nicole."

"Pretty name."

"Who are you?"

"My name is Smoke. This is Preacher."

"Smoke? Preacher? Are those real names?"

Smoke smiled. "My real name is Kirby Jensen. His real name is Art, but he doesn't like to be called that. He only wants to be called Preacher."

"Did you see my father, my two uncles?"

"Yes," Smoke said, grimly.

"They are all dead, aren't they?"

Smoke nodded, but said nothing.

"What about my aunt? Did you see her?"

"Looks like the savages took her," Preacher said.

"What will they do to her?"

"Depends a lot on her. Was she a looker?"

"I beg your pardon?"

"Was she a handsome woman?"

"She was beautiful," Nicole answered.

Preacher shrugged. "Then they'll probably keep her."

He didn't tell the young woman her aunt may have been, by now, raped repeatedly and then tortured to death.

"They'll work her hard, beat her some, but she'll most probably be all right. Some buck with no squaw will bed her down. Then again, they might trade her off for a horse or rifle."

"Or they might kill her?" she asked.

"Yep."

"You don't believe I'll ever see her again, do you?"

"No, darlin', it just ain't likely," Preacher said.

Nicole put her face in her hands and began to weep. "I don't know what to do. I have a brother somewhere, but I don't know where he is. I don't have anyone else."

Smoke put his arms around her. "Yes, you do, Nicole. You have us," he said.*

Smoke, Preacher, and Nicole built a cabin and shortly after the cabin was built, Preacher rode on, leaving Smoke and Nicole alone. Preacher didn't return that winter of 1870–71, then one day Nicole came to Smoke.

*The Last Mountain Man.

"We have to get married, Smoke," she said.

"We're going to get married. But didn't we say we wanted to wait until Preacher got back?"

"Have you considered the idea that he might not come back?"

"I don't like to think about it."

"How old is he?"

"In his seventies, I think. He's never really told me. I know he's too old to be spendin' another winter alone."

"Smoke, Preacher has spent a long, exciting, and very fruitful life. He wouldn't want to die in bed, would he? He would want to leave this life the way he has lived it, in the wilderness. And do you think he would really want you to be worrying about him?"

Smoke smiled. "You're right, Nicole, as usual."

"So, you don't think we have to wait for Preacher for us to get married? The reason I ask is, I'm pretty sure we're going to have a baby."

"What? No, Nicole, we can't! We're more than a hundred miles from the nearest doctor."

"There is nothing to having a baby, Smoke. That is a natural process that's been going on since the beginning of time. Besides, I went to nursing school. It's just that I want the baby to have a legal name. I want to be married. So, where can we go?"

"We're too far from Big Rock, wouldn't want you traveling that far. But Preacher told me there was a little settlement of Mormons just west of here, over in Utah Territory. We could go there."

It was still cool when they left the valley, heading for Utah.

"Smoke, do you think we'll see any Indians?"

"I don't know. I've never been this way before, I've never been in Utah. I reckon we'll just have to find out together."

On the fifth day of their travel they reached the settlement Preacher had spoken of, but all they found were half a dozen rotting and collapsing cabins. They found no sign of life.

"Preacher said there was a going settlement here back in '55. I wonder where everyone went?"

They saw an overgrown cemetery and going over to check it, saw a handful of rotting grave markers. The latest date they could find was fourteen years ago.

"Must've been some disease come to kill most of 'em off," Smoke suggested. "And the ones that didn't die, left."

They went back to explore the buildings, and finding a nail, Smoke built a fire, heated the nail, then with a hammer flattened the nail, then curled it into a crude ring. When the ring cooled, he showed it to Nicole. "Not much of a ring, I'm afraid."

"I would rather have this than a band of gold," Nicole said.

Smoke slipped it onto Nicole's third finger of her left hand.

"Nicole, I love you. And with this ring, I declare you to be my wife."

"And I declare you to be my husband," Nicole said.

They kissed.

Old Main Building

"That's when I learned that I had warrants out on me, and that there were bounty hunters on my trail, particularly Potter, Stratton, and Richards."

"I don't want to bring up unpleasant memories," Professor Armbruster said. "But weren't those men involved in Nicole's murder?"

Smoke's mouth tightened, and he nodded. "Yes," he said. "But you're getting a little ahead of the story."

"Sorry."

"That's all right. It's just that I haven't told this story, I haven't even thought about it, in many, many years. I think it might be good to get it all out of my system now. It started with Preacher."

CHAPTER 18

Del Norte, Colorado—Fall 1870

Preacher was walking toward a saloon when he saw a young man wearing a brace of pearl-handled pistols.

"Hey, grandpa! You a little old to be out by yourself, ain't you?"

Preacher didn't say a word in response to the young punk, nor did he look at him, or even change his stride. But as he walked by, he drove the butt of his rifle into the loudmouth's stomach. The young man bent over double, puking in the street. Unable to resist, Preacher pulled the two pistols from the loudmouth's holsters. He dropped the pistols into the horse trough, then went into the saloon, where he ordered a whiskey with a beer chaser.

A moment later the town marshal came into the saloon and stepped up to the bar.

"You're the one they call Preacher, ain't you?"

"Yes."

"You have a young friend, a gunman named Smoke, I believe. Thought you might like to know that the bounty's been upped. Someone's wantin' him real bad."

"Who is it that's a-wantin' him?"

"That would be Potter, Stratton, and Richards. Potter is

into politics, Richards is in mining and cattle, and Stratton owns the town of Bury. They want the boy, and they got the money to get the job done. What did the boy do, to get 'em so mad?"

"He knows where a lot of gold is buried, gold that them three stole from the Confederacy, then the boy's papa stole back from them," Preacher said.

"I figured it had to be somethin' like that. There's a couple of gunfighters out on the front porch, Felter and Canning, and they got some more hardcases with them, camped just north of town."

"I thank you," Preacher said.

Preacher left town a short while later.

He knew he was being watched, but he thought it was Indians, and the Indians didn't worry him, because, for the most part, he and the Indians had gotten along well for the last fifty years. He was surprised when he felt a hammerblow to his shoulder, the heavy slug tearing through the tissue to come out his back.

"Get him alive, don't kill him! He can tell us where Jensen is!" someone shouted.

Preacher felt a second slug tear into his leg, careen off his leg bone, then rip a big hole in his hip, taking a piece of bone with it. Now Preacher saw the three men who were following him. He snaked his Henry from the sheath, and began firing, jacking a new shell into the chamber after each shot, getting off three rounds in less than four seconds. Two of the men were knocked from their saddles, and he knew that it had been killing shots that took them down. He shot the horse of the third man and it went down, crushing its rider beneath him.

With the three men down and Preacher badly wounded, he rode on, barely able to stay in the saddle. When night came he picketed his horse and wrapped himself up in a blanket, not sure if he would live through the night, but determined to do so, so he could warn Smoke.

Old Main Building

"Preacher did survive the night, and though I don't know how he did it, managed to stay alive long enough to get back to the cabin I had built for Nicole and me," Smoke said.

"He was badly shot up, his leg was infected, I don't know how he could stand the pain. Finally he put on his best buckskins, then telling us good-bye, rode off, presumably to die."

"But he didn't die then, did he?" Professor Armbruster asked.

"No. For the life of me, I don't know how he survived, but he did."

"Then, your baby was born?"

"Yes, the baby was born with the first snow that winter, and we named him Arthur, after Preacher. There was nobody there but Nicole and me. She told me how to cut the umbilical cord. I did that," Smoke chuckled, "then she sent me outside because she thought I was getting sick.

"We were taking a chance on staying there, but I knew that as long as the passes were filled with snow, that the bounty hunters looking for me wouldn't be able to get through. That meant that, for the time being at least, we were safe . . . but come spring we were going to have to move.

"Then, come April, just before we were going to leave, a really bad thunderstorm broke, and it scattered the herd of horses we were raising. I had to get them back. I hated leaving Nicole and the baby but . . ." Smoke stopped speaking for a moment, and waved his hand.

The professor moved the toggle switch on the speaker box. "Wes, hold it for a moment, would you?" Professor Armbruster said.

"Yes, sir," Wes replied, his voice coming back over the box. "Take your time, Smoke."

"It's been fifty-two years," Smoke said. "You wouldn't think I would still feel it this intensely. I'm sorry."

"Nonsense, you have nothing to be sorry about," Professor Armbruster replied. "Some memories are so firmly embedded that they aren't just a part of our minds, they are also a part of our souls."

"Yes. I love Sally, very much, and we have had a wonderful marriage. But there will always be a part of me that loves, and misses, Nicole and our baby."

"Would you like a drink of water? A cup of coffee?"

"A cup of coffee would be good."

Again, Professor Armbruster spoke into the box. "Wes, we're going to take about a half-hour break."

"Very good, sir." Wes replied.

Smoke followed Professor Armbruster into the staff and faculty lounge, where there was a table on which stood a big coffeemaker and a large silver tray of doughnuts.

Professor Armbruster drew a cup of coffee and handed it to Smoke, then made another for himself. Smoke walked over to look through the window, out onto the campus. He saw half a dozen young men wearing raccoon coats, straw hats, and white spats, and he chuckled.

"Raccoon coats," he said. "They came along too late for the trappers of my generation. Beaver and marten, that's all anyone wanted then. About the only thing coon was good for was eating, and making caps. Now look."

"It started back East in the Ivy League schools," Professor Armbruster said. "Now, no college man is worth his salt if he isn't wearing a raccoon coat."

"Preacher and John would have had a big laugh over this."

"Have you ever seen a football game, Smoke?" Professor Armbruster asked.

"I've seen a few of the high school games in Big Rock. The Trappers, they call themselves."

"Yes, we've gotten some players here, from Big Rock. Have you ever seen a college game?"

"No."

"You absolutely have to see one while you are here. I do hope you and Mrs. Jensen will be my guests for the football game this weekend."

"Yes, we would be pleased to come to the game," Smoke said.

A car drove up in front of the building, a Model T Ford, sporting fox and raccoon tails and bearing painted signs: STRUGGLE BUGGY, 23 SKIDOO, IT'S THE BERRIES, IT'S A LOLLA-PALOOZA, and of course, GO BUFFALOS, referring to the Colorado football team.

The driver, who was also wearing a raccoon coat, squeezed the bulb on the horn mounted on the door of his car, and several laughing young men and women hurried toward him.

Smoke shook his head as he watched them, and wondered how many of them could survive one year in the Rockies on their own. He finished his coffee, then took the empty cup back.

"Professor, I'm ready to go back, if you are."

"Absolutely," Professor Armbruster replied.

CHAPTER 19

"All right, Wes, we're ready to go again," Professor Armbruster said into the little intercom box.

"Very good, sir," Wes replied.

"Now, Smoke, if you are up to it, we'll continue with where we left off."

"Yeah," Smoke said. "I wasn't gone very long. By the second day I had found most of my herd and I closed them up in a canyon, keeping them there until I could find the rest of them. Then, late in the afternoon of the second day, I thought I heard gunfire. But when I stopped to listen, I didn't hear anything, so I figured it must just be wind blowing through the trees.

"I started back home on the third day and . . ." Smoke stopped and shook his head, "I don't know how to explain it, but I suddenly got the strongest feeling of dread. I knew something had happened.

"When I got there, I saw one of them, a man named Grissom. I shot him. Then I saw someone just pushing open the door to the outhouse, and I shot him. The next one was a young punk, would-be gunman who called himself Kid Austin.

"When I ran to the back of the house I saw"—Smoke

paused and took a deep breath—"I saw my baby, lying dead in the grass. He had just been tossed out like trash.

"Someone started taunting me from inside the house. I had Preacher's Sharps with me. I wasn't worrying about hitting Nicole; I knew she was dead. So I fired through the wall, and heard someone screaming. I found out later that the big Sharps had torn his arm off.

"A moment later, several men rode off at a gallop. But there was one left, a man named Clark. He was taunting me from the house, but he was crouching, looking out the back door, when I came in through the front. I got the drop on him, and when I saw Nicole, and what they had done to her, scalping her, partially skinning her, I felt an anger unlike anything I had ever felt before or since.

"Clark was on his hands and knees, begging me for mercy. I kicked him in the side of head, and knocked him out. Then I took him outside, stripped him naked, smeared his body with honey, and staked him out over a big hill of fire ants.

"I could hear him screaming the whole time I was digging a grave for Nicole and the baby. He was still screaming when I rode off, and I could hear him for at least half a mile."

"So you set things right. You avenged her murder."

"Nicole had been raped, murdered, scalped, and partly skinned. My boy was killed and tossed out the back door of the cabin like so much trash. There's no way you can make that right."

"I'm sorry, of course I didn't mean it like that. But you did kill the ones who murdered your family, did you not? I don't mean just the ones you killed at the cabin. I mean, one of the stories about you is how you tracked down and killed all the others as well. Is that true, or is it all a myth?"

"The story is true."

"Because of the research I'm doing, I have a repository of books about you, many of them pertaining to that very event.

And of course, there is the Jack Holt movie about it . . . *Where There Is Smoke, There Is Fire.*"

Smoke chuckled. "It was Sally who came up with that title. A couple of the people associated with the film didn't like the title but Jack loved it, and he is the one that managed to get it through."

"It is a clever title," Professor Armbruster said.

"I think so," Smoke agreed.

"The problem with all these accounts, the movie, the books, the many articles, is that they vary so widely. Some say you killed fifty men that day, some say a hundred. I don't suppose anyone knows for sure."

"I know."

"Well, how many was it?"

"Eighteen."

"Eighteen?"

"I killed four of them there at the cabin. Then I went after the others and caught up with them at the silver-mining camp near the Uncompahgre. The four I killed at the cabin, and the fourteen more I killed in town, make eighteen."

"That's quite an accomplishment. I can see why so much has been written about it.

"After your wife and son were killed, you remarried though. I believe she was a schoolteacher?"

"Yes, but that wasn't for two more years."

"And you had two children?"

"We did. We had twins, Louis Arthur and Denise Nicole."

"I'm sorry to keep bringing up unpleasant memories, but they are both deceased now, aren't they?"

"Yes. They went to Europe to be educated. Denise died and was buried there. When Louis came back, he decided to stay East with Sally's family, where he became a lawyer. Sally and I didn't see much of him after that. We were never actually estranged, we just sort of went our separate ways. Ironically, Louis also died in France, and is buried there."

"Yes, I have done some research. He was a pilot who received the Medal of Honor."

[*I have located the citation which accompanied the Medal of Honor award, and post it here for the edification of the reader:*

"After having previously destroyed a number of enemy aircraft, Captain Louis Arthur Jensen voluntarily started on a patrol after German observation balloons. Though pursued by eight German planes which were protecting the enemy balloon line, he unhesitatingly attacked and shot down in flames three German balloons, being himself under heavy fire from ground batteries and the hostile planes. Severely wounded, he descended to within one hundred fifty feet of the ground, and flying at this low altitude near the town of Murvaux, opened fire upon enemy troops, killing six and wounding as many. Forced to make a landing and surrounded on all sides by the enemy who called upon him to surrender, he drew his automatic pistol and defended himself gallantly until he fell dead from a wound in the chest."—ED.]

"Do you know what I find particularly fascinating about your son receiving the Medal of Honor? I mean other than the obvious intrepidity he displayed."

"What is that?"

"There were no American witnesses to his action. All the facts of his heroism, including notarized eyewitness accounts, were from the Germans themselves. I find it fascinating that the details of his heroism were sent through the lines, along with his body, by the German army. They were that impressed with his bravery."

"I spoke to one of the Germans who was there that day," Smoke said.

"You did?"

"Yes. Last year Sally and I crossed the Atlantic onboard the ocean liner *Homeric.*"

"That must have been fascinating."

"It was. But, Professor, we are getting way afield here. Don't you think we should get back to John Jackson?"

"Yes, of course. Where did we leave off with Mr. Jackson?"

"He and Claire had just built themselves a cabin."

Upper Missouri River

John began chopping down trees and sizing the logs, and Claire debarked them, using a crowbar and a spud, which was like a hoe . . . but with a straight blade. John used ropes and his horse and mule to pull the logs into position, then, when he had the walls up, Claire chinked in between them with twigs and mud. While Claire was filling in between the logs, John made a roof of smaller-diameter limbs. When the roof was completed, it was covered with sod.

The cabin had a single room that was twelve feet square. The floor was dirt, but John promised that they would have a wood floor as soon as he could get around to it. There was only one door and no windows. John put the fireplace at one end of the cabin and built the chimney of wattle and daubed mud. Stone and clay were used for the hearth and the interior of the fireplace.

It took a lot of hard work, but two weeks after the first log was cut, they were able to spend the night in their own house. For the next month, John and Claire built furniture for their house, a bed, a table and some chairs, and some shelves.

By the time the first snows came, they were warm and snug in their house, and Claire announced that she was pregnant.

"Wow! Then we have to celebrate!" John said. "You know what? I think it must be nearly Thanksgiving. Yes, I'm sure it is. I'm going to kill us a turkey, and we'll have an old-fashioned Thanksgiving Day dinner, just the two of us."

John did kill a turkey and the aroma of it cooking filled the inside of the little cabin so that by the time it was ready to eat, they were both ravenous. John smiled as he carved up the turkey for them.

"Happy Thanksgiving," he said.

"What is Thanksgiving?"

"You've never heard of Thanksgiving?"

"No."

"Well, then I'll tell you the story."

For the rest of the afternoon John told the story of the Pilgrims, and their voyage to America on the small ship, the *Mayflower*. He told of the men and women who left England in search of religious freedom.

"They thought they were going to the Virginia Colony, where some Europeans had already settled, but in November, they reached Cape Cod, Massachusetts.

"There were a hundred and two passengers on the ship," John said. "And the ship remained at anchor while they built cabins where they could live."

"Like this," Claire said, taking in their cabin with a proud smile.

"That first winter was brutal, and more than one-half of them died the first year, from starvation and disease. The Pilgrims held secret burials for the ones who died, so that the Indians wouldn't realize how few were remaining."

"Indians?" Claire asked. She pointed to herself.

"These were Wampanoag Indians. And they eventually began helping the Pilgrims, because if they hadn't, I believe every one of them would have died. And think how that would have changed history."

"And they ate turkey?" Claire asked, not making the connection between the Pilgrims, half of whom had died, and the turkey they were eating now.

"Yes. You see, after almost dying of starvation, they had a good harvest, and to celebrate the harvest, and the fact that at least half of them were still alive, they held a feast. And the Indians came to join them," John said. He smiled, and made a motion with his hand to take in the two of them.

"It's like us," he added. "Indian and white man coming together to give thanks."

"The baby will be a Thanksgiving thing," Claire said. "The baby will be Indian and white," she added, touching John on the face, then putting her hand on her stomach.

"Yes, it will indeed be a thing for thanksgiving," John said.

John ran his traps every day that winter, beaver traps in the water, and marten traps hanging from trees near the water. The reason the marten traps had to be hung from trees was to prevent rodents from chewing on the martens once they had been caught.

The trapping was bountiful, much more even than he and Smoke had brought in the year before. He would skin the beaver, and hang the meat out so the wild animals couldn't get to it. Claire would scrape and clean the hides, then stack them. She also cooked the beaver meat, sometimes frying it, sometimes baking it, sometimes grilling it over the open flames of the fireplace. She also boiled the beaver and made a soup, cooked with wild onions, mushrooms, cattail, and sun root tubers.

John kept a close count of his furs and before winter was half over, had over a thousand dollars' worth of pelts, based on the prices they paid the previous year. But he had also heard that the St. Louis market paid twice as much, and at that rate it would be worth his while to go there.

CHAPTER 20

Boulder

"The team in red is the University of Denver," Professor Armbruster said. "So far this season, we haven't lost a game. As a matter of fact, nobody has even scored on us this year and . . . oh, oh, this isn't good."

On the field one of the players wearing red broke free from the rest and started a long run, with players wearing black chasing after him. There were loud cheers from the other side of the field, and groans from this side. "I spoke too soon," Professor Armbruster said.

"Why?" Sally asked.

"Denver just made a touchdown."

Despite Denver's score, Colorado won the game, twenty-one to seven, and there was much celebration on the campus that evening.

Smoke and Sally had been invited by Professor Armbruster to dine with him and his wife, as well as Dr. and Mrs. George Norlin. Dr. Norlin was president of the University of Colorado.

"I have been listening to recordings of your account each evening," Dr. Norlin said. "And I must say that I am finding

452 *William W. Johnstone and J.A. Johnstone*

the story very fascinating. You will truly go down in history as one of our most valiant men."

"You are embarrassing me, Dr. Norlin," Smoke said with a smile. "I just spent most of my life trying to stay alive."

"Dr. Norlin won't say anything about it, but he has been in a fight as well, with the state legislature," Professor Armbruster said. "They have been taken over by the KKK, and they are demanding that he fire every Catholic and Jew on the campus. And to his credit, he has refused to do so."

"Good for you, Doctor," Smoke said.

"It has been at some cost, I must say," Dr. Norlin said. "The state has stopped all financial aid to the university. We are having to subsist on what income we can garner from tuitions, and such revenue-producing programs that we have, such as our football team."

"Sally, give me the . . ." Smoke started to say, but Sally had already gotten the checkbook from her purse and was handing it to him, with a smile.

"Would ten thousand dollars help?" Smoke asked, as he started writing the check.

"What? Why, yes, of course. But please, Mr. Jensen, I hope you don't think this was a request for a donation."

"It doesn't matter whether it was a request or not," Smoke said. "It's something I want to do."

"I'm serious," Wes said over Monday morning breakfast at the TKE house. He was talking to Philip McGrath, the Grand Prytanis of Tau Kappa Epsilon. "You come up with any name in the history of the American West, and this guy knew them. Wild Bill Hickok, Falcon MacCallister, Buffalo Bill, Monte Carson, Calamity Jane, Wyatt Earp, Doc Holliday. He knew them all! Not only that, he's lived the kind of life that you read about in novels. You need to meet him just so that someday, fifty or sixty years from now, you can tell your grandchildren that you met Smoke Jensen."

"I heard about what he did at the speakeasy, an old man like that," McGrath said.

"I tell you what, Phil. It might be that he's been around for a long time, but I wouldn't exactly call him an old man," Wes said. "No, sir, not by a long shot. And certainly, not to his face," he added with a laugh.

"I remember reading books about him when I was a kid," Phil said. "But they were all novels. I didn't know there really was such a person."

"When Professor Armbruster asked me if I would make the recordings, I tried to get out of it," Wes said. "I mean, who wants to sit around and listen to some old man mumble on with his stories. But I wouldn't trade what I'm doing for the world. Sixty, seventy years from now, if I'm still alive, I'm going to tell everyone I know that I met Smoke Jensen. Why . . . it's like meeting Abraham Lincoln, or Davy Crockett, or Andrew Jackson. I mean, you name someone from our history . . . anyone, and I wouldn't get any bigger a thrill meeting them than I have gotten by meeting Smoke Jensen."

"I can tell he's made quite an impression on you."

"Yes, he has," Wes admitted. "I'm telling you, Phil, you need to meet this man."

"Do you suppose he would come to dinner at the fraternity house and give us a little talk?" Phil asked.

"I don't know. That's all he's doin' all day long now, is just talking into the microphone. I wouldn't want to ask him to come give us a talk. But we might ask him to come have dinner with us."

"Good idea," Phil said. "All right, I will."

"Mr. Jensen," Wes said, greeting Smoke as he stepped out of his car in front of the Old Main building. "I would like for you to meet Phil McGrath. He is the Grand Prytanis of the fraternity I belong to."

"He's the what?" Smoke asked with a chuckle.

"He's the president."

"Well, why didn't you say so? Hello, Mr. McGrath," Smoke said, extending his hand.

"Mr. Jensen, it is a great pleasure meeting you," McGrath said, taking Smoke's hand and pumping it enthusiastically.

"You are also on the football team, I believe," Smoke said. "I watched you play, Saturday. You played very well."

"Thank you," McGrath said, smiling in obvious pleasure at the accolade. "Oh, uh, I wanted to ask . . . that is, uh, I was wondering if you would have dinner with us tonight at the fraternity house?"

"Oh, I'd better not. My wife is here and I'm gone from her all day long. I don't know how she would take it if I left her alone in the evening as well."

"What about lunch?" Wes asked quickly. "You have to eat lunch somewhere, don't you?"

"I suppose I could. But today is Monday, isn't it?"

"Yes, sir, it is. Does that matter?" Wes replied, confused as to what difference it would make what day it was.

"Well, I always eat beaver on Monday, so if you would tell your cook to fry me up some beaver tail in a little bear grease, I'd be glad to join you for lunch."

Wes and McGrath looked at each other with a rather desolate expression on their faces.

Smoke laughed. "Well, I suppose I can make an exception. I'll be there and I'll eat whatever you have."

Wes and McGrath weren't the only ones who greeted Smoke that morning. There were even more students in front of the Old Main building today than there had been the morning after the speakeasy episode the night before. Several went out of their way to shake hands with him.

"What is all this about, Wes?" Smoke asked when, finally, they had run the gauntlet and were safely inside the building.

"It's you, Mr. Jensen. Everyone wants an opportunity to see history, firsthand."

"Boy, are you saying I'm history?" Smoke asked with a snarl.

"Oh, uh, no, I mean, uh, it's just . . ."

Smoke laughed. "I'm teasing you, Wes. At my age, I have seen a lot of history, so I guess, in a way, that does make me history."

"Uh, yes, sir," Wes said, somewhat awkwardly. "I'll, uh, just get everything set up for the recording session today."

"Good morning, Smoke," Professor Armbruster said when Smoke arrived, going directly to the recording studio.

"Good morning, Professor. Wes and a young man named McGrath have invited me for lunch at their fraternity house. Am I taking a risk by eating there?"

"Smoke, after everything you've been through, they could be serving bugs and I don't think it would bother you."

"Depends on the bug," Smoke said. "Grub worms can be quite tasty."

Professor Armbruster laughed. "I figured you would say something like that. When we left off, I believe you said that John was considering a trip to St. Louis to sell his furs. Did he go to St. Louis?"

"Yes," Smoke said. "And it proved to be quite profitable for him."

[*After the Civil War, steamboat traffic on the Missouri River became a common sight. The boats were considerably different in design from the Mississippi River* boats, with few of the fancy fittings. The most important feature of a Missouri River boat was that it be of light weight. From 140 to 170 feet long and 30 feet wide they had a shallow hull, and spoonbill-shaped bow. With this design they could carry two hundred tons of cargo through waist-deep water, safely navigating over anything from sandbars to whitewater rapids. In addition, this type of vessel was less expensive to fuel and much easier to steer.

Steamboat captains in the late 1870s could charge as much as $1,200 every month for their services, an enormous sum, compared to the average income of $40 per month for the rest of America. They had to be extremely skilled captains and a good hand at striking a deal with merchants. The payoff was huge, however, since a steamboat could carry cargo worth a profit of up to $40,000.

A few words about the history of the city of St. Louis might enlighten the reader, and thus help in understanding the significant role the city played in the lives of not only the mountaineers and the fur trappers, but all of the western frontier.

The first steamboat arrived in St. Louis on July 27, 1817, which proved to be only the beginning of St. Louis as an important river city. By 1859, river traffic had increased to such an extent that St. Louis took its position as the second-largest port in the country, with only New York exceeding St. Louis in total commercial tonnage moved. Often as many as 170 steamboats could be counted on the levee.

Because of the junction of the Missouri River, St. Louis was uniquely positioned to truly become the gateway city to the West. It was fed by boats from the east, traversing the Ohio River, then entering the Mississippi River at Cairo, Illinois, to beat their way upstream to St. Louis. There was also a very busy schedule of boats

*that plied the Mississippi between St. Louis, Memphis,
Vicksburg, and the seaport at New Orleans.*

*By the time the construction of the railroads began in
the early 1850s, St. Louis had a population of almost
eighty thousand people. The first westbound train left
St. Louis in 1855. It was the railroads that eventually led
to the diminution of the importance of the riverboats in
the city's economy.—ED.]*

Upper Missouri—1872

John built a raft, onto which he loaded his winter catch of
furs, then he, Claire, and their son, Kirby, rafted downriver to
Yankton. There, they boarded a Missouri riverboat, the *Nellie
Peck*, for passage to St. Louis.

When John purchased the tickets, he was given a sheet
of paper with the title, "Helpful Hints for Steamboat Passengers."

Welcome Aboard the Missouri River Steamboat, NELLIE PECK.

*This guide is published as a service for the traveling
public. Careful attention to its information and suggestions will insure the riverboat patron a memorable
journey. This guide describes the many accommodations found on the boat, and gives warnings about possible unpleasant situations.*

Departure Time

The NELLIE PECK will leave terminal ports on sched-
uled times. The arrival and departure times change at
ports along the river. Your steamboat captain, Captain
Milton Saddler, prefers early morning departures. This
will provide the NELLIE PECK with as many daylight
hours as possible. It is not feasible to operate at night
unless the moon is very bright. There is too much danger
in navigating in the dark, especially in low water.

Cabin Passengers

Enjoy the best of steamboat travel. Staterooms for the NELLIE PECK are on the cabin deck. They are ten feet square with doors at each end, one to the interior passage and the other to the deck. The NELLIE PECK also provides clean mattresses and sheets on the berths. Curtains at cabin windows provide privacy to the passenger while dressing.

Toilet

Toilet facilities are vastly improved on the NELLIE PECK with a washstand and basin in each of the staterooms. For the deck passengers there are two washrooms, one each for ladies and gentlemen, located near the wheel-house. Each deck washroom is equipped with a wash-basin, one hair brush, a comb, a community toothbrush, and a roller-type towel. The crew keeps the pitchers filled with river water. The toilets are like the outdoor variety and placed next to the wheel.

Warning

Thieves, con agents, and gamblers ride the steamboats. Many of these undesirable citizens hang around levees, wharves, hotels, and taverns in the river towns. Travelers are advised to buy bank drafts. Some prefer letters of credit from their own bank. If you need to carry a large sum of money, wear a money belt. Avoid games of chance on the riverboats.

Wooding

A passenger can reduce his fare by wooding on a trip. However, the job of cutting and carrying wood is a hard one, and should only be attempted by those used to hard work.

St. Louis

The *Nellie Peck* approached the riverbank, then just before it got there, reversed the paddle, causing the water to froth at the stern. The boat glided in, until the bow bumped against the cobblestone levee. A crewman on the front of the boat tossed out a thick hawser, and someone on the bank made the boat fast.

The riverfront was alive with activity, not only the scores of other boats that were tied up, but the amount of traffic ashore: carriages, buggies, surreys, buckboards, coaches, and wagons of all sizes. There was noise from the steam relief valves of the boats, some of the venting sounding almost like cannon fire. Men were shouting back and forth to each other, and the air was rent with the clops of steel-shoed horses and mules on the paved streets.

Claire had never seen anything like this in her life, and she stood at the railing of the boat with her hand to her chest.

"Are you all right?" John asked.

"I . . . I have never seen so many people," Claire said.

"I should think not. If you put every person you had ever seen in your whole life, together, they wouldn't make but a fraction of what you are seeing right here, right now, just on the riverfront."

"How can so many people live so close together? Don't they step on each other's feet?"

John laughed. "I imagine they do," he said.

Claire reached out to grab John's arm. "John, do not leave the baby and me alone here. I am frightened by so many."

"Don't worry, Claire. I have no intention of leaving you alone."

"Mr. Jackson," the boat's purser said, approaching them then. "I have secured a wagon for your cargo."

"Thank you, Mr. Adams," John said.

John and Claire stood by, watching as bale after bale of

beaver and marten pelts were loaded onto the wagon. Then, leaving the boat, John secured a cab, and they followed the wagonload of furs as it made its way through the city to the St. Louis Fur Exchange, on Lafayette Street.

Claire was in awe of the huge buildings, many of them five and six stories high. They passed by the Christian Staehlin's Phoenix Brewery, a huge building with towering smoke-stacks.

"Why don't I just let you and Kirby out here?" John suggested. "I'll come back for you later."

"No!" Claire said, grabbing his arm even tighter.

John laughed quietly, then kissed her on the forehead. "Don't worry, my sweet," he said. "I'm just teasing you. I have no intention of letting you go."

When they reached the fur exchange, John let the cab go, then he, Claire, and Kirby went inside to make arrangements to sell the pelts.

CHAPTER 21

"I must say, Mr. Jackson," O. D. Clayton said a few minutes later as he examined the pelts. "These are in remarkable condition, much better condition than the ones I normally get. I think that's because the fur traders don't always take that good of care of them."

"How much are you willing to pay for them?"

"Five dollars apiece for the marten, three dollars for the beaver."

"Will you take all of them?" John asked.

"How many do you have?"

"I have six hundred beaver, and three hundred twenty-five marten."

O. D. Clayton did some figuring, then looked up. "That comes to three thousand, four hundred, and twenty-five dollars," he said.

"Three thousand, four hundred, and twenty-five?" A huge smile spread across John's face. "Claire!" he said, embracing her. "We're rich!"

"Do you want it in cash, or by check?" Clayton asked.

"I expect I'd better take it by cash," John said. "There aren't a lot of banks near my cabin."

Clayton chuckled. "No, I don't expect there would be," he said. "Is paper money all right?"

"Yes, where I do business, they take paper money."

"I'm never sure. Paper money is as good as gold all over St. Louis. But I've heard that there are some places where they won't take it."

Clayton counted out the money, and John, with a big smile, put it in his pocket.

"Now," John said. "Suppose you tell me where we can find an elegant place to eat in St. Louis."

"You might try the Delmonico on Olive," Clayton told him. "That's just three blocks over. Truth is, I've never been there, but I've heard it was an elegant place."

With his money in his pocket, John, Claire, and baby Kirby walked the three blocks to Delmonico. Smiling, they stepped into the restaurant.

"I'm sorry, but you aren't welcome here," a waiter said, stopping them just inside the door.

"Oh, I'm sorry," John said, touching his buckskin shirt. "I wasn't aware there was a dress code."

"No, sir, you are fine," the waiter said. "You can come in. It's the squaw and papoose who can't. They will have to wait outside."

John reached up and grabbed the man's collar with his left hand, then he twisted it so that it was choking him.

"What did you say?" he asked. Though the expression on his face was fearsome, and he did have a tight grip of the man's collar, the question was spoken quietly, and coldly, the more frightening because of that. "Do you seriously think I'm going to leave my wife and child outside while I come in?"

"I . . . uh . . . the owner has a policy that only whites can come in. I'm sorry, sir, there's nothing I can do about it. No colored, no Indians, and no Chinamen."

"John, please, let's go," Claire said.

"Mister, I don't know who you think you are, but we don't want squaw men comin' in here," a man sitting at the first table said. He pulled a pistol and was about to point it at John, but before he could, John pushed the waiter away, drew his knife, and threw it. It pinned the man's sleeve to the table, and he dropped the pistol. John stepped over quickly, and picked up the pistol.

The man who had drawn the gun reached over with his left hand to pull the knife free.

"Leave the knife where it is," John ordered. "I'll remove it when I decide to." He pulled the cylinder from the man's pistol, dumped all the shells onto the floor, and kicked them away. Only then did he recover his knife, unpinning the man's jacket sleeve.

Then, doing it so quickly and smoothly that the would-be gunman had no time to react, John sliced through the man's septum. It started bleeding profusely.

"Ahhh!!" the man shouted out in pain, sticking his hand to his nose. "You cut my nose!"

"Yes, I did, didn't I? Well, that's just a reminder to make you think twice next time you want to stick your nose into somebody else's business," John said.

He used the man's shirtsleeve to wipe the blood away from his knife.

"If you good folks don't mind, I'll just find another place to spend my money," he said. "Let's go, Claire."

They started toward the door, but just before they left, John turned to address the others.

"By the way, if anyone so much as sticks a head out the door in the next minute, I'll shoot you dead."

Not one word was spoken by anyone in the restaurant, but all stared at him with expressions that ranged from curiosity, to shock, to outright fear.

The next restaurant accepted them without question, and not until they were seated at a table in the back of the room did Claire allow herself to laugh.

"Why are you laughing?"

"Did you see their faces? They were like this." Claire lifted her eyebrows, and opened her mouth, simulating an expression of shock.

"Yes, I suppose I did go a bit too far there."

Claire giggled again. "Yes, cutting his nose here"—she put her finger to her nose septum—"is a bit too far."

"Claire, will you marry me?" John asked.

"What? But we are already married."

"No. I mean will you marry me by the law of the white man? My father is an Episcopal priest. I want to find an Episcopal church and I want us to get married. No, wait, if we do that, we'll have to post banns and that will take too long. I'll find us a circuit judge, he can marry us, then I'll get a priest to bless the marriage. When we go back, we will go back as legally married husband and wife."

Two hours later, having been married by a circuit court judge, John and Claire, with Kirby, stepped into St. Mark's Episcopal Church in south St. Louis. John dipped his fingers into the basin of holy water and crossed himself. Because he had taught Claire some of the liturgy of the church, she did so as well.

They walked to the front and knelt at the altar rail. They were there when the priest stepped out of his study and saw them. The priest waited until they both rose.

"Good afternoon," the priest said. "May I help you?"

"Yes, Father. We are married, but it was a civil ceremony. I would like to ask that you bless our marriage."

"You are Episcopalian?"

"Yes, my father is an Episcopalian priest back in Pennsylvania. His name is Nathaniel Jackson."

The priest's eyes widened. "Is he by chance the author of

A Book of Rites for the Use of Congregations of the Protestant Episcopal Church?"

"He is," John said.

The priest smiled and extended his hand. "My name is Sharkey. Bill Sharkey. I am most pleased to meet you, sir."

"I am John Jackson, and this is my wife, Claire, and our baby, Kirby. I have baptized both of them, simply because we live so far from any church. I would like you to validate the baptisms as well."

"I would be happy to do so," Father Sharkey said.

It was as Mr. and Mrs. John Jackson that they, with their baby, boarded the train in St. Louis for the long trip back. Because he had enough money to do so, they took passage on the Palace Car.

For the first part of the trip, there were only six people in the car: John, Claire, and Kirby, plus one other couple, and a man dressed as a clergyman, who was traveling alone. The clergyman kept staring at Claire and the baby with an obvious look of displeasure on his face. Finally he spoke.

"You are in violation of God's law," he said.

"I beg your pardon, Parson, did you say something?" John asked.

"I said you are sinners, both of you. Cohabitation without marriage is a sin. Whoremongers and adulterers God will judge."

"Well, Parson, it's none of your business, but it so happens that we are married."

The parson shook his head. "No, that ain't possible. God don't hold with white men marryin' savages."

"Oh? Would you mind telling me where, in the Bible, it says that?"

"Ezra 10:2–3. 'We have taken strange wives of the people of the land, yet now there is hope in Israel concerning this thing. Now therefore let us make a covenant with our God to put away all the wives, and such as are born of them,'" the parson said, sanctimoniously.

"Colossians 3:11. 'There is no distinction between Greek and Jew, circumcised and uncircumcised, barbarian, Scythian, slave and freeman, but Christ is all, and in all.'" John replied

"How dare you, sir!" the parson said, pointing a long, bony finger at John. "How dare you quote scripture to a man of Gawd?"

"You call yourself a man of God. Yet 'you love all words that devour, oh deceitful tongue.' Psalm 52:4," John said.

"You . . . you know your scripture, sir," the parson said, surprised by John's Bible acumen.

"I do."

"Then why in Gawd's name would you marry an Indian whore?" he shouted at the top of his lungs.

"Mister, and I'm not calling you parson anymore, because by your words, you have proven yourself to be unworthy of that title. So I'm telling you now to leave this car, and don't come back in until either you, or we, leave this train. And we won't be leaving this train for a thousand miles."

"I will not leave this car," the parson said, angrily. "I paid for my passage."

"Here is ten dollars," John said, handing the parson a bill. "Now, get out of this car and stay out."

"You have no right to order me out."

"Oh, it isn't a question of whether I have the right," John said. He smiled, but it was a taunting smile. "It's a question of whether I am capable of grabbing you by the scruff of your neck and the seat of your pants and bodily throwing you off this train. And believe me, sir, I am. Now your choice is simple. Leave this car now, of your own accord, or I will throw you off the train."

"You wouldn't dare, sir!" the parson said, confidently.

"Shall we see?"

John walked over to him and grabbed him by his shirt and the seat of his pants and started moving him toward the door. "I wonder if you will bounce," John said.

"No! No! God in heaven, man, don't do it! Don't do it!"

"You'll leave of your own volition?"

"I will, I will!"

John took his hands away.

"Here's another thing," John said. "Don't let me see you again. When we are in the dining car, don't you come in. If we get off the train for a few minutes in some station, don't you be where I can see you. Do you understand that? I don't want to see your ugly face again, ever, anywhere."

"You . . . you have no right . . ."

"I thought we had already discussed that," John said. He shook his head. "I told you, I don't care whether I have the right or not. Now, get."

The preacher licked his lips a couple of times, then, turning, he hurried out through the front door of the car.

John looked at the other couple in the car, an older man and woman who had been watching the whole thing.

"Ma'am, sir, I'm sorry about that," he said. "But I've always believed that it was the duty of a man to look after his wife and family. And that means to shield them from all hostility, whether by word or action."

"Young man, you have nothing to apologize for," the elderly man said. "You had every right to protect your family."

"And your wife and baby are beautiful," the elderly woman added.

"Thank you, I think so myself. Of course, I might be just a little prejudiced," John said with a smile. "Would you care to join my family and me in the dining car for lunch? I would be delighted to have you as our guests."

"Why, yes, we would be happy to. Thank you very much, young man."

A few minutes later, John, Claire, Kirby, and the man and

woman who had accepted John's invitation were enjoying their lunch in the dining car. Their names were Mr. and Mrs. George Upton. Mr. Upton was a retired college professor from Washington University in St. Louis. They were on their way to California because, as Upton explained, he had always wanted to see what was beyond the setting sun.

"I remember as a young man, seeing so many people coming through St. Louis, bound for California," Upton said. "That is how St. Louis acquired the name the Gateway City, you know."

"So I've heard," John replied.

"I almost joined one of the trains, but I was only fourteen at the time, and the wagon master would not let me come with them without my parents' permission. Oh, what an adventure that would have been."

"I have told him, many times, I am quite satisfied to be making the journey in the comfort of a Palace Car," Mrs. Upton said.

"Are you a . . . and please don't take offense, but my curiosity is piqued. Are you a mountain man?"

"No offense taken, Professor. I am indeed a mountain man," John said.

"But your language, your Bible acumen, that isn't something one would associate with a mountain man."

"I am a graduate of the University of Pennsylvania," John said. "But, I have taken a postgraduate course in mountaineering."

"My word, a postgraduate course in mountaineering? Where does one find such a course?"

"In Colorado and Montana," John said. "And I've had excellent professors, a man named Preacher, a man named Smoke, and a woman named Hanhepiwi."

Claire smiled.

CHAPTER 22

Tau Kappa Epsilon Fraternity House

Smoke was given a position of honor at the head of the table in the dining room of the TKE house. Every member of the fraternity treated him with awe.

"Mr. Jensen, how many men have you killed?" a plebe asked.

"Booker! You are dismissed from the table!" McGrath said, angrily.

"No, please," Smoke said, holding up his hand. "It's a legitimate question, given the number of books that have been written about me, and many of them stressing only that part of the story. The truth is, Booker, I'm not quite sure how many men I have killed. It's not something I've ever wanted to keep a tally of, as some perverted badge of honor. But I will say this. I have never killed a man who didn't need killing."

"But what gave you the right to determine whether he needed killing or not?" Booker asked.

It was more of a challenge than a question, and everyone sitting around the dining room table looked toward Smoke to see how he would react.

"That is another good question," Smoke said. "For the most

part, survival gave me the right to make the determination," Smoke said. "I killed men who were trying to kill me. But there have been times when I purposely set out to hunt men down for the sole purpose of killing them."

"There is no statute of limitations for murder," Booker said. "Are you afraid that some zealous prosecutor might bring charges against you today?"

Smoke chuckled. "Mr. Booker, do you, by any chance, plan to be a lawyer?"

"Yes, sir."

"Then, let's make a deal, right here. If some zealous prosecutor decides that he would like to try me for killing someone like oh, let's say, Ted Casey, I would like to hire you to defend me."

"Ted Casey is the one you lynched, isn't he?"

"Lynched?" Wes said. "Listen, I heard that story firsthand. If ever any man deserved to hang, it was Ted Casey."

"But he was hung without a trial, wasn't he?" Booker asked.

"He was."

"Looking back on it now, would you do things differently?" Booker asked.

"Yes."

"Ha! I thought so. What would you do differently?"

"I wouldn't have used a new rope," Smoke said.

The others laughed, then, when Booker started to speak again, McGrath held up his hand.

"Booker, Mr. Jensen has been more than generous with you. We'll have no more inquisition."

"Yes, sir," Booker said, contritely.

Old Main Building

"How was your lunch?" Professor Armbruster asked.

"Quite interesting," Smoke replied without further elaboration.

"Well, are you ready to resume the session?"

"I am."

"We left off with John and Claire going back home," Professor Armbruster said.

"Yes."

John's cabin

After John, Claire, and the baby returned from St. Louis they put in a garden. As John explained, "Wild plants will do in a pinch, but there's nothing improves the table like fresh radishes, onions, tomatoes, lettuce, potatoes, carrots, beans, cabbage, and watermelon."

John worked hard on his garden, and soon he was raising a bountiful crop. Already they had radishes, and the tomatoes were coming along as well.

Because trapping was nonproductive in the summer, John had a lot of time to work in the garden and he enjoyed it. He also enjoyed Claire's genuine enthusiasm at seeing the plants grow. She had no experience whatever with gardening, so it was all new and exciting to her.

John was also enjoying his son, particularly the infant's reaction to everything around him. Claire had made a flute from a sumac branch, and John was learning to play it.

"Now, listen to this, Kirby," he said, lifting the flute to his lips. He began playing, and to Claire's surprise, was actually playing a song.

"What is that song?" she asked.

"It is called 'Old Folks at Home.' Some call it 'Suwanee River.'"

"How can you do that? You have not played the flute before."

John chuckled. "Once you know how to play the scale, the rest is easy," he said.

He played a few more songs, then handed to flute to Claire, who played music from her background. The music was melodious, consisting of a lot of halftones, but there was a soulful, almost mournful quality to it.

"That was beautiful," John said when she finished. "What was it?"

"It is a prayer to the Great Spirit. It has words. Would you like to hear them?"

"Yes."

Claire sang the song, first in her own language, then again, this time in English.

> *"Oh Great Spirit whose voice I hear in the winds*
> *Whose breath gives life to the world*
> *I come to you as one of your many children*
> *I am small and weak."*

"Why, that is beautiful, Claire," he said. He embraced her. "I never thought, when I left Pennsylvania, that I would wind up with an Indian woman, let alone, that I would fall in love with her. I love you, Claire."

"I did not think I would ever love," Claire said. "It is only a word, I thought. But you have taught me that it is much more than a word."

John embraced her again, then he heard the sound of approaching horses, and he separated from her, and, picking up his rifle, stepped out in front of his cabin. It wasn't that he feared every sound, but the cabin was so remote that any visitor became suspect.

There was only one direct approach to the cabin, and he jacked a round into the chamber of his rifle and watched, and waited.

He saw a body of men approaching and he knew, immediately, that they were soldiers. He assumed they might be lost, and he put his rifle down, and waited until they approached. What he saw was eight soldiers, being led by a lieutenant.

"Excuse me, sir. Are you John Jackson?" the lieutenant asked when they reached the front of his cabin.

"I am. What can I do for you, Lieutenant?"

"Mr. Jackson, I am Lieutenant Murphy, from Fort Shaw. Major Clinton's compliments, sir, and he wonders if you and your wife would do him the honor of paying a visit to the fort?"

"Would this be anything more than a courtesy call, Lieutenant?" John asked.

"I believe the major has a favor he wishes to ask of you, sir. But I have not been made privy to what that favor might be."

"All right, Lieutenant Murphy, we'll join you," John said.

"What is it?" Claire asked when John went back into the cabin.

"Major Clinton wants us to pay a call on him at Fort Shaw," John said.

"Why?"

"I don't know, the lieutenant didn't say. I'm not sure he even knows. But, it's never a bad thing to have a good relationship with the military, so I think we should go."

"What about the garden?"

"It'll be all right for a few days."

With baby Kirby riding in a cradleboard hanging from the side of Claire's horse, John and Claire rode back to Fort Shaw with Lieutenant Murphy and his military detachment.

Fort Shaw was located on the south side of Sun River, constructed of palisade logs, and perched high on the end of a bluff that protruded over the water. There were projecting blockhouses on corners opposite each other, from which the soldiers had a good view of the approach.

The front gate to the post was tightly closed as Lieutenant Murphy and his party approached.

"Hello, the post!" Lieutenant Murphy shouted. "Open the gate!"

The gate was opened early enough so that there was no need for the group to break stride. They rode right through with Lieutenant Murphy returning the salute of the private at the gate. When they reached the parade ground, Lieutenant Murphy halted the detail.

"Dismount!" he ordered.

Claire looked at John, and he smiled. "That's not us," he said.

The soldiers dismounted.

"Fall out!" Lieutenant Murphy ordered.

As the soldiers led their mounts to the stable, Lieutenant Murphy indicated than John and Claire should follow him. They rode to the headquarters building then dismounted, and tied their horses off at the hitching rail.

John took Kirby from his cradleboard, and handed him to Claire, then they followed Lieutenant Murphy inside.

"Sergeant Major, is Major Clinton in his office?" Lieutenant Murphy asked.

"Yes, sir," the first sergeant major answered.

Murphy went over to the door leading to the commanding officer's office, tapped lightly, then pushed it open and stuck his head in.

"Sir, I have Mr. Jackson."

John couldn't hear the major's answer, but he did hear the lieutenant's response.

"Yes, sir, she is with him." The lieutenant turned toward John. "Come ahead," he said.

"John, the baby and I will wait here," Claire said.

"No," Lieutenant Murphy said, quickly. "The major wants to see both of you."

"Both of us?" John asked. He wasn't sure what this was about, but he wasn't sure he liked it. If the major planned to give him some trouble because he was married to an Indian woman, he wasn't going to put up with it. Taking Claire by the arm, he led her into the commanding officer's office.

"Mr. Jackson, Mrs. Jackson," the major said with a broad smile. He was standing and he came toward them with his hand extended. "I'm Major Clinton. Thank you so much for coming."

The major's demeanor allowed John to dismiss his apprehension. He wasn't acting like someone who was going to give him any trouble.

"Please," he said, "I know you have had a long ride. Have a seat." He extended his arm toward the side wall, where there was a sofa and a chair.

John and Claire sat on the sofa, and she held Kirby on her lap. Kirby stared at the major, his dark brown eyes open wide.

"I know you are wondering why I asked you here," Major Clinton said. "I have a favor to ask of you and, if you choose not to do it, I will certainly understand. In the meantime, I've made quarters available for you here, on the post, for the night, so you can start back, rested, tomorrow."

"What do you want, Major?" John asked.

"I want you and your wife to be an emissary for me," Major Clinton said.

"What sort of an emissary?"

"A peace emissary to the Crow Indians. I thought, with your wife, you would be an ideal ambassador."

"My wife is Lakota, not Crow," John said. "The Lakota and the Crow are traditional enemies."

"Can you speak the Crow language?" Major Clinton asked.

"I can speak," Claire said.

"It could save hundreds of lives," Major Clinton said. "All I need is for the Crow to understand that we will not encroach on their land, that we will in fact protect their land from any white men who try to violate their borders. Try and make her understand that."

"I won't try to make her understand anything," John said. "She will make her own decision, and I will honor it."

"I understand," Major Clinton said. "Well, I do hope you and Mrs. Jackson will be our guests for dinner this evening. And I promise you," he said, holding up his finger and smiling, "I will make no further petitions. As I said, whether or not you and Mrs. Jackson consent to do this, will be up to you."

"Thank you," John said.

The major's wife was a rather plump, blond woman with bright blue eyes. "Oh, it is so wonderful to have dinner guests," she said when John and Claire arrived.

"I must apologize for our dress," John said. "We had no idea we would be invited to your beautiful home."

"Oh, nonsense, you are dressed just fine. And what a lovely thing you are," she said, gushingly, to Claire. "Oh, may I hold the child for a moment? Our own son is back East, attending the Military Academy at West Point," she said. "It's been so long since I held a little one."

"Yes, you may hold him," Claire said, extending the baby to her.

"Oh, my, what a handsome creature you are," Mrs. Clinton said. "Yes, you are. Indeed, you are." Kirby smiled at her and a line of spittle trailed from his mouth.

True to his promise, Major Clinton made no more mention of the mission he wanted John and Claire to undertake. Instead they talked about St. Louis. John and Claire had just come from there, and Major Clinton had been stationed there at Jefferson Barracks.

After a pleasant dinner, and because Kirby had fallen

asleep, John made his excuses, and said they needed to get the baby to bed.

"In regard to your request, Major, I will give you an answer in the morning," he said.

"Good, thank you, that's all I ask," Major Clinton replied. "I'm gratified that you are still thinking about it, rather than an outright dismissal of the request."

The empty quarters of what would normally be the residence of an unmarried junior officer, was for them. As they walked back to the quarters John heard the first note of the bugle.

"What is that music?" Claire asked. "It is so beautiful. But it is sad."

"It is called 'Taps,'" John said. "It is the bugle call that puts the soldiers to bed at night. Would you like to know the words?"

"Yes."

John sung the words, softly, as the bugler repeated the call.

> *"Day is done,*
> *Gone the sun,*
> *From the lakes, from the hills, from the sky.*
> *All is well, safely rest,*
> *God is nigh."*

"Those are good words," Claire said.

Looking around the garrison, John saw that all the buildings, the officers' quarters, and the soldiers' barracks, were dark and quiet.

"Come," he said. "We must be to our bed."

Later, after Kirby was asleep, John and Claire lay together in bed, with Claire's head on John's shoulder.

"John, do you want to do what the major has asked us to do?"

"It is up to you, Claire. You are the one who will have to do the talking."

"Yes, I will do the talking, but you will give me the words to say."

"As I said, it is up to you."

"If it will make peace, I say we should go."

"All right," John said. "I'll tell the major in the morning. We'll go."

CHAPTER 23

In the village of Iron Bull

When John, Claire, and the baby rode into the village, every villager crowded around them, men, women, and children. One of the older boys, who was about fourteen, ran up to touch John's leg. Then, with a loud shout he ran back into the crowd.

"I have counted coups! I have counted coups!" he shouted, proudly.

"Claire, where do we go now?" John asked quietly.

"They will lead us to the place of the village council," Claire replied.

Almost immediately, two men came up, and one took the bridle of John's horse in hand, as the other took the bridle of Claire's horse. The two men led them through the camp until they stopped in front of a teepee. There was a council fire and several men were sitting around the fire. One was sitting by himself, just in front of the teepee opening, making it obvious that he was the head.

"That is Iron Bull," Claire said.

John held up his hand. "I come in peace, Iron Bull."

"*Taŋyaŋ yahípi,*" Iron Bull replied.

"He welcomes us."

Iron Bull spoke again.

"He asks that you join the council, but I cannot, as I am a woman."

"Tell him I must have you beside me, because you are my words."

Claire translated John's words.

Iron Bull nodded, and made a motion indicating Claire could join them.

"Philamayaye," Claire replied, thanking him.

"Tell him that we come from the soldier chief. That the white man wants to live in peace with his Indian brothers."

Claire translated, then Iron Bull spoke, and she gasped.

"What is it? What did he say?"

"He said that you have killed some of his people. That you, and one called Smoke have killed Crow."

"That is true, but only because we were attacked by Crow. That is why we are here now, to make peace so that our people will not kill each other anymore."

"You have come to me in peace, and you may leave in peace. But there can be no peace between us."

"What do you think, Claire? Do you think there is any chance in getting him to change his mind?"

"I will ask," she replied, then, to Iron Bull.

"Great Chief, how strong is your conviction that there can be no peace?"

"It is very strong. Why do you live with a white man?"

"I was sold to a white man, by my own people. It was not my choice."

"Were you sold to this man?"

"No. John Jackson is a good man. I came to him because I wanted to. This baby is our baby. I wanted to have our baby."

"The baby is white."

"The baby is white and Indian. It is a fine baby, and it is a symbol of peace between the Indian and the white man."

"You may leave the village in peace. But after you have left, there can be no peace."

Claire turned to her husband. "I think we must go now," she said. "We can do no more, here."

"All right," John said. "If that is what you think."

"Iron Bull, have we your word that we can leave without fear?"

"My word is good only as far as the village," Iron Bull replied. *"After you leave the village, there will be no peace."*

"Oh!" Claire said.

"Claire, what is it?"

"John, we must go, now."

John stood, then took the baby, and with Claire moved slowly and deliberately to their horses.

"Tie the baby in very tightly," Claire said. "For after we leave the village, we must ride as fast as we can ride."

"Claire, what is it? What did he say?"

"He said we are safe only until we are out of the village. Then we will be in great danger."

They rode quietly out of the village then, when they were clear of the village, someone shouted something.

"John! He said we must run!" Claire said.

Quickly they broke into a gallop, riding as fast as they could. Behind them they heard the cries and calls of Indians in pursuit, and when John looked around he saw several mounted Indians chasing them.

"In there!" John said, pointing to a narrow draw, as arrows flew by them.

The draw was so narrow that only one horse at a time could pass, and that was good, because that meant that only one Indian at a time could be in pursuit.

Claire and the baby went in first with John behind them. He knew this draw well because he had been trapped here last winter. He knew where it came out, and he also knew that if they could make it out the other end, he could seal it off so that the pursuing Indians couldn't get through.

Pulling his rifle from the saddle sheath, John twisted around in the saddle, raised the Henry to his shoulder, aimed, and fired at the horse the Indian was riding. The horse went down, throwing its rider over its head. The dead horse had the effect of blocking off the draw. That brought the Indians behind to a complete stop, enabling John and Claire to put a little more distance between them.

One Indian managed to get through, and he galloped after them. This time John shot at the rider, rather than the horse and that bought them enough time to make it all the way through to the other end.

"Keep going!" John yelled. "I'm going to stop them here!"

John dismounted, then climbed up to the top of the opening. There, using his rifle as a lever, he managed to roll a rock loose, which had the effect of starting others down, until there was a rockslide of sufficient quantity to block up the entire pass.

Climbing back down he stayed just outside the blocked-up pass for a few minutes to make sure none of the Indians were able to get through, then satisfied that he had stopped them, he remounted and joined Claire, who was half a mile away.

By now their horses were panting hard.

"We need to dismount and walk them for a while," John said.

"Do we go back home, now?" Claire asked.

"Yes, but first we should go by the fort to tell Major Clinton that we didn't have any luck with our peace mission."

"But you don't need me," Claire said. "I want to go home." She smiled. "I want to make a soup with vegetables from our garden."

"All right, you and Kirby go on home. I'll stop by the fort to see Major Clinton, then I'll come on home."

"Tonight?"

"Yes, tonight."

"I will have soup ready for you. It will be a very good soup."

"I've no doubt but that it will," John said. He leaned over toward her, and kissed her. "Going to Rendezvous and finding you, is the best thing I ever did in my entire life."

By now the horses had resumed their normal breathing.

"I think we can ride them now," he said. "You go on home, I'll be back as soon as I can."

"*Thechihila,*" Claire said.

"*Thechihila.*" John replied. Lakota for "I love you," it was one of the first Lakota phrases John learned.

Fort Shaw, Montana

"Well, I'm very sorry to hear that, Mr. Jackson," Major Clinton said. "I was rather hoping that we might be able to come to some kind of an accommodation with them."

"I'm sorry as well," John replied.

"You can use the same quarters tonight and start home tomorrow."

"No, my wife and child have already gone home. I promised I would be back tonight."

Major Clinton laughed. "Well, I can't say as I blame you. I do thank you for your effort, even if it wasn't successful."

Before he left, John went into the sutler's store, where he bought a straw hat with a wide brim for Claire to wear as she worked in the garden. He was sure she would like it. He also bought some chocolate, and a small toy horse for Kirby. Kirby was too young to be able to appreciate it now, but he was sure that he would within another few years.

He thought about his friend Smoke, and thought he would be pleased to know that there was someone named for him.

[*Fort Shaw was established June 30, 1867. It was located on the right bank of the Sun River, some twenty-five miles above its junction with the Missouri, and five miles above the point where the Fort Benton–Helena stagecoach road crossed the Sun River. Fort Shaw was established to protect the route between Fort Benton and Helena and to prevent the movement of hostile Indians into the settled area to the south. Four companies, under the command of Major William Clinton, 13th U.S. Infantry, selected the site. First called "Camp Reynolds," the post was designated "Fort Shaw" on August 1, 1867, in honor of Colonel Robert G. Shaw, 54th Massachusetts Infantry, killed before Fort Wagner in 1863. Abandoned on July 21, 1891, the military reservation was transferred to the Interior Department on April 30, 1892. The former post served as an Indian school from 1892 until 1910.—ED.*]

Boulder

Smoke couldn't believe he had let Sally talk him into coming to the Jordan car dealership.

"Yes, sir," the slick salesman said. "There she is, the Jordan Playboy. The niftiest car on the road today."

"What do you think, Smoke?" Sally asked. She got into the car, sat behind the wheel, and flashed a big smile.

"Why don't I just buy you a jar of perfume?" Smoke proposed.

Sally laughed. "A *jar*? A *jar* of perfume? Honey, do you think they put perfume up in jars, like a jar of pickles?"

"I know it comes in little bitty bottles, but for what this thing would cost, I could buy you ten jars of perfume."

"I can see that I'm getting nowhere with you," she said. She got out of the car. "Okay, take me out to dinner. And if you aren't going to buy me this car, then I want the most expensive dinner in town."

"That, I will do," Smoke replied.

Boulder's newest, and quickly one of its finest, restaurants was Summer's Sunken Gardens, a European-style eatery. The focal point was a large pool-like fountain in the center of the dining area.

"Please don't tell Pearlie or Cal that we ate lamb," Smoke said as they began on the entrée, crown roast of lamb. "I'll never live it down."

"How are your sessions with Professor Armbruster going?"

"It's funny," Smoke said. "But talking to him like this, I mean bringing things out in great detail, not just a quick story here and there, it's as if I am actually reliving it."

"Are you all right with that?" Sally asked as she carved off a bit of lamb.

"Yes, I suppose I am. Some of it, I'm actually enjoying. But some of it has been hard, much harder than I would have thought."

"I know you talked about Nicole and Arthur, and I know how difficult that had to be for you."

"Yes, it was difficult. And, it was also difficult talking about Denise and Louis, especially Louis, since it hasn't been that long since he was killed."

"At least we have our grandchildren, Frank and Elyse," Sally said.

"How old are they now?"

"Frank is eleven, Elyse is nine."

"They're living with their mother and her new husband, and we never get to see them."

"The trains run in both directions," Sally said. "We could

go back East to see them easier than they could come here. They do have school, after all."

"Yeah, we can, can't we? Sally, what do you say that after I'm finished with this business with Professor Armbruster, that we go see the grandkids?"

"Oh, Smoke, I think that would be wonderful!" she said. "Yes, let's please do it!"

"We will," Smoke promised.

CHAPTER 24

Old Main Building

"Do you need to listen to where we left off yesterday?" Professor Armbruster asked Smoke the next morning when he showed up at the Old Main building to continue with the narrative.

"No, that won't be necessary," Smoke said. "I know exactly where I left off, and I know where it's going next."

Smoke was silent for a long moment.

"Is something wrong?"

"The part that is coming up isn't going to be easy," Smoke said.

"Do you want to take a few moments to compose yourself before we begin?" Professor Armbruster asked.

"I've had all night to compose myself, Professor. A few more minutes won't make any difference."

"No, I suppose not."

"Tell Wes I'm ready."

Professor Armbruster reached down to click the toggle switch. "We're ready, Wes," he said.

Through the window Smoke saw Wes nod, then bring his hand down. Smoke resumed the story.

John's cabin

Whips His Horses held his hand up as a signal for the others to be quiet. He didn't have to say anything, though, because they were all good warriors, and they well knew the value of stealth. Then, they saw the woman come from the house with a basket. She walked into the garden and began picking vegetables.

Whips His Horses signaled to three who were armed with bows and arrows. All three fired, and Whips His Horses watched the rapid and graceful flight of the arrows. All three arrows struck the woman and she dropped the basket, took a couple of stumbling steps, then fell.

"Ayiee!" Whips His Horses shouted, hoping the shout would bring out the man who had killed his brother.

But no one came from the white man's house.

They waited for a few moments, then they heard a baby crying. The baby cried for several minutes without letup.

"I think the man is not here," one of the others said. "He would not let the baby cry for so long. He would come for the woman, but nobody has come for the woman."

"We will see," Whips His Horses said.

There were six others with him. Eight had started in pursuit of the man and his woman when they left the village, but two were killed in the pass. Then, the rocks fell, and it took a long time to move the rocks so they could continue. Now they were here, and Whips His Horses did not think the man they had followed was here.

He started toward the cabin, moving in a crouch, and on the balls of his feet, ready to run if need be.

But the man did not appear.

One of the other Indians in the party darted quickly up to the cabin, stood with his back to the wall near the door, then, cautiously, looked inside.

"Only the baby is here!" he called back to the others.

"Bring the baby out," Whips His Horses said.

The Indian by the door went into the cabin, then came out again, carrying the baby upside down, holding him by his foot. The baby was still crying.

"What shall we do with the baby?" the man holding it asked.

"Throw it on the ground by the woman."

With a huge smile, the Indian holding the child swung his arm back and forth a few times to get the momentum he needed, then he let the baby go. It flew through the air, then landed, hard, on the ground, next to its mother. There it lay quiet and still.

"Shall we burn the house?" one of the other Indians asked.

"Yes," Whips His Horses said, then he changed his mind. "No. Leave the house as it is. When the man returns, I want him not to know what has happened until he sees the woman and the baby."

"Will we wait for him?"

"No," Whips His Horses said. "If we wait for him, we will kill him, but he will die only one time. When he sees his woman and his baby dead, he will die two times. Then, we will kill him a third time."

"Yes, he will die three times. That is very good," one of the other Indians said.

"Let us return to the village now. It will be good to let him find his dead woman and child and weep over them."

It was dark by the time John returned to his cabin. All the way home he had been thinking about the soup Claire had promised him, and he thought it would be very good, with the vegetables grown in his own garden. He even thought he might be able to smell it when he got close enough.

He smelled nothing and was disappointed. Then, when he got to the little clearing where he had built a home for himself, Claire, and the baby, he was surprised to see no light shining through the window. Instead the cabin sat there, gleaming silver under the full, bright moon.

Why could he see no light from within the house?

Then he thought of what a hard ride it had been for Claire and the baby, and with a smile, he realized they must already be in bed.

That was all right. The soup could wait until tomorrow. He was tired too, and it would be good to climb into bed beside his wife. And if she wasn't too tired . . . he smiled at the implications of that.

He took his horse around to the lean-to attached to the back of the house, unsaddled him, then tied him to the hitching rail alongside Claire's horse. The watering trough had water, and he pitched some hay into the feeding trough, then he went inside.

"Claire, I'm home," he said, speaking just loudly enough for Claire to hear, but not to wake the baby.

"Claire?"

John went over to the baby's crib and felt down inside. The baby wasn't there, and he realized that he must be in bed with Claire. He lit a candle. If he was going to move the baby back to his crib, he didn't want to trip over something.

"Claire, I'm going to put the baby back . . ." He stopped in mid-sentence. There was nobody in the bed, and in fact, the bed was still made.

"What?" he asked aloud.

She couldn't have gone anywhere, her horse was still in the lean-to.

John stepped outside. "Claire?" he called. "Claire, are you out here?"

John heard something from the garden, low and guttural, like the sound of wolves, feeding.

"Get the hell out of my garden!" he shouted loudly, and, with yelps, the animals ran.

John started out to the garden to see what kind of damage

the wolves might have done. That was when he saw the two bodies . . . one large, and one small. Or at least, what was left of the bodies.

"NO!!!!!" The agonizing cry of horror and despair rolled back from the walls of the little canyon. "God in heaven . . . no!!!"

John fell to his knees in the garden beside the bodies of his wife and baby, and wept aloud as he hadn't done so since he was a small boy.

Old Main Building

"Please, stop the recording," Smoke said.

Professor Armbruster waved at Wes, who stopped the session.

Smoke sat there for a long moment, his eyes closed as he pinched the bridge of his nose.

"Are you all right, Smoke?" Professor Armbruster asked.

"I need to walk around a bit if you don't mind," Smoke said.

"No, I don't mind at all. Go ahead, walk around the campus all you want. I'll be in my office when you are ready to resume recording. You do intend to continue, don't you?"

"I don't know," Smoke said. "This has become . . . difficult," he said. "Much more difficult than I ever imagined it could be."

"I understand."

Smoke forced a smile. "I'm glad you understand, because I'm not sure that I do. In the first place, this happened many years ago. And in the second place, I've told this story before without it affecting me as it is now."

"But the way you are telling it now is different," Professor Armbruster said. "You have never before been as powerfully absorbed in the story as you are now. This intense immersion has heightened your reaction to the events so that you are, in effect, reliving, rather than merely retelling the details. There is a psychological explanation for this. It is called 'cognitive context-dependent memory.' You see, you lost your own wife and child by an act of violence, much in the same way as John Jackson lost his. And now, in the retelling of this story you are, in effect, redoubling and experiencing again, your own trauma."

Smoke smiled, wanly. "Yeah," he said. "Something like that."

As Smoke walked around the campus he heard the sound of an engine from above, and looked up to see an airplane passing overhead. Across a landscape covered with fallen leaves, and under a tree he saw a group of college students. They were listening to music on the radio, and two young girls, wearing bobbed hair and short skirts, were doing some sort of dance that seemed to require a lot of kicking.

He couldn't help but think what drastic changes there had been within his lifetime, and as he looked at the students, he wondered how many of them could have stood up to the ordeal of a two-month-long wagon train trip, or a winter in the mountains with nothing but their own wits for survival.

But even as he contemplated such patronizing thoughts, he recalled the Great War so recently concluded, and he realized that despite the outside trappings, nothing had really changed. The principles of courage, honor, and self-reliance were still present, and he was satisfied that these young men and women would be able to rise to whatever challenges they might meet in the future.

He wished he could go into Longmont's Saloon for a beer, but knew that, even if he were back in Big Rock, that option wouldn't be open to him. He wondered if the country would ever come to its senses and repeal the idiotic amendment that was prohibition.

Finally, the melancholy he had been experiencing since the moment he told of John finding the half-eaten bodies of

Claire and Kirby passed. He turned and started back toward the Old Main building, the fallen leaves crackling under his feet.

When he returned to the recording room, he saw a glass of amber liquid sitting by the microphone, and he smiled.

"Something tells me this isn't tea," he said.

"I thought you might need a little . . . what is it you men called it in the old days? Snort?"

"Snort, yes," Smoke said. He picked it up. "And, yes, I do need a drink right now."

He tossed the drink down, wiped his lips with the back of his hand, and nodded.

"I'm ready when you are," he said.

On the other side of the window, Wes brought his hand down, and Smoke resumed talking.

CHAPTER 25

Montana

John carried Claire and the baby back into the house and he laid them both on the bed. The same bed that he and Claire had shared, the same bed on which Kirby had been conceived. He covered their bodies with a bright red blanket, then he pulled a chair up beside the bed and sat there, staring at the covered mounds on the bed.

As John sat there, unbidden, episodes of his past flashed through his mind. He saw himself as an acolyte in his father's church, and as a student at the University of Pennsylvania. Terrible images of the war tumbled by, as well as his difficulty in adjusting when he came back. He recalled his rejection by Lucinda, and his experiences in Annam.

But nothing, nothing in his entire life, had ever hurt him to the degree he was hurting now. The pain was unbearable, and he wanted to scream until he had no voice left.

"God, why?" he asked aloud.

He remembered asking that same question to his father after he came back from the war, when he was having such a difficult time adjusting.

"Why, if He is a just God, would He allow such evil things to happen?" John had asked.

"God allows things to happen for His reasons, whether or not we understand them," John's father had answered. "Above all, however, we must remember that He is a good, just, loving, and merciful God. I know that things have happened to you that are beyond your understanding. But you must trust in the Lord, and put aside all doubts."

Nathaniel's short homily had done nothing to ease John's inner turmoil then, and recalling his words was doing nothing toward easing his pain now.

"Why, God! Why?" John shouted at the top of his voice. Then, in an angry snarl he added, "Never mind. I'll set things right on my own."

When the sun rose the next morning, John went out into the garden where he gathered every flower that had been planted. Bringing them in, he spread them on top of the bed until the bed was covered with colorful blooms and petals.

That done, John emptied a container of kerosene, then he set fire to the house. He stood out front watching the flames leap up around the logs that he and Claire had cut, shaped, notched, and put into position to build the house.

He could feel the heat of the flames, and even though it was uncomfortable, he made no effort to back away. He stood right there, until the cabin was completely consumed by the fire, so that there was not one recognizable thing about it remaining. He looked where he thought the bed might be, but could see nothing but blackened ash. He made no attempt to look closer.

Not until the last wisp of smoke had died, did he mount his horse and ride away. In less than twenty-four hours, his life had taken a turn that closed off his previous thirty-five years, as if none of it had ever happened. He was now a man consumed with hatred, and a determination to avenge his wife and child.

Old Main Building

Smoke stopped talking and Professor Armbruster waited for a moment, then he reached down to flip the toggle switch on the intercom box.

"Wes, this will be all for the day," he said.

"Yes, sir," Wes replied.

"Are you okay, Smoke?"

Smoke nodded. "Yeah, I'm fine. I guess it's just a little more of this *cognitive context-dependent memory* you were talking about earlier."

"Yes, it can be very intense. Look, why don't you take off early today. You and Sally take in some of the sights of the town."

When Smoke returned to the hotel room, Sally was sitting on the sofa, her legs curled up under her, reading *Babbitt,* a novel by Sinclair Lewis. She looked up in surprise when Smoke came in.

"Hello," she said. "You're back early."

"Yes," Smoke said without further explanation. "Enjoying the book?"

"To be honest? Not particularly. There's no plot to the story, it's almost like a diary . . . we're just following him around, but he isn't going anywhere."

"Then if I suggested we go somewhere, you wouldn't necessarily be against it?"

"Where do you want to go?"

"You'll know when we get there."

* * *

Fifteen minutes later, Smoke turned into the large lot of the Jordan automobile dealership.

"Smoke, what?"

"Didn't you say you wanted a sports car?"

"Yes, but . . ."

"But nothing. You're my wife, I love you, we can afford it. So what is there to argue?" Smoke said.

Parking the Duesenberg, Smoke and Sally went inside, then walked over to stand beside a bright, shining, red car.

"Pretty car, isn't it?" a salesman asked, coming over to them.

"Beautiful," Sally said.

"It has a 127-inch wheelbase, a finely louvered hood, low-slung beltline, and steeply sloped tail."

"Where is the top?" Smoke asked. "If it starts raining, do you just get wet?"

"Oh, no, it has a top. But the top is completely removable. That way, you don't have a bulky folded top to spoil the car's lines."

"Is it fast?" Smoke asked.

"Fast? Mister, this car has a flathead six cylinder engine of sixty-five horsepower. Why, on a straight, flat road, you could get her up to seventy miles per hour, easily."

"We'll take it."

"Smoke! Are you serious?"

"Very serious," Smoke said.

Half an hour later, with the Duesenberg parked at the hotel, Smoke and Sally drove their new sports car up to the top of Flagstaff Mountain. There, they sat in the open-top car and looked down onto the blazing lights of the city of Boulder.

"Why?" Sally asked.

"Why what?"

"You know what I'm asking. Why did you come home early, with the sudden urge to buy this car?"

"Didn't you want it?"

"I had already put it behind me as a foolish notion. No, you bought this car, and it had nothing to do with me. I just want to know why?"

"It was a pretty rough day today," Smoke said. "I talked about John finding Claire and his baby, killed, and half eaten by wolves." Smoke half laughed. "I thought maybe buying this car, and driving it, might help me put it out of my mind."

Sally reached over to put her hand on his.

"Smoke, why don't you tell Professor Armbruster you've had enough and we're going home?"

Smoke didn't answer.

"I mean really, you've spoken about losing your father, about Nicole and Art being killed. And now this? It's too much. Your life was hard enough, and dangerous enough, Smoke. You've reached the point to where you should be able to just relax, and drive like a fool if you want to."

"What? What do you mean, drive like a fool?" Smoke asked with a chuckle.

"I mean you drove like a fool. Do you think you drove cautiously coming up here?"

"The salesman said it would do seventy miles per hour," Smoke defended.

"Yes, but just because the salesman said this car would go seventy miles per hour, that doesn't mean you should drive that fast on a winding mountain road."

"I'll be more careful going back down," Smoke said.

"I should hope so."

A meteor streaked across the sky.

"Look," Smoke said. "When you see a meteor, you're supposed to kiss a pretty girl."

"So now we're going to drive back in town so you can kiss a pretty girl?" Sally teased.

"I don't have to go to town for that. Don't you know, Sally, that when I look at you, I see the same beautiful young schoolteacher you were when I first met you?"

"I'm an old woman, Smoke," Sally said. She put her arms around his neck. "But I'm glad you still see me that way."

They kissed.

Residence of the President of the University

"How are your sessions with Mr. Jensen going?" Dr. Norlin asked.

Once again Armbruster had been invited for dinner with the president of the university, but this time the invitation omitted Smoke Jensen. The reason Smoke was left out of the invitation was so Dr. Norlin could speak frankly with Armbruster.

"It's, uh, going fairly well," Armbruster replied.

"Fairly well? That's certainly a measured response. What is wrong?"

"There's nothing actually wrong, it's just that . . . well, some of the stories are very intense, and as Smoke shares them, it is as if he is reliving the experiences. And not just of his own life. He just told the event that started John Jackson on his killing spree, his coming home and finding his wife and child out in the garden. They had been killed by the Crow and half consumed by wolves."

"Would you mind a suggestion from me?" Dr. Norlin asked.

"No, I wouldn't mind at all."

"Take the conversation in another direction for a while. Then come back to Jackson."

"Yes," Armbruster said. "I was thinking about doing that. Your suggestion just reinforces it."

Old Main Building

"Are you ready to go on?" Professor Armbruster asked the next morning.

"As ready as I'm going to be," Smoke replied.

"I have a few questions, if you don't mind."

"I don't mind at all. That's why I'm here."

"This business with the Crow Indians, that was two years after you and John Jackson separated, wasn't it?"

"Yes."

"Just so we can fill in the gap, I'd be interested in catching up on what you were doing during that time."

"Besides marrying Sally, you mean?"

"Well, that's significant, yes. But more specifically, I was wondering if you might tell about Fast Lennie Moore. I've only read one account of it, and to be truthful with you, I don't even know if it really happened, or not."

"It happened," Smoke said.

[*On May 25, 1871, Lennie Moore (whose real name may have been Will Bachman) was drinking heavily in Tucson, Arizona, with his friend Larry Wallace, and eight or nine other cowboys. Wallace insulted Moore's friend Deputy Marshal Billy Baker. Baker ignored Wallace, but Moore took offense and insisted that Wallace accompany him and apologize to Baker. When Wallace refused, Moore threatened to kill him. Wallace complied, but Moore afterward heaped abuse on Wallace, announcing, "You son of a bitch, I think I'll just kill you anyhow."*

Moore had already demonstrated his speed and skill with a pistol, and Wallace wanted no fight with him, so he left the saloon. Moore followed him. Feeling threatened, Wallace turned and shot Moore, wounding him in the cheek and neck. Marshal Baker arrested Wallace but the court ruled he acted in self-defense.

A Tucson doctor treated Moore, who had not been seriously wounded. When Moore recovered, he called Wallace out and killed him. Later he killed Michael and Isaac Paterson, cousins of Wallace who had come for revenge. Moore's reputation began to grow after that, and it is believed that he had killed nine men before his fateful encounter with Smoke Jensen in the small town of Perdition, Arizona.—ED.]

CHAPTER 26

Perdition, Arizona—1872

When Smoke Jensen had ridden into town a few minutes earlier, news of his arrival spread quickly. Even though he was still a young man, his fame had spread, and grandfathers held up their grandsons to point him out as he rode by, so that the young ones could remember this moment, and, many years from now, tell their grandchildren about it.

Smoke had earned this not-always-welcome notoriety, because of his prowess with a Colt. He was in the Rattler's Cage Saloon now, and had just ordered a beer. Picking it up, he looked around the interior of the saloon. Half a dozen tables, occupied by a dozen or so men filled the room, and tobacco smoke hovered in a noxious cloud just under the ceiling. It was now twilight, and as daylight disappeared, flickering kerosene lanterns combined with the smoke to make the room seem even hazier.

Smoke had come to Perdition because he had heard that his sister, Janey, was here. He and his sister had never been close, not since she ran away from home during the war, leaving a young Smoke to try and run the farm, and deal with their dying mother, all by himself.

He had encountered Janey again, briefly, in the town of

Bury, Colorado, just before his showdown with Richards, Potter, and Stratton. Then, he had sent her away. But, at Sally's urging, he decided to make at least one more effort to find her, and to see if he could patch up things between them.

It had been a false lead though. She wasn't here and she hadn't been here, so his trip to Perdition had been a waste of time. He sent a telegram back to Sally, telling her that his search had been fruitless, and he was coming back home.

"Would you be the one they call Smoke Jensen? The famous . . . gunfighter?" It wasn't a friendly question, or even a question of curiosity. In fact, it was less a question than it was a challenge.

In Smoke's young life, he had already encountered dozens of men like this: angry, belligerent, challenging. He said nothing in reply to the question, but simply held his beer glass out in sort of a salute.

"You too good to talk?" the challenger asked.

Smoke sighed. "Mister, I've ridden a long way on a wild-goose chase. I hope you aren't going to make any trouble."

"Make trouble? Make trouble, you say?" the young man replied. He turned to address the others. The saloon had grown deathly still now as the patrons sat quietly, nervously, and yet titillated too, by the life-and-death drama that had suddenly begun to unfold in front of them. "You don't want me to make any trouble for the great gunfighter, is that it? Do you think I should just shut up and be scared of you because I am in the presence of the great Smoke Jensen?"

Smoke put his beer down with a tired sigh and turned to face his tormentor.

"What's put the burr under your saddle, mister? Have I killed someone close to you? A brother, perhaps? Or maybe your father or just a friend?"

"No, it ain't that. It ain't nothin' like that, at all," the young man answered. "I'm just a-thinkin' that if I killed the great

Smoke Jensen in a fair fight, why, folks would be sayin' my name the way they say yours now."

"And is that what you want?"

"Oh, yeah," the man said with a sardonic grin. "That's what I want."

"What is your name?"

"The name is Moore. Lennie Moore, though you've probably heard of me as Fast Lennie. That's what most folks call me."

"Fast Lennie, huh?"

"Yeah. Have you ever heard of me?"

"As a matter of fact, I have," Smoke replied.

Moore's smile broadened. "So, you've heard of me, have you? What have you heard?"

"I've heard that you are an ignorant young punk, trying to pass yourself off as a man."

Moore's smile quickly turned to an angry snarl. "Draw, Jensen!" he shouted, going for his own gun even before he issued the challenge.

Moore was quick, quicker than anyone else this town had ever seen, and quicker even than anyone Smoke had encountered for some time. But midway through his draw Moore realized that he wasn't quick enough. The arrogant look of confidence on his face was replaced by the knowledge that he knew he was about to be killed.

The two pistols discharged almost simultaneously, but Smoke had been able to bring his gun to bear whereas Moore had not. Smoke's bullet plunged into Moore's chest. The bullet from Moore's gun smashed the glass that held Smoke's drink, sending up a shower of beer and tiny shards of glass.

Looking down at himself, Moore put his hand over his wound, then pulled it away and examined the blood that had filled his palm. By the time he looked back at Smoke the fear had been replaced by acceptance, and a little expression of surprise.

"Damn," he said. "You're good. I would have bet my life that I could beat you." Moore tried to chuckle, though the chuckle ended with a cough. "I guess I just did that, didn't I?" Moore fell on his back, his right arm stretched out, his forefinger still sticking through the trigger guard.

Moore had been wearing a black hat, with a silver band from which protruded a red feather. The hat was upside down on the floor behind him. The eye-burning, acrid smoke of two gunshots hung in a gray-blue cloud just below the ceiling.

Smoke turned back to the bar where all that was left of his drink were pieces of broken glass and a small puddle of beer.

"Damn, he spilled my beer," Smoke said.

"Yeah, it looks like he did," the bartender said. Grabbing a new mug, he opened the spigot of the beer barrel, and a golden liquid began climbing the sides of the glass.

The saloon had grown silent in the moments just before the gunfight, but since the gunfight it had become a buzz of excitement as everyone shared with each other what all had just seen. Smoke was only halfway through his drink when the sheriff and one of his deputies arrived.

"What happened here?" the sheriff asked.

The question wasn't directed to anyone in particular, so everyone started answering at once, availing themselves of the first opportunity to tell a story they would be telling for the rest of their lives.

"Hold it, hold it!" the sheriff said, holding up his hands. "Don't everyone talk at once." The sheriff looked over toward the bartender. "Abe, what happened here?"

"Moore tried to brace Jensen."

"Moore started the fight?"

"Oh, yeah, Moore started it," Abe replied.

"Abe's tellin' it true, Sheriff," one of the saloon patrons

said. "All this feller here done"—the patron pointed toward Smoke—"was try 'n have hisself a drink in peace. Next thing you know, why Moore there, is gnawin' at 'im."

The sheriff stroked his chin as he looked down at Moore's body. Death had made the young would-be gunman's face appear slack-jawed and distorted.

"Let me guess," the sheriff said. "Moore recognized Jensen, and was trying to make a name for himself, wasn't he?"

"That's exactly what it was," Abe said.

The sheriff walked back down the bar toward Smoke, who hadn't spoken a word since the sheriff and his deputy came in. He was calmly drinking his beer.

"Mr. Jensen, I thought you told me when you found out your sister wasn't here, that you would be goin' back up to Colorado."

"I am going back," Smoke said. "Train's leavin' tomorrow."

"Too bad it didn't leave an hour ago," the sheriff said.

"I would have been on it," Smoke said.

"And Moore would still be alive," the sheriff said.

"For now. But with his attitude, he was sure to get himself killed, sooner or later."

"I expect you might be right."

"I know I'm right."

"I reckon you've run across people like Moore before."

"More often than I want to," Smoke said. "Most of the time it's all jaw. Not ever'one has the guts to actually make the try, like Mr. Moore did."

"And you say your train leaves tomorrow?"

"That's right."

"What are your plans now?"

"My plans are to go back home."

"No, I mean from now until your train leaves tomorrow."

"I thought I might have supper and get a good night's sleep," Smoke said. "Unless you need me to stay around for an inquest or something."

"No, no, that won't be needed. Uh, but it would be good for all of us, if you'd maybe have your supper and turn in early. You wouldn't want to sleep late and miss your train tomorrow, would you?"

Smoke chuckled. "No, I don't think I would want to do that."

A tall, very gaunt-looking man dressed in black tails and a high hat came in then. Two other men were with him.

"Hello, Gene. I see it didn't take you long to get here," the sheriff said. "Gene Ponder is our undertaker," he added, speaking to Smoke.

"Oh, my, I do believe that is young Mr. Moore, isn't it?" Ponder asked. "He has given me business before, but always before it was the other gentleman I would be carrying away."

"Get him out of here," the sheriff said.

Ponder nodded toward his two associates, and they picked the body up and carried him out. Immediately after the body was moved, one of Abe's workers began cleaning up the blood.

"Mr. Jensen, I apologize for this," the sheriff said. "And I do hope nobody else gets the idea to come after you."

"Yes, I hope so as well."

Sugarloaf Ranch

Smoke and Sally were sitting in a porch swing watching the light show on the mountains as the sun dipped lower in the western sky.

"And this man, Moore, just challenged you for no reason?" Sally asked.

"Oh, he had a reason all right. He wanted to be known as the man who had killed Smoke Jensen."

Sally shivered. "That's no reason."

"It was to Moore, and it is for other men just like Moore."

"Smoke, will you ever be able to just hang up your guns and become a gentleman rancher?" Sally asked.

"Oh, I don't know. That's pretty hard."

"What's so hard about it?"

"The 'gentleman' part," Smoke said, teasingly.

"Oh, pooh, you know what I meant," Sally said with a little laugh, hitting him playfully on the shoulder.

"To answer your question, truthfully, I don't know," Smoke said. "It seems to me like my trail has already been blazed. I don't know as I have any choice but to follow it."

"But wouldn't you like to see Sugarloaf become a productive ranch?"

"It will become a productive ranch, Sally, I promise you that. The day will come when Sugarloaf will be one of the biggest and the best ranches in all of Colorado."

"But if someone is always trying to kill you?"

"I'll deal with it," Smoke said, confidently.

CHAPTER 27

Old Main Building

After Smoke finished with his account of the encounter with Fast Lennie Moore, he, Professor Armbruster, and Wes went into the faculty lounge, where they had coffee and freshly made bear signs.

Over coffee, Smoke told them about the Jordan automobile he had bought for Sally, and Wes, particularly fascinated by it, asked him all sorts of questions, most of which Smoke couldn't answer.

"I'm not all that familiar with modern gadgets," Smoke said. "For example, I'm barely able to understand how a telephone works, let alone a radio, or even how, when I speak into the microphone, you can play my voice back to me. All I know is that the man who sold the car said it had a sixty-five horsepower engine. But I don't understand that either, because even if you hooked sixty-five horses to the machine, they wouldn't be able to run at seventy miles an hour. The car will run seventy miles an hour though. I know this, because I drove it that fast."

Professor Armbruster and Wes laughed.

"Well," Armbruster said as he put his cup down. "Are you ready to continue the account of John Jackson?"

"Yes," Smoke said.

The three men returned to the recording studio, and as soon as Wes was ready, he gave the sign to Professor Armbruster.

"What happened after John burned the cabin, in effect cremating his wife and child?"

"John went on the warpath," Smoke said. "That's what happened."

Montana—1872

John saw smoke drifting up through the trees ahead, and he heard the sound of Indians talking. He had no idea whether these were the same ones who raided his cabin or not, but he didn't care. They were Crow, and it had been Crow Indians who had killed Claire and Kirby. And in John's anger and hatred, all Crow were the same.

Pulling his pistol, he urged his horse into a gallop, heading straight for the campfire of the Indians. He didn't know how many were there, and he didn't care. He intended to kill as many of them as he could before he was killed, and the idea that he might be killed disturbed him not in the least.

With a loud and enraged scream, John burst into the clearing. There were three Indians sitting around a fire, cooking some kind of meat. They looked around at John in shock and fear.

John began shooting. He killed two of them instantly, but the third managed to get to his feet and start running.

John put his pistol away and took out a hatchet that hung from his belt. Easily overtaking the running Indian, John swung his ax, blade first. He split open the fleeing Indian's skull, and his brains began pouring from the wound, even before he fell.

John left him where he lay, and he returned to the campfire to make certain than the two he had shot were dead.

They were dead, and John dismounted and stared at their bodies, wondering what he could do to send a signal to the other Indians, to let them know that this was more than just a random killing.

Then he recalled something Claire had once told him.

"To the Crow, the liver is the most important part of the body," she had said. "Without it, they don't believe they can make it to the afterlife."

John carved open the stomach of one of the Indians, then he cut out his liver. He did the same with the other two. Then, he skewered the three livers on a stick, and put them over the fire to cook.

Once they were cooked, he took a small bite from each of the livers, then cut the rest of them up in small pieces and scattered them about to be consumed by animals and insects.

The Indians had been cooking a rabbit, and he ate what he could, then wrapped the rest of it up in a piece of cloth and took it with him.

Two days later he saw a couple of Crow Indians hunting, and he rode quickly to be able to put himself in position in front of them. He waited until they were almost on him, then he suddenly jumped out in front of them, shooting them both.

Again, he carved out their livers, and again, he roasted them over a fire, taking but one small bite from each of the livers before carving them to spread them around.

Fort Shaw

"He's doing what?" Major Clinton asked, shocked at the report that had been delivered by two old mountain men.

"He's killin' Injuns 'n he's eatin' their livers," Emerson said.

"Who is doing that?"

"Whoever it is that's doin' it," Seth replied. Seth was one of the two mountain men who had come to the fort.

"You don't know who it is that's supposed to be doing this?"

"There ain't no supposed to be doin' it about this. Whoever it is, is actual doin' it," Seth said.

"You're telling me that someone is killing Indians, and eating their livers," Clinton said.

"Yep, but not all Injuns. From what we're a-hearin', it's only the Crow that's gettin' their livers et," Seth said.

"Is it supposed to be a white man who is doing this?"

"That's what the Injuns is sayin'," Emerson said.

"Well now, that just doesn't make any sense at all," Major Clinton said.

"Well, yeah, it does when you stop and think about it," Emerson replied. "You see, most Injuns don't pay that much attention to such things. Oh, they figure if they take a scalp, well you'll be wanderin' around in the Happy Hunting Grounds without your hair. But now the Crow, they figure you can't even get there at all if you ain't got your liver."

"Where did you hear about this?"

"It's all over the mountains," Seth said. "All the other trappers, all the peaceful Injuns, is all a-talkin' about it."

"An' here's the thing, Major, this has got all the Injuns spooked. So far whoever it is, is only killin' the Crow," Emerson said. "But what if he is somebody who's suddenly got hisself a big taste for Injun liver? 'Cause I reckon when you get right down to it, one Injun liver probably tastes pretty much like any other Injun liver. So if this here Liver-Eatin' feller can't get him a Crow, why, more 'n likely he'd settle for just any Injun."

"Leastwise, that's more 'n likely what all the other Injuns

is thinkin' right now, the good ones an' the bad ones," Seth said.

"But so far he has just been killing Crow, right?" Clinton asked.

"That's right," Emerson said.

"There must be a reason."

"I figure it's revenge," Seth said. "Whoever it is that's a-doin' this was more 'n likely done wrong by the Crow. And he's doin' this to get back at 'em."

"You men have your ear to the ground. Have you heard about anything that the Crow may have done to get someone angry enough to do this?"

"Hell, Major, the Crows is always a-doin' somethin'," Emerson said. "I ain't got enough fingers and toes to cipher up how many men I know that's got a bone to pick with the Crow. Includin' me, but I ain't the one that's a-doin' this."

"I ain't either," Seth said. "But I don't mind tellin' you that whoever is doin' it, I say, good for him."

"We need to find out who this is," Major Clinton said. "And when we find out, we need to put a stop to it."

"What fer?" Emerson asked. "The Crow is some damn evil Injuns. And I figure whoever it is that's a-doin' this, is doin' us all a favor."

"No," Major Clinton said. "Don't you see? Whoever is doing this could set off a full-scale Indian war."

"Yeah, I reckon he could at that."

"You must do what you can to find out who this is, so we can find him and put a stop to it," Clinton said.

In the village of Iron Bull

"It is a ghost," Running Bear said. "It is a ghost and he can stay alive only as long as he can eat the livers of the ones he has killed."

"We must kill him before he kills any more of us," Iron Bull said.

"You cannot kill a ghost," Running Bear insisted.

"And so, what would you have us do, Running Bear? Would you have us continue to give him the liver of Apsáalooke to eat?"

"We must do something," Brave Horse said. "Our women and our children are frightened, and they cower and weep in the lodges."

"There will be much honor to the one who kills Liver Eater," Iron Bull said.

"There will be much honor to the one who kills Liver Eater." The words of Iron Bull resonated in Two Leggings's mind as he searched for Liver Eater.

"Hear me, people of the Apsáalooke!" Iron Bull would say at the council fire. "We are here to speak aloud the name of Two Leggings! Songs will be sung and his name will be spoken in all the lodges because of his bravery!"

Two Leggings composed Iron Bull's speech as he waited on the trail for Liver Eater. He had seen Liver Eater earlier, coming toward the mountain. He would have to come along this trail on the only pass that would let him through. And when he did, Two Leggings would be waiting for him.

Two Leggings began to chant, quietly, the song of a warrior.

"As a warrior I must go bravely into those dark places within myself. I must learn the truth of my being. It takes much courage to do this, and I have the courage within."

Two Leggings knew that in order to have the greatest honor in the campfire circle, he must kill Liver Eater with his own hands, and not shoot him from afar. He could hear Liver Eater approaching, and he climbed onto a rock and waited.

* * *

John saw several birds fly from the trees just ahead of him. Something had spooked them and though he knew it could have been a mountain lion, or a wolf, or even a coyote, it put him on guard. If it was a coyote he would run when John approached. And, more than likely, even a mountain lion or a wolf would give him room, if there was no food source to contend.

But John felt a tingling in his skin, an awareness that was beyond that of any animal. He had seen nothing more than the sudden flight of birds, but he had a distinct impression that someone was waiting for him in the path ahead. And, just as strongly, he believed that it was only one person.

John loosened the pistol in his holster. Unlike his friend Smoke, John had never mastered the art of the quick draw. But even as he thought about that, he chuckled, because he realized that no one was Smoke's equal in the speed with which he could draw his pistol.

John was an excellent shot with pistol and rifle, and for his purposes, that was enough.

As John was deep in contemplation he rode by a large rock. Suddenly, and without warning, an Indian leaped down from the rock, grabbing John and knocking him off his horse. The horse whinnied and moved ahead quickly, its steel-shod shoes clacking loudly on the rocky pathway.

John felt a sharp pain in his shoulder as he, and the Indian who had a tight hold on him, hit the ground. He reached for his pistol, hoping to be able to pull it and shoot the Indian at point-blank range, but the pistol was no longer in his holster.

John and the Indian rolled around on the ground, each trying to get the advantage of the other. The Indian was holding a war club, but John was holding on to him so securely that he couldn't free his arm to use it. But if the Indian couldn't use his war club, neither could John free his hand long enough to get to his Bowie knife.

The two rolled on the ground for a moment, then John was able to bend his knees and get his feet into the Indian's stomach. Because he was on his back, beneath the Indian, it gave him leverage and he straightened his legs, throwing the Indian away from him.

Quickly, John got to his feet and pulled his knife. The Indian had regained his own feet almost as quickly, and now the two men were facing each other. John was in a crouch and armed with a knife, which he was holding low with the blade parallel to the ground; the Indian was more upright, and he was holding a war club.

They moved around each other in a rather macabre dance, the Indian making a few motions with the war club, while John merely moved his knife back and forth like the head of a coiled rattlesnake.

Suddenly the Indian, with the club raised over his head, rushed at John. John leaned to one side so that when the Indian brought the club down, he missed. John counterthrusted with his knife, and the blade penetrated the Indian's stomach all the way to the hilt.

John withdrew the blade then, and as the Indian clamped both his hands over the belly wound, John made a slicing motion, cutting the Indian's throat. The Indian collapsed, and died quickly. John removed the Indian's liver, threw it away, then remounted and rode on.

CHAPTER 28

Irwin, Colorado—1872

Smoke had come for Preacher, issuing him a personal invitation to come visit him so he could see the new house he had built for Sally at the ranch he was calling Sugarloaf. They were at least a day's ride away from Sugarloaf, and so stopped for the night in Irwin.

"Here's your food, gentleman," one of the bar girls said a moment later, carrying the two plates to the table.

"Thanks," Smoke said. He handed the young woman a quarter.

"Thank you, sir," she said, smiling broadly.

"How's your new ranch comin' along?" Preacher asked.

"It's coming along real good," Smoke said. "I've hired me a few hands to help out around the place."

"You goin' to raise cattle or horses?"

"Well, I tried raising horses when I was married to Nicole. They can be plumb ornery critters, there's no getting around that. I may raise some horses, but most likely it'll be cattle."

"I expect that's the best way to go," Preacher said.

Preacher's buckskins were nearly black, his long white hair and beard were matted and, no doubt, Smoke thought, filled with critters, and there was a leatherlike patina to his skin that Smoke knew was an accumulation of dirt. For himself, Preacher's appearance wasn't a problem. Smoke had lived with him for a long time and he knew there were many times when he looked just like Preacher did now.

But, he was taking Preacher home with him to see Sally. And Sally, coming from the East, and not only from the East, but from a fine family, was used to being around people who paid a little more attention to their personal appearance. Smoke himself had developed a habit of good hygiene, at least when he could satisfy that habit. And he knew that he had to do something about Preacher's appearance before they reached Sugarloaf.

"Preacher, what do you say we get us a hotel room and take us a bath after we eat?"

"I had me a bath," Preacher said.

"What? Just when did you have a bath?"

"I don't know . . . three, maybe four months ago."

Smoke laughed. "Four months ago?"

"All right, maybe it was six months ago, what difference does it make? I mean, just how many baths does a feller need in one year, anyhow?"

"I tell you the truth, Preacher, your stink don't bother me none at all. But Sally can be just real particular about things like being clean 'n smelling good, and all that. And she'd probably like it better if you took a bath, and got cleaned up some before we get there."

"Hrummph," Preacher grunted. "If I had known you was goin' to turn into such a fancy Dan about bathin' 'n all, I woulda never took you in to raise."

"Yeah, you would've," Smoke said. "You liked havin' someone to train and boss around."

"Boss around? When did you ever do anything I asked you to do?"

* * *

Leaving the café, the two men went into the hotel and walked up to the counter.

"Yes, sir, can I help you gentlemen?"

"We'd like a couple of rooms. And a bath," Smoke said.

The clerk looked at Preacher with an obvious sense of displeasure in what he was seeing. "Both of you will be wanting a bath, I take it?"

Before Smoke could answer, Preacher spoke up. "Yeah, both of us will be wantin' to take a bath. What do you think, that we're some kind of heathens what don't never bathe?"

"Very good, sir. That will be three dollars. A dollar apiece for the rooms, and half a dollar apiece for the baths."

Smoke lifted a small buckskin pouch to the counter, then poured out a pile of gold and silver coins. He moved the coins, many of them twenty-dollar gold pieces, around with his finger until he found three silver dollars.

"Here you are," he said.

Sitting in the lobby of the hotel was a man named Angus Flatt. When he saw the sack of gold coins emptied on the check-in desk, he took in a deep breath. There had to be several hundred dollars there.

He left the lobby, then hurried down to the Hog's Breath Saloon, where he found Moe James, playing solitaire.

"Hey, Moe, how much money you got?" Angus asked.

"I ain't got no money a-tall, so don't be askin' me to lend you any."

"I ain't askin' to borrow any money," Angus said. "What I'm askin' for is, I just seen me a way to make two or three hunnert dollars real easy. And I was wonderin' if you wanted in on it?"

"If it's all that easy, why are you offerin' me a chance at it?" Moe replied.

"On account of because it would be a lot easier for the two of us to do it. And I'm tellin' you, there's enough money we could divide up, 'n still have more money than either one of us have had for a whole year."

"Where is this easy money?"

"Some man come into the hotel a little while ago, and when he paid for it, why, you shoulda seen all the gold coins that poured out of his bag. I'll bet there's three or four, or maybe even five hunnert dollars there."

"So we're just goin' to ask him to give the money to us?"

"Yeah," Angus said, as a big smile spread across his face. "We're goin' to ask him while he's takin' hisself a bath."

The hotel had a bathing room, complete with a large bathtub as well as a water-holding tank and a small wood-burning stove by which to heat the water. Smoke started the fire, then went back to his room to wait for the water to heat. He walked over to the window and stood there, just looking out over the town, watching the commerce for a few minutes. Leaving the window, he lay down on his bed for about fifteen minutes, until he was sure that the water would be warm enough for a bath. Then, taking a change of clothes, a bar of soap, and a towel with him, he started down the hall toward the bathing room.

Just before Smoke opened the door, he stopped. He had the soap and the water was hot. There was no excuse Preacher could come up with for not taking a bath now, so he was going to let Preacher go first. He walked back down the hall, then knocked on Preacher's door. "Preacher?"

The door opened. "Yeah?"

"I've filled the tub with hot water for you. Here's your soap and towel."

"What'd you do that for?"

"Let's just say I respect my elders," Smoke said.

"Do you now?"

"And I respect them more when they're clean," Smoke added with a chuckle.

"All right, all right, you don't have to hit me on the head with it," Preacher grumbled. "Your woman wants me clean, so I'll clean up. But it ain't for you, you understand. It's for your woman."

"I understand," Smoke said with a smile.

Preacher reached down to pick up his Sharps .50 caliber.

"You need a rifle in the bathing room, do you?" Smoke teased.

"I don't go nowhere without I have this with me. You know that."

Smoke held up his hands. "Take it. You never can tell but what you might run into a grizzly in there."

"It wouldn't be the first time I seen a grizzly while I was bathin'," Preacher said.

Smoke chuckled. "Considering where you do your bathing— that is, when you do bathe—that's not particularly surprising."

Angus and Moe were in the lobby of the hotel.

"I seen him headed toward the bathing room just a couple of minutes ago," Angus said. "By now he's prob'ly in the tub, and, more 'n likely, he took his money in there with 'im."

"How do you know he took his money with 'im?"

"You don't think he'd just leave it in his room, do you?"

"No, more 'n likely he wouldn't."

"That's why, it won't be nothin' to take it from 'im."

"You know he ain't goin' to just be quiet about it," Moe said.

"They's two of us, only one of him. He'll be nekkid in the tub. All we got to do is hold his head under water till he stops movin'. Folks don't make a lot of noise while they're drownin'. And once he's drowned, why we'll get his money and slip out just real quiet-like."

Angus and Moe looked over toward the check-in clerk, and when they saw him step away and walk into a room just behind the desk, they moved quickly to the steps and hurried up to the second floor.

The bathing room was at the back end of the corridor and Angus and Moe walked quickly down the carpeted hallway until they reached the door. They stood there for just a moment, listening.

"Yeah, he's in the tub, all right. I can hear the splashin'," Angus said. "Let's go in."

Angus tried the doorknob, found that it wasn't locked, then pushed it open and stepped inside.

"This ain't the one," Angus said when he saw the old, white-haired and white-bearded man sitting in the tub.

Smoke stepped out of his room just in time to see two men going toward the bathing room. He didn't know who they were, or what they wanted, but he was absolutely certain that Preacher wouldn't welcome their presence. And, because it was hard enough to get Preacher to take a bath anyway, he figured he had better see what's going on.

Smoke started toward them, and saw them open the door then step inside. He figured he would hear Preacher's bellow any moment now. And he wasn't disappointed.

"Get the hell out of here! Can't you see that I'm takin' a bath?" The words were loud and angry.

The two men who had stepped into the bathing room had their pistols in their hands, pointing them at Preacher.

"Where's the young one? The one with the gold?" one of the two men asked.

"That would be me," Smoke said from behind them.

Spinning around, they saw Smoke. They also saw that he wasn't wearing a gun.

One of the two men smiled. "Well now, Angus, look at this. Looks like these two men have got their selves into a situation. One of 'em is nekkid, 'n the other 'n ain't got hisself a gun."

"Tell you what, Moe. You go with this feller to get the money. I'll stay here and keep a gun on the old man," Angus said. "If you ain't back with the money in one minute, I'll shoot the old man."

"Yeah," Moe said. "Good . . ."

Whatever Moe was about to say was cut short by Preacher. While Angus's and Moe's backs were turned, Preacher had picked his rifle up from the floor, stood up quietly, then drove the butt of the rifle into Moe's back, between his shoulder blades.

The commotion distracted Angus and when he looked toward Moe, that gave Smoke all the opening he needed. He brought down the would-be thief with a hammerlike right cross.

"What do we do with 'em now?" Preacher asked.

Smoke took the pistols away from the two men and handed them to Preacher.

"When they come to, keep them covered until I get back. I'm going to get the marshal."

Sugarloaf Ranch

Unlike the cabin he had personally built for Nicole, Sally had wanted a house, and Smoke bought the material and hired two carpenters to build it for him. The main house, or "big house" as the cowboys called it, was a rather large, two-story Victorian edifice, white, with red shutters and a gray-painted porch that ran across the front and wrapped around to one side. The bunkhouse, which was also white with red shutters, sat halfway between the big house and the barn. The house was so new that it still had the smell of fresh-cut wood about it, though for the moment, the most predominate aroma was that of Sally's cooking.

"My, Preacher, I don't believe I have ever seen you looking so handsome," Sally said, greeting the two when they arrived.

"Hrrmph," Preacher said. "It ain't natural being all spiffed up like this."

"Oh, pooh," Sally said, kissing him on the cheek.

"'Course now, if I'm goin' to get a kiss from a pretty woman, and get fed to boot, why, it's worth gettin' unnatural ever' now 'n then," Preacher said. "Could that be apple pie I'm smellin'?"

"It could be," Sally said.

"I don't rightly recollect the last time I had me an apple pie. I hope you made one for you 'n Smoke too. I'd sure hate to be eatin' in front of you without you two didn't have no pie of your own."

Sally laughed. "Don't worry, I made more than one. How long will you be staying with us?"

"I don't know. Three, maybe four days. But if that's too long, why you can kick me out anytime you want . . . after the pie is all gone."

CHAPTER 29

Arrow Creek, Montana

Whips His Horses gave the reins of his pony to another man, then he climbed to the top of the hill. He knew the warrior's secret of lying down behind the crest of the hill so that he couldn't be seen against the skyline, so he lay on his stomach, then sneaked up to the top and peered over. There, on the valley floor below him, he saw the three wagons. It was obvious that the whites had no idea they were in danger. It would be easy to count coups against them.

Whips His Horses smiled, then slithered back down the hill into the ravine where the others were waiting.

"Did you see them?"

"Yes," Whips His Horses answered.

"When do we attack?"

"Now," Whips His Horses replied. He pointed down the ravine. "We will follow the ravine around the side of the hill. That way they will not see us until it is too late."

For the moment the three wagons were stopped, because one of them had a broken front wheel. A long pole had been put under the front part of the wagon. Using a rock as the pivot, two men were using the pole as a lever to hold the wagon up. A third man had crawled under the wagon with a jack and, as soon as the wagon was high enough, he was going to put the jack in place.

"Can you get it, Dan?" James asked. His voice was strained because he and Steven were struggling at the end of the long pole.

"Just a little more," Dan said from beneath the wagon. He was in some danger at this point, because if James or Steven lost his grip, or if the pole should slip, the wagon would fall on him.

Straining hard, the two men lifted the wagon another couple of inches.

"There!" Dan called. "I think I can get it now."

"All right, slide out from under there so we can lower this thing down," James said, and his voice almost cracked under the strain.

Dan rolled over, then crawled out and, with a mighty sigh of relief, James and Steven set the wagon down on the rock.

"Whew," James said, wiping the sweat from his forehead. "I'm glad that part is over."

"You and me both," Steven said.

Dan started to remove the broken wheel. "I appreciate you two holding up your wagons for us, it was . . ."

"Hush up! Listen," James said, interrupting Dan in midsentence.

"What is it?" Steven asked. "I didn't hear anything."

"Listen," James said again.

Not only the three men working on the wagon were quiet but, at the warning, so were the women and children. For a long moment there was only the sound of the ever-present prairie wind moaning its mournful wail. Then, they all heard what James had heard, the distant thunder of pounding hooves.

"Get the women and children behind the wagon," James

said. "We've got company comin', and I don't think it's anyone we want."

The battle was short and violent. Whips His Horses had twenty warriors with him, which was more than the total number of people—men, women, and children—with the three wagons. Within a short time after the initial attack, the wagons were in flames and the men and women were falling, mortally wounded. The Indians galloped, whooping and shouting, through the remains of the wagon train.

Whips His Horses leaped over the rocks, and in and out of the gully, shouting with joy as he pursued the fight. The men, and even the women of the wagon train, fired at him, but it was as if he were impervious to their bullets. He leaped upon a burning wagon and looked at his handiwork, chortling in glee as the last white defender was put to the lance. Now that all the men, women, and children of the wagon train were dead, he and his warriors cut the livers from the body of everyone they killed.

Dog Runner, a Blackfoot Indian, was in the camp of Iron Bull when Whips His Horses and the raiding party returned from their attack on the wagon train. The raiders were excited by what they had done, and they began to dance around the council fire.

"Hear me!" Whips His Horses shouted. "Hear the victory song that I sing!"

The others of the village gathered around as Whips His Horses, dancing, and brandishing a war club began to sing.

> *"The white man who came for peace*
> *Now eats our livers.*
> *For every liver of the Apsáalooke he eats*
> *Our anger will grow."*

As Whips His Horses sang his song the others of the raiding party, who were dancing with him, suddenly pulled from pouches, the bloody livers of the white men, women, and children they had killed. Waving the livers long enough for all to see, they threw them into the fire.

> *"With each white that we kill*
> *We will kill Liver Eater.*
> *We will kill many whites.*
> *Liver Eater will die many deaths."*

The singing, dancing, and celebration lasted far into the night. When Dog Runner left the next morning, many were still asleep. The campfire had burned down and was now only glowing embers, but the smell of the cooked human livers permeated the camp.

Dog Runner mounted his horse and rode away slowly. Not until he was far away did he urge his horse into a gallop. He rode hard all the way to Fort Shaw.

Fort Shaw

Dog Runner was held up at the gate.

"Where are you going, Injun?" the guard asked.

"Philbin," Dog Runner said. "Philbin." He then began talking rapidly in his own language.

"Corporal?" the gate guard shouted. "This Injun is talkin' about somethin', but I don't have no idea what it is he's a-talkin' about."

The corporal came over to the front gate.

"Philbin!" Dog Runner said, again following it with a long, excited stream in his own language.

"Philbin? Lieutenant Philbin?"

"Han, han!" Dog Runner said, at the same time shaking his head yes.

"Keep him here, McMurtry. I'll go get the lieutenant."

Dog Runner paced back and forth for a few minutes until Lieutenant Philbin arrived. Philbin was chief of the Indian scouts, and could speak to Dog Runner in his own language.

"Dog Runner," Philbin said, smiling with his hand up, palm out. "It is good to see you."

"It is not good," Dog Runner said. "The Crow have attacked wagons and killed many white people."

"What? Where? When?"

"Today," Dog Runner said. "I will take you."

An hour later Lieutenant Philbin and ten soldiers arrived at the scene of the massacre. They found five men, four women, and nine children lying in a pool of blood where they had fallen.

"Lieutenant, this don't make no sense," Sergeant Dawes said. "I mean, there ain't a one of 'em been scalped, nor cut up in any other way. But all of 'em's got their stomach cut open, even the kids."

"Yes," Philbin said. "I'll admit, that is quite odd."

Later that evening, with all the bodies returned to Fort Shaw, Major Clinton asked his post surgeon, Dr. Urban, to examine the bodies, to see if there was any pattern to all of them being cut open in such a way.

It was the next morning before Dr. Urban got back to Major Clinton.

"What did you find out?" Major Clinton asked.

Urban shook his head. "It's the damndest thing I believe I've ever seen," he said.

"What is?"

"The liver has been removed from every one of the bodies."

"What? From every one of them? Even the children?"

"Yes, sir."

"Well, that doesn't make sense," Major Clinton said. "Why would the Indians cut out their livers?"

"Major, I don't have the slightest idea. All I know is, the livers have been cut from all of them."

"Sergeant Major Porter?" Major Clinton called.

"Yes, sir?"

"Find Lieutenant Philbin and that Indian that told us where to find the bodies. Bring them to me."

"Yes, sir," Sergeant Major Porter replied.

Less than ten minutes later, Lieutenant Philbin and Dog Runner were in Major Clinton's office.

"Yes, sir?" Philbin asked.

"Lieutenant, the livers have been removed from every single body."

"Yes, sir," Philbin said.

"'Yes, sir'? You mean you knew that?"

"Yes, sir. Well, Dog Runner couldn't come up with the word in English, and I don't know the word in his language, but we finally managed to put it together enough that I understood what he was saying. I was just about to come see you, when Sergeant Major Porter found me, and asked me to come over."

Major Clinton shook his head. "Would you mind telling me why in the Sam Hill would the Indians be cutting out livers?"

"Because John Jackson is carving out the Indian livers and eating them," Philbin said, easily.

"What? Why, that is insane! Are you sure it's John Jackson?" Major Clinton asked, refusing to believe what his chief of scouts said.

"Yes, sir, I've talked with several of my scouts and they all say the same thing. It's out in every village in the territory.

All the Indians call him Liver Eater, because after he kills an Indian, he cuts out, and eats, their livers."

"No, surely there is some mistake. They must be thinking of someone else," Major Clinton said. "I met the man, I was quite impressed with him. He is well educated, well spoken. And a finer gentleman I have never met. I can't imagine someone like John Jackson killing Indians and eating their livers. Why do you suppose he suddenly went on a killing binge like that?"

"It's because of his wife," Lieutenant Philbin said.

"What do you mean? I met her as well. She's Indian, yes, but she isn't Crow. And her manners are such that I expect she would be welcome in just about any level of society, back East. Why would she want her husband to go on such an inhuman killing spree?"

"I didn't say she wanted it, Major. You said why would he do such a thing, and I said it's because of his wife. And his child. You see, the Crow killed them both."

"When?"

"As I understand it, they were killed shortly after Jackson and his wife visited Iron Bull's camp to talk peace with the Indians."

"After he visited their camp?"

"Yes, sir. Jackson delivered your message to Iron Bull, who granted them a pass only as long as it took them to get out of camp. Once they left the camp, Iron Bull sent Indians after them. According to Dog Runner, Jackson killed one of them in the chase.

"Then, Jackson came here to report to you, that he had failed. And while he was here, talking to you, Whips His Horses went to Jackson's cabin. There, he killed Jackson's wife and child."

"My God!" Major Clinton said with a gasp. "My God, that means I'm to be blamed! I'm not only to be blamed for

Jackson's wife and child being killed, I'm also to be blamed for the attack on the wagons."

"Why would you say that, Major?"

"Because I am the one who sent them there!"

"I don't think there is anyone who actually blames you, Major."

"I don't care whether anyone else blames me or not," Major Clinton said. "I blame myself . . . not only for what he is doing now . . . but for what happened to precipitate this."

CHAPTER 30

[*Warrior societies were an important aspect of the life of the Plains Indians. The tribes' fighting men were divided into distinct units which provided their members with prestige. They fell under two categories, graded and ungraded, and though the warrior societies of the Apsáalooke (Crow) were, theoretically, ungraded, there was, by recognition, a definite graduation among the three societies of the tribe. Those three societies were the Lumpwood, the Fox, and the Big Dog. There was a fierce rivalry between them and, in battle, each society strove to strike the first coup.*

There were, in addition, ranks within the individual societies which, while they conferred great honor, also demanded a personal sacrifice or commitment from the warrior upon whom the rank had been bestowed.

The Big Dog Warrior Society gradually emerged as the most prestigious. Members of this society would wear a belt of bearskin, complete with claws. They also daubed their bodies with mud, and rolled their hair into tight balls, imitating bear's ears. They made a commitment to walk upright straight toward the enemy, never to retreat, and to come to the aid of any tribesman in danger.—ED.]

In the village of Iron Bull

Stone Eagle wore two vertical stripes on his right cheek, one red and one black. The stripes ran from the bottom of his eye to the top of his lip, and they denoted his rank as chief of the warrior society known as the Big Dog Warrior Society. He had asked for a meeting of the council and now all were gathered before the council fire.

Stone Eagle pointed to Whips His Horses, and spoke derisively of him.

"Whips His Horses boasts of his feats," Stone Eagle said. "But what has he done? He has killed women and children. He has killed men who are not warriors. He has done this while Liver Eater continues to go free, to kill our braves."

"And what have you done?" Whips His Horses replied, angrily. "You have done nothing!"

"Liver Eater is but one man. I have thought, until now, that one brave warrior would be his equal, but ten have tried, and ten have died. And you," Stone Eagle said, pointing to Whips His Horses, "you have not even tried. You are afraid to fight Liver Eater, so you fight those who cannot fight back."

"Whips His Horses has asked a question that must be answered," Iron Bull said. "What have you done?"

"I have done nothing," Stone Eagle admitted. "But now I am ready to lead the Big Dog Warriors to find and kill this man who has killed so many of our own."

"How many will you take?" Iron Bull asked.

"He has killed ten. We will be two for every one that he has killed. We will be twenty."

"I will be one of the twenty," Whips His Horses said.

"You are not a member of the Big Dog Society," Stone Eagle replied.

"Then I will be a member."

"If you become a member, you must follow me. Do you agree to that?"

"I will also be a leader," Whips His Horses said. He pointed to his chest. "I am chief of the Fox Society."

"To be a Big Dog Warrior you must leave the Fox and become a Big Dog. You can be a member, but you will not be a leader," Stone Eagle insisted.

"I ask the council!" Whips His Horses said. "Hear me. I am chief of the Fox Warrior Society. Is it not fair that if I join the Big Dog Warrior Society that I shall be a chief, equal in authority to Stone Eagle?"

The members of the council discussed it among themselves, then Iron Bull spoke.

"Stone Eagle, would you agree to a test with Whips His Horses to determine if he should be a chief?"

"Yes, I will agree to a test," Stone Eagle replied.

"Whips His Horses, will you agree to a test?" Iron Bull asked.

Whips His Horses looked at Stone Eagle with an expression of hatred on his face.

"If we are to test, then let it be a final test. Let us fight until the death," Whips His Horses said.

"Stone Eagle, you have been challenged," Iron Bull said. "You cannot deny the challenge and remain chief of the Big Dog Warrior Society. What is your answer?"

"I accept the challenge," Stone Eagle said.

Iron Bull held up both his arms and called out loudly so that all in the village could hear what he had to say.

"Hear me!" he called. "A challenge has been issued, and accepted. Whips His Horses and Stone Eagle are to fight. The fight must be until the death of one. The winner of the fight will be chief of the Big Dog Warrior Society."

A circle was drawn and the two warriors entered the circle, each armed with a knife. Facing each other warily, they held their arms crossed in front of them, the palm of their left hand open, while grasping the knife in their right hand. They moved around in the circle, first one, and then the other, leaning forward to make, mostly futile, downward stabbing motions with the knife.

On one of his thrusts, Whips His Horses made a slashing cut on Stone Eagle's arm. It wasn't a deep cut, but it did bring blood. A moment later Stone Eagle opened a cut on Whips His Horses' shoulder and now both men were bloodied as they faced each other.

Whips His Horses made another thrust but Stone Eagle stepped aside, then stuck out his foot, tripping Whips His Horses. Whips His Horses fell facedown and dropped his knife. Stone Eagle reached down and grabbed it, quickly, before Whips His Horses could recover. Now, with both knives, he reached down and laid the flat of the blade on the back of Whips His Horses' neck.

"I claim coup," he shouted, and turning his back to Whips His Horses' prone form, he held both his arms up over his head, his knife in one hand and Whips His Horses' knife in the other. "I have won!" he claimed, triumphantly.

Whips His Horses got to his feet quickly, then reaching out of the circle, grabbed a lance from one of the warriors who had been watching. With a shout of triumph, he rushed across the circle and thrust the lance into Stone Eagle's back, doing so with such force that the bloody point came through Stone Eagle's stomach.

Stone Eagle looked down in surprise, grabbed the lance point, then fell dead.

"Ayiee! It is I who have won!" Whips His Horses shouted.

There was some discussion among the elders of the council, but it was pointed out that the requirement was a fight to the death. And it was obvious that Whips His Horses had met that requirement. He was now the new head of the Big Dog Warrior Society.

"Will you now do as Stone Eagle would have done?"

Iron Bull asked. "Will you take twenty warriors to kill Liver Eater?"

"I will do this," Whips His Horses said.

"Send runners to all the villages," Iron Bull declared. "Let the word go out to the Gros Ventre, the Piegan, the Lakota, and the Blackfeet, that twenty Big Dog Warriors of the Apsáalooke village of Iron Bull will avenge the death of our brothers!"

Fort Shaw

"What would you have me do about it?" Major Clinton asked the two civilian representatives from Helena. "Wage a full-scale war?"

"But don't you understand? The Indians attacked three wagons of whites. That is already an act of war," Babcock, one of the two civilians, said.

"From all that I've been able to learn, it was no more than a few renegade Indians," Major Clinton said. "It wasn't a full-blown war party. I have four companies of infantry here. And I stress that we are infantry, not cavalry. We are not a mobile force. I can detach one company of infantry and assign them to protect the town of Helena, but I don't really think the town of Helena is in any danger. Do you?"

"I don't know," Babcock said. "Is it true that what has gotten them all riled up is some crazy mountain man who has turned cannibal? He's actually eating the bodies?"

"From what I've heard, he's only eating their livers," Major Clinton said.

"Then I think if you can do nothing about the Indians, you should do something about this crazy mountain man," Jones said. Jones was the other civilian from Helena.

"Do something about the mountain man?" Major Clinton replied. "Do what? What are you suggesting?"

"I'm suggesting that you find him and kill him," Jones said.

"Definitely not!" Major Clinton said. "I'm appalled that you would even suggest such a thing!"

"It seems like a pretty good bargain to me," Jones said. "One crazy white cannibal against the lives of how many more whites will the Indians kill?"

"I'm going to ask you two men to leave this post, now," Major Clinton said, angrily.

"You've got no right to order us off this post," Babcock insisted. "We have come to seek army protection."

"You have two choices," Major Clinton said. "You can leave of your own volition, or I will have you escorted off this post under armed guard."

"All right, all right, we're going," Babcock said. "But I intend to write a letter to the War Department protesting your refusal to protect us."

"Sergeant Major?" Major Clinton called.

"Yes, sir?" Sergeant Major Porter replied, stepping into Major Clinton's office.

"See that these"—Major Clinton paused, setting the next word apart from the sentence to show his disdain—"gentlemen . . . are shown safely off this post."

"Yes, sir," Sergeant Major Porter said. "This way, gentlemen."

Major Clinton walked to the front of the headquarters building and stood in the doorway as he watched the two civilians cross the quadrangle toward the gate. Lieutenant Philbin approached him with a salute.

"Do you know what those two men wanted?" Major Clinton asked.

"No, sir, not exactly. I know they were concerned about the people who were killed at their wagons."

"They wanted me to send the army out to kill Mr. Jackson. The very idea."

"Yes, sir, well, it might all be beyond our hands anyway," Lieutenant Philbin said.

"Why? What do you mean?"

"My Indians tell me that Iron Bull is sending twenty of his Big Dog Warriors out to find and kill Jackson."

"Do you think we should warn Jackson?"

Philbin chuckled. "In the first place, I'm damn sure Jackson already knows that he is the enemy of the Crow right now. In fact, I'm pretty sure he welcomes it. Major, he brought this war on himself, you know."

"No, he didn't," Major Clinton said. "I did, when I sent him and his wife to meet with Iron Bull."

"If he had just killed the ones who killed his wife and child, that would have been the end of it," Philbin said. "But he didn't stop there. He has made a personal war on all the Crow. And, don't forget, he is eating their livers. That is a slap in the face of every Crow alive."

"We don't know that he is actually eating their livers."

"It doesn't matter whether he is or not, now," Philbin said. "The Crow believe that he is, and that's enough."

CHAPTER 31

[*One of the mysteries of the last century is how quickly information could spread from place to place. In a time before telephones were commonplace, before radio, and even when newspapers were few and far between, there was something referred to as the "underground telegraph." John Jackson's activities were limited to Montana, but word of his unique and very personal battle with the Indians spread quickly, from Montana through Wyoming, into Colorado, Utah, Nevada, California, and even down into Arizona, New Mexico, and Texas.—ED.*]

Buford, Colorado

The Pair of Tens Saloon in Buford, Colorado Territory, was already filled with customers, even though it was no later than three o'clock in the afternoon. A clean-shaven man whose eyes were enlarged by the thick lenses of the glasses he wore was plinking away on a piano in the corner of the room while a glass of warm beer, its head gone, sat beside him. Two cowboys who were standing at the bar, were engaged in a vociferous discussion.

"They say the reason the Injuns attacked and kilt them

folks in the wagons, is 'cause this feller, whoever it is, is a-killin' Injuns, then he's carvin' out their gizzards and eatin' 'em."

He put an exclamation mark to his statement by spitting out a large quid of tobacco into a nearby spittoon, making it ring with the impact. A soiled dove, whose profession had already caused dissipation beyond her years, had stopped making her rounds of the tables, just to listen in on the discussion the two cowboys were having.

"You don't mean he's actual eatin' human beings, do you, Pete?" she asked.

"Well now, I reckon that all depends on whether or not you call Crow Injuns human bein's. They's some that say that Crow ain't nothin' but heathens, through 'n through, 'n the words 'human bein'' don't quite fit with them. You take Ned, here. He don't hold much truck for Crow, do you, Ned?"

"I don't want nothin' to do with no Crows," Ned said. "Are you sayin' Crows is the only ones this here fella is killin' an' eatin'?"

Before the first cowboy could answer the question, two men slapped the batwings open, stepped into the saloon, and crossed over to the bar. Everyone in the place paused and stared at the pair as they made their way across the room. They looked like before and after pictures of what life in the mountains would do to anyone crazy enough, or antisocial enough, to endure it. The older of the two had fought in the Battle of New Orleans as a fourteen-year-old boy. That was close to sixty years ago, and he showed the effects of strenuous living for all that time. The younger of the two was a boy during the Civil War, which had been over now for seven years. They were both dressed in buckskins; the old one had a full beard and long hair that hung down almost to his shoulders, the beard and hair white as snow. The younger of the two was clean shaven, with neatly trimmed hair.

Mountain men weren't all that rare in this part of the Colorado Territory, but these two men did capture the attention of all who were in the saloon. They were both armed, as if they were about to go to war. The older of the two was carrying a Sharps Big Fifty cradled in his arms, and a Navy Colt .36, not in a holster, but stuck down in his belt. The younger of the two had a Colt .44 tied low on his thigh in a right-hand rig. A matching Colt was butt-forward in a high holster on his left hip, and a twelve-inch-long Bowie knife rested in a scabbard in the middle of his back. He was also carrying a rifle, in this case a Henry repeating rifle.

When the older man sat his rifle down and they both leaned on the bar, all the rest of the saloon customers went back to what they'd been doing, ignoring the two newcomers.

"Seems to me like you two fellas stopped by here not much more 'n a week or so ago, didn't you?" the bartender said as he slid down to wait on them. "You're Preacher, and you're the one they call Smoke."

"You got a good memory, pilgrim," Preacher said.

"Yeah, maybe, but it ain't good enough for me to 'member just exactly what it was you two fellers are likin' to drink."

"We'll both have beer," Smoke said.

"Two beers comin' up."

The two cowboys, after no more than a cursory glance at the two mountain men, resumed their conversation.

"They say the feller doin' all the killin' and the gizzard eatin' is doin' it 'cause the Injuns kilt his wife 'n kid," Pete said, continuing to impart the information as he had heard it.

"But they don't nobody know his name?" Ned asked.

"Nope. Don't nobody know nothin' a-tall about him. Onliest thing is, they say he's one of them mountain men. Up in Montana, he is."

"Hey, let's ask them two," Ned suggested. "They look like

they're mountain men. Leastwise, the older feller looks like that."

"I wouldn't be gettin' them two men riled up if I was you," the bartender said. "Don't you boys know who they are?"

"Nope, ain't never seen neither one of 'em," Pete said. "They ever been in here before?"

"Oh, yeah, they been in here before. They stopped in here a week or so ago on their way to Big Rock. The young one has him a ranch there. The other 'n is pure mountain man, lives in the High Lonesome all by his ownself."

"That means you know them then, so who are they?" Pete asked.

"Well, sir, the young one there is Smoke Jensen," the bartender said.

"Smoke Jensen? Wait a minute! Are you talkin' about the gunfighter Smoke Jensen? The one that kilt Fast Lennie Moore a month or so back?" Pete asked.

"Yeah, that's who I'm talkin' about."

"Fast Lennie was supposed to be the fastest there was, couldn't nobody hold a candle to him, they said. But from what I heard, Fast Lennie started his draw first, and Smoke still beat him."

"That's true," the bartender said.

"But you just said he has a ranch near Big Rock," Ned said.

"That he does."

"What do you reckon he's doin' runnin' around with that old man?"

"You don't know who that old man is?"

"Can't say as I do."

"Well, I don't know his name. His real name, I mean. Long as I've known about 'im, I ain't never heard him called nothin' but Preacher."

"Preacher? Wait, are you talkin' about the old mountain man that's been here for, what? Forty, fifty years?" Pete asked.

"That's him."

"I'll be damn. I thought he was dead."

"Yeah, there's been two or three times I've heard he was dead too, but he's like a cat with nine lives or something. He always seems to show up again, to put to lie that idea."

"What I don't understand is how someone like Smoke Jensen would be runnin' with an old mountain man like Preacher," Pete said.

"Smoke is pretty much a mountain man his ownself," the bartender said. "You see, that old man most raised Smoke. Leastwise, that's what I've always heard. They're what you call tight, so I wouldn't be doin' nothin' to get airy a one of 'em riled," the bartender said.

"Ain't Smoke the one that kilt fourteen men at that silver mining camp near the Uncompahgre a couple years ago?" Ned asked.

"That's him, all right."

"Yeah, you're right, he ain't the kind of man you'd want to get riled up at you," Ned said.

"Well, come on, Ned, it ain't like he kilt all them men 'cause they got him all riled up by askin' a question, is it?" Pete asked.

"No. The way I heard it, them men kilt his wife 'n kid," the bartender said.

"So then he had hisself a good reason for killin' 'em. Sounds to me like they was needin' killin'. So how is it you think we're goin' to rile him just by askin' him if he's ever heard of some mountain man up in Montana that's killin' Injuns 'n eatin' their gizzards?" Pete asked.

"I don't know. If you want to ask him, you go ahead and ask, but I'm tellin' you, I ain't goin' to do it," Ned said.

"What do you think?" Pete asked the bartender. "You think a question like that would get 'em riled?"

"No, they're both good men. They sort of like their privacy, especially the old one. But I don't reckon there won't neither one of them get all riled up just from you askin' a question."

Pete looked down at the far end of the bar where the two men stood, talking quietly to each other as they drank their beer.

"All right," he said. "I'm goin' to do it. I'm goin' to ask 'em if they ever heard of this fella."

Pete fortified himself with the last of his beer, then, wiping his mouth with the back of his hand, moved down the bar to ask his question.

"Beg your pardon, gents, but I've got a question that I'm kinda hopin' you can answer," Pete said when he approached Preacher and Smoke.

"What is the question?"

"Well, sir, it's all over ever'where now, that there is a feller up in Montana, a mountain man like I expect you two is, who's killin' Injuns 'n eatin' their gizzards. And I was wonderin', that is, me 'n my friend"—he nodded toward Ned, who hadn't moved from the far end of the bar—"we was wonderin' if either one of you fellers had heard about it, and could maybe tell us who it is that's a-doin' such a thing."

"You're saying there's a mountain man killin' Injuns 'n eatin' 'em?" Preacher asked, his voice showing his incredulity.

"Yes, sir. Well, no, not quite. He ain't eatin' ever'thing of the Injuns he's kilt now, mind you. From what I hear, the onliest thing he's eatin' is their gizzards."

"People don't have gizzards," Smoke pointed out.

"They don't?"

"Nope."

"I'll be damn. Wonder what it is then, that that feller is eatin'?" Pete held up his hand, then turned toward his friend, who was sitting at the other end of the bar. "Hey, Ned, people don't have gizzards. So what is it this feller up there is eatin'?"

"Livers," one of the bar girls said. "He is eating their livers."

"Does folks have livers?" Pete asked Smoke.

"Yes, they do. But why would someone do something like that?" Smoke asked.

"Well, sir, from what I heard, the Injuns kilt his wife 'n kid, 'n he just kind of went crazy and is killin' as many of 'em as he can. Well, sir, I'm sure you can understand somethin' like that."

"Oh?"

"I mean, what with what happened at that silver mining camp near the Uncompahgre, 'n all."

Pete put his hand to his mouth as soon as he spoke the words, and his eyes grew wide in fear. Had he said too much?

"Yes," Smoke replied. "Yes, I can understand."

"Hope I didn't make you mad or nothin' by bringin' that up," Pete said, anxiously.

"No, why should I be mad? It happened, and just about everyone knows that it happened."

"Yes, sir, just so's you know I don't mean nothin' bad by it. Anyhow, what I've heard now is that Iron Bull, he's the chief of the Crow, has rounded him up twenty warriors from the Big Dog Warrior Society to hunt this feller down and kill him."

"But there is something I don't understand. If the Indians killed this man's wife and child, why isn't the army involved?" Smoke asked.

"I don't rightly know why the army ain't involved, but reckon it's 'cause it was a squaw and a papoose the Injuns kilt, bein' as that was who the mountain man was married to. And it's more 'n likely that the army don't really care that much about a squaw and a papoose, even if they are married to a white man."

"I see," Smoke said. He shook his head. "But I'm afraid I can't help you. I have no idea as to who it might be."

"The thing is, whoever it is, what I've heered now is that the Crow is out to kill 'im, and they're sendin' whole war parties out. It's come down to bein' purt' nigh that feller all by his ownself agin the entire Crow nation. Don't seem like no fair fight to me."

"Maybe he'll leave the country so's the Crow can't find 'im," Preacher suggested.

"No, sir, I don't think so. This here feller seems to have hisself a lot more guts than he's got brains, if you know what I mean. He's bound to just stay up there 'n keep on killin' Injuns an' eatin' their gizzards, till he gets kilt his ownself."

"I hope that fella didn't disturb you men none," the bartender said after Pete went back to join Ned.

"No, he didn't disturb us. What have you got in the kitchen?"

"Ham and beans."

Smoke pointed to an empty table. "Bring us some. We'll be back there."

"Yes, sir," the bartender replied.

Smoke and Preacher took their beer with them, then walked back to the table in the far corner.

CHAPTER 32

"It's him," Smoke said. "I know it is."

"Who are you talking about?"

"The man that's killing the Crow and eating their livers. That has to be John Jackson. Though, I'm not sure he is actually eating their livers."

"It's just like you told that cowboy back there," Preacher said. "You don't really have no idea who it is. It don't have to be John, why, it could be purt' nigh anyone."

"But I know that John took the Indian girl to be his wife. And there's been plenty of time for them to have had kids. But there's something else about it."

"What's that?" Preacher asked.

"I feel it."

Preacher made no teasing response to that. He well knew the value of intuition, though that wasn't a word he had ever heard. For him, it was best described as feeling it in his gut. And his life had been saved more than once because he had reacted to a feeling in his gut.

"Yeah," Preacher said. "Well, there is that."

"I think I'll just mosey on up there and see for myself."

"Do you want me to come with you?" Preacher asked.

"No, there's no need."

"Do you think I'm too old? Sonny, I was dealing with

Injuns long before you were born. Even before your pa was born."

"Preacher, I don't doubt your courage, your skills, or your ability in dealing with, or fighting against Indians. But John and I may well find ourselves in positions where we have to move fast. You've slowed down a mite, and if you are honest with yourself, you'll admit that."

Preacher was quiet for a moment, then he nodded, and stood. "I guess I'd better get myself on back up to my cabin now. As old and as slow as I am, it'll more 'n likely take me a month or two to get there."

For just a moment, Smoke thought Preacher was hurt, then he saw the smile on the old man's face.

"You take care, young 'un," he said, grabbing Smoke's hand.

"I will," Smoke promised.

[*It was the underground telegraph I alluded to in my previous editorial insert that first alerted Smoke Jensen to the fact that his friend was in a personal struggle. Jackson had killed at least ten braves and Iron Bull sent twenty of his most fearsome warriors to kill Jackson.*

Smoke valued friendship and loyalty above all other personal traits, so he left Colorado to look for Jackson, not to stop him, but to help him. He wasn't sure he believed the part about John eating the livers of the Indians he killed, but there was no doubt that his friend was being hunted. Smoke rushed in to help, knowing it wouldn't be easy.—ED.]

Old Main Building

Professor Armbruster laughed. "Gizzards? Did that cowboy really think that human beings had gizzards?"

"Well, you have to understand, Professor, most cowboys had seen the innards of animals and people, but except for the heart, and maybe the lungs, most of them wouldn't know the difference between a pancreas and a spleen." Smoke laughed as well. "Hell, I'm not sure I could pick out a liver from any of the other human organs. But at least I've always known that we didn't have gizzards."

"What did you think when you learned that the army had no intention of intervening on behalf of your friend?"

"To be honest with you, Professor, I don't really know that I gave it much thought at all. I just sort of figured that this was a personal war between John and the Crow, and I calculated that the odds were way against him, so I decided to go up and see if I could lend him a hand."

"Did you go up to Montana and look for John Jackson as soon as you heard that he was in trouble?" Professor Armbruster asked.

"Yes," Smoke replied. "Well, I say yes. I didn't actually leave until after I returned home to tell Sally what I was doing."

"How did she feel about that? I mean, you hadn't been married all that long then. Did she understand that this was something you had to do? And was she all right with that?"

"We hadn't been married too long then, that's true," Smoke said. "But Sally always was a very smart woman, and she knew, right away, what kind of man I was. From the very beginning she told me that she wouldn't get in the way if I had to do something that, in her words, 'was a matter of conscience or honor.' So, yes, she was all right with it."

Sugarloaf Ranch

Smoke and Sally were sitting on the front porch watching a couple of the cowboys pitching horseshoes.

There was a clang, then a yell of triumph. "Ha! I got me a leaner!"

"Yeah? Well watch this."

The next cowboy threw and his horseshoe knocked the leaner away, then fell down, ringing the stob.

The other cowboys yelled in approval.

"Look at that, would you? Mack is good!"

"He ain't good, he's just lucky," the first cowboy said, dejectedly.

"You've got something to tell me, don't you, Smoke?" Sally asked.

"What makes you think that?"

"I know you, Smoke. I can read you like a book."

Smoke chuckled. "I guess I better never lie to you, huh?"

Sally laughed. "You couldn't lie to me if you tried. Now, what is it you have to tell me?"

"You remember me telling you about John Jackson?"

"Of course I remember. You spent a year with him, teaching him how to become a westerner."

"I need to go see him."

"Well, why didn't you say so? I'd love to meet him. Didn't you say he got married? Oh, don't tell me," she added excitedly. "They have a child now. Of course you must go. We must go."

Smoke shook his head and put his hand out on Sally's hand. "It's not that kind of visit, I'm afraid. And we aren't going, I'm going."

"Oh," Sally said, obviously disappointed by the reply. "What is it? Is John in some sort of trouble?"

"Yes."

"What kind of trouble?"

"From what I can gather, the Crow killed his wife and child, and he has gone on a personal vendetta. But now the Crow are fighting back. They've sent twenty warriors after him."

"I see," Sally said, quietly.

"Sally, I can't just . . ."

"I know," Sally said, interrupting him. She put her other hand on top of Smoke's hand. "I know that you have to do what you have to do."

Smoke lifted her hand to his lips and kissed it. "Thank you for approving."

"I'm not sure that I do approve," Sally said. "But I understand. God help me, I do understand."

It took Smoke two weeks to get to the upper Missouri River valley, but it only took him one more week to find John, once he arrived. That was because Smoke had spent enough time with John, right here, in this very location, that he had a pretty good idea as to where he should look. And once he got into the area, he was able to track him.

Smoke smelled the cooking meat, and he knew, intuitively, that it was John. He approached slowly, though not necessarily quietly. He wanted John to hear him approaching, and he wanted him to realize that it was a measured, rather than a secretive approach.

He found John squatting by a small fire on the banks of Porcupine Creek. He had a piece of meat on a green twig, leaning out over the fire.

"What are you cooking?" Smoke asked.

"Become finicky, have you?" John replied.

Smoke dismounted and walked over toward the fire. "Well, when I come this far to be your dinner guest, I like to know what I'm eating."

"Something I found dead."

"Smells good, anyway."

John stood and stuck out his hand. "I guess you've heard about my particular situation." It wasn't a question, it was an observation.

"Hell, John, there isn't anyone between here and El Paso who hasn't heard what's going on."

"Yeah," John said. "I sort of thought it might be getting around."

"Let me ask you something . . ."

"No, I'm not eating livers," John said, answering before the question was completely asked.

"Why does everyone think that you are?"

"I took a bite of them, the first time. And I've been letting the Crow think that I'm eating the livers." John chuckled. "It seems to have gotten them a little upset."

"A little upset? You are their biggest enemy right now."

"Good. That's what I wanted. If you've heard about this, you also know what those bastards did to Claire and little Kirby."

"Yes, I heard," Smoke said. He smiled. "Kirby? Your baby's name was Kirby?"

"I didn't think you would mind."

"I'm honored," Smoke said. "But I'm also saddened that he had such a short life. And I'm saddened by what happened to Claire."

"Then you can understand why I'm doing what I'm doing," John said.

Smoke sighed. "What do you know about the Big Dog Warrior Society of the Crow?"

John shook his head. "I don't know anything about it. I've never heard of it."

"Well, of all the Indians, the Sioux, the Cheyenne, the Apache, the Comanche, the Big Dog Warrior Society of the Crow is the most fierce. When they set out to make war against an enemy, they take an oath, to kill that enemy, or to, literally, die trying. John, twenty of them are after you."

"I may have already run across them; I've killed a few Crow, here and there."

"No," Smoke said. "If you've killed a few here and there, you have not encountered the Big Dog Warriors. They won't come after you, here and there. There are twenty of them, and they will all come after you all at the same time."

John carved off a piece of the meat and tasted it.

"It's done," he said, pulling it away from the fire. He carved it up, then gave a big piece of it to Smoke.

"Uhmm," Smoke said. "This is very good. You've come

some distance from when I first saw you, losing a fight to a turkey."

"I've worked at it," John replied.

The two men ate in silence for a moment or two before John spoke again.

"If these fierce warriors are coming after me, en masse, as you say, I expect you had better put distance between you and me soon as you finish eating."

"Uh-uh," Smoke said. "I'm not leaving."

"Smoke, I'm the one they're after. There's no need in you getting yourself killed."

"Didn't you name your son after me?"

"I did."

"Then, like I said, I'm not leaving. I have a personal stake in this now."

"All right," John said. "I welcome your company."

"John, when we first met, I was the teacher, and I taught you everything I know about living in the mountains, trapping, hunting, and just generally surviving. But you are the soldier. You went through the same war my pa did, and you were over in Asia with the French Foreign Legion, so now, you are the teacher. We've got twenty armed men coming after us, and we are but two. Do you have any suggestions as to how we find them and deal with them?"

John smiled. "Yeah, I do. First of all, we let them find us. And I know exactly where we need to be found."

"Where?"

"It's a small cabin I discovered not too far from here. The walls are thick, we'll have good cover as long as we are in there."

Smoke shook his head. "I don't know as I want to be confined in a cabin," he said. "If they burn it down around us, we'll be trapped."

"Ah, my friend," John said, holding up his finger. "This cabin can't be burned down. It is made of adobe."

"Adobe? Up here, in the woods?"

"I know. I was surprised too, when I found it. But it's there all right. Now, all we have to do is leave a trail they can follow, so they'll come to us."

"I agree. But the trail can't be too obvious," Smoke said. "We have to make them think that we are trying to cover it up. We don't want them to know that we want them to find us."

John smiled and nodded. "You'd make a good army officer, Smoke. You catch on fast."

CHAPTER 33

With the Big Dog Warriors at Elk Prairie Creek

Whips His Horses and the Indians in his raiding party had spent last night on the banks of Elk Prairie Creek. During the night Whips His Horses had gone off by himself to construct a sweat lodge. When he returned the next morning he called the others together so he could share with them what he had learned during his meditation.

"I have sought wisdom in the sweat lodge," he said when the others had gathered. "I asked for knowledge, so that I might know what to do, and that knowledge has been given me. I asked for a special power to guide me in finding Liver Eater, and that special power has been given me. I asked for the courage to face our enemy and to kill him, so we can remove his liver and bring it back to our village so that Iron Bull and the others can see what I have done, and know that Liver Eater is dead and can harm us no more. In the sweat lodge I was given the knowledge, the power, and the courage to do this thing before me."

[It may give the reader some insight to understand something about the sweat lodge ceremony. It is, and has been for some time, central to most Indian cultures.

It is a place to get answers and guidance by asking spiritual entities for wisdom and power.

The entrance to the sweat lodge always faces to the east and the sacred fire pit. This is significant to the Indians, because each new day begins in the east with the rising of the sun, which the Indians see as the source of life and power.

Between the entrance to the lodge and the fire pit, where the stones are heated, is an altar upon which is often placed an animal skull atop a post. At the base of the post is a small raised earthen altar upon which are placed other items of significance, such as sage, grass, feathers, and, always, a pipe.

While subjecting themselves to heat intense enough to cause a sweat, the participant asks for such things as knowledge, power, courage, and endurance.

It is not at all unusual that Whips His Horses would have gone to the sweat lodge to seek such assistance as he searched for John Jackson.—ED.]

"We will find Liver Eater, this I know, for I was told this in a vision," Whips His Horses said.

The nineteen other men of the Big Dog Warrior Society who were with Whips His Horses became very excited, not only because Whips His Horses had shared his vision with them, but also because success seemed so assured. They began painting their bodies for the war party.

At the adobe cabin

Smoke and John had reached the cabin the day before. After they located a safe place for their horses that night, they brought into the little cabin everything they might need to withstand a prolonged siege. They filled two big earthen vessels, found in the cabin, with water from the creek. They had all their food, as well as what ammunition they had.

"If there is no set-piece battle, I think we are in an advantageous enough position to be able to defeat the Indians by attrition, if need be," John said.

There were two windows in front of the cabin, one on each side of the door. There was at least one window on all the other sides of the cabin, but it seemed unlikely that any Indian would approach them from the back, as the cabin was built so close to a sheer wall of a cliff, that there was no room for them to maneuver.

They had slept in shifts during the night, and now, early in the morning, Smoke stepped outside. That was when he saw a large dark mass advancing slowly out of the gray dawn. He realized at once that it was the Indians.

At almost the same moment he saw them, the Indians saw him, and a loud, collective war whoop emerged from their throats. They began riding toward the cabin, their horses thundering across the ground.

"John, here they come!" Smoke shouted at the top of his voice.

On came the Indians, their horses leaping, gliding over obstacles, the half-naked, painted bodies of the warriors shining in the first brilliant rays of the morning sun.

"Get in here!" John shouted, holding the door open.

Smoke dashed in through the door, then it was closed and bolted.

Smoke hurried to his window and looked outside. At that precise moment one of the Indians had ridden all the way up to the building. Smoke shot him, his bullet striking the Indian just under his left eye, killing him instantly.

The Indians greatly outnumbered the two defenders and, perhaps because they had such superior numbers, they were overconfident, and foolishly bold. They would ride all the way up to the walls of the building, then lean over and try to shoot through the windows, or they would dismount and run up to try and force the door open. Because of such foolish activity, they were making themselves very easy targets, and Smoke and John were cutting them down like a scythe through wheat.

The Indians withdrew, dragging their dead and wounded back with them. After what had been a thunderous roar of gunfire for nearly half an hour, there was absolute silence.

"You said only one man would be here. There are two," Swift Hawk, one of the Indians, said, protesting to Whips His Horses. "Where is your medicine?" He pointed to the dead and dying. "Do you see that your medicine does not work?"

"My medicine is strong," Whips His Horses insisted. "We will go again!"

"Here they come!" John said.

The Indians came again, three abreast this time, galloping through the dust, shouting and whooping their war cries. Again they charged all the way up to the little cabin. The Indians fired from horseback, shooting arrows and bullets toward the open windows. Two of them jumped down from their horses and tried to force the door open by hitting against it with the butts of their rifles.

Again, the marksmanship of Smoke and John was deadly, and riderless horses whirled and retreated, leaving their riders dead or dying on the ground behind them.

"Damn," John said. "Is this to be *ngôi nhà trang trại*, again?"

"The Nogy what?"

"You remember, I told you about the business in Annam?"

"Oh, yes. Well, there the army came just in time," Smoke said. "We're on our own, here." He chuckled.

"Yeah, I guess we are," John replied with a laugh. "The problem is, just like at the fight at *ngôi nhà trang trại*, I'm running out of ammunition."

"How much do you have left?"

"Five rounds for the rifle. Two rounds for the pistol. How about you?"

"I'm not much better. Three rifle rounds, one pistol is empty, four rounds in the other."

Throughout the rest of the day the Indians attacked several more times. But they prefaced each attack with loud screeches and war whoops, and that enabled Smoke and John to be ready for them. They made every shot count.

"If we can just hold on until dark, maybe they'll go away," John suggested. "I've heard that Indians don't like to fight in the dark."

"They may not attack, but that doesn't mean they are going to go away," Smoke said.

Smoke was right. The Indians didn't go away, and all night long Smoke and John—who took turns sleeping just in case—could hear singing, and see the campfires.

"I wonder how long they'll stay?" John asked.

"Hard to say," Smoke answered. "How many rounds do you have now?"

"Two. What about you?"

"One pistol round, one round in the Henry."

"Damn."

The next morning the Indians had pulled back, and were now milling around on top of a hill. They were making no attempt to conceal themselves, because they were well out of range.

"Bold bunch of bastards, aren't they?" Smoke asked.

John had a pair of binoculars and he used them to study the Indians, only one of whom was mounted.

"I'll be damn," John said.

"What is it?"

"The Indian on the horse. Take a look at him. Look at his face. Do you see the black and red vertical lines on his cheek?"

"Yes."

"Claire pointed that out to me when we visited Iron Bull's camp. That means this man is the leader."

"Is he now?"

"I wonder if we killed him . . ."

"Would the others leave?" Smoke finished.

"It's worth a try."

Smoke looked at him. "That's a hell of a long shot. Six or seven hundred yards, easily."

"But if we both shot at the same time?"

"I've only got one rifle round left," Smoke said.

"Then, one of us had better hit him," John suggested.

"Wait," Smoke said. "I'm going to try a trick Preacher showed me once. It might improve our chances of hitting him. But it's all or nothing, because if we miss, we are going to be in a bad fix."

"What do you have in mind?" John asked.

Smoke took out the bullet from his pistol, and the one from his rifle. Then he separated the two bullets from their casings. Looking down into the rifle casing, he saw that there was room to add more powder. He filled the rifle casing the rest of the way, with powder from the pistol casing.

"Good idea," John said, and he did the same thing, combining the powder from two bullets into one.

John chuckled. "But this is absolutely an all-or-nothing draw of the cards."

When both were ready, they rested the barrels of the rifles on the windowsills and took long and careful aim.

"I'll count to three," Smoke said. "One, two, three."

Swift Hawk was standing next to Whips His Horses when he heard an angry buzz, then a loud pop. Looking up he saw blood squirting from Whips His Horses' head, and from a wound in his chest. Whips His Horses fell at Swift Hawk's feet.

"How can this be? How can they kill from so far?" one of the Indians asked in awed fear.

The Indians were disoriented. Whips His Horses' medicine had not protected him, which meant it could not protect them.

"Swift Hawk, there are but five of us now. And surely the spirits are angry with us, for no ordinary man can kill from so far away."

"And the bullets of both men found their mark," another said.

"Their medicine is strong," another said. "Swift Hawk, what shall we do?"

"We will make peace," Swift Hawk said.

Swift Hawk mounted his horse then, slowly, very slowly, started riding toward the adobe cabin.

"Here they come," John said. "What'll we do now?"

"Wait," Smoke said. "Look!"

The approaching Indian held his hand up, palm forward, and he continued to ride.

"I believe he wants to make peace," John said.

"They don't need to know we are out of ammunition. Hold your rifle by your side in your left hand," Smoke said. "We'll go outside to meet him, with our right hands up in the sign of peace."

Swift Hawk rode to within twenty yards of the cabin, all the while holding his hand up. Smoke and John stood out front, holding their hands up as well.

"No more will the Crow make war against Liver Eater!" Swift Hawk said in English.

"No more will I will eat the liver of the Crow," John said.

Swift Hawk nodded, then turned and rode away.

EPILOGUE

Some may think, upon reading this study of two of Colorado's most colorful characters, that I have taken what might be considered a soft approach to history, using words that are more sensual than cerebral. And because of this, some readers might suggest that this is a substitute for academic research.

I assure you that nothing can be further from the truth. No amount of scholarly inquiry, particularly of the kind that requires poring over the printed word, whether it be the work of earlier scholars, newspapers, diaries, or letters, could be more accurate than getting the story directly from one of the actual participants. As of the time of this writing, Smoke Jensen is still alive, and still one of Colorado's living treasures.

The peace negotiated between Swift Hawk and John Jackson held up, and never again was there trouble between them. In fact, John Jackson eventually declared himself to be a brother to the Crow.

He never married again, so there are no direct descendants of this storied legend. He was, during his lifetime, a soldier in the Union army, a soldier of fortune with the French Foreign Legion, a scout, hunter, and trapper. In the end, he returned to Pennsylvania where he died, alone, in a veteran's hospital on December 21, 1900.

Jacob W. Armbruster, Ph.D.
Professor of History, University of Colorado
Boulder, Colorado
April 9, 1925

JOHNSTONE ON JOHNSTONE

"When the Truth Becomes Legend"

William W. Johnstone was born in southern Missouri, the youngest of four children. He was raised with strong moral and family values by his minister father, and tutored by his schoolteacher mother. Despite this, he quit school at age fifteen.

"I have the highest respect for education," he says, "but such is the folly of youth, and wanting to see the world beyond the four walls and the blackboard."

True to this vow, Bill attempted to enlist in the French Foreign Legion ("I saw Gary Cooper in *Beau Geste* when I was a kid and I thought the French Foreign Legion would be fun") but was rejected, thankfully, for being underage. Instead, he joined a traveling carnival and did all kinds of odd jobs. It was listening to the veteran carny folk, some of whom had been on the circuit since the late 1800s, telling amazing tales about their experiences, which planted the storytelling seed in Bill's imagination.

"They were mostly honest people, despite the bad reputation traveling carny shows had back then," Bill remembers. "Of course, there were exceptions. There was one guy named Picky, who got that name because he was a master pickpocket. He could steal a man's socks right off his feet without him knowing. Believe me, Picky got us chased out of more than a few towns."

After a few months of this grueling existence, Bill returned home and finished high school. Next came stints as a deputy sheriff in the Tallulah, Louisiana, Sheriff's

Department, followed by a hitch in the U.S. Army. Then he began a career in radio broadcasting at KTLD in Tallulah, Louisiana, which would last sixteen years. It was there that he fine-tuned his storytelling skills. He turned to writing in 1970, but it wouldn't be until 1979 that his first novel, *The Devil's Kiss,* was published. Thus began the full-time writing career of William W. Johnstone. He wrote horror (*The Uninvited*), thrillers (*The Last of the Dog Team*), even a romance novel or two. Then, in February 1983, *Out of the Ashes* was published. Searching for his missing family in the aftermath of a post-apocalyptic America, rebel mercenary and patriot Ben Raines is united with the civilians of the Resistance forces and moves to the forefront of a revolution for the nation's future.

Out of the Ashes was a smash. The series would continue for the next twenty years, winning Bill three generations of fans all over the world. The series was often imitated but never duplicated. "We all tried to copy *The Ashes* series," said one publishing executive, "but Bill's uncanny ability, both then and now, to predict in which direction the political winds were blowing brought a certain immediacy to the table no one else could capture." The Ashes series would end its run with more than thirty-four books and twenty million copies in print, making it one of the most successful men's action series in American book publishing. (The Ashes series also, Bill notes with a touch of pride, got him on the FBI's Watch List for its less than flattering portrayal of spineless politicians and the growing power of big government over our lives, among other things. In that respect, I often find myself saying, "Bill was years ahead of his time.")

Always steps ahead of the political curve, Bill's recent thrillers, written with myself, include *Vengeance Is Mine, Invasion USA, Border War, Jackknife, Remember the Alamo, Home Invasion, Phoenix Rising, The Blood of Patriots, The Bleeding Edge,* and *Suicide Mission.*

It is with the western, though, that Bill found his greatest success and propelled him onto both the *USA Today* and the *New York Times* bestseller lists.

Bill's western series include The Mountain Man, Matt Jensen:The Last Mountain Man, Preacher, The Family Jensen, Luke Jensen: Bounty Hunter, Eagles, MacCallister (an Eagles spin-off), Sidewinders, The Brothers O'Brien, Sixkiller, Blood Bond, The Last Gunfighter, and the upcoming new series Flintlock and The Trail West.

"The Western," Bill says, "is one of the few true art forms that is one hundred percent American. I liken the Western as America's version of England's Arthurian legends, like the Knights of the Round Table, or Robin Hood and his Merry Men. Starting with the 1902 publication of *The Virginian* by Owen Wister, and followed by the greats like Zane Grey, Max Brand, Ernest Haycox, and of course Louis L'Amour, the Western has helped to shape the cultural landscape of America.

"I'm no goggle-eyed college academic, so when my fans ask me why the Western is as popular now as it was a century ago, I don't offer a 200-page thesis. Instead, I can only offer this: The Western is honest. In this great country, which is suffering under the yoke of political correctness, the Western harks back to an era when justice was sure and swift. Steal a man's horse, rustle his cattle, rob a bank, a stagecoach, or a train, you were hunted down and fitted with a hangman's noose. One size fit all.

"Sure, we westerners are prone to a little embellishment and exaggeration and, I admit it, occasionally play a little fast and loose with the facts. But we do so for a very good reason—to enhance the enjoyment of readers.

"It was Owen Wister, in *The Virginian* who first coined the phrase *'When you call me that, smile.'* Legend has it that Wister actually heard those words spoken by a deputy sheriff in Medicine Bow, Wyoming, when another poker player called him a son-of-a-bitch.

"Did it really happen, or is it one of those myths that have passed down from one generation to the next? I honestly don't know. But there's a line in one of my favorite Westerns of all time, *The Man Who Shot Liberty Valance,* where the newspaper editor tells the young reporter, 'When the truth becomes legend, print the legend.'

"These are the words I live by."

Now that the war's over, Trace and Chaw
travel the West together, taking on odd jobs.
They're handy with six-guns and gut-shredders, fond of
women and liquor, and always ready to raise hell.
Somehow, the unlikely partnership works—until Trace
and Chaw sign up with a freighting company run by a
beautiful woman. Her company is caught in the crossfire
of two rival mine owners who want to control
the freight routes. Like it or not, Trace and Chaw
are stuck in the middle of another war. And this one's
going to be every bit as bloody—and maybe their last. . . .

**NATIONAL BESTSELLING AUTHORS
WILLIAM W. JOHNSTONE
and J.A. Johnstone**

THE BEST OF ENEMIES
A Trace and Chaw Western

First in a New Series!

Live Free. Read Hard.
williamjohnstone.net
Visit us at kensingtonbooks.com

On sale now, wherever Pinnacle Books are sold.

CHAPTER 1

The first thing the man felt was heat, heat from the unforgiving sun baking down. By the time he came around, it had already reddened his upturned face and blistered his lips.

The next thing he noticed was yet more heat, but this time it came from within himself, from below himself, as if from the earth on which he lay.

He forced his eyes open, just a crack at first; all he could see were stinging pinpricks of light through a gauze of pink that edged out to redness. Jagged, brittle snatches of memory drizzled back to him at the same time. And not a bit of it impressed him.

All this told him was that he had to be dead, given what he was recalling. He almost wished he had lost his ability to recall anything, so awful were the bits of memory, of what he had seen and lived through. Or had he?

Then sound flooded in and became more pronounced. But at first, all he could hear was a whooshing and thudding.

With more effort than he bet he'd ever expended on anything in a coon's age, the man lifted his head. It wobbled on its feeble stalk of a neck. He cracked his right eye wider than its slit and saw bright, warm light, and little else. How on earth did he get here? And where was *here*?

All he could recall was fighting. Seems that's all he'd done since he was born. What did that mean?

Notions, facts, or perhaps they were fabrications, he could not yet tell, flitted in and out of his mind. He gritted his teeth and fought to keep his eyes open. There, he looked down along the length of his body and saw himself, stretched out on his back in the sun. His clothes looked sodden—*must be sweat*, he thought.

And then, as if someone had clapped their hands and awakened him fully, he remembered who he was. And from that revelation, it was a short jump to how he got here. Wherever *here* was. He figured that in time, that too, would come.

And then he remembered—the war. The war and the cursed Yankees who started it. And there he was, all laid out, baking in the sun, not certain how alive he was, or if he was on his way out. The latter possibility seemed the most likely, given the pain he felt, the light burning away at him, and the rush of memories flooding into his mind.

But right then, he figured he knew who he was, and that was pretty good. He was Chaw Dagworth, private in the army of the Confederate States of America.

He glanced down at himself again as he struggled to raise himself up onto an elbow. And if he was in the Confederate Army, then that meant his uniform would be gray. And if that was the case, why was it so sodden looking? Ah yes, the fighting. The cursed, fool Big War Twixt the States a protracted fracas, as his old Colonel used to say, caused by Yankee bellicosity.

Chaw grunted and felt a stinging in various parts of his body that quickly gave way to lancing pains, as if someone were sliding knives in and out of his arms, his sides, his legs. What was happening? And then he knew that he wasn't seeing a sweaty uniform, he was seeing a blood-soaked uniform. And as soon as that dawned on him, the rest of his situation became as clear to him as a cool mountain stream.

As he shoved himself up, despite the constant throbbing all over his body, more memories came gushing on in. Uninvited, but there they were anyway. . . .

His company had been taking a ridge, below which was a hollow, what was it called? Deadeye Gap, that's it. And then he'd seen a bluebelly and had taken off after him. That's right, that bluebelly and Chaw got into it pretty good. For a Yankee, the man was brute enough. Must have had Rebel bark somewhere in the woodpile.

In fact, Chaw recalled shouting that at the man as they tore into each other, each giving as good as they got. That comment sure got that bluebelly riled. That foul Yankee had called Chaw a slave trader and a child killer and all manner of raw names, none of which was true. Chaw found this humorous, considering the Yank was a foul traitor and a child killer and a secret slaver himself!

Of course, Chaw had no way of verifying such, but he didn't doubt that bluebelly was guilty of that and a whole lot more. He was a foul Yankee, after all, wasn't he? That alone was reason enough to pin the entire mess on him.

As he lay there, Chaw pulled in as much of a breath as he could—it wasn't a deep one nor was it clear. Sounded to him as if he was breathing through a ragged pig's bladder. That reminded him of pig killin' time, when the men folk back home used to inflate and tie off the bladders for the kiddies to bat around.

None of that much mattered now. He was likely dying and would as likely never see his poor old family ever again. Not Ma, nor Pa, nor Jube, nor dear old Daisy the hound.

Chaw grunted and swung his gaze slowly over to his left. What he saw somehow did not surprise him, although it should have. But he reckoned some part of him knew what he would see before he looked there. And what he saw did not fill him with satisfaction, as he had expected it should. Nope, seeing that dead Yank not but a few yards to his left only made Chaw Dagworth feel almighty awful.

Even if the man was a foul Yankee, that carcass left Chaw hollowed out inside, even more than before. Because it only meant that, as bad as he felt, that Yank was worse off. For he was already dead.

And so, that meant that Chaw had given away his own life, and for a cause that had become so muddied and confused for him and most of his fellow Rebs, most had, at one time or another, considered running off in the night. Even though it meant risking getting shot in the back. And now, here he was, surely about to die himself, and that was a raw, hard thing to take.

The Yank, in Chaw's brief glimpse of the man, and then on repeated forced looks, appeared to be in particularly rough condition. The bluebelly, too, was sprawled out on his back, and he, too, was covered with what looked to be a whole lot of dried blood from gashes and rents in his once-blue uniform. He knew this because there were a few spots of blue wool still visible through the darkened blood.

Was this it, then? Nothing more than kill or be killed? How on earth, he wondered, would his death or the death of that foul Yank beside him, be helpful to the cause of the South, or the cursed North, for that matter?

Chaw closed his eyes a moment and worked to breathe a bit more. And he came to the conclusion that there wasn't a single scrap of usefulness in his sacrificing himself for the dang cause. No sir.

And then he heard a sound. From his left.

Chaw grunted and worked to angle his gaze back over in that direction. He blinked hard and opened his eyes again, forcing them wide. Couldn't be. He could swear he saw that foul Yank move!

* * *

Long before he opened his eyes, Private Fullcup Trace, of the Union Army, lay awake. Keeping his eyes closed on waking each morning was a lifelong habit, and something that, even in the much-abused state he knew his body to be in, he nonetheless maintained.

He found it beneficial to slowly, over the course of several minutes, allow himself to come around to full consciousness. In this way he could take account of who he was, what had happened to him, and where he was at that moment.

All of this came to him as he lay there, sipping air between parted lips. He knew who he was—Trace, he was called—for he became aware of such as if someone had whispered it to his mind.

But it also soon became obvious to him that his normal method of waking was not going to cut it this day. For memory reminded him in the harshest way just what it was that had landed him where he was, and in the state he suspected his body of being in.

First, he felt a thudding building within him. It started down low, deep in his guts, and rose as if it were marching right into his chest, and on up his gullet. By the time it wormed its way into his mouth and nose, he had begun to ache all over.

And then, the memory of the events leading up to all of this flooded into his mind. The lashing agonies that come with what surely were a thousand cuts, stabs, cracked ribs, broken fingers, and more thrummed with a sudden and searing pain over all his body. As bad as was that pain, it bowed down before the thudding of the cannonade playing out betwixt his ears.

With more effort than he felt capable of, Trace cracked open his eyes. The sunlight that had been there, awaiting this moment with supreme impatience, drove forward and inward. As Trace squeezed his eyes shut once more, although too late to avoid this fresh, raw wash of pain, it felt as if forge-fired daggers were jamming themselves like steel vipers into his skull.

An unbidden moan, low and fragile, was accompanied with a deluge of memories that flooded over him. And he knew without doubt where he was. The battle atop that cursed ridge above Deadeye Gap, it was called. They'd found that holdout Reb company they'd been chasing for weeks.

Those foolish graybacks fought like cornered lions, with claws out and fangs slashing and with a hard pistoning of their gunfire that seemed to not let up. Trace recalled wondering out loud, with some of the other Union men, if maybe the Rebel soldiers truly didn't know that the war was all but over for them.

No, there hadn't been any surrender as such, at least not yet. But it was bound to happen soon. That's what they had all thought going into the latest fracas with the elusive, dastardly Rebs. The enemy numbers were raggedy and slowly dwindling, but they nonetheless fought at every turn as if they were freshly minted men.

Trace groaned again as the rest of the preceding events came back to him. He recalled how he had made his way down past the far side of the battle, chasing after a pair of Reb snipers. He knew from experience that they'd been looking to sneak up around to where the Northern Army was encamped. That would not stand.

Trace had gotten the drop on them, sure, but instead of letting him take them as his prisoners, they'd put up a fight. He'd expected that, anyway. He didn't recommend it to anyone, even a foul Rebel, but he could hardly blame them, now, could he?

As he fought, trading shots with the two snipers, Trace realized from the sounds of the battle above and behind him, atop that ridge, that the melee was not about to end in favor of these maddening Rebels and the rest of their Southern ilk.

He was all but through with these two, having pinned

them pretty well, despite being a lone soldier against two men. He had the landscape to thank, in part, for that, too. He had been able to position himself behind a boulder the size of a wagon while the two Rebs he'd been pursuing had found themselves at the bottom of a gulley with nothing but knee-height rocks and crusty pines no thicker around than a man's arm.

Then, he had touched finger to trigger and had been about ready to send those two Rebel curs barking to the netherworld. Despite how he felt about them and their cause, there was that flicker of a moment when he regretted ever being involved in this foul mess to begin with.

It had less, far less, to do with the individual solders, no matter the side, than it had to do with the cause each side fought for. And for all that, he knew that all these deaths could be laid at the feet of the leaders on both sides for their failure to keep talking, keep shouting at each other across the back-room negotiation tables.

Trace didn't care how how angry they got or how many days or weeks or months or years it would have taken. All of it would have been breath and time well spent if it had saved a single life of one of the soldiers on either side. Instead, they had ended up fighting, either by choice or, as had proved the case, by force, to fight and die for their respective so-called causes.

And Trace knew he wasn't the only man in the Union Army who felt that way. And he had it on good authority that most Rebs felt the same darned way, too. Fat lot of good it had done any of them.

All of that flooded into and out of his mind in that whisper of a moment before he squeezed the trigger to take yet another Rebel man's life. And at that moment, a shot whipped by his head from behind him. It spun Trace's gaze hard over his right shoulder. At the same time, instinct drove him down to one knee.

There he spied yet another grayback. This one, however, wasn't oblivious like his fellow soldiers. Trace had, after all, gotten the upper hand on those two Rebs down in their gully, looking this way and that.

In recalling that day, however many days before, Trace now realized that moment could have well ended it all, and in eyeblink speed. But for some reason that crazed Rebel he'd seen over his shoulder, with his rifle aimed right at Trace's head, had decided not to shoot him.

What he did instead genuinely surprised Trace. The man had delivered that shot at him. And when he faced him, Trace saw that the Reb hadn't been far enough away to have missed him. *Why hadn't I heard the rascal sneaking on up behind me?* thought Trace.

As if in answer to the question of why echoing in Trace's skull, the Reb who'd shot at him from behind, and who held a revolver aimed right at him—he must have used his rifle to deliver that first, too-close-to-have-missed shot—shouted from about sixty feet away.

The Reb eyed him down the short barrel and barked, "I am a son of the South and as such I am too proud to shoot a man in the back, even if he is a foul, yellow, blue-bellied Yankee!"

By then, of course, Trace had his own gun aimed right at that Rebel's gut. He rose once more to a standing position. Behind and below his big boulder, he heard a voice shout to another, "Let's git gone back to the fight! That Yank's done for!"

That told Trace he didn't have much to worry about from those two. He could concentrate on dealing with this crazy Rebel. A man who had him dead to rights, but who made him turn to face him before he would shoot him was a crazy man. Or a man with a conscience.

Make that a Rebel with a conscience. He knew there were a good many of them because he'd learned a whole lot since he started in on this war, with all its marches and lousy, maggoty food, and surly officers and lack of leadership with brains.

He'd learned that most Rebs were just about the same as most Yanks. That was to say they were all just men. Men with wives and children and parents and cousins and friends and homes and farms, all of it.

And now here was one who wanted to fight him, face to face, fair and square. All right then, thought Trace. Let's get to it.

He rose back to standing height, keeping his rifle aimed at that man's chest, and said, "What's it going to be, Reb? We have each other square on!"

"Shut up and approach. We'll see how far you make it, you stinking Yank!"

And so they had advanced on each other, slow step by slow step, their respective barrels not faltering, their boot steps sure and well placed, their eyes never leaving the other's, their trigger fingers ready to dole out the last sound the other man would ever hear.

But neither man pulled a trigger. Neither man dared to be the first, apparently, for they each advanced and strode with caution and unwavering concentration right toward the other.

And then they were close enough to see the grime caked in the lines on their faces, to see that they each could use a real shave, a haircut, a month's worth of sleep, and the same of food.

"Enough!" growled Fullcup Trace, flinging away his rifle. He didn't care any longer.

They'd been staring each other down for long, long minutes, slowly circling, and the situation had grown more than tiresome. A vital need had grown in him that they fight like men, men who were unafraid to cower behind the false cowardice of a gun.

As Trace regarded the other man, the grayback sneered, and he, too, sent his own gun spinning to the dirt. That's when things really began to head off into an interesting direction.

Again, as if by mutual unspoken agreement, the two men each sneered, their lips pulled back over tight-set teeth. Their eyes narrowed and growls crawled up out of their throats.

Arms drew up fast and their hands sought each other with clawlike fingers, fingers that closed on the other, on arms and chests. They balled wool tunics and at the same time jerked the other man this way and that, hoping to gain the upper hand.

They each gave voice to deep rage that, while directed at the other man, really represented the anguish and frustration and fear and confusion they had each felt for the past couple of years of being forced to kill or be killed.

Propelled by a clot of such feelings fueling their rage, the two men grabbed onto each other hard and fast, neither uttering any sounds that could be recognized as words. Instead they were growls and barks and the utterances of seething anger.

They circled, breaking their holds, only to collide again, one arm grasping clothing or hair, it mattered not. The other was curled into a thick fist that drew back then drove forward like a sledge wielded by a railway man.

Their blows staggered each other, sent blasts of starlight even during the day before the receiver's sweat-riddled eyes. The punches and cudgel-like shots staggered each other, and yet neither man relented. Once they had agreed to brawl it out, neither man gave the other a moment's peace. Legs kicked, circled around other legs, seeking to trip.

Once, the Reb was able to use his momentum to drive the Yank backward. One of the man's blue-clad legs lay pinned beneath him, and the Reb knew something had happened to that bent knee. It had not broken, for the man would have yipped like a kicked dog, but nonetheless he knew something very painful had overtaken the man.

He grinned, his gritted teeth stained yellow and gray, as if to match his uniform, and he used the moment's pain to his advantage, jamming his own knee into the Yank's midsection.

But his hubris at finding himself atop the other was short lived, for he had lost, for a moment, his accounting of the Yank's left arm. And as the Reb bent low to deliver a pulled-back punch, he left his own right side exposed.

The desperate Yank's left fist slammed into the right side of the Reb's ribs with the force of a hickory log being jammed, butt end first, into the man's torso, with deadly, unexpected momentum.

The blow shoved any air the Reb had in his chest up and out in a rush that ended in a wheeze. The worst of it for the Reb was feeling the sickening, sharp, lancing pain deep inside. He'd been down that painful road before and knew he'd just received a broken rib or three from that foul Yank.

The Reb collapsed to his left, falling off the pinned Yank long enough that the man in blue could roll to his left. Again, as if by mutual consent, the two men rose to their knees, facing each other, panting their rasping breaths. Hatred, directed at each other, glowed through their narrowed eyes, their chests working like bellows.

The Yank put little weight on his bum knee, for it pained him already and he knew it was swelling. He bet that something inside, the stringy bits in a man's body that hold flesh to bone, had torn or separated somehow.

The Reb raised his left hand to rest against the right side of his rib cage. He knew it showed a weakness, a wound dealt by the Yank, but he had to do it. Trace probed gingerly and again could not help the sharp-dawn breath of limping forward. With the Reb sipping shallow breaths, they drove at the other. Now each was intent of furthering the damage he had already inflicted on the other man.

How long they fought, neither man knew. Not that either of them cared. The brawl had become far more than two enemies having it out to some sort of end. It was the long-pent result of years of hardship shoved on them each day by their superiors, by the weather, by other soldiers, by bad food and worse water, by unforgiving terrain, and by the long-forgotten reasons behind why each was told they must kill other men.

And so it went, for hours or days or weeks, neither man knew nor cared. At some point, one of them, neither could recall later which, tugged free his knife barely an eyeblink's worth of time before the other did.

Thus the fight went on, continuing with each man guessing the move of the other, growl for growl, punch for punch, kick for kick, driving knee for driving knee, butting head for butting head, lunging, snapping teeth for the same. And now was the deadly promise of honed steel.

The appearance of blades in their scar-knuckled, brawl-reddened hands kindled in each man a renewed fire, a burning rage to kill, and to not be killed. It was no surprise to either man that his opponent wore a sheath knife on his belt. Most soldiers did, and frequently these tools were brought from home, cherished items that a man regarded with as much or more fondness than his gun.

A hip knife was perhaps a man's most-relied upon possession. It was a tool he used many times a day. Men shaved with them, used them to cut hair and trim beards, to skin, gut, and slice fresh killed critters for the fry pan or pot, from turtles to swamp rats to rabbits, and more.

A big-bladed knife also could be used to split lengths of branch wood for kindling, for sharpening sticks, for cooking and hewing stakes for tents. And as long as a man had a whet stone in his possibles sack, it could also be used to dig a cat hole in the steel-dulling earth, should a man care that much about covering his leavings with more than forest duff.

Occasionally, although the men agreed it was happening

more and more as the war dragged on, these knives had begun to be used to defend one's life, and to attack a foe as well.

As each man, Trace and Chaw, lifted free his knife, a sneer rose unbidden on each face. Without warning, they rushed at each other, snarls of rage ripping from their mouths.

They fought with bedraggled bodies sporting bloodshot eyes, bruised and bloodied mouths from split lips and smacked noses, and sweat-plastered hair. They wore the grime of repeated slammings and rollings in the dust and churned soil of the small, scree-riddled plateau they each had been stomping and trampling and kicking and furrowing for hours.

They fought as beasts, coming together amidst howls and clouds of dust, slashing and driving, peeling apart and wielding keen blades afresh with each parry and thrust. Over and over they attacked, not seeming to lose the renewed, whetted appetite for blood they each shared.

Their thirst for killing clouded their usual individual sensibilities and they fought hard and viciously. They rarely fell apart without leaving hacked slices in the arms of woolen tunics, on through into the sweat-soaked long-handle underwear beneath, finally drawing blood in scarred skin befouled by war and hard living.

Cuts more than gashes, although there were plenty of those as well, covered each man's head, face, torso, arms, hips, backsides, and calves. It seemed to each man as if they were covered with the denizens of a huge hive of deadly hornets, for with every move they made, their bodies screamed from the constant, stinging pain of a thousand lacerations.

Over time, neither man knew how much, the welter of agony each found himself mired within began to take its due toll.

Each man, the Reb and the Yank, after hours of cutting and slashing, howling and colliding, clubbing and flailing at the other, hammer and tong, staggered backward.

Trace, the Yank, had no idea how he had managed to stay upright for so very long, as his knee had somehow endured far beyond ordinary pain.

When he had been able to steal a quick glance at himself, he had been shocked to see, through the slashed fabric of his trousers, that they were no longer showing any trace of blue. They were matted with a reddened black, and were sodden with sweat and blood. His own and that of the foul, determined Reb.

What had shocked him most was the size of his knee. It had swelled to what seemed the size of a man's head. The ragged trouser leg about it, although slashed, had also brought with it a cold dose of luck. The knee had been able to swell and not be constricted by the fabric itself, for good or ill.

The Reb, leaning against the boulder before which the Yank had begun the fight, felt his breath wheezing in and out of his damaged breadbasket and rib cage. He hated to admit it, but that Yank had delivered into his side one mighty wallop, a pummeling such that the Reb was certain he might never again breathe as a normal man.

That thought had been from who knew how long before. Before the brutality their knives had inflicted. Now the Reb was a gasping, wheezing mess.

It was all he could do, now that they had fallen back apart from each other once again, to maintain his tender hold on his knife. He glanced down at himself and saw nothing he recognized.

Not his right hand, nor the knife in its grasp. He knew there was a knife there somewhere, hidden under a thick, syrupy coating of red-black gore that streamed and sluiced in steady rivulets down his drooped arm. The hand and fingers were covered with their own slick gore, beneath which dozens of cuts screamed at once. As did his entire body.

Chaw glanced up once more, as he held his left hand to his

right-side rib cage, the tenderest spot on his entire savaged form. "If I . . . look . . ."

He swallowed and licked his lips, his voice a cracked, croaking thing. My how he longed for a long sip of cool, clear water. "If I looked as bad . . . as you . . . Yank . . . I'd up and die already."

The Yank regarded the Reb while he leaned against the trunk of a much-scuffed pine. What he wanted to say was: "Of course you would! You're a weak-kneed Rebel!" But what came out, between huffing gasps was: "Could say the same . . . to you, Reb. . . ."

In all the time of that fight, neither man had done much more, sound-wise, than to grunt and shout sounds that were not words. But they did not much care. But now, hearing their voices, after hearing nothing but raw animal sounds from themselves, surprised each of them.

It also seemed to trigger something within each of them once more, yet another animalistic lunge to satisfy the unreasoning rage each felt at nearly being killed by the other.

They bolted forward, once more as if they had nodded in agreement with one another, and yet they hadn't. This did not slow them down, but the wearing, atrophying pain of the protracted battle had shown its strain as each man shoved up and away from the only things that were really keeping them upright—the boulder and the tree.

They lurched forward, staggering and eyeing each other through blood-flecked eyelashes, blinking and wheezing, their knives held halfway up in weak grasps. Each man with his eyes fixed on the other advanced. Paltry, feeble step by lurching, halting step, they drew closer, slowly, grunting and wheezing, bleeding and groaning.

And, as had happened since they began their attempt at mutual destruction, they each faltered within ten feet of each other, and the last thing each man saw was the other, his sworn mortal foe, sagging and collapsing. Eyes rolled back in heads, knees buckled, heads slopped backward on their weak stalks as their bodies slowly sank to the churned, bloodied earth.

Each man slopped to the side, then flopped sprawled flat on his back, but a couple of yards apart. Each still held his dagger in a death-clench grip, stiffened into place by the sticky, drying blood.

When Chaw Dagworth, Private of the Confederate Army, came to, and as he gazed on what he assumed was a dead Yank not but a few feet to his right, a Yank he had apparently killed, the entirety of the brutal fight came back to him. And he did not feel one sliver of goodness about it, not one slender thread of pride or satisfaction in having laid low yet another Yankee soldier.

Instead, he thought about how evenly matched they had been. Too much so, it seemed, for it had been one heck of a fight. And as much as he had tried to outmaneuver that blue brute, the fellow had done the same to him, as if they were each reading the other man's thoughts.

How long had they fought? Had it been mere minutes? Hours? The way he looked and the way he felt, it surely must have been days, days in which neither man was aware of light or dark passing. When neither one broke away, despite the fact that they yearned for a drink of water so badly from their respective canteens.

But now, with the thought of water, the wetness of it touching his lips, cooling his parched, burning throat, now all Chaw could think of was water, of getting a sweet, sweet drink into himself.

Where was his canteen?

He looked down at himself, but no, it was not strapped about his chest as usual. Nor was the rest of his gear. Where was it all?

And then he remembered—he had shed the canteen, the blanket roll, his pack in the dried grasses at the base of the tree. That tree that somehow the Yank had ended up closer to than Chaw.

He glanced back that way, beyond the Yank, and Chaw saw he'd been wrong. For the man now looked not to be alive but dead. Deader than dead, as his old Pap used to say. If he could only get on over there, past the Yank, over to the tree, where his gear still lay in a heap. Get to that canteen.

Then he saw what he had assumed was trickery of his eyes, that cursed Yank was moving again. Yes, he was alive! His chest was rising, falling, rising.

Chaw could not understand two things—how the man could possibly be alive, for Chaw had convinced himself that he alone had survived the awful fight. And the second thing he could not fathom was why he felt relief, immediate and flooding through his mind, as he saw that bluebelly breathe.

Hadn't he fought such men for years now? Hadn't he vowed over and over again that he would kill every Yankee he came across?

Chaw groaned and squeezed his eyes shut, then opened them again, the dried blood cracking slightly about them. Back to the water, he thought. Concentrate on getting water or nobody, not you or the Yank, is going to live for much longer.

And then Chaw had what at that moment he knew was the very best idea he had ever come upon in his whole life. He turned his head slowly painfully to the left and saw that massive boulder where the Yank had been standing when Chaw had first popped off that warning shot. And there, at the base was the Yank's own gear pile. And among it, not but a few yards to Chaw's left, sat a canteen.

He grunted, trying to shove himself over onto his left side, pinioning himself from behind with his bloody right hand. That's when Chaw felt his knife still gripped tight in his hand.

He tried to let go of it but it stayed there, attached somehow to his palm.

He raised it and saw that it was glued to his hand, then he knew—it was blood, likely his own, thick and mostly dried, holding the knife there. The sight of it made his head and guts churn. He flopped back to the earth with a gasp from his wounded ribs, his wind pinched and painful.

Why hadn't he shot the cursed Yank when he had the chance? What stayed his hand? Surely it wasn't just not wanting to shoot a Yank, even in the back. He'd done it a few times before. Yeah, it left a sour taste in his gut and mouth and mind for days after, but then he'd seen a new atrocity committed on a Reb by a Yank, and he'd gotten over it right quick.

A few feet away, Private Fullcup Trace, of the Union Army, managed a good few pulls of breath and worked at trying to open his eyes all the way. Something not unlike what a child felt when he awakened with eyes half-crusted shut following a night's sleep.

But this was different, and something he'd not felt before, not in all his adult years. He scrunched his eyes and worked his cheeks until whatever it was freed up a bit, enough for him to force, then pop open first one eye, and then the second.

He tried to raise a hand, but neither wanted to respond. And then, with a bit more concentrated effort, he was able to twitch life into first his left and then his right. But the left felt heavier. He gritted his teeth and forced his eyes open wide. It was a mighty effort and he didn't want to let his mind trail down the path of finding out why. Not yet. First he had to find out what that new sound was, off to his left.

Instinct told him to keep his movements as quiet as he could, but for all that, he grunted as he worked to raise himself up onto his left elbow. He looked down at his left side and saw that his hand, a blood-crusted claw, was curled tight around what looked to be a knife. Yes, it was a knife, his hip dagger.

Trace looked at his fingers, but somehow could not make them do his bidding. He'd have to use his right hand, which seemed to be working all right. He again heard a sound from his left, and, reminded of why he had been roused in the first place, he looked over to the left.

The first thing he saw was the big boulder, and he recognized it as the one he'd been hiding behind . . . for some reason. What had it been? And then he saw before the rock a body, but it was moving, faced away from him, doing something. . . .

On seeing it, in a fingersnap of time it all came back to him and Trace recalled everything that had happened. Chasing those two Rebs, pinning them down in the draw, then being jumped and surprised from behind as he hid by the boulder.

He'd spun and seen that Rebel. He was a tall, rugged-looking, scruffy, gray-clad fellow who'd gotten the drop on him. But instead of shooting to kill Trace, he'd missed him, missed him with intention.

It had made no sense to Trace then, and it still didn't. Despite the fact that the Reb had shouted something about how he'd not resort to shooting a man in the back, even if that man was a lousy Yank.

Trace almost grinned at the thought of him being referred to as "lousy." He reckoned he'd been called a whole lot of things in his life, but not quite that. And then . . . then they had fought. Oh, how they had fought.

Hammer and tong, as the old timers used to say it. Neither man had been willing to give in, let alone give up. It had been the hardest, rawest, most brutal fight of Trace's life.

A hawk's piercing call from high-up sounded. Other than that, and the slight sounds the Reb was making—what was that fellow doing?—there was no other sound. Nothing. Not even battle noise. There should be that, at least. It was . . . Deadeye Gap, that's right.

Something seemed . . . not right. He should hear something, should feel something. But all he felt was . . . numb. As if he'd spent a week inside a whiskey bottle and still hadn't reached the bottom of the thing.

He looked around himself, down at his bloodied mess of a body, and saw his right leg, puffed at the knee. So much so, in fact, that it looked as though there were two limbs in that trouser leg. If I'm that bad off, why can't I feel it?

He squinted and tried to see what the Reb was up to, but the man was faced away from him, looking at the boulder, but doing something over there.

So why, thought Trace, can't I feel something, anything at all other than this fuzzy, sort-of numb sensation? And then a thought came to him: I must be dead. This must be what it's like to be gone. Or maybe in that limbo place, because I have not been sorted out yet by whoever was in charge up there. Or . . . no, can't be down there. Can it?

I'm stuck in this middle layer of whatever this was, neither dead nor alive. He'd read about this, he thought, or maybe he was just recalling it from his Gran's growled interpretations of the Bible. Either way, here I am, thought Trace. Dead or dying.

Had that Rebel bandit killed him? As bad as Trace was beginning to feel, it must be so. He must have been killed in the fight. He sure knew it was a fight for the ages. And yet, when you're dead, or nearly so, what did that matter? You might well have fought for some cause you believed in, sure, but when you're dead, what good is that cause to you?

Heady stuff, he figured, but the upshot of it was that Trace was convinced more and more with each second that passed that he was sitting, or laying down, on Death's doorstep. And the Rebel?

Trace wagered that if he himself was dead, it stood to

some sort of reason that his licks had laid the Reb low, too. But then why was that rascal here as well? Must be he had killed the Reb at the same time the Reb had done for him. Must be that one of his licks managed to find purchase on the Reb's body, a blow that surely had laid low the man.

As memory trickled, then flooded in, so had his begrudging admiration for the Rebel. As with most of his kind that Trace had come across, he was a scrapper.

"Hey!"

Trace jerked as if slapped. What had that been? Or who?

"Hey, you! Yank!"

Trace had heard that, hadn't he?

"Hey now, Yank!"

The voice had come from his left. He looked over that way once more and saw that the Reb was now facing him and looking his way. And he held a canteen below his lips.

At the thought of that word, Fullcup Trace felt a quick zing of something charge into him. Water. He would kill all over again for a drink of water.

"Yeah, I see you heard me."

Trace looked at the man once more. Was the Rebel smiling? Can a man smile when he's dead? Oh, but this felt all too confusing.

"You best do what I did and crawl on back there behind yourself. My pack's there, not but a few feet behind you, at that tree. Got a canteen there."

The words, somehow, leached through the gauzy, thick scrim that Trace felt covering over himself, and he knew that even if he was dead he had to try to act on those words. They were important somehow. For they meant there was water at the end of them, and even if he was well and truly dead, which seemed pretty likely to him, he sure could use a drink of water.

"Wake up now, man, and go get that water. We ain't through tussling with each other yet."

Trace glanced once more at the Rebel to his left, then shifted his body such that he looked to his right instead. Sure, there was the tree, it was the tree the Rebel had been standing before when Trace had been tipped off by that shot that should have, by rights, killed him.

But it hadn't, and now here he was, and the Reb was telling him he needed to go get water. If Trace was understanding all this correctly, that meant the Reb was telling him to go get the Reb's water. And that sounded like a trap. A trick. Rebel treachery.

But then it occurred to Trace that the Reb was drinking water, and it was Trace's water. His very own canteen. Why was he doing that? But did that mean that he trusted Trace? No, it only meant that he was thirsty.

All of this thinking amounted to nothing more than confusion for Trace. He glanced at the Reb's dropped gear at the base of that tree, not all that far from him, to the right, and he thought he could see the man's canteen. And the sight of it gave him an overwhelming urge for water.

He grunted and worked to flip himself over onto his right side. Even as he did this, he stuck his thick, swollen tongue slowly out of his mouth and touched his lips. He had to get to that canteen.

Ever since Fullcup Trace was a child, he could recall no time when he did not accomplish a thing once he set his sights on it. And that water waiting for him was no exception. He saw it and he wanted it and that was all there was to it. That and crawling on over there.

In his mind he was nearly there. But when he glanced quickly down at himself, he had only planted one elbow, his right, to the dusty earth. He still needed to get himself righted and angled so he could make it over there.

He squeezed his eyes shut and gritted his teeth and somehow he managed to get the top half of his body angled where it should be, aimed for that water. He made for it, somehow, and felt himself actually moving forward, slower, he was certain, than an ant. But then again, he was dead or nearly there, so why should he complain? He was moving pretty well for a dead man.

He almost laughed at this, but somehow he hadn't the strength. He moved forward with one elbow and then the forearm of his left arm. And there was that knife, still gripped in his locked fingers, and he couldn't figure out how to let go of it.

Maybe it was best he didn't. That Reb might be sneaking on over to ambush him at that moment!

Trace wondered about this and figured that as bad as that man looked, he wasn't going to be moving any faster than was Trace. And besides, he was nearly to that water.

Then he felt something down low that he hadn't felt before. It was on his legs, no, just the one leg, ah yes, he thought. That swollen right leg. It was paining him something awful.

Could that be right? If he was on his way to death, just waiting for someone to tap him on the shoulder, would he be able to feel that pain?

As he crawled, now no more than a few feet from that water, that leg began to throb hard. He groaned again, and let himself do it. It was a sound, after all, and that might lead to him being able to say something. Or to shout, should he need to call for help from one of the boys. They'd take care of that Reb, and right quick, too.

Trace saw it now, just ahead of him, jumbled with a small pile of gear that looked a whole lot like his own. He spied a bedroll and a pack, and leaning against the pack, a canteen, round and carved wood and bound with what looked like rawhide, tight and shrunk to fit. A strap handle of some sort of grimy cloth, knotted and looking as if it had been through a war.

At that thought, Trace did snort, just a bit. His lips split as he did so and he felt the stinging anew.

He brought his left hand up to grab that canteen, which sat right there before his face, but that blasted knife was still part of his hand. He shifted his weight over to the left elbow and reached with his crusted, filthy right hand.

It was a shaking thing that looked like it should be attached to some old dead man. But it did the job, after a couple of grabs, and he felt that canteen jostle, heard the water inside, felt the promising weight of it—it felt more than half full.

He drew it to his face and leaned it against his nose while his fingers fumbled with the wooden bung. It was attached with a strip of string and he grunted and made a slight, squealing sound deep in his throat trying to get it dislodged.

When he finally was able to drizzle that soothing, although warm, liquid onto his lips and into his mouth, he nursed on it like a feeding piglet, and he didn't care who heard him. Never, never, never—and he could not be convinced otherwise—had anything in the history of the world tasted as good to anyone. Ever.

He sipped and slurped and guzzled and although he knew he really should ration that precious stuff, somehow he could not make himself aware, could not make himself do the thing he knew he needed to do.

Which was to ease off on the water and. . . .

"Take 'er easy, Yank, or you're liable to get a gut ache and throw it all up again. Then where will you be?"

Trace paused when the man first began to speak. It reminded him of what he had forgotten, namely that he was not alone. He angled himself to face the man, finding it easier to move and maneuver now that he had been somewhat revived due to the water.

He saw that the Reb was still where he'd last seen him, over by the boulder. But now he was seated and leaning against it.

"Huh?" said Trace, surprised on hearing his own voice.

"Huh?" he repeated, more to hear his voice falter. But at least he could still hear and feel.

All of his senses appeared to have been rejuvenated by the water. It was a lesson he'd long known, but as he'd experienced throughout life, it often paid to be reminded.

"I said to back off the water. Rest up!"

Trace let these words sink into his mind a moment, then said, "Why?"

"Got to take care of you. . . ."

"Why?"

The Reb chuckled. "So I can kill you fair and square, that's why!"

"Don't count on it, Reb."

And so it went, with each man resting and occasionally nibbling on the canteen of his enemy. Remembering, in their fatigue, to look across the few yards toward the other, taking stock and planning just how he would, with very little strength and a body sliced and stabbed and broken and bruised and aching, renew his attack. That was about all they had strength for.

This kept up for hours, and the sun began its descent.

"Reb!"

"Yeah?"

"You got food in this pack?"

"Not much. Hard tack. Coffee. You?"

"About the same. No coffee, though."

"Have at it, Yank."

"You, too, Reb."

Neither man did much more for long minutes as the shadows grew. Trace had been able to pry the fingers of his left hand from around the handle of his knife. He still couldn't flex them fully, but they were moving bit by bit a little better than they had been.

Then the Reb said, "If we built a fire, we could have ourselves coffee."

"I don't have any coffee," said the Yank.

"I do, like I said. In my pack. But no flint nor steel."

"I have those."

"All right then," said the Reb. "Where?"

Silence, then Trace, the Yankee, said, "Best by that boulder where you are."

"Yeah. All right. Bring my gear?"

"I will," said Trace, trying to figure out how he was going to do that and get himself on over to the rock where the Reb sat with Trace's own gear. But he did it.

At the same time, the Reb managed to get himself up to his feet, although he leaned heavily on the rock, and worked to toe up tinder and duff from the ground.

The entire knobby plateau on which they sat was sparsely treed, mostly with low, stunty growth, but there was enough of that. There were also a few dropped branches, and a long, dead tree, brittle and dry. So finding fuel for the fire did not look to be a problem to two men used to scavenging for such on behalf of their respective outfits.

Trace managed to also get to his feet, although his swollen knee proved a painful hinderance to his being able to move any faster than a snail with no ambition. Still, he pressed on, dragging the Reb's pack and canteen and blankets, as well as the man's rifle, lugged by its sling, along with him so a return trip to the base of the tree would not be necessary.

Although they had spent the past few hours but twenty or so feet apart, the two men approached each other with slow caution and grim looks. Each once more held his knife, and Trace was relieved to see that the Reb looked about as bad as he did.

He'd wondered earlier, since the Reb was so chatty, at least compared with himself, that maybe the man wasn't as bad off as Trace felt.

He knew that wasn't a very charitable way to think, but after all, this was a man who was a member of a group he'd been told to hate, so much so that he must kill him. But at that moment, seeing the haggard Reb before him, a man who, when he'd had the opportunity to shoot Trace, had not done so, gave Trace a strange sense of calm and relief.

He knew then that, at least for the time being, however long that might be, they had reached a truce of sorts and would break bread and share coffee. After that . . . well, that was a bridge they would cross when they reached it.

Together they managed to kindle a fire and keep it fed. All the while, from opposite sides of the fire, the two men stole glances at each other, stern faces not slipping a bit.

They exchanged snatches of speech and answered the other's brief questions without much elaboration. Soon, it became apparent to each man that the other was tired. Dog tired and bone weary, as Chaw's old Gramps used to say.

Darkness descended on them, and while they had dragged back to the fire enough snapped wood and half-rotted lengths and sticks and such, they knew they would be unable to keep it fed through the night.

Trace fought to keep his eyelids open. Finally, he sighed. "Am I safe?" There was a brief pause and he realized he had likely just awakened the Reb from a cat nap.

"Safe? From me?" The Reb chuckled. "Yeah, I reckon. As long as I am from you."

"Yeah, okay. Truce for sleep."

"Truce for sleep. . . ."

Visit our website at
KensingtonBooks.com
to sign up for our newsletters, read
more from your favorite authors, see
books by series, view reading group
guides, and more!

Become a Part of Our
Between the Chapters Book Club
Community and Join the Conversation

Betweenthechapters.net